"All that mattered to Sarai was what ⸺ imply with regard to Adam. If this was an opulent room, did that mean Abram would be treated well? Or did the favor extend only to her, so that his life was in danger if he resisted whatever Pharaoh might want of her?

"Do *you* have any idea what any of this means?" Sarai asked the servant girl.

Hagar looked at her blankly.

"Is my accent so bad you can't understand me?"

"I can understand you," said Hagar—in heavily accented Egyptian.

"So you're a native of Egypt," said Sarai. "What language do you speak, then, from birth?" She tried Amorite first, and the girl seemed pleased enough.

"If Mistress wishes to speak the tougue of desert thieves, it's all one to me," said Hagar. Her tone was sweet, but the barb was obvious. Had the girl sized her up and decided Sarai wasn't dangerous?

In Hebrew, Sarai said, "Is this a good room or an ordinary one?"

The girl paused a moment before she got what was said. "That is for Mistress to judge."

One more language to try. In the Arabic of spice traders from the south, Sarai said, "Is this your tougue"

Hagar's eyes widened, and suddenly a torrent of words poured forth. . . .

TOR BOOKS BY ORSON SCOTT CARD

The Folk of the Fringe
Future on Fire (editor)
Future on Ice (editor)
Hart's Hope
Lovelock (with Kathryn Kidd)
Pastwatch: The Redemption of Christopher Columbus
Saints
Sarah
Songmaster
The Worthing Saga
Wyrms

THE TALES OF ALVIN MAKER

Seventh Son
Red Prophet
Prentice Alvin
Alvin Journeyman
Heartfire

ENDER

Ender's Game
Speaker for the Dead
Xenocide
Children of the Mind
Ender's Shadow
Shadow of the Hegemon

HOMECOMING

The Memory of Earth
The Call of Earth
The Ships of Earth
Earthfall
Earthborn

SHORT FICTION

Maps in a Mirror: The Short Fiction of
Orson Scott Card (hardcover)
Maps in a Mirror, Volume 1: The Changed Man (paperback)
Maps in a Mirror, Volume 2: Flux (paperback)
Maps in a Mirror, Volume 3: Cruel Miracles (paperback)
Maps in a Mirror, Volume 4: Monkey Sonatas (paperback)

SARAH

❧WOMEN OF GENESIS❧

ORSON SCOTT
CARD

FORGE®

A TOM DOHERTY ASSOCIATES BOOK
NEW YORK

This is a work of fiction. All the characters and events portrayed in this book are either products of the author's imagination or are used fictitiously.

SARAH

A Forge Book
Published by Tom Doherty Associates, LLC
175 Fifth Avenue
New York, NY 10010

www.tor.com

Forge® is a registered trademark of Tom Doherty Associates, LLC.

ISBN-13: 978-0-765-34117-4
ISBN-10: 0-765-34117-4
Library of Congress Catalog Card Number: 00-044005

First Forge edition: September 2001

Printed in the United States of America

0 9 8 7 6 5 4

*To Jill Locke, whose voice has been heard
reading aloud, filling our home
with the language of love, and whose music
is gold that we hold in our hearts*

❧ CONTENTS ❧

ACKNOWLEDGMENTS ix

I. OUT OF THE DESERT 1

II. IN A DRY SEASON 41

III. PHARAOH'S WOMEN 75

IV. MA'AT 105

V. DIVISION 159

VI. KINGS AND JUDGES 203

VII. FIRE FROM HEAVEN 253

VIII. ISAAC 295

AFTERWORD 331

ACKNOWLEDGMENTS

It was bold of Cory Maxwell at Bookcraft to decide to contract with me for three historical novels based on the lives of the wives of the patriarchs. His boldness became even more evident when, to my own surprise but perhaps not to his, I began the manuscript almost on time, but then took so long to get past several serious story hurdles that it ended up being submitted more than a year late. By that time, Bookcraft had been purchased by Deseret Book, but Sheri Dew showed as much patience and boldness as Cory Maxwell did. I thank them both for making it possible for an old science fiction writer like me to have a chance to write a novel aimed at a very different, but (I hope) overlapping audience.

I very much appreciate the helpful comments of those who read the manuscript chunk by chunk as I was writing it, especially Erin Absher, who was my bellwether when I wandered into dangerous territory. Other readers who deserve my heartfelt thanks are Erin's husband, Phillip Absher, my son Geoffrey, and my friends and fellow writers Kathryn H. Kidd (encourageuse extraordinaire) and Jill Robinson.

Every word I write is read first by my wife, Kristine, and while I remain responsible for whatever foolishness survives her careful reading, she deserves my readers' thanks for all the foolishness she caught before you saw it. Besides, if I have any understanding of what a good marriage can and should be, it is because we have spent so many years trying to make one for and with each other.

And if I have any understanding of what it meant to Abraham and Sarah to have children, regardless of the cost or the delay, it is because of Kristine's and my five children, Geoffrey, Emily, Charlie Ben, Zina, and Erin, who have each taught us a complete course in why raising children is the most important enterprise one can embark on in this life, and the one in which we most closely approach an understanding of the work and glory of God.

❧ CHAPTER 1 ❧

Sarai was ten years old when she saw him first. She was mistress of the distaff that day, and was proud of the steadiness of her spinning, the even quality of the yarn she drew from the spindle. She had a gift for closing off the outside world, hearing nothing but the words that raced through her own mind, seeing nothing but woolen fibers as she transformed them into yarn. And today she worked with wool of the finest white, for it would be woven, undyed, into the bridal dress of her sister Qira.

Into the yarn, from time to time, she added a red-gold hair plucked from her own head. It would be almost invisible, yet in the sunlight there would be the slightest sheen of color in the dress. Her sister would be embraced by Sarai even as she was given to her husband; a part of Sarai would go with her to the distant places where she would live.

A desert man, a wanderer. What was Father thinking? And all because the man was supposed to be of an ancient priestly lineage. "There's power in their blood," Father said. "My grandchildren will have it." As if Father were not the rightful king of Ur, with plenty of godly power in his own blood. The difference was that Father still lived in a city, with many servants around him, while this desert man lived in a tent and surrounded himself with goats and sheep. Let us buy his wool, Father, and pay for it with olive oil, not with the life of my dear sister, my truest friend!

As she thought of words she wanted to say, her eyes filled with tears and she had to stop the spindle, lest she mar the yarn through her blindness.

Only now, with her spinning stopped, did she notice the flurry of voices at the door.

"Then come to the courtyard! My younger daughter will draw you water from the cistern."

Father's voice. Which meant that Sarai was the daughter who must draw the water for this visitor.

She laid aside distaff, wool, and yarn, and blinked her eyes to clear them.

Two feet stood before her, greyish-white with the dust of travel, creased and cracked from the dry air. She had never seen feet so weary-looking.

"I'm afraid I've interrupted you," said a voice. A gentle voice, pitched so only she could hear. But also a strong voice, full of confidence. Already she knew that she wanted her name to be spoken by this man, so she could hear the sound of it spoken with such authority and yet such kindness. If the gods could speak, this would be the voice of a god.

"Sir," she said, "will you have water from our cistern?"

"I would have water from your hands," said the man, "since you are to become my sister."

At once the tears leapt back into Sarai's eyes. This must be the desert man, her sister's husband-to-be. She should have known at once, from the feet! Who but a desert wanderer would have feet like these? And he smelled like goats and donkeys!

But his voice . . .

I don't want to see his face, she thought. For what if he is beautiful, so my sister will love him and not be sorry to leave me? And what if he is ugly, and I have to be afraid for her, going off into the desert with a monster?

"I will draw water for you, sir." Not looking up, she strode to the cistern—walking boldly, so he would know she did not fear him, though she would not raise her eyes to see him.

She climbed the short ladder and pulled upward on the waterdoor. She could hear water gurgling out of the cistern, splashing down into the jar. It would take much to wash those feet, so she left the water flowing until she could hear the pitch of the falling water begin to rise, telling her the jar was growing full. Then she put all her weight onto the waterdoor; it slid downward and closed off the flow from the cistern.

When she had climbed down, she turned to the jar and, to her surprise, looked the stranger in the face. For instead of standing, he had sat down on the tiles of the courtyard and now looked, smiling, up into her eyes. "You're so serious at your task," he said.

Was he mocking her? "I'm not serious when I play," she said, "but I prefer to work. There's pride in work, when it's done well. And someone gets the use of it."

She ladled water out of the jar and poured it over his feet. The dust on his legs turned into black mud, and then into slime. He immediately put his hands right in it, scrubbing away the dirt.

Ubudüe, the courtyard servant, at once protested. "Sir, it is for my hands to wash your feet."

"*Your* hands?" asked the man. "They're as clean as the king's dishes. Whereas *my* hands need washing almost as much as my feet do."

"And your face," said Sarai. The words came out of her before she realized how outrageous they were. She blushed.

"Ah!" cried the man. "My face! I must be as pretty as a locust." He held out his hands to her.

She poured water into his cupped hands, and he splashed it at once on his own face. And again. And again. Only then did he take the linen cloth from Ubudüe's hand and vigorously rub his cheeks and brow. When he pulled the towel away and revealed his face to her, his eyes were crossed and his mouth deformed into a grotesque shape. "Better?" he asked.

She couldn't help it. She had to laugh. "A little," she said.

He rubbed again with the towel. This time he made a much more threatening face. "Do I need more water?"

"I'm not sure it will help."

He held out his hands all the same, and she poured more into them, and he washed again, and now when the towel came away, he was grinning.

It was the face of a god, his eyes so bright, his smile so warm, his cheek so golden with sunlight.

"I see that my sister will do well," said Sarai. She said it politely, but inside, her heart was breaking. Qira will forget me quickly, with this man as her husband.

"She *will* do well," said the man, "and better than you think. For I am not Lot. I'm only Lot's uncle, come with the bride-price for your father and to help prepare for the wedding. Lot is much better looking."

"His uncle?" asked Sarai. "But you're so young. He must be a child."

"He's the son of my elder brother Haran. My *much* elder brother. My *late* elder brother. Lot grew up in my father's tent, as if he were my own brother. He *is* my brother, in truth, since my father adopted him—and more to the point, he's the same age as me. Twenty years in the world our gracious Lord has given us."

"I'm ten," said Sarai, wondering even as she said it why she imagined that he would care.

"Before your age is doubled, I expect I'll be coming back for *you*."

"Why? Have you another nephew?"

He laughed at that as if it were the cleverest thing she could have said. She had no idea why.

"No more nephews," he said. "But still these two feet, much in need of washing."

She poured more water as Father came into the courtyard, followed by servants carrying cups of beer and a basket of bread. "Barley for the traveler," said Father. He took one cup from the servant's hand and gave it to the visitor himself.

"If the elder daughter is as pretty as the younger," said the visitor, "my brother Lot will be the happiest man in the world."

Sarai was astonished. No one spoke of her as pretty.

"Oh, now, don't be getting thoughts," said Father. "The younger is already spoken for."

"Before the elder?" asked the visitor.

"Spoken for by the goddess Asherah."

At once the visitor's face was transformed into a mask of rage. This was no game of making faces with a child, either. "You mean to slay this child?"

"Abram!" said Father. "You misunderstand me! She is marked to be a priestess. One daughter of the king's house has always tended a shrine of Asherah."

Abram was his name.

His body relaxed a little, but he was still upset, Sarai could see it. "Even though you live six days upriver from the city where your great-grandfather was once king?"

"The duty of kings does not end just because the gods are pleased to let another have our throne. A king is a priest before he is a king, and he still must intercede for his people, even if he no longer rules them. What right would I have to return to the throne of ancient Ur, if I slack in my duty now, with my people under the harsh rule of the Amorite?"

Sarai poured another ladle of water over Abram's feet and lower legs. The dark slime was almost gone, and the bronze color of his sunworn skin was visible now. His legs were strong—this man ran as much as he rode.

"You speak the truth," said Abram. "But God does not ask parents to give their children to him. He asks people to give themselves, by their own free choice."

"Well," said Father, "it's not as if we're going to force her. But she was god-chosen from her infancy. She sang in the cradle. She danced before she walked."

"One can be chosen by God, and yet still marry and raise children. The soul with many children is rich, though there is no bread, and the one without is poor, though there is oil enough to bathe in."

This idea struck Sarai like a thunderclap. Who had ever heard such a thing? Marriage was fine, and these princes of the desert had their own sort of prestige. But to be a priestess of Asherah was the highest work of all. She would make music in the temple and sing before the goddess and minister in her holy name. Yet this man seemed not to understand it.

No, he understood—he simply did not believe it.

"Sarai," said Father, "I fear that our visitor is too weary for company right now."

"I have spoken too boldly," said Abram. "I did not mean to give offense. But you see, your news came as a surprise to me, for I had already promised Sarai that I would return in ten years to marry her."

Sarai dropped the ladle. To marry her? *That* was what he meant when he said that he'd be coming back?

"My daughter is normally graceful," said Father. "But look—you've made her clumsy. Leave the ladle, Sarai. Go inside with your spinning."

Still blushing, Sarai strode to her distaff, gathered up wool and yarn and all, and rushed into the house.

But she did not stay indoors—it was too dark for good work, wasn't it? In moments she was on the roof looking down into the courtyard. Without quite planning it, she found herself positioned so that Father's back was to her and she could see the face of this earnest stranger, this Abram, who had been so furious when he thought that

Father meant to slay her in sacrifice to Asherah. It was as if he thought himself fit to judge a god. To judge a king in his own house!

Was he joking when he said that he would return to marry me?

No matter. Sarai knew her life's work. It had no marriage in it.

But such a man as this. Filthy from travel, yes. But there was a light inside him that even the dust of the desert could not hide. Everyone in Ur-of-the-North treated Father with great respect and honor, even though he was a king without a city. But this Abram did not need to have others give him his honor. He carried it within himself. He was more a king, arriving filthy from the desert, than Father was, here in his fine house.

The disloyalty of this thought made Sarai blush with shame. She would never speak it aloud. But she would never deny it, either. If the desert is traveled by such men as this, no wonder they are fit husbands for the daughters of kings.

❧ ❧ ❧

Qira was born to be a queen, and this marriage covenant with a desert man was the disaster of her life. When Father returned from the temple of the Lord of the city full of talk about a desert priest named Terah, Qira had to fight to stay awake. Why would Father bore her with talk about some Amorite who claimed a special kinship with Ba'al? It was Sarai who was going to be a priestess. Qira was going to be a queen!

So when Father said, "And I want you to marry his heir, Lot, the son of his eldest son," Qira did not quite understand.

"Whom?" she asked. "You want me to what?"

"Marry him. Terah's grandson, the heir to his great and ancient priesthood. Not to mention the greater portion of his flocks and herds."

"*Marry* him? What city is *he* king of?"

"Not king of any *one* city. He says that the Ba'al of one city is only a statue that reminds us of the true Lord, who has a true name known only to a few, written in signs known to none outside the lineage of the true priesthood."

Qira could not resist throwing some of Father's own teachings back in his face. "It's an arrogant man who says that 'the worship of others is false, and only his own is true.' "

Father shook his head. "Daughter, theirs is the lineage of Utnapishtim, who rode above the flood. What is the royalty of a mere city, compared to him who is priest to all the world?"

"If they don't live in a city, how are they any better than the wandering Amorites?"

"The Amorites are barbarians who raid from the desert and destroy what they cannot conquer. As we know to our sorrow."

"What cities has this Terah conquered?"

"He is no Amorite; that is my point, Qira. There is no need for him to conquer cities, when he is the chief priest of God in the world!"

"Father," said Qira, "with all respect, I must still point out to you that a beggar could say the things this man said to you, and it doesn't make him a king unless there are people somewhere who obey him."

Father's face turned red then, and Qira realized that in denigrating this Terah, she had said the unspeakable thing: She had denied that a king without a city could truly be a king. "I did not mean . . ." But there was no way she could put a good face on what she had said.

"Very well," said Father. "Let me speak no more of priests and kings. Let me speak of money. A real prince, to marry you, would demand a dowry, and we have no dowry for you, living as we do on the gifts of my brother, king of Ur-of-the-North. While this Terah is rich in herds, and promises me a very sizeable bride-price for you."

"Everyone knows the Amorites trade in slaves," said

Qira savagely, "but I never thought you would sell your own daughter to one."

"As a slave," said Father coldly, "you wouldn't be worth two shoats, since you do no work and have no skills."

"Should I callus my fingers with spinning, like a common woman?"

"Your sister is not ashamed."

"Sarai is born to be a temple servant. I am born to be consort to a king!"

"And I was born to rule a great city," said Father. "We don't always live the life we were born for. Would you rather marry some tradesman who will put you in the house behind his shop and trot you out to show his visitors that he has married royalty?"

"Once you decide that my shame can be purchased for money, what difference does it make?"

At once she saw that she had goaded Father too far. "Your tongue is enough to drive a man to beat a woman!" shouted Father. But he quickly got control of himself. "If I marry you to Terah's grandson Lot, you will be the wife of a wealthy man with a claim to an ancient priestly lineage. No one will say you married down."

"Yes they will," she murmured.

"Despite the fame of your beauty and the majesty of my rank," said Faither dryly, "there has been no queue at our door of ruling princes begging for your royal company."

Qira burst into tears. "I will not live in a tent!"

"Is that all?" said Father. "I'll make that a condition of the wedding—that you never have to live in a tent. But this is the best marriage I will ever be able to arrange for you."

Qira was no fool. She might be bitterly disappointed, but she knew that Father would not lie about such a thing. "I will do my duty," she said miserably.

And so it was that she consented to this miserable wedding, wrecking all her hopes, discarding all her dreams.

Ever since then, she had wondered: What god was it who hated her so much?

Still, for days at a time she had been able to forget what lay in her future. Desert men were unreliable. They changed their minds. They broke their word. Or perhaps her future husband died in battle and would never come for her. Or starved to death out in the deep desert where not even grass could grow. She had all sorts of hopeful fantasies like that.

But now the filthy uncle was here, and Father insisted on parading her forth as if he were selling a milk cow.

"Wear the scarlet," Father said.

Her most precious gown. Well, she would not wear it, not for the mere uncle. What did desert men know of scarlets and other bright and precious colors? Everything was the yellow of grass and sand to them, everything smelled of the hair and dung of animals, and the only music that they knew was mooing and bleating. Scarlet would be wasted on him. If Father was unhappy that she disobeyed, what would he do? Beat her with a stick in front of the uncle? Father could insist on the marriage, but she would show her independence where she could. Qira was not one for submissive obedience, and Father had better remember it.

So it was her blue and brown woollen dress that she pulled on over her linen shift, only one step up from what a tradesman's wife might wear.

"Qira, what are you doing?"

Sarai stood in the door of her room, looking stricken.

"Showing proper respect to my uncle-to-be," said Qira, feigning innocence.

"You mustn't," said Sarai.

"He's a desert man—what will he know?"

"He *will* know," said Sarai. "He's not what you think. He doesn't talk like an Amorite—his speech is as pure as ours, the speech of Ur the Great. And he's a man of refined senses, I know it—he'll understand what you mean by this coarse dress."

"It is a dress belonging to the daughter of a king," said Qira. "All my clothing is far above *his* station." Why she was bothering to argue with a ten-year-old was beyond her, anyway.

Sarai stood in the doorway, contemplating her.

"Yes, after all, I think you're right," said Sarai.

Since Sarai never changed her mind easily, Qira grew suspicious. "What do you mean?"

"It's good to begin your marriage with honesty, not pretending," said Sarai. "With this dress you'll show him that you're the daughter of a fallen, beggarly house that lives on the gifts of another king. The royal scarlet would be nothing but a sham."

"I hate you," said Qira. "Asherah may never forgive Father for giving him such a nasty daughter."

"You don't hate me," said Sarai. "You love me because I remind you to do what you already know that you should."

"I don't *like* doing what I should."

"Neither do I," said Sarai. "But we both do what we must."

Qira burst into tears and embraced her sister, who also wept. But as they clung to each other, Sarai spoke softly. "If your bridegroom is like his uncle, you'll not be cursed by this marriage, you'll be blessed. The uncle is a handsome man, and he speaks like one who is born to rule." She told Qira all about Abram, saying several times that since this was only the uncle, the husband was bound to be even better.

But Qira saw the truth behind the words, and she was astonished. "You've fallen in love with the uncle!" she said.

Sarai looked startled, then embarrassed. "I *like* him," said Sarai.

"I know all about such 'liking,' " said Qira. "You're all set to keep him in your dreams, I know it from the way you talk!"

"The servant of Asherah has only such dreams as the goddess might send."

"You aren't bound over to Asherah's service yet."

"I'll help you put on the scarlet dress," said Sarai.

"You know I'm right. That's why you change the subject."

"I know that the uncle is waiting, and Father is impatient to show you off to him."

"Ten years old, but you have a woman's heart."

"It would do me no good to love him," said Sarai. "You know that if one who is intended for Asherah should turn away and marry a man, the goddess will never give her children as long as she lives."

"So I've heard," said Qira. "They say such things to keep temple-bound girls from wishing for a wedding. But who knows if it is true?"

"I don't intend to find out," said Sarai.

"And yet you *will* dream." Qira began to hum and sing a wordless melody as she held out the voluminous skirt of the scarlet dress and turned and turned.

Sarai could not help laughing. "You are such a foolish child," she said.

"The ten-year-old says this to her almost-married sister?"

"*You're* a dreamer," said Sarai. "So you think everyone dreams."

"You're telling me you don't? I won't believe it."

"I'm a very practical person," said Sarai. "I keep my hands busy with work. I keep my thoughts on what my hands are doing."

"And you speak nonsense all day long."

"Come now," said Sarai. "Father's waiting."

"Down to earth," said Qira. "Practical. Handy. What a sturdy wife you'd make for a desert man."

"Don't say any such thing in front of him," said Sarai, suddenly angry. "Don't you dare shame me like a little child who has no feelings!"

"But you *are* a little child," Qira teased. "And you just

said that you had no feelings for this desert uncle."

The fury in Sarai's face would have been frightening, if she were not so small. "If you mock me in front of him I will never forgive you!"

"I do what I want," said Qira, and she flounced on out of the room, Sarai scampering furiously at her heels.

🌿 🌿 🌿

Sarai knew that Qira would do it, and she also knew that getting mad at Qira would only make it worse, but it's not like you could stop being angry; it just filled you up and you couldn't think about anything else until you either used up the anger or something else happened to take your mind off it. And Sarai meant what she had said. It was silly of her to care what this desert man thought of her, but she did care, and even though she knew he was only teasing when he spoke of returning someday to marry her, she could not bear the idea of being made ridiculous in his eyes. For he alone of all adults had treated her, not as some sacred godbound object to be reverenced, and not as some little toy human to be petted and chuckled at and then ignored or sent away, but rather as a person worth talking to.

And if he teased her a little, it was flirtatious and not condescending. He didn't tell her what she looked like or ask her what her favorite toy or game might be. He didn't talk about her hair or comment on how adult she sounded when she talked, as if children should talk a separate language. Instead he talked to *her*. And if Qira spoiled that by reducing her to a child in his eyes, then she would see what it was like to lose a sister. There would be nothing between them from then on. They would be like strangers forever. Sarai's memory was very long.

When they got to the courtyard, however, Father and Abram were not alone. A new visitor had arrived, a man in strange clothing that Sarai recognized as Egyptian— white linens, with more of his body showing than a man would usually let other people see. The Egyptians who visited Ur-of-the-North were like that, flaunting their disdain for local customs. Their clothing was the only true clothing, their language the only true language, their gods the only true gods. Others had to learn their language to do business with them, though in truth Father had told her once that the Egyptians only pretended not to understand the accented Akkadian speech used here, so that others would speak freely in front of them, thinking their secrets would be safe. That was why Father made a habit of speaking the ancient holy language of Sumeria in front of Egyptians, even though few in this city but the priests could speak it fluently.

Who was *this* Egyptian?

"Suwertu, these are my daughters, the princess Qira and the godchosen Sarai."

Even as she knelt before the visitors, Sarai remembered that Suwertu was the name of the priest of Pharaoh who dwelt here in Ur-of-the-North. He was not actually born Egyptian. He had been a priest of Elkenah until the day he won his appointment as the priest of Pharaoh for this region. Father said he spoke Egyptian with a woeful accent. Officially he merely ministered to the religious needs of Egyptian traders and travelers. In fact, though, he watched over the interests of Pharaoh in the land of the upper Euphrates. These days all the cities of the region had ties to Egypt almost as strong as those of Byblos, which some said was practically an Egyptian city.

"Is he a spy, then?" Sarai once asked Father.

"Something between a spy, a teacher, and an overseer," Father had answered. "He tells Pharaoh who his friends and enemies are, so that gifts and influence can be used wisely. He encourages the local people to learn Egyptian ways and even give respect to the Egyptian gods. And if there are signs of Ur-of-the-North getting out of line, he will crack the whip."

"What whip can he crack, so far from Egypt?"

"The Amorites have broken up all the trade routes that used to make this city prosper. You can no longer be sure

of carrying goods from here to Ashur or Akkad, to Ur-
of-the-South or anywhere beyond the Tarsus. And as for
Canaan, the cities of that land are empty, and the people
hide in caves for fear of the raids of the Amorites. The
only trade that remains strong is between Byblos and
Egypt, for that is done by sea, where the Amorites cannot
go. So Ur must trade with Byblos if it is to prosper. And
if Egypt should tell the king of Byblos that Ur-of-the-
North is not a friend to Egypt, will our traders have any
part of this trade? That is the whip. It has cracked more
than once. There are those who act as if Egypt ruled here.
They go to Suwertu to learn the Egyptian language, to
worship Egyptian gods, to *become* Egyptians as best they
can." Father said this with disgust, as if becoming Egyptian were as foolish as trying to become a lion or an el-
ephant.

And here was this same Suwertu, in the courtyard of
their home. What was his business? And why today, of
all days, when Abram had come to deliver the bride-price
in preparation for the wedding?

Despite the presence of the Egyptian, Sarai could see
that Qira only had eyes for Abram, and Abram frankly
stared at Qira in return. Qira was no doubt trying to guess
whether Lot was going to be as handsome as Abram—or
was she noticing only the dirt of traveling that still clung
to him here and there? And Abram was probably judging
what kind of wife Qira would make, and whether his father Terah had chosen well.

But Sarai knew that having Suwertu here had to mean
something, and it was unlikely to be coincidence that he
was here at this exact moment. For some reason Egypt
was taking interest in the marriage of a daughter of the
ancient house of Ur with the heir to this priestly family
from the desert. Which meant that Terah's claims must
have substance—or at least enough substance to kindle
Suwertu's interest.

At first the conversation was mere chat—talking about
Qira's charms as if she didn't understand plain speech,

telling stories about things that went wrong at weddings in the past, commenting on the bride-price and how Father was going to dispose of such flocks when he had no shepherds among his servants.

Finally, though, Sarai's close attention was rewarded, as she heard Suwertu turn to the subject that must have brought him here. "I wondered, though, that a man of such wisdom as yourself, O King, would give such honor to an obscure family of Amorites, no matter how many cattle they brought to your house."

Sarai noticed how Abram, rather than growing angry at this insult—a veiled accusation that his father was a liar— merely seemed to relax further onto his bench, paying, if anything, *less* attention to the conversation.

"A king is a priest before he is a king," said Father, as he had so often said before.

"But not all who call themselves priests have any claim to speak for God," said Suwertu.

"There are many gods and many priests," said Father.

"There are many names for gods," said Suwertu. "But we all know that the great god whom the people of this land call merely *Ba'al* 'the Lord,' is the same as Osiris, the god who dies and is brought back to life by his son Horus with the help of the goddess Isis."

"I know little of Egyptian names for the gods," said Father. Sarai could see his wariness increase even as he kept his tone of voice mild. "Terah knows the secret name of Ba'al. And his priesthood comes from Utnapishtim, who rode above the flood, upheld by the hand of the Lord."

"But how can *he* be the rightful possessor of this priesthood, when this can be claimed only by Pharaoh?"

At once the air in the room seemed to crackle as if a thunderstorm were about to strike.

Abram's eyes were fully closed.

"I have never heard such a claim made by a priest of Pharaoh before," said Father.

"Who would need to *claim* what everyone knows, until

someone is bold enough to deny it? Out of Canaan came the first Pharaoh. Osiris gave the land of Egypt to him, because only Pharaoh had the true priesthood from the lineage of him you call Utnapishtim."

"Forgive me, Suwertu," said Father, "but how could the priesthood of Utnapishtim have anything to do with the land of Egypt, or Pharaohs with Canaan?"

It was only then that Abram spoke, though he still did not open his eyes. "Suwertu says many true things. The first Pharaoh *was* a descendent of a son of Utnapishtim. He did indeed come from Canaan, where his claim to the true priesthood was one of the tools he used in taking control of upper Egypt."

Sarai could see how surprised Suwertu was by this admission. "If you admit this, then how can your father claim that his house has the true power of God?"

Abram sighed. "My father has many mistaken ideas, I'm afraid. For instance, Ba'al is not just another name for the true God. Once upon a time it may have been so, but now Ba'al is the name for statues erected in every city. The people do not sacrifice to God, they sacrifice to the statue. But my father persists in thinking that these idols can somehow be used in worship by servants of the true God."

"So you admit that your father's claims are false," said Father, looking stunned.

"*Which* claims?" asked Abram.

"That he is of the lineage of Utnapishtim, that the true priesthood is his by right."

"Oh, the priesthood is indeed Father's birthright. And the birthright of Lot, through my brother Haran. As long as he is worthy. And I can assure you that Lot is as worthy an heir to that birthright as you're likely to find."

Suwertu chuckled. "If this man's father lied about one thing, who is to say he doesn't lie about—"

Abram sat bolt upright and swung around to face Suwertu. "My father lied about nothing. I believe him to be mistaken about the relationship between Ba'al and God.

I have tried in vain to persuade him to remove all idols from his house. We *disagree*. But my father is an honest man."

"And a pious one," said Suwertu. "While you deny the power of the Ba'al of . . . well, of this city."

"And every other one," said Abram.

"If you deny that Ba'al is God, then you deny the power of the king," said Suwertu.

"When the king commands, the priests and the soldiers obey," said Abram. "I'd have to be a fool to deny that."

"You deny the *priestly* power of the king."

"In every city, the king rules over the priests. Why would I deny that?"

"You deny that the king has *divine* power."

Abram looked startled. "But . . . are you saying that kings are *gods*? I thought they were *priests*."

Sarai finally understood the game that Abram was playing. Suwertu thought that he was examining Abram, but it was really the other way around. Abram was giving Suwertu a long string, and Suwertu was tying himself in knots with it. She smiled. Father glanced at her right then, and winked. He, too, understood.

"What is the priesthood," said Suwertu, "if not the power to do what God does."

"God does what God does," said Abram. "The priesthood is the power to do what God *says* for men to do in his name."

"I fail to see the distinction," said Suwertu.

"Does God offer sacrifice?"

"Of course not."

"But priests and kings offer sacrifice. So they aren't doing what God *does*, they're doing what God *says* to do."

"*Some* kings have so much divine power that they do what only God can do."

"You mean Pharaoh," said Abram.

"I mean that just as Horus went into the underworld and raised his father from death into spiritual life, so also does the son of Pharaoh go into the underworld and lift his dead father into heaven. They do what Horus did, and then, as Pharaoh, they will do what Osiris did. The Father and the Son."

Abram nodded slowly. "Well, there it is. *That's* why Egypt is the only place where the story stands on its head. Very clever."

"What are you saying?" said Suwertu.

"In every other land, we know that the King who dies and is raised up from the dead is the Son, and the one who raises him up is his Father, the God of heaven. Only in Egypt is it the father who dies, and the son who raises him up. For the very good reason that the kings of Egypt wanted to make the claim you just stated—that they have more divine power than anyone else. Pharaoh has no power to let his son be slain, and then raise him from the dead—only God can do that. But if you just change the story in this one tiny detail—have the son raise the father from the dead—then you can act out the story all you want, generation after generation. The father dies, the son does a ritual descent into the underworld and comes back to report that his father has been raised from death up to eternal life, to dwell among the gods forever. Of course, no one but Pharaoh sees this—Pharaoh doesn't actually have to *produce* his resurrected father. That, too, would be very hard to do."

Father smiled at Abram's words. Sarai could see that Suwertu didn't like that.

"When you think about it," Abram went on, "it's amazing that other kings had never thought of it before. If you don't actually have the power to do what God does, then you simply change the story of what God does, to make it something that you *can* do. Perhaps those other kings actually believed in God, and therefore were afraid to tell lies about him."

Suwertu's loathing was clear, but he maintained his composure. "So you accuse every Pharaoh in the entire history of Egypt of being a liar."

"Not at all," said Abram. "I accuse only the first. The rest were simply repeating the story they were taught. Old lies are passed along, not by new liars, but by new fools."

Sarai thought Suwertu might burst. But still he contained his hatred. "You yourself said that Pharaoh had the birthright," said Suwertu. "So who are you to say that the story as it is known in Egypt is not the true one?"

"I never said Pharaoh had the birthright. I said he was descended from Noah—the one the Sumerians call Utnapishtim. But through a son who was specifically denied that birthright, whose children were forbidden to hold the true priesthood. A sad old story, but a true one. The birthright doesn't always follow the lineage."

"If the birthright doesn't follow the lineage," said Suwertu, "what happens to your father's claim?"

"The birthright passes from the father to a worthy son."

"And how do we know who is worthy? Especially when different sons claim to have the birthright?"

"When a man has the true priesthood, the power of God is visible in his life," Abram said.

"But that is what I said before," said Suwertu. "I will believe your father has the priesthood if he can raise his son from the dead, as you say your god can do."

"God does not give us his priesthood so we can submit to foolish tests."

"Listen to him," said Suwertu, laughing. "He sees now the danger he is in, and so like a rabbit he dodges left and right, trying to avoid the hawk."

"I'm in no danger, Suwertu," said Abram. "You're the one who is tempting God."

"You are most definitely in danger, Abram," said Suwertu. "In Egypt, when the king dies his son goes to the underworld to bring the king into eternal life, as Horus did for Osiris. If your priesthood is more true than Pharaoh's, you must prove it by doing what you say your God does."

"We sacrifice animals as a symbol of the death and resurrection of the Son."

"Look at the rabbit dodging," said Suwertu. "Your father pretends to have the kingly priesthood—to be the only man in the world with the right to that priesthood—but *kings* offer kingly blood in sacrifice."

"Your Pharaohs die of old age," said Abram. "Not as a sacrifice."

"But the son of the king is young. For him to be resurrected, he must be helped to pass over into death."

"Don't be ridiculous," said Father, interrupting. "I want Lot as a husband for my daughter, not as a sacrifice."

"Lot is Terah's *grandson*," said Suwertu. "Abram here, this man of effrontery, *he* is a son of Terah. So let this Abram be offered up in sacrifice, and then let Terah show us he can raise him up. Pharaohs do this every generation. If Terah cannot do as much, then this marriage has nothing to do with kings, and everything to do with sheep."

"Suwertu," said Father, "you pervert the idea of religion."

"There are many kingdoms where the king's blood is shed," said Suwertu mildly.

"Barbaric ones," said Father. "Or they name a man as king for a day, so they can kill him, and then the real king resumes the throne. I do not require any such foolishness!"

"No, but you do require a royal marriage for your daughter," said Suwertu. "I will explain this situation to the King of Ur-of-the-North, your host and benefactor. I think he will agree with me that unless Terah passes this test, his claim to be of royal blood will not be recognized. Then if you marry your daughter to this grandson, this *Lot*, it will be seen for what it is—selling your daughter to an Amorite shepherd in exchange for sheep."

"Why are you doing this?" said Father. "Why does Egypt care?"

"Because Pharaoh is the only king on earth with the true power of God in him!"

"Are you going to say *that* to my friend and brother-king? He'll enjoy hearing it, I'm sure."

"The King of Ur-of-the-North cannot afford to lose the right to trade with Byblos, and the king of Byblos will not trade with someone that Pharaoh deems to be his enemy. This Terah's claim is in direct conflict with Pharaoh's authority."

Abram laughed. "By this very action you prove that Pharaoh has no authority. God has never allowed human sacrifice. Never. It cannot happen. A father does not kill his son in the name of God. So by asking for this, you prove that you and your Pharaoh are the enemies of God."

"We are the enemies of *your* god," said Suwertu. "I have a suggestion, Abram. Get out of Ur-of-the-North tonight, while you still have time. Because if you're here by morning, you will be taken and offered up as a sacrifice. Your father will, of course, be given every opportunity to raise you from the dead."

Suwertu rose, bowed to Father, and swept from the house.

Abram sighed. "I see that this marriage is going to cause political complications. Who would have thought Pharaoh would care so much?"

"It's not Pharaoh, it's his meddling priest," said Father. "You'd better leave, Abram. Give me time to work out the political problems."

"Forgive me," said Abram, "but you have no lever that you can use to pry us out of this. If I leave, the marriage is off—the king of Ur-of-the-North will be forced to bow to Pharaoh's will, because Byblos is more important to him than you are. I speak offensively, sir, but I speak the truth."

"Your words sting," said Father, "but yes, it *is* the truth. So I release you from the marriage vow. Go. You can take the flocks with you."

"On the contrary," said Abram. "I came here to seal the marriage promise between the daughter of a king of great and ancient lineage with the grandson and heir of another. Nothing has changed, as far as my errand is concerned, except some interference from the lying priest of a false god. What does this nonsense have to do with Lot and Qira?"

"Didn't you hear him? He'll kill you."

"There is more than one way for God to show his power," said Abram. "Just because Suwertu has a plan does not mean that the plan will be carried out."

"And just because you trust in your God does not mean that God will regard your life as being important enough to be worth saving," said Father.

"I trust in God," said Abram, "not to save me from death, but to save my soul when I die. I expect my father to see to it that the priest of Pharaoh does not shed my blood on an altar in order to perform some stupid test. God does not give signs to prove things to liars."

"I think you are in grave danger," said Father.

"I think you're right," said Abram. "But there are bears in the mountains, and lions on the savannah, and diseases that kill men in their sleep. Do you know why I can't die now?"

"Why is that?" asked Father.

"Because I promised Sarai that I would come back for her in ten years."

Father's face reddened. "Sarai is promised to Asherah."

"Asherah is just another name for mother Eve. She was a woman of greatness and nobility, but she was never a god, and she has no use for your daughter, except to see her be married and raise her children to serve God."

"Are you trying to make me as angry as Suwertu?"

"I speak truth," said Abram. "I speak the same truth to powerful men that I speak to weak ones. That's why you can trust every word I say. How many men do you know with whom *that* is possible? But now, if you'll excuse me, I must go and see to my other business in the city."

"I hope you will have sense enough to leave Ur at once," said Father. "Next time have your father send a trusted servant, and *not* a son. Especially not such an honest and forthright son."

Abram smiled. "My father has sometimes told me that

nothing is more annoying than the inconvenient virtues of one's children. God be with you, King of Ur."

In moments he was gone. Sarai was left gasping at all that she had heard. This man called into question all that she had been taught, all that she believed, and he did it with such authority that it was impossible not to listen to him. Even when Father glared at her and demanded to know what she did to allure this man, Sarai could only answer feebly, "I don't know, I don't know." For as of this day, she was no longer sure of anything. Except this: Abram said he would be back to marry her, and somehow it would happen, for today she had seen for the first time in her life the true power of a king. It was the power of word: To speak, knowing that the thing spoken would come true.

❧ CHAPTER 2 ❧

The next few weeks were maddening for Sarai. Everything happening to Abram in Ur was important to her household—and certainly not least to her!—but no one thought to tell her each bit of news as it came into the house. Instead she had to quiz the slaves, who never quite got the story right, since they didn't understand it themselves, and who also tended to change the details to make stories more interesting—which usually meant more awful.

But the truth, when she finally learned it, was awful enough. Because Suwertu declared Abram to be the enemy of Pharaoh's authority and therefore a danger to the authority of all kings, Abram was taken prisoner. Within a day, his father, Terah, came and camped in the grassland half a day's run from Ur. His messengers passed back and forth, trying to win Abram's release.

Suwertu, though, was pulling strings behind the negotiations, and the choice became clear. Terah had to renounce his claim to the true priesthood, confess that

Pharaoh was the only heir to the birthright of Noah, and swear never to make such a claim again. Otherwise, he could prove the power of his priesthood by raising his son Abram from the dead, after he was sacrificed to Ba'al—or to Horus, or to Pharaoh himself as a divinity, depending on who was telling the story.

Until the gossip about Suwertu and Abram began, Sarai had never heard of offering a human being as a sacrifice. To her, worship was about incense and music, and now and then, from a distance, the ashy smell of burnt meat. But the meat was always an animal—a bullock, a he-lamb—and a year or so back, Qira had explained to her that only parts of the animal were burnt, while the rest of the meat was used by the priests. "What do you think they eat, silly?" asked Qira. But Sarai had never thought about it. She had only had some vague idea that the god they served provided for them. Instead it was the people.

But when she realized that they were seriously planning to sacrifice Abram, her first terrible thought was that the priests would eat him. Qira quickly dispelled *that* notion—but provided her with information that was even more horrifying. "It's not like anyone in Ur sacrifices babies to Molech." If she intended to reassure Sarai with this information, she failed. It broke Sarai's heart just to imagine that somewhere there were people who would kill their own baby—and that they would do it in service to a god. And now that Abram had raised in her mind the possibility that priests might be making up some of the stories about the gods, she was even more confused. For she could not believe in the existence of a god who wanted the murder of children. Yet she could also not believe that a priest could make up such a terrible thing.

Sarai thought of all the babies that she had known—an infant suckling at a servant's breast, a toddler playing beside his mother as she worked. She saw how mothers loved their children, even when they were annoyed with them, even when they were angry. Though she didn't understand why the mothers got angry. Everything children did, at every age, fascinated and delighted Sarai. And somewhere, either a god or a priest decided that people should be commanded to offer their own babies as sacrifices.

All of this preyed on Sarai's mind, and many times she almost convinced herself that it was all pretend, that nobody ever really killed people in the name of a god. Certainly it never happened with the worship of Asherah—though there were things that went on at the temple of Asherah that they didn't talk about in front of her. Could it be that even there, something or someone was killed? Impossible.

But the rising tide of gossip made anything seem possible. Now she heard for the first time that Suwertu had sacrificed a child as a thank offering, burning the child's body on a hill near Olishem. This story was told in support of the idea that there really wasn't anything unusual about human sacrifice, though to Sarai it seemed that if human sacrifice were normal, no one would need to prove that it was normal, because everyone would already know.

Most of the stories horrified or puzzled Sarai. Only one really frightened her. It was the tale that Suwertu had sacrificed three young sisters. It wasn't the fact they were young like Sarai that made her afraid. It was that they were the daughters of a man named Onitah, who just happened to be making a claim that he was the rightful heir of the first Pharaohs.

If this story was true, it meant that Suwertu made it a habit to kill people in order to punish their fathers for claiming the birthright of the priesthood. That was the reason this story was told—those who repeated it always made comments about how murder was murder, even when a priest did it and called it sacrifice. "This has to be stopped," they would say.

But Sarai never heard them mention any *plan* to stop the sacrifice of Abram. They might deplore it, but they weren't doing anything. Not even Father. And why? Because he was afraid that he might lose his safe haven in

Ur-of-the-North if he spoke up against Suwertu's "sacrifices."

This is how it happens—how bad people can do terrible things, right out in the open, and everyone stands away and lets them do it.

There were even people who were helping Suwertu. The priest of Shagreel, for instance, claimed that Abram had also blasphemed against *his* god, which was, after all, only the sun. By saying that only the priests of his father's God had authority, Abram had as much as said that all other gods were false. "And yet we see the sun in the sky every day!" the priest was said to have declared. "We are warmed by it! And Abram denies that the sun is a god!"

At last Sarai could stand it no more, and went tearfully to her father to ask him why no one was doing anything.

"But many of us *are* doing things," said Father kindly. "We do them quietly, where you don't see. But if it hadn't been for our intervention with the king, Suwertu would have pierced Abram's heart already."

"So you're going to stop him?"

"With so many jackals pulling at the deer, how long will it stay on its feet?" Father shook his head. "I'm sorry you have to know about such things."

"Why don't people hate Suwertu?"

"They do hate him. But they fear him more. So they don't stand against him."

"*You* stand against him, Father! I don't care if he sacrifices me."

"He couldn't sacrifice *you*," said Father. "You belong to Asherah."

Only then did she realize—if Father openly opposed Suwertu, it might be Qira on that altar, just like those three daughters of Onitah.

So because they fear it happening to their own families, everyone will let this murderer have his way.

And he does it all in the name of a god.

It made Sarai ponder long and hard about the life she had been pledged to live, as a priestess of Asherah. If the worship of Ba'al or Osiris or Elkenah or Shagreel could be used as a mask for the murder of a foreign king's enemy, then which gods were genuine? Only Abram seemed to be acting out of faith instead of private advantage, and his God had no statues. His priests were herdsmen like Terah and Abram and Lot, who worked with their own hands instead of leading the washed and perfumed life of a temple priest.

Will I have to become a liar and hypocrite like Suwertu in order to serve Asherah? Or are the priestesses somehow holier than the priests?

Abram said that Asherah was just another name for a real woman, Mother Eve, who was not a god at all. Why then would she need priestesses?

These questions rankled her and bothered her, getting all mixed up with her confusion about Abram's promise to marry her and her own feeling of rage and revulsion at what was being done to that good man.

Finally a day came when she could stand no more of it. She set aside her distaff and ran up to the roof. Three servants were there spreading out clean clothing to dry, but she sent them away so she could be alone there. She knelt and raised her arms to heaven and prayed, not to Asherah or Ba'al, but to the God whose name she didn't even know.

"O God, spare the life of Abram! If thou dost this miracle, O God, then I will know thou art the only true God, mightier than kings and false priests, and I will worship only thee forever. I will repudiate my promise to Asherah. I ask only the life of Abram. He doesn't even have to keep his promise to come marry me—I know that a man can sometimes be prevented from keeping his word, however honestly given. I ask nothing for myself. Only save his life, and I will be thy servant in all things forever."

Over and over she said the prayer.

That night, as she slept, Sarai was suddenly awakened by a great shaking of the ground. Her bed bounced on the floor. She heard the roofbeam creaking above her, and ran from her room into the courtyard, so nothing could fall and crush her. The servants ran there, too, and Father, and Qira. Some of them had bloody knees because they had fallen when the ground shook so hard. And some had bloody heads or shoulders, because of tiles or bricks that had fallen on them.

When the earthquake ended, no one would go back inside. It was common knowledge that God rarely shook the earth just once. So even though the night was not warm, they slept outdoors, servants lying down right among the royal family. Sarai stayed awake after most of them slept, but not because she was afraid. At first she wanted to see whether the servants slept in some vulgar manner that would explain why they were not allowed to sleep in the same rooms as the royal family. And when she satisfied herself that servants were no cruder in their sleep than the royal family, she used the time to pray.

At last she did sleep, though only fitfully. No one slept deeply or long. She lay on her mat on the stones of the courtyard as the adults woke, speaking softly, repeating news of the city. The earthquake had broken down this house or that one; this person had been killed, or that one. The reports of disaster made Sarai imagine what it might be like to have someone in her own family killed by the shaking of the earth. Surely there could be no clearer sign that a god wanted you dead than to have him shake the earth to accomplish it.

She listened with her eyes closed, so no one would realize she was awake and cease speaking plainly in front of her. So she heard the glorious news at the same time Father did.

"Suwertu was on the hill where he does his sacrifice when the earthquake struck," said the breathless visitor. "The earthquake knocked down all the statues he had gathered there, shattering them all. And Suwertu was directly under the statue of Osiris, which fell on him and crushed him to death."

Father gave one bark of laughter, and then composed

himself. "I am sure the king of this city will have a day of mourning for this noble servant of Egypt. There will be weeping and wailing throughout the land!"

"No doubt," said his visitor.

"What about the sacrifice of my son-in-law's uncle?" asked Father. "They can't be going on with it, can they?"

The visitor chuckled grimly. "Since his own chief god crushed him to death while he was preparing to conduct that very sacrifice, I think it's safe to say that no one else is at all interested in going ahead and daring the gods again. No, there'll be no sacrifices today. I hear that Abram has already fled the city and gone into the desert."

"Yes, *now* he goes," said Father. "I tried to get him to do that days ago, but would he listen?"

"If he had left when *you* told him to, Suwertu would not have been at the altar when the earthquake struck, and so he would not be dead, and so the human sacrifices would have continued."

"You think they'll stop?"

"He's the one who got people back into that kind of worship when he was nothing but a priest of Elkenah. He showed everyone the danger of giving any man the power to kill his enemies in the name of God. No, I think that when the next priest of Pharaoh is chosen, it will be carefully explained to him what he may or may not do without the consent of the king of Ur-of-the-North."

"So," said Father. "It looks like my daughter's marriage will go ahead after all."

"If you still want to marry your daughter to the grandson of such a weak man."

Sarai perked up her ears.

"It was not weakness for Terah to refuse to repudiate his own claim, even if it cost the life of his son," said Father. "It was great courage and faith. More than I have. For I would never allow my own child to be sacrificed, as Terah was doing, just for the sake of preserving my own estate."

For the first time it occurred to Sarai: Isn't that exactly

what you did, Father, when you pledged me to Asherah the day I was born?

Then, condemning herself for even having such a thought, Sarai bounded to her feet and ran once again to the roof. Behind her she could hear Father saying, with an irked tone, "Was she listening the whole time?"

On the roof Sarai fell to her knees to pray again. "O God of Abram, I know Thou art faithful to Thy true servant, Abram. So I will keep my vow. I will not give myself to the service of Asherah. How could I, when I know now that Thou art the only true and living God. Thou, O Shaker of Earth, art my God forever. For Thou hast heard my prayer. Thou hast spared the life of Abram."

❧ CHAPTER 3 ❧

In the spring, Lot finally came in person and married Qira under the gaze of their fathers—two kings without kingdoms. It was a joyful time, and Sarai was especially happy for her sister, for she was going to have everything she wanted: Lot seemed to be a kind man, he was even more handsome than Abram had been, and he promised to live in Ur for the near future, leaving his steward and servants with Abram out in the empty grasslands.

For Abram did not return to Ur, even for the wedding of his beloved nephew. There were those in Ur—especially priests of other gods who had joined their cause with Suwertu's—who would never forgive Abram for having humiliated them. Never mind that what humiliated them was proof that there was indeed a God who did not want Abram murdered. There was too great a chance that someone would try to finish the job—Abram would never enter Ur again.

And I will never leave, thought Sarai. He will forget me. But I will never forget him.

It took two years, but she finally persuaded her father that it wasn't a whim—she was determined not to enter the service of Asherah. It was a delicate task, persuading him to release her from the vow, for by releasing her he was as much as confessing that he was not, in fact, king of anything, and so his daughter had no responsibilities to the gods. Father never quite admitted that openly. He found some pretext about Sarai's unreadiness or unworthiness—Sarai did not care, as long as she did not end up bound into the service of a god in whom she no longer believed.

The years passed. Sarai watched as her father tried to arrange this or that marriage, but always it was the bored son of a rich man trying to add some luster to a family that had no standing. Father tried to persuade her that each one was really a good husband, but in truth he was never even able to convince himself.

By the time Sarai was eighteen, she had no idea what was going to happen to her. By her age, most women were already married. Almost every day Sarai was reminded of how well her older sister had married—with Lot's wealth to back her up, she was head of a worthy household in Ur. But to Sarai, the prizes in Qira's household were the two little girls who, truth be told, saw more of their aunt than of their mother. Is this my destiny, Sarai wondered, to be a spinster living in my sister's house, tending her children and someday her grandchildren, always subservient, never to have a child of my own in my arms?

The one thing she could not let herself think of was the man who had come from the desert so long before. Lot sent messages back and forth to Abram at least every week, and servants made the journey often. Sarai heard of every movement Abram made, each new encampment. He would be in the ruins of this or that city in Canaan, empty because all the years of drought and windborne dust had forced the people to flee to other lands. Or he would be selling cheeses in Akkad or wool in Babylon or leather in Ur-of-Sumeria, and the next month, south of the Dead Sea in Sodom or Zoar, he would be selling jewelry or clothing from Akkad, Babylon, and Ur. She heard of him trading along the Phoenician coast in cities like Tyre or Byblos, or north among the Assyrians or the Hittites or the Hurrians. Not once did Lot ever tell Sarai that Abram had so much as asked about her. Not once did she receive a letter or a message or a gift or even a glance from a servant that would tell her that perhaps her name had been mentioned in Abram's tent.

And yet . . . she knew he was a man of honor. He had said he would come for her. She had promised nothing to him. Yet even if his words were merely a jest with a child, it did not change this single fact: If he did come, she was determined that he would find her waiting, ready to be a good wife, ready to be the mother of his children. And she would never be like Qira, making him live in a city so she could wear fine gowns. No, she would live in his tent, travel when he traveled. If he came for her, she would go with him, and stay with him forever.

If the ten years passed, and then an eleventh, and he did not come, she would never send word to him, either, nor give a hint to anyone, not even Qira, that she had waited for him. She would simply decide, then, what to do with the rest of her life. By then it would probably be too late for her to marry any other man. But having once known Abram, she could not be content with a lesser man, and apart from Lot, she knew of none that came close to being Abram's equal.

Did it hurt her? Yes, there were times when she felt a pain so sharp that it was all she could do to keep her weeping silent and secret in her room.

But then, in the midst of such suffering, she would remember: Abram told me the truth about God, and saved me from a life wasted in the service of false gods. I would rather have had that hour of truth with Abram than any other possible life in which I did not have the truth and never met that man. She would pray at such moments, and soon her heart would be lighter, and even though she had no sign from God that her future was being watched over, still she was content. She could wait to see what life would bring.

It was a hot day in summer, the kind of day where there is no shade except indoors, and indoors there was no air that one could bear to breathe. No breath of wind—the dust from travelers or animals moving on the roads would rise in a cloud and hang there, unmoving, settling so slowly that it seemed to be a brown-grey fog. Sarai could not remain inside, and in the courtyard there was so much yammering from the servant women that she couldn't think. The dust of the streets made the air unbreathable; she could not walk to Qira's house. So she took her distaff to the roof, and with a white linen hood over her head to give her shade, she spun, while thinking her thoughts and glancing out over the desert, over the city, over the nearly dry riverbed. Would the drought, which had already consumed so many years that she had never known a season when the river ran full, finally do to Ur-of-the-North what it had done to the cities of Canaan? Was it going to kill the grasslands and turn them into desert like the rumored empty lands of the far south, where only sand covered the earth as far as the eye could see?

And who is that coming from the driest part of the desert, raising dust so thick that he must have an army with him? Does no one else see this marauding army? Why are there no trumpets of alarm, warning of a raiding party of so many Amorites that they will swarm over Ur like locusts?

Then they came near enough that she could see that it was not an army at all, but a huge herd of cattle and a vast flock of sheep. What Amorite would be mad enough to assemble such a large herd in one place? Where would they find grazing? If all these animals were sold at once in the markets of Ur, they would force the price down so low that the animals would have almost no value. Even Sarai knew that much about trade.

On they came, and on, and on, and finally riders went forth from the city, and then the riders came back from the herd, and after a very short while there was talking and shouting in the streets and riders came to the door of Father's house and Sarai heard her own name being shouted down below in the courtyard, in the rooms of the house, but she did not need to be told anything—she already knew. Abram had come for her, and with a bride-gift so large that no woman in all of Ur would be able to claim that so much had been given for her.

Father himself came to the roof and handed her a sealed wax-stick. "For you only," he said, and his eyes danced with happiness, for he had been worried about his younger daughter.

Sarai tremblingly opened the stick and exposed the two waxen surfaces. Very little was written there. But it was enough.

> I am almost two years early, Sarai, but I can delay no longer. I wait for you outside the walls of the city, with a gift for your father but none for you except my love and my faith and my future, which I ask you to share with me for-ever.
> Abram

Sarai looked up from the stick. "Father," she said, "I think my husband has brought an inconvenient number of cattle and sheep for you to dispose of."

"His message to me," said Father, "spoke of plans to divide this herd and take the animals to a dozen other cities, where they will be sold and the proceeds brought to me. My only fear for you, Sarai, is that your husband will be poor, having given so much to me. And yet the gift does not begin to make up for the great loss to me when you leave and the light goes out of my life."

Sarai burst into tears and embraced her father. "He remembered," she said. "He remembered me."

"No one, having known you, could ever forget you," said Father.

"Many men have forgotten me," said Sarai, "and far more have never noticed me."

"Abram noticed you," said Father. "And God has noticed Abram."

"And God has noticed *me*," said Sarai. "Or I would not be so blessed, to go from the house of such a father to the house of such a husband."

Two days later, under a canopy that shaded the bright calm sun of morning, she and Abram were married, with Father, Terah, Lot, and Qira looking on. She did not know what the future would bring, but because she was married to Abram, she knew that her life would matter, that the world would change and she would be a part of it.

PART II

IN A DRY SEASON

❧ CHAPTER 4 ❧

I n the desert, wealth was not measured in cattle after all. Calves were born, and kids, and lambs, but they didn't live long without pasturage for their mothers, and there was no grass where it did not rain. And rain was rare.

There were storms—plenty of storms, as many as ever. But there was no moisture in them. Instead, when clouds appeared on the horizon, people shuttered their windows and brought their animals inside so they would not be suffocated by the dust. The lands to the north were so dry that every storm scooped up their soil and carried it out across the land between the rivers, down through Canaan, choking cattle, burying fences and fields, blinding travelers, and turning the feeble drought-stricken rivers into beds of mud. Grasses struggled to rise above the dust, sheep to graze through it. The beards of goats were caked with mud, as if they had been trying to eat the very soil. In a dry season, storms brought no relief, they only forced the drought inside houses, tents, mouths, noses, ears, and eyes.

Abram had not impoverished himself with his extravagant bride-price. Indeed, Sarai soon realized that his gesture had been wise. There wasn't water enough or grass for the vast herds that Abram once had owned. If he had sold them all at once, the price would have been so low that everyone would have known he sold from desperation. The cruel laws of the marketplace would have guaranteed that he would be charged higher prices for everything, and paid less for what he sold. But by using the cattle as a bride-price, Abram rid himself of herds he could not feed while enhancing his reputation for wealth. His credit and reputation everywhere were enhanced.

Early in their marriage, Sarai had moments when she wondered if that was the only reason he had returned for her. But he was such a loving husband that she could not believe such a thing for long. In all his labors, in all his traveling from well to well and herd to herd, in all his sending of servants and taking account of those who returned, he always had time for her. Nor did he keep her from knowing of his business. He would meet with his men or with his visitors at the door of his tent, so that she could sit in the door of hers, just across from them, and spin or sew as she heard all that passed. She kept her silence; they did not notice or soon forgot that she was there. But afterward, Abram would come to her tent and talk with her until she understood what she had heard, and it was not too long before she knew the work of a nomadic chief as well as she had understood the protocols of a king's house, or the mysteries of Asherah.

He included her in his life, and she in turn longed to include him in her own. But of course a bride had no life at first, except the gossip of her aging handmaid, Bitute, a Sumerian slave who had passed all her years serving the women of Sarai's mother's family. What could Sarai tell Abram of her day? "Bitute brushed out my hair and then we both carded wool until our hands were raw. Then we spun and spun until I see the distaff before my eyes even when I close them. All the while, Bitute kept reassuring me that I'll have a baby soon, that it's just a matter of time, some women conceive slowly but it means the child will be a boy, and very strong, don't worry about it, your husband will love you at last when you give him his first son, and is that true, Abram, will your love for me only begin when I conceive a child?"

No, she made no report to him of days trapped with a well-meaning old woman who did not know how her words cut Sarai to the heart. "And don't you believe those who say that Asherah dries up the wombs of girls who break their oaths. It wasn't *you* who took the oath, young mistress, and besides, Asherah has many priestesses, she can spare such a beautiful young princess, she's not spiteful." Sarai did not bother to explain to Bitute that there was no such god as Asherah, and therefore no possibility of her drying up wombs or filling them. Nor did Sarai ask Abram for reassurance—she already knew what he believed, and it would only trouble him to think that his wife was nagged by the worry that an imaginary god was wreaking vengeance on her.

She did try to find out how he felt about it, especially after the first year of their marriage. "Does it worry you that God has not yet blessed you with a son?" she asked him. He looked up, distracted, as if the question were utter nonsense. "God has never failed me before," he said. "Why would he start now?" And when he saw that this did not reassure her—after all, it was not God but Sarai who had failed him in this—he took her in his arms and laughed and said, "I married the woman, not the babies she might have. But there *will* be babies, lots of them I imagine."

He was sincere, but she knew that his words were false all the same. He might *think* he married the woman, but a man marries to have sons—all the more when he needs men-children to receive his priesthood and carry it on. God was tied up in every part of Abram's life, this not least. Abram must want a child in his arms, a child on little legs, to be hoisted up to the back of a donkey and taken with his father to the hill to see to the sheep, or to the riverbed to watch over the cattle, or to the altar to witness the sacrifice.

Sarai saw the servants' babies, and every happy cry, every fitful squall, every greedy slurp at the breast was like a knife in her heart.

Patience, she told herself. Have faith as Abram has faith. Qira has had two children—girls, it's true, but it was a sign that her family did not have barren daughters.

And thus she passed her days, and her months, season after season, until she could not call herself a girl anymore, could not tell herself that it was just as well, she was too young to bear children, being hardly more than a child herself. Girlchildren born the year of her marriage were ten years old now, eleven. When they began to marry and bear children the reproach would be unbearable. Maybe then she would have to tell Abram they could pretend no longer, that it was time for him to put her aside and marry a woman who could bear him sons.

On nights when she thought such thoughts, she tried to pray, but found the words bitter in her mouth. I gave up all for You, God of Abram. But now my womb tells me that Asherah, not You, has all the power over me.

She covered her mouth with her hands, but knew that God had heard her already. It was too late to call back the words she had spoken to a god, even when they had not come to her lips, for the gods could hear the words that were whispered in the heart. O, forgive me, God of Abram. I have faith only in Thee.

That was in the night. By day those fears faded in the heat of the morning. Each pasture was smaller, the grass shorter than it had been the year before, and even with far smaller herds the pasture was too soon exhausted. Years before, Abram and Lot had separated their herds, because their men had begun to quarrel over whose cattle were being allowed to overgraze. But now, though Lot had sold most of his herds and now lived as a man of land and wealth in the city of Sodom, Abram's herds alone were too many for what grass remained. Little was said, but Sarai could see from the grim faces of the men how things were going. From their faces, and from the fact that they feasted on goat or mutton or beef every night. They grew sick of meat, and not just from having too much of it. It was Abram's wealth, his future they were eating, because the rain had not fallen, and the grass was not growing, and the cattle were starving. They were devouring the inheritance of the children Sarai had not yet borne.

"What if," said Abram one hot afternoon, sprawling wearily beside her on the rugs piled in her tent, "what if we went to Sodom with Lot?"

"You love the city life so much," said Sarai.

Abram sighed. "Sodom least of all. A vile place. But I don't have connections anywhere else."

"My father's city," Sarai reminded him, then realized her error at once. "I forgot. He has no city."

"Ur of Sumeria is in the hands of his enemies, and Ur-of-the-North is full of mine," said Abram. "Ah, Sarai, I've already written to him, asking what's possible there. This drought is too much for me. Already we stray so far out of our range that the risk of war is constant. We'll come to a well where they've never heard of me or my family, and those who think of the water as their own will draw swords, and what then? Will I spend my life with my sword against every man, stealing water from them in order to keep my own herds and house?"

"Surely the drought will pass soon," said Sarai.

"I hear that often," said Abram, "but it isn't so. This drought has already lasted longer than I've been alive."

"No, Abram, there was rain often in my childhood."

"No, Sarai. I *know* what the rainfall has been for the past fifty years."

"How can you remember what happened before you were born?"

He shook his head. "A woman who can read and write, and still she wonders."

"Your family kept records of the rain?"

"So do priests in every city," said Abram. "They learned their duties from my ancestors—how could they pretend to be priests if they didn't do what we did? This is the same drought that killed my brother Haran, Lot's father, all those years ago, choking his life out in the dust that filled the air day after day, month after month. This is the drought that killed the grasslands and drove the Amorites from the desert to conquer your father's city. This is the drought that emptied the cities of Canaan and left only herdsmen to wander the half-buried streets."

He made the desolation of the land sound like poetry. "But there are good years," said Sarai.

"There are years not quite as bad," said Abram. "My father remembers a day when the land was green as far as the eye could see. You could stand on a mountain and see herds of deer and antelope running free right along with the herds of cattle. There were even elephants then— giant beasts like hillocks. The most daring goats would take shelter in their shadows in the afternoon. There was land and water enough for all in those days, and no one envied the people of the cities, huddled in their little huts, digging ditches for the river water because their crops couldn't live from the rain, even though it came as regular as daylight. In all our lives, we've never seen such times, because they're gone. The world my father knew is gone. And I don't know if we can hold on to such a way of life for another year. It isn't about the cattle anymore. I have all these people in my house. I can't hold them here, where their children live ever closer to the edge of star-vation, of death by thirst when the next dust storm buries the last well."

"They'll stay with you."

"I don't doubt that," said Abram, "for a long time, any-way. But when I say I can't hold them, I speak of my duty, not of their obedience."

"What of the dangers of the city?"

"I know," he sighed. "What good is it to save the lives

of their children, only to lose their souls in Sodom?"

Sarai realized now why he had chosen this moment to come to her and say these things. "Eliadab is back from Sodom," she said.

"I saw his red cloak far off," said Abram. "He'll have letters from Lot and Qira."

"From Qira." Sarai could not restrain a dry laugh.

"It's good that your sister can write to you," said Abram.

"Just because she can mark the syllables doesn't mean she has anything to say."

Abram laughed. "What she says, even when she says nothing, is that she cares for you."

"Oh, Abram, must I be virtuous *every* moment?"

"Virtue is supposed to be alive in the heart, not put on and off like a burden."

"Sometimes, my love, virtues conflict."

Abram raised an eyebrow.

"Do I speak kindly of my sister at all times, or do I speak honestly to my husband?"

"Just see to it that you speak kindly of the husband."

"So loyalty is better than honesty?"

He roared at her, pounced on her, all in play, but it was a delight to see him light-hearted at such a heavy time. Soon enough the distant red cloak became a dust-covered man on a weary donkey, handing a bag to Abram.

They read sitting in the doorway of the shadier tent—hers, at this time of day. Other men might have tried to conceal that their wives could read, but Abram was proud of Sarai's learning, and so they set aside the letters from Qira and sat together reading Lot's letter.

It was bitter news.

Strangers aren't welcome here. More and more wells are failing, and we're importing grain from Egypt. Every stranger is regarded as a thief, stealing water. I can't bring you here, or to any of the five cities of the plain, not till we see whether the spring rains come. Indeed, I was about to write to you, to ask if we could take refuge with you until this drought ends. I see now that we are better off separated. At least my wife consented to leave the city. Thirst for water is apparently stronger than dread of boredom.

"He doesn't understand Qira," said Sarai. "It isn't boredom she fears, it's loneliness. She needs faces around her, lots of them, and the sound of many voices."

"I've seen a tree full of monkeys that would do very nicely for her," said Abram. "I'm glad I got the sister who doesn't need chattering."

"Oh? And what do I need?" asked Sarai.

"You are the lioness standing alone over the kill, waiting for her mate to come and dine before her, driving off the jackals and the vultures."

Sarai was not at all sure how she felt about this image of her, but she'd think about it later. "We aren't going to Sodom," said Sarai. "And we can't stay here."

"I wondered about building a boat," said Abram. "It worked for my ancestor Noah, when he had too much water. Why not try it again when there's too little? Get out on the sea and float before the wind until we find a land that no one else has known."

"And do what?"

"Create a great nation," said Abram.

"To do that," said Sarai, "you would need children."

There. It was said.

But he didn't notice or didn't care how fearfully she had said it. "We'll have children," Abram answered simply.

She accepted his reassurance without argument. Until he understood what it meant to her, there was no use trying to prolong the discussion. "Do you want to read Qira's letter with me?"

"Will you forgive me if I don't?" asked Abram. "Unless I decide I'm serious about boatbuilding, I must find some more practical solution."

He got up and crossed the way to his own tent. To

pray, Sarai knew, and between prayers to read the books that were unreadable, the ones he seemed to spend his life copying over, so that not one word would be lost. Unreadable words, for they were in a different script from the wedges of the Akkadian or the painted figures of the Egyptian language. He tried to explain it to her, that this language was written with only a few marks—one mark for the sound "buh," no matter whether it was "bee" or "bah" or "boo" or "bay." It made no sense to Sarai—how could you tell these syllables apart, if all the "buh" syllables used the same mark? "Bee-bah" and "bo-boo" would look exactly alike. Abram just laughed and said, "What does it matter? No one speaks the language they're written in, anyway."

"Then why do you copy it?" she asked. "If no one can read it?"

"Because the words of God can be written in any language, and He will give His servants the power to read it," said Abram.

"So you can read any language?"

"When the words are from God," said Abram. "And when God wants me to read."

"Why don't you write it down in Akkadian? Or Sumerian? Or Egyptian, so many could read it?"

"I will if God commands it," said Abram. "And not, if not."

It made Sarai feel like an illiterate after all, because she could read common messages, the tallies of the shepherds, the laws of the temple, the tales of great deeds that must be remembered. But she could not read the words of God, and Abram only sometimes read to her what was written there. "The hand of Noah wrote this," said Abram once, and then read her something that did not sound like the words of a man who had watched the world destroyed around him. When she said so, Abram answered impatiently, "This was written before the flood. When he was still trying to save the people from destruction."

"When he still had hope," she said.

"When he still had hope for *them*," said Abram. "He never lost hope for himself and his family."

Sarai laid out the tiles of Qira's letter. As usual, Qira took no thought for the quality of the clay on which she wrote. Or perhaps water was so scarce that they used less of it for clay-making. Three of the six tiles had cracked, and one had crumbled. It was hard to figure out in some places what she had written. Large pieces could still hold syllables, but once the clay became dust, the syllables vanished. It was a good thing that she never said anything that mattered. Sarai murmured her sister's words, uttering them in the same pitch and at the same speed that Qira herself would use.

> Beloved sister, I write in a rush because the girls are such hungry birds, and even though I refuse to give them the breast the moment they have teeth they still will take nothing except from my hand. The burden of motherhood is a heavy one. There's never time to yourself.

Sarai's eyes stung at this. Qira had no thought of how her words might affect the one who read them. And it would only get worse.

> Your messenger says you still have no baby in you, but I think they have no business calling a woman barren when for all you know your husband is casting dead seed into fertile ground, why should the woman get all the blame?

The disloyalty of this was unspeakable. Did Qira blame Lot, then, for the fact that they had only daughters?

> After all, Lot's the one who planted girl seeds in me.

Apparently yes.

> And the way people look at you in Sodom, I sometimes think it's better to be barren than to have only girls to show for

all that fattening up and screaming and bleeding and stink. It's a lot of trouble to go to, and I don't know how Father put up with the comments people make. You wouldn't believe how insensitive people can be.

Yes I would.

Of course Father is a king and people don't speak to him the way they speak to women. I swear in Sodom you'd think women were made of sticks the way we get ignored. There are festivals for men every night of the year, while the women sit home and spin. And the fine fabrics from the east and the bright colors from the north, those end up on the men's backs, like peacocks they strut. I understand it though because the women really are dull. I miss my dear sister because you were never dull. Well, you were often dull but not as dull as they are, I can't even make them angry by saying outrageous things, they just look at each other as if I were a silly child who doesn't understand a thing that's happening, when it seems to me I'm the only one who even notices the world around me; they just stay indoors and take care of their babies. Those that have babies, because you'd fit right in here in Sodom, so many women are barren, only nobody ever mentions it, even though it's as obvious as can be, not a baby in the house, and these women aren't even ashamed of it, can you imagine? Not that there's any shame, but you know what I mean.

How many times can barrenness be mentioned in one letter?

Lot says you shouldn't come to Sodom after all even though I think you would get along just fine here, it's Abram who'd get in trouble, he can't ever seem to keep from pointing out sins even though everybody knows about them anyway so why point them out? Lot is finally getting used to city life though I think. He doesn't make trouble by accusing people, he just gets along with everybody. They all like him. I think

I got the better bargain in husbands, thank you very much.
I am the most sought-after woman in Sodom already, can
you imagine? I call on a dozen women a day, and they're all
at home! How can they bear it? What is a city for, if not to
go out and see the faces of a hundred people every day?
Visit me visit me visit me, the messenger gets here from
your camp in only two days, so why has it been years and
you never found your way here? Is Abram so poor at navi-
gating by the stars? Lot knows the name of every star. Visit
me!

Sarai picked up the tiles, dumped them back into the
bag, and crumbled them. There was nothing in that letter
that she would want to read again. She loved her sister,
but when she imagined spending hours in her company,
it made her too tired and sad.

She waited outside the tent door for another half hour,
spinning and spinning, while the life of the camp went on
around her. Now and then someone would approach
Abram's tent, wanting to speak to him, but Sarai, keeping
watch just across the way, would hold up a hand and
smile. Some would smile, nod, and go away. Most came
to her and told her what they wanted.

At first it was only in an emergency that they would
tell her their business, so she could decide whether to
interrupt her husband. Sometimes, though, she simply decided what to do, knowing that her decision was exactly
what Abram would have done. Only rarely had he con-
tradicted her later, and then only because he knew of circumstances she didn't know—and he made it a point to
explain this, so that she would not lose authority. Now
Abram was able to spend many hours undisturbed in his
tent, while Sarai's tent gradually became the center of the
camp. She enjoyed this, partly because it was a kingly
role, to govern and judge, so she felt she was living out
the role she was born for. But mostly she was glad that
she could free Abram to do the work he cared most

about—to study and copy out the holy writing, to pray, to listen to the voice of God in his heart.

She had spun a sheepsworth of wool, it seemed to her, and dealt with a dozen minor questions, by the time Abram emerged. His face had that curious shine to it— not light, really, but it seemed like light from his eyes, drawing her like a moth to the fire.

"What does the Lord say?" asked Sarai.

"Years ago," said Abram, "the Lord told me to get out of my father's house and go to Canaan. He said he would make a great nation out of me, and make my children a blessing to the world."

After Qira's letter, these words stung doubly. "You're getting a slow start," said Sarai.

He waved off her words, a little annoyed with her for hearing only the implicit reference to her barrenness. She couldn't help it—he never complained about it and someone had to.

"I'm explaining to you why I've refused to go far from Canaan," he said. "Why I don't go dwell in a city, why even when I have to range far beyond Jordan, I always return within a year. This is the land God has given me."

"Does he plan to let anyone else know this?" asked Sarai. "Or will they take your word for it?"

"With the Lord, things don't happen all at once," said Abram. "It might be my children or my children's children who inherit the land—I'm content having the Lord's promise." He put his fingers to her lips to stop her from mentioning that his grandchildren could not inherit anything unless she first bore him a child or two to get things started. "Sarai, I'm explaining something."

"And I'm listening."

"For just a moment, my love, listen with your ears, and leave your lips out of it."

His grin almost kept his words from stinging.

"Sarai, the Lord today affirmed his promise. He said that he would bless those that bless me, and curse those that curse me."

"Did he mention rain?"

Abram looked heavenward in supplication.

"Sorry," said Sarai.

"The Lord *mentioned*," said Abram, "a journey."

"Your life is a journey," said Sarai. Then she clamped her hand over her mouth and between her fingers mumbled, "Sorry."

"To Egypt."

She sat in silence.

"Well, don't you have anything to say to that?" he demanded.

She rolled her eyes and made a great show of trying, and failing, to pry her mouth open.

"Egypt!" said Abram. "So much wisdom there, I've heard."

She made a face and rocked her head back and forth derisively.

"Just because you didn't like the Egyptians who came to Ur-of-the-North doesn't mean there's anything wrong with Egypt itself," said Abram. "Only lowborn and ambitious Egyptians, or the highborn without ambition, end up so far from the Nile. The best of them remain in Egypt, because it's not just the oldest kingdom in the world, to them it's the *only* kingdom."

Sarai mimed falling asleep.

"They have water in Egypt, Sarai," said Abram. "The Nile is low, but it still flows, and the flood comes every spring."

"Why would they give any to us?" she said.

"Ha! I knew you couldn't keep that silence going forever!"

"Why should I bother to speak, when you don't answer my words?" asked Sarai.

"They will give us water and food and fodder because they value knowledge. They will tell me what they know, and I will tell them what I know."

"Or they'll kill you and steal your books and read for themselves."

Abram laughed. "That would be silly. They can't read it!"

"Make sure to tell them that very quickly," said Sarai, "because they might be disappointed to discover it later, but you'll be dead."

"What kinds of stories do they tell about Egypt, there in Ur-of-the-North?" asked Abram. "They don't kill every stranger who comes."

"But strangers who come from the desert with vast herds and a mighty host—how will they know, from the look of us, whether we're supplicants or invaders?"

"When I explain who I am—"

"The last time you explained to an Egyptian who you were," said Sarai, "he tried to sacrifice you."

Abram shrugged. "If the Lord chooses to let them kill me in Egypt, then that's where I'll die."

"That's well for you," said Sarai. "God knows your name, you're old friends. What happens to the rest of us?"

"He knows your name, too," said Abram.

She smiled. But inwardly she argued: Does He? Does He know that I exist? I'd rather think He didn't, that He simply hasn't noticed me, and when He does He'll say, Oh, Sarai! How could I forget a good woman like that! She needs some babies! Who was supposed to remind me of that? While if He does remember me, then my barrenness is not by chance. He must hate me.

A little voice, deep inside, said, It isn't the God of Abram who hates you. It's Asherah who tends to the wombs of women, who remembers that you belong to her.

To silence that voice, Sarai laughed. "Then let's go to Egypt, Abram. I ask only this—that you share a few crumbs of your learning with me."

"Learning is the only bread that you can share without lessening your own meal," said Abram.

"If that isn't already in your books, I hope you'll write it down," said Sarai. "It sounded very poetic and wise."

He touched her nose, then kissed her lightly. "You shouldn't mock me, you know."

"Someone has to," said Sarai, "and no one else would dare."

He sighed, but smiled, too. "That's you, Sarai. Always willing to bear the heaviest burden."

❧ CHAPTER 5 ❧

For years, Abram had made his camp in the best lands—the deepest wells, the everflowing springs, where grass grew, where trees gave shade. Sarai thought she had seen the worst of the drought, seeing how many of those trees were scant-leafed now, and how many bare-limbed; hearing the hollow echo of stones thrown down empty wells; tasting the soupy water of a dying spring.

But in truth she had been sheltered from the worst destruction of this endless dry season. For now they moved through lands that had once been farmed, through villages that once had known the voices of children shouting in the streets, women chattering at the well, men grunting as they practiced the skills of war in a field outside the wall. Now the only sound was the echoing footfalls of the flocks and herds, the bleating and mooing of beasts, the murmurs and occasional shouts of herdsmen. These were sounds she had lived with for years, but now they came in the wrong place, which made them desperately sad.

At first she would succumb to the impulse to go into one of the houses, but it was always the same. Old spider webs near the ceiling, rooms half-filled with dust swept in by wind, but no sign of human habitation. It was not a hasty departure, not the ruins of war or plague. These people had lingered until there was no more hope, and then they had moved out, taking all that they could, leaving nothing of value to them. And then their neighbors had scavenged even the valueless things, and burned what could be burned to roast the last scrawny animals or boil the last weedy soup.

The last time she entered a house, Abram came in after her. "Why do you do this?" he asked. "It only makes you morose."

"I can't decide," said Sarai, "if I should feel despair for those who left this place, or hope that someday it will be occupied again."

"Someday this village will be peopled by our grandsons and granddaughters, and the land will be full from the river to the sea."

He looked so happy and hopeful that it was all she could do to keep from screaming. She had been feeling pity for the losses of strangers; he turned it into a prophecy to be fulfilled by her drought-stricken womb. Today the time of women had come upon her, five days late. Those past five days she had allowed herself some hope, but today she had none. It will rain first, Abram, there'll be water rushing down these streets before you hold *my* baby in your arms.

Still, she said nothing, because his words came from God, and hers from grief. To him, it was as if what the Lord had promised were already fulfilled; he thought of himself as a man with many children, and it didn't occur to him that she did not live in that world. From then on she went into no more houses. She passed through each village without looking to left or right, for now it was her sons' voices that had fallen silent in the streets, her daughters' hands that spun no distaff in the houses. What a miserable life, she thought, to spend it mourning for the unconceived.

At last they left Canaan behind, and proceeded through the desert lands again. This time Abram had to consult old writings to get his bearings, for he had not come this way in many years, and the blowing dust had hidden or transformed many a landmark. Still, where there was a well to be found, he found it. But more and more of them were dry.

After a week of losing a dozen animals a day, they topped a rise and saw, in the distance, the shimmering of water. Not a mirage above burning sand this time. There was marsh grass growing in patches, then reeds, tall and topped with seeds. The beasts could not be held back— they ran, those that could, or shambled, the neediest arriving last, but there was water enough for all. Not from the marsh itself—that water was brackish, too salty to drink. Near it, though, the men hurried to dig shallow depressions into which water quickly seeped. There the animals drank greedily, the men watching to make sure all got a chance at the water, and to keep them from fouling it.

Abram did not need to watch them drink. He stood looking westward, across the water, toward Egypt. "They call this marsh the Sea of Reeds," said Abram. "We have to go around it, and the water we get this way isn't very good. But it's fresh enough for the animals, and reliable even when springs and wells fail."

"This is the boundary of Egypt?"

"Oh, I suppose we've been in Egypt for days. But off the main road."

"Why? Are we hiding?"

"Egypt is in the midst of its own troubles," said Abram. "Too many people coming because of the food and water here. They might try to keep us out."

"Compared to the herds we once had, these are only a bedraggled few," said Sarai.

"As you yourself once pointed out, it's hard to know

how they'll see us," said Abram. "We might look like an invading host. We might look like a horde of locusts. Or we might look like a weak band of travelers, easy to rob."

"Rob? I thought Pharaoh kept the peace." What she had most hoped for in Egypt was to be in a land where kings ruled and streets flowed with commerce and conversation. The city life that Qira could not live without, Sarai also sometimes missed. But cities were only worth visiting when the king maintained good order.

"Pharaoh keeps whatever Pharaoh wants," said Abram. "Or rather, Pharaoh's servants take what they want in his name. That's the tale, anyway."

"So is Pharaoh stronger in Ur-of-the-North than he is in Egypt?"

"In Ur-of-the-North, Pharaoh has influence because people wish his servants to make a good report of the city. On the borders of Egypt, Pharaoh's servants do as they wish because they are the very ones he relies on to report on their own doings."

Sarai tried to reconcile this with her own understanding of how kings must trust their servants. "They would lie to their king?"

Abram looked at her oddly. "The first skill a good king has to acquire is to learn how to find the truth behind the lies he's told."

"But your men don't lie to *you*."

"Because there are only a few of them, and the lives of their own families depend on my making wise decisions based on true knowledge. Egypt is vast, and the great system of granaries runs itself, year after year. Pharaoh's ignorance costs them nothing, individually. But a king who has no idea what is happening reels back and forth like a drunken man, and finally he will fall."

"My father fell because of invaders from the desert."

"Your father ruled wisely, and the invaders won only because they were too many for his defenses. If it's true that Pharaoh rules ignorantly, then he might be brought down by a much smaller force."

"If this place teeters on the brink of chaos, then why are we here?" asked Sarai. "Why didn't we go north, to the Hurrian lands? Or east into Elam?"

"Because the Lord is with us," said Abram, "and this is where He said that we should go." He put his hand on her arm. "Sarai, I told you of the dangers so you'd know why I'm being cautious. But in all likelihood, we look strong enough that we won't be molested, and yet not so strong as to make Pharaoh fear us. It will go as the Lord wills, but I try to be prudent all the same."

They camped well back from the lake, so they would not be tortured by the biting flies that lived on the edges of the water, and so the stupider beasts would not drink from the salt marsh and die. The next day they moved south, skirting the marsh until at last they rejoined the road.

They were spotted almost at once by two men who took off running.

"We must be frightening after all," said Sarai.

"No," said Abram. "They're just doing their job. They watch until there's something to see, then they run back to report on us."

"They're naked," said Sarai.

"Didn't I mention that?" said Abram. "Egyptians aren't much for clothing. They use it more for ornamentation than modesty."

"But all the Egyptians I've known wore clothing."

"And so will the wealthy Egyptians you meet here," said Abram, "though slaves and poor farmers are as likely to be naked as not. And even the wealthy—well, you'll see. White linen is the rule here, finely woven. Very cool and comfortable, keeping off the sun while letting in the air. Almost as easy to see through as water."

"No."

"Pretend that it doesn't bother you," said Abram. "If you look away, they'll tease you. If you stare, they'll get angry."

"If they're naked, how can they hope that no one will stare?"

"Because no one does," said Abram. "If no one looks at you, then you aren't really naked, are you?"

"A person with no clothes on is naked, whether anyone's looking or not."

"That's because you're not an Egyptian." Abram laughed again. "Sarai, it's not as bad as you think. This is a civilized country, as long as you adapt to their customs. They'll even tolerate our strange foreign ways—all this extra clothing we wear—as long as we don't seem to be criticizing them."

Egypt was not sounding half so enticing to her now. Why hadn't he mentioned this before? Perhaps he hadn't realized it would bother her. Or perhaps he simply knew that they were going to Egypt no matter how she felt about it, and he simply refrained from warning her until the last possible moment, to spare her weeks of dread along the road.

Well, that just proved that he didn't understand her yet. Because she always preferred to know. She could have been preparing herself for weeks. Instead, this matter of clothing came as a shock.

The sun was still a good three hands above the horizon when a group of soldiers came jogging along the road toward them.

"Good," said Abram. "Enough force to show respect, but not so many as to imply they fear us." He gave commands to his men to move the animals away from the road, into the grassier land nearer the water, while he talked with the soldiers.

The commander was a young nobleman named Kay—very young, but not all that noble, Sarai could see that at once. He was still unsure of his station, which made him a little belligerent as he spoke to them in a mixture of Egyptian and Amorite words. But he was not a fool. While Abram was busy reassuring and calming him, Sarai could see that Kay was taking inventory of Abram's household, counting the men capable of fighting, and counting the women and children as well. Abram had made sure that they would be in plain sight. Now Sarai realized why. The Egyptians would be suspicious if there were not families enough for all the men of fighting age, for then this might be a party of raiders.

And something else. Sarai wasn't sure, but she thought that Kay had recognized Abram's name. That concerned her. What report had come back to Egypt, after the attempt by Suwertu to have Abram killed? Surely those events in Ur-of-the-North all those years ago could not be remembered now.

When Kay had already formed up his men to escort Abram's household into Egypt, he asked, almost as an afterthought, "And this is the princess, yes? Your wife, yes?"

Abram hesitated for only a moment, and then answered with a laugh. "My wife, come on such a journey? You don't know princesses! This is my sister, Milcah."

Sarai had long since learned how not to let her face or body reveal surprise—or anything else. A king's daughter must master *that* skill, at least, even if she *was* intended for the temple.

Kay turned to her. "The sister of Abram is very beautiful," he said.

"Pharaoh's voice at the border is sweet as honey," she replied.

"Where is the lady's husband? Is he not with this party?"

Abram laughed. "Husband? And where would I have found a husband for my sister? You see how my herds are depleted. I haven't the bride-price for a great man, and I love my sister too much to give her to a peasant."

"Some women are their own bride-price," said Kay.

But he had gone too far, even for an official of a great king. "You speak like a suitor," said Abram coldly, "and not like a soldier."

Kay did not seem at all abashed, or even embarrassed.

He simply bade them stay near the road and follow him and his men toward the first town.

Sarai was careful not to confer with Abram for some time, waiting until the soldiers were some distance ahead. By then Abram had already passed the word through one of his servants that Sarai was to be addressed by the name of Abram's sister-in-law Milcah, who lived in Haran, in the house of Abram's father Terah far to the north.

"How did I become your sister?" she asked him softly.

"When he asked me about you," said Abram, "I knew by the power of God that if I told him the truth, I would be killed."

"But you already told him your name," said Sarai. "If they blame Abram the son of Terah for the death of Suwertu, what difference does it make who *I* am?"

"This isn't about Suwertu," said Abram. "He knew that Abram son of Terah had married Sarai the daughter of the king-in-exile of Ur, and I knew in that moment that if they thought I was bringing you into Egypt as my wife, you would soon be a widow."

"Why?"

"So Pharaoh could marry you himself."

"But . . . that's absurd. Pharaohs marry their sisters, everyone knows that."

"Yes. Which means that something is terribly wrong here."

"One thing, certainly. You just presented me as a single woman, and here I am dressed like a married one."

"And he said nothing about it, though if he knows anything about the way we dress, he could see the difference," said Abram. "So he's no doubt wondering if I lied, or if you're married, or perhaps widowed."

"Abram, if the daughter of an exiled king is desirable, why wouldn't the sister of a desert priest-king be just as useful?"

"Do you think I haven't thought of that?" said Abram.

"So there's no danger?"

"No danger?" He looked grim. "There's very grave

danger. The first Pharaohs originally came from our country, the grasslands of the east—that's why the Egyptian language is so close to ours. Perhaps Pharaoh is trying to assert that ancient authority. Or perhaps he fears it. And . . . I *have* the very authority the original Pharaohs claimed to have. Pharaoh might regard me as a threat, or he might regard me as someone worth linking himself to. As my sister, you may be even more useful to him than you would have been as my widow."

"Useful?" said Sarai. "How am I to be useful to Pharaoh without dishonoring myself and betraying you and disobeying God?"

"I tell you what Pharaoh might be thinking. What God is thinking, I don't know."

This was not the comfort Sarai had been hoping for. "What will I do?"

"Trust in God," said Abram.

"That's your whole plan?"

"It was God who told me to come here, and God who told me to tell him you were my sister," said Abram. "Beyond that, what do I know?"

"What are you and God doing to me?" asked Sarai. "I'm not your sister, in case you've forgotten, and I'm not a single woman, eligible to be snagged by kings in order to prop up their dynasties." Finally, though, she got a good look at Abram's face, and saw that he was as upset about this as she was.

"For now, you must pretend to be single," said Abram, "or I'm a dead man. I'll plead with the Lord to keep you safe."

Sarai heard this in silence, and walked in silence for half a mile before she found her voice to answer. All the while she was in turmoil, frightened and angry but not sure whom to be angry at, God or Abram. And when she did speak, she didn't say at all what was in her heart. She didn't plead with him to turn around and leave. She didn't beg him to protect her himself. She didn't demand that he go back to God and get an alternate plan. Instead, she answered with a voice that she had never heard herself use before. Qira's voice, sarcastic and cutting. "And if there had been a battle, would you have handed a sword to me and pushed me ahead of you into the fray?"

Abram felt the accusation like a blow—she saw him stagger under it. "I did not choose this way," he said.

Try as she might, she could not get that nasty tone out of her voice. "The thought came to you that calling me your sister would keep you safe. What I wonder is, was it really God that gave you the idea? Or fear?"

Before she could say more to wound him, she strode faster, moving ahead of him. Part of her wanted to turn back and cling to him, weeping, assuring him of her love for him. But it would not do to let the soldiers see her act so wifelike. And besides, a part of her was very, very angry and meant every nasty word that she had said. What exactly would Abram do if Pharaoh decided that he wanted a woman from an ancient priestly house as his wife? What would *she* do? Kings were not inclined to take no for an answer. If she did not bend to Pharaoh's will, even in such a terrible sin, Abram might end up just as dead as if Pharaoh thought that she was his wife.

The thought of Abram murdered was unbearable. At once her anger at God was swept away in fear for her husband. Do whatever you must to me, she prayed silently, but let no harm come to Abram!

And another thought: Maybe God means to take me away from him, so he can marry a woman who will bear him sons.

❧ CHAPTER 6 ❧

From the first, the palace officials did their best to separate Sarai from Abram. As they first came to the green and settled lands near the river, Kay suggested that Milcah and the other women and children might want to rest in the shade while Abram went ahead to meet with Sehtepibre, Pharaoh's most trusted steward.

"My sister is as wise as any man," said Abram, "and I will not be without her counsel."

Kay did not press the point. But when they reached the river, where a servant from the palace awaited them with ten ships, again there was an attempt to separate them. Abram made it clear he would leave only the herders' own families with them. "Milcah" would stay with her brother. "Does a man leave a precious jewel among cows and sheep?"

"But floating on the river makes women ill," said Khnumhotpe, the servant from the palace. "At least let your sister's boat travel more slowly, so she and her maidservants do not suffer, while the oarsmen make *your* boat leap ahead to take you to lord Pharaoh."

"Those who have ridden on dromedaries will not be sickened by a bit of wobbling in a boat," said Abram. "And I wish to see the greatness of the river with my sister, whose eyes are my own, as mine are hers."

Abram's statement might have been true, but Sarai had never actually ridden on a dromedary—only those who crossed the great stretches of pure sand far to the south of their rangeland ever needed those towering beasts. But to these city people, utterly without experience of the desert life, anything was possible.

On the lead boat, oarsmen poled them up the edges of the river while boats and rafts floated down the middle current. Abram and Sarai sat together, watching the farms of Egypt endlessly pass by them. "It could be the Euphrates," she said. "But here, there isn't a cubit of land that is not farmed or dwelt on. Where will your herds graze?"

"There must be grassland beyond the farms," said Abram.

"No, lord Abram," said Khnumhotpe. "The farms run to the desert edge. That's what the drought has done to us. All the grasslands are buried in sand or burned away by the sun. Where the river's flood puts mud, we farm; where it doesn't, there is no life at all."

"But I've seen many desert people living here," said Abram. "From their clothing, at least, they seemed like those who once lived in Canaan or on the range. Where do *their* herds live?"

"Those who wish to keep their animals buy fodder. Others rent some scrap of surviving rangeland from great lords or from Pharaoh himself. Most, though, came to Egypt because their herds were gone."

"How do they live, then?" asked Sarai.

"As servants, of course." Khnumhotpe did not seem surprised that Sarai spoke up as if she were their conversational equal.

"They give up their freedom?" asked Sarai.

"Many were captured in war," said Khnumhotpe.

"Many others, though, sell their freedom for gruel and beer. We have it, they don't. And they have nothing to buy it with except their labor. They survive, and Egypt has more servants than it knows what to do with." Khnumhotpe chuckled, as if this surplus of slaves were amusing.

But Sarai had seen the Canaanites and Amorites, too, and very few of them seemed to be servants. Khnumhotpe was either lying, or he was himself ignorant of the life of the desert people. Which was quite possible. *Hsy*, the term he used for Canaanites and Amorites, Hittites and Sumerians and Libyans interchangeably, was not uttered with any special contempt—but the word meant "vile" or "shameful." It was clear that Egyptians regarded even the great cities of the east as nothing compared to the majesty of Egypt.

Well, what city did not think itself the best of all possible places? The difference in Egypt was that it was not a series of cities vying with each other for supremacy. That issue had been settled long ago. Egypt was a single kingdom, and all who held office in any city did so at the pleasure of Pharaoh. People did not belong to a mere city, they belonged to a great nation whose king was a god who ruled from the far reaches of the high river to the coasts of the sea. So when an Egyptian spoke of foreigners as contemptible people, it was not just empty brag. Egypt was whole, and all other nations were in pieces.

"Egypt seems to find something for every man and woman to do," said Sarai. "I've seen no idle hands . . . except our own."

Khnumhotpe laughed at that, laughed without derision. He seemed genuinely to enjoy her company. But when Sarai glanced at Abram, she saw him roll his eyes. Apparently he did not take Khnumhotpe's jovial disposition at face value. Sarai wondered if Abram was right. After all, they were no longer in the desert. They were with royal servants now, and that was something Sarai understood, having grown up in a house that, despite its poverty and lack of power, was nonetheless royal. Was it not possible that Abram was distrustful because he was on less familiar ground?

He *had* held his own in encounters with her father, Sarai remembered that, and Abram often did business in cities. Still, she had been raised in a king's house, and it was to a king's house they were going. She liked Khnumhotpe, and Khnumhotpe seemed to like her. Why was that a matter for suspicion? If Abram wanted to act the jealous husband, he might have declared her publicly to be his wife.

She smiled at Khnumhotpe. "Then again, we are the sort of people who work by thinking and speaking. So while our hands may do little labor at this moment, yet we are not at rest."

Again she glanced at Abram, but now he was not looking at her at all. He was gazing out over the water, toward a large brightly painted building that opened onto a great sweep of steps leading down into the river. The boats were steering toward a jetty that flanked the stairs.

"So this is the king's house," she said to Khnumhotpe.

"One of them."

"Will he see us, do you think?"

"Without question," said Khnumhotpe. "He has a keen interest in your brother. His name is not unknown here."

That set off a silent cry of alarm in Sarai's heart. Khnumhotpe was a man who chose his words carefully. And he had carefully avoided saying whether Pharaoh's "interest" in Abram was kindly or threatening. Yet Khnumhotpe gave no sign of any but the cheerfulest of attitudes. Perhaps Abram's suspicions had been wiser than Sarai's trust.

Khnumhotpe leapt to the jetty as soon as the boat drew near enough. He held out a hand as if to help Sarai, but while she was still gathering her skirts about her for the leap from bouncing boat to solid land, Abram bounded to the jetty with such force that, had she been in midstep, she would have plunged into the water. "Abram," she said in consternation.

"I wanted to help my sister to shore myself," Abram explained to Khnumhotpe.

In reply, Khnumhotpe clapped Abram on the shoulder. "Oh, no need of that! Milcah will be taken to the house of Pharaoh's wives to be given a chance to rest and refresh herself in the company of women."

Sure enough, the boat was drawing back from the jetty; it was already impossible for her to make the leap, and Sarai could not swim. Neither could Abram, though as he stood there on the dock, she could guess that he was furiously trying to decide just how hard swimming could be, since so many children of servants here by the Nile could do it. Khnumhotpe had outmaneuvered them. Abram had understood the Egyptian well enough to know not to trust him. But Khnumhotpe had understood Abram even better, well enough to manipulate him into allowing the separation he had so adamantly refused. And Sarai—clearly she had understood nothing at all.

"No, Abram, you go with Khnumhotpe," Sarai called to him. "Pharaoh does not want to meet your sister covered with the dirt of travel." She was warning him not to try to fight this right now. This was the moment of greatest danger. If they were going to kill him, they would do it now, the moment Sarai was out of sight. "Think nothing of me," she insisted, her voice now echoing from the stone steps as she shouted over the growing expanse of water. "Let your thoughts be on your own imminent meeting with Suwertu's master." The name of the priest who had sought to kill him was the only warning she could give him. And she was now too far away to be able to see, from his face, whether he had understood.

O God of Abram, she prayed. Forgive my selfishness in resenting the deception thou didst urge upon us, and my vanity in thinking I was wise in the ways of a royal house. I will bear whatever burden Thou placest upon me, but keep my husband safe. Let him live, O God, to have the children of Thy promise to him. It matters not to me that I be the mother of those children, as long as Abram is their father.

But even as she prayed the words—and surely she meant them—another voice, one that could not find words, was crying out in anguish in the deep recesses of her mind. To think of another woman as the mother of Abram's children was unbearable. Was this the vengeance of Asherah?

Yet with the part of her mind that she could control, she outshouted that wordless wish. Better that it be Asherah avenging a broken oath and reclaiming a lost servant than to have it be Pharaoh, avenging the death of Suwertu and claiming the life of an escaped sacrifice. God, hear the words I pray, not the unworthy, selfish cry of my inmost heart.

PART III

PHARAOH'S
WOMEN

❧ CHAPTER 7 ❧

What impressed Sarai most was the cleanliness. How did they manage it? The same wind blew here as anywhere else, carrying dust, fine sand, fleas, and flies. Yet in the house of Pharaoh, the stone floors held no dust, the tapestries on the walls were unfaded by dirt or sunlight, and water stood in pools so clear she could see the mosaics on the bottom. Everyone moved swiftly and quietly about their tasks. She could hear the laughter of children as she passed one door, the low throaty chuckle of a gossiping woman as she passed another, but the work of the house—the work of banishing every grain of sand—went on silently, invisibly.

In such cleanliness, where does anyone live? Children are dirty, work is dirty, *life* is dirty, so when you ban the dirt, where does the life of the house go? And yet there was that laughter, that chuckle; there was pleasure and delight in this place. And Sarai felt, for the first time in her life, like a country bumpkin, for in Ur there was no such luxury as this, to banish the desert.

It was men who brought her here—obsequious men in command, bored soldiers giving teeth to their authority. Sarai said little and tried to smile benignly as if being kidnapped and carried off to Pharaoh's house were exactly what she had expected in a place as benighted as this. She tried not to let herself gawk at the size of the house. She refused to ask questions. And so she found herself now following a servant girl through the labyrinth of rooms, with no idea where she was going or what was expected of her.

They entered a room where a woman sat in conversation with a man. The woman wore a linen drape so light that Sarai could see the shape of her breasts as easily as if she were naked. The man wore a kilt of linen, but it was apparently long enough to be wrapped twice around him, so it was not so transparent. Still, even from behind she knew more about his body than she wanted to. On the way here, she had seen that the workers in the fields were naked, but they were far away. The soldiers wore kilts, but of rougher, thicker fabric. It seemed that the rich wore clothing, but clothing that left them as close to the nakedness of the poor as possible.

I would not dress like that even if I were dead.

"Ah," the woman said. "The desert princess."

"No princess," said Sarai.

"If you stay in this house, you're a princess," said the woman. "But the desert, we'd prefer to leave that outside."

"So would I," said Sarai, "but I was brought here with no chance to rest or change my clothing after a long journey."

"How untidy," she said. "I am told you are Milcah. My name is Eshut."

"Are you the queen?" asked Sarai.

She gave a brief glance at the man, but neither showed any sign of what they thought of her question. "No," said Eshut. "I am a cousin of Pharaoh. I manage his household and see to it that the women and children of the house are provided for. This is Sehtipibre, who manages Pharaoh's kingdom and sees to it that the people of Egypt are provided for."

Sehtipibre smiled slightly. "Pharaoh and his brother gods provide for Egypt," he said. And then, without so much as a pause, he continued in thickly accented Sumerian: "They do a better job of it than the gods who pour water into the Euphrates, I hear."

Sarai did not have to pretend to be straining to understand—Milcah would not understand Sumerian at all, but even Sumerians would have a hard time understanding Sehtipibre. "I'm so sorry," she said. "My Egyptian is so bad that I didn't understand a word you said."

He grimaced slightly. "No one ever does. I hoped that, being from the upper Euphrates, you might have some knowledge of Sumerian."

"Oh, that's a very hard language, and few speak it even in Sumeria now—it's all one Amorite dialect or another."

"You don't consider yourself an Amorite?"

"You don't consider me one, either," said Sarai. "You think of me as Hsy."

This earned her a thin smile, but not a nice one. "I can see that Abram's sister is unmarried for good reason."

"If you are proposing to me," said Sarai, "I'm afraid I must ask you to take your petition to my brother."

His face reddened slightly, but he did not speak—perhaps because of his iron self-control, or perhaps because of Eshut's hand lightly touching his arm. "My lord Sehtipibre," she said, "you have made the mistake of sparring with a great lady, who is weary from traveling and annoyed at the abrupt way our hospitality was imposed on her."

"When you make your report to Pharaoh," said Sehtipibre, "please point out that I did not call her Hsy. It was a term she chose herself."

"I'm so sorry," said Sarai. "I thought it was an Egyptian word, since I heard it so many times in the muttering of my hosts."

"Go, go," said Eshut. "Let us not fight a border skirmish here in the House of the Women."

"Am I dismissed from the sacred presence?" Even though the language was not easy to understand, Sarai grasped his irony. It was he, not she, who normally would do the dismissing.

"No," said Eshut, "I and the whole house are dismissed from your presence. But the house is too big to move, so it would be a kindness if you would remove yourself instead."

Sehtipibre smiled then, with warmth—but the smile became chilly when he turned from Eshut to Sarai. He murmured a brief blessing and walked from the room.

"How would an Egyptian man learn a language like Sumerian?" asked Sarai.

"Sehtipibre told me once that his goal is to know everything and do everything."

"I assume that he will do death last."

"He does not expect to achieve his goal. Still, he can't help but profit from the attempt. Now let us cease this conversation and get you to your room. Will you have wine? The barley beer of Egypt? Or is there some concoction of goat's milk and sheep's blood that you drink?"

Eshut looked completely cheerful, but Sarai understood now that she was in the house of her betters and would be criticized or ridiculed whatever she did. So be it—since the condemnation was assured, she might as well please herself. Besides, she was a hostage here, wasn't she? So she answered with a light laugh, "Oh, dear, no. I doubt that anyone here would have the skill to make *that* drink."

That broke Eshut's poise, for a moment at least. Sarai could imagine her gossiping later. "I joked that she might want to drink something of goat's milk and sheep's blood and—can you believe it?—apparently there *is* such a drink!" Someday, perhaps, someone would point out to Eshut that in fact there was no such drink, and Eshut would realize, belatedly, how Sarai had mocked her to her face.

"I'll have the beer, please. It's what Egypt is most famous for." Again, a little jab. Let her wonder if it really was their nasty barley drink, and not the Nile or the pyramids, that foreigners talked about.

"By the way," said Eshut, "we asked among your company and the only maid they could find for you was a woman so old I doubt she could dress herself, let alone you."

"I've been dressing myself since childhood," said Sarai.

Eshut gave Sarai's clothing a brief glance. "And there's so much of it."

"But it doesn't require a miracle to keep it on," said Sarai.

"Ah, yes, I'm aware that you desert people think that our clothing is improper."

"Not at all," said Sarai. "It's just that our men have enough imagination or memory that they don't need constant reminders of what women look like under their clothes."

Eshut sighed. "He's had desert women before, you know."

"Before what?" said Sarai. "Surely you do not imply that he has 'had' or will 'have' *me?*"

"As a guest, of course," said Eshut. "Let's not quarrel, shall we? He may have an infatuation with all things Mesopotamian, but in fact he is Egyptian, and he prefers the women in his house to be clean—and their clothing as well, even your exotic desert clothing."

"You keep speaking of the desert," said Sarai, "but I have spent my life passing easily between grassland and city, while I have only seen true desert here, in *your* land. Start from the assumption that I have not spent my entire life among cattle, and perhaps we can cease our banter before one of us gets offended."

Now was the moment for Eshut to break down and smile and embrace her as a sister. Instead, she merely grew chillier. "Perhaps it is time for me to assign you a maid who will find your exotic ideas fascinating." She glanced over her shoulder. "Hagar," she said.

A tall young woman—still a girl, really, from her boy-ish hips and scant bosom—entered through the door be-hind Eshut, her head bowed, her hands clasped before her.

"Hagar, this is Princess—oh, pardon me, *Lady*—Milcah. She's to be a guest in the house. Do show her where to bathe and get her clothes to the laundresses. You'll be with her while she's here."

Hagar bowed deeply to Eshut, and then again to Sarai.

"Thank you for your help," Sarai said to the servant girl.

She stood there, in midbow, obviously unsure how to respond. Had no one ever thanked her?

"You see how pleasant it will be, Hagar, learning the charming customs of desert people," said Eshut. "Go now, Hagar. Lady Milcah is no doubt eager to wash the filth of travel from her body."

"If only a mere bath," said Sarai, "could make me as beautiful as Lady Eshut." She spoke without allowing even a trace of irony into her voice.

Eshut looked at her sharply for a moment, then raised an eyebrow—as eloquent as another woman's shrug. "Our house is richer for your presence here, Lady Milcah. And I know Pharaoh will be delighted with your . . . charming conversation, as I have been."

Hagar was at the door now, waiting for Sarai to follow, which she gratefully did.

You may put on airs, Eshut, but I'm a captive here, and that makes you my jailer.

❧ CHAPTER 8 ❧

Hagar led her to a room not far away, one with
windows overlooking a lush garden. The smell
of the blooms reached even into the room,
though the windows were so deep that only the sun's light
and very little of its heat made it through. If there had
been such a room in her father's house in Ur-of-the-North,
that is where he would have brought his visitors, for such
constant extravagance with water would have spoken
more of his wealth and power than any other display he
might have made. Yet here in the house of Pharaoh's
women, this room was no doubt quite an ordinary one.
Or was it? It was hard to know whether she was being
treated with honor or disdain. Quite probably both—
outward respect and secret contempt.

All that mattered to Sarai was what this might imply
with regard to Abram. If this was an opulent room, did
that mean Abram would be treated well? Or did the favor
extend only to her, so that his life was in danger if he
resisted whatever Pharaoh might want of her?

"Do *you* have any idea what any of this means?" Sarai asked the servant girl.

Hagar looked at her blankly.

"Is my accent so bad you can't understand me?"

"I can understand you," said Hagar—in heavily accented Egyptian.

"So you're not a native of Egypt," said Sarai. "What language do you speak, then, from birth?" She tried Amorite first, and the girl seemed pleased enough.

"If Mistress wishes to speak the tongue of the desert thieves, it's all one to me," said Hagar. Her tone was sweet, but the barb was obvious. Had the girl sized her up and decided Sarai wasn't dangerous?

In Hebrew, Sarai said, "Is this a good room or an ordinary one?"

The girl paused a moment before she got what was said. "That is for Mistress to judge."

One more language to try. In the Arabic of spice traders from the south, Sarai said, "Is this your tongue?"

Hagar's eyes widened, and suddenly a torrent of words poured forth. Sarai was not fluent in Arabic, and though it was close to Hebrew and Amorite, there were enough differences that she only caught a few phrases—enough to know that Hagar was asking her if she had come only recently from Arabia and did she know anything of Hagar's father. A boatmaker? A sailor?

"You must talk Arabic more slowly for me," said Sarai in a mix of Egyptian and Arabic. "I have never visited your homeland. I only know the few words I learned from spice merchants."

"The desert Bedu is no merchant, only a trader," Hagar said scornfully. "My father is a real merchant, with three fine ships." She looked away as if to hide emotion. "If they were not all seized when I was captured. That is the only reason I can think of that my family has not ransomed me. The pirates ruined their fortune, and with nothing to pay ransom, the pirates could only profit from me by selling me into slavery here in Egypt."

"How long have you been in bondage?"

Hagar looked at her oddly for a moment, then replied. "Six years."

"Then you were a mere child when they took you!"

"I was a child until that day, but on that day I became old. I have lived since then with one foot in the grave."

"Why? Is your health bad?"

Hagar looked at her in amazement. "I was once the daughter of a rich house, and you ask why I feel myself to be dead?"

"Rich or poor, orphan or daughter, you are still a daughter of God, still yourself."

Hagar laughed derisively. "Which god? A weak one, if he protects me no better than this."

"Ah. So *you* are the one mortal soul who should suffer nothing and lose nothing, while all the rest of us struggle on."

"What have *you* lost, king's daughter?"

"I am also a captive here," said Sarai.

"Then where are the scars of your beatings? Why are your cheeks plump while those of the other captives are gaunt?"

"It pleases them to pretend that I am their guest. But I may not go when I wish, and my brother may or may not be killed by Pharaoh's men. He may already be dead."

"I've already lost brothers, sisters, parents, myself," said Hagar. "I hope you don't mind if I fail to cry for you."

"I never asked you to cry for me. I merely tell you why I will not cry for *you*."

"Good. I don't want your tears." Hagar looked away, angry.

"Do you speak to all of Pharaoh's guests this way?"

"None but you ever tried to pry into my life, or to judge me."

"I meant only to encourage you," said Sarai. "For God *does* look over you, and if you live by His will, He will turn all things to good."

"If you really believed that, you wouldn't be afraid for your brother."

Her words stung Sarai. "God is perfect, even if my faith is not."

"You speak as if you expected me to believe in *your* god."

"I expect nothing," said Sarai. "But since the God of Abram is the only god that actually exists, you might as well believe in Him, for it is He and He alone who hears the prayers of the righteous." She meant what she said, but in a tiny corner of her mind she harbored the dread that Asherah had heard her.

"No god has ever heard my prayers."

"Or you have never recognized God's answers."

"Oh, his answers are familiar to me," said Hagar heatedly. "To every favor I beg, the answer is no. To every plea for understanding, his answer is confusion."

Sarai laid her hand on the girl's head, meaning only to stroke her hair. Hagar jerked her head away.

"If I had beaten you with a stick," said Sarai, "you would have borne it without flinching. But the hand of friendship . . ."

"That was not the hand of friendship," said Hagar. "That was the hand of pity."

Sarai took a deep breath, to hold back the sharp answer she wanted to give. "You already know that I am your friend," said Sarai.

"I do not."

"It's obvious you trust me, or you wouldn't dare speak so boldly to me."

Hagar almost blurted out a sharp answer, but Sarai's words caught her, made her wait. "Why would I trust you?"

"Because you know that I am like you at least in one way—I am in dire need of a friend, and in this place the only hope of one is you."

"How can a slave be a friend to a princess?"

"I'm no princess," said Sarai.

"I'm supposed to trust you when you lie to me?"

"How could you know whether it's a lie or not?" demanded Sarai.

"You gave away the truth when you spoke to Eshut, and then to me."

"But I spoke to you both exactly the same."

"Yes. That's what gave you away."

Sarai tried to imagine what she had said or done. She spoke to both of them with respect, not condescending to them in any way that she was aware of.

Hagar laughed at Sarai's consternation. "You're used to speaking to anyone, man or woman, as if they were your equal. That is an attitude that only those who are born of the noblest blood can have. Eshut must always put her inferiors in their place, because she is so keenly aware that there are people above her, so afraid that people will not give her the respect she wants. You *know* that no one is above you."

"Or I know that no one is beneath me."

Hagar shook her head. "Slaves *must* understand whose authority is greatest, so that we can know whose command takes precedence. You know from the start that you have authority. In this house, only Pharaoh's queen and her daughters have such confidence."

"You compare me to Pharaoh's wife?"

"Actually, you're more confident of your place than she is," said Hagar.

"I wish I were," said Sarai. "I wish I knew from one moment to the next what would happen to me and my . . . brother." She stammered in fear for Abram. She was going to give him away. Milcah would never act as Hagar had seen. Her disguise had not lasted a whole day in court. She began to cry, half-stifled sobs that racked her body but hardly made a sound.

Hagar came to her, put an arm around her. "Mistress," said Hagar. "You have nothing to fear from Pharaoh. He's fascinated by the gods and kings of the east. He believes that the first Pharaohs who united Egypt were of the east, of the land between rivers. He believes that the blood of the Pharaohs runs thin and weak, and the gods have sent famine to the east in order to bring the strong blood of the desert peoples to reinvigorate Egypt. You are in no danger here. Pharaoh has brought you into his house so you might give him vigorous royal sons and daughters."

At those words, Sarai burst into tears in earnest.

"Mistress, what did I say?"

"Sons and daughters," said Sarai bitterly. "What have I ever asked of God, except sons and daughters?"

"But you're not married, Mistress, how . . ." And then Hagar understood. "Abram is not your brother."

"Tell no one," said Sarai. "God told him he must pretend I am his sister."

"I will keep your secret," said Hagar. "But if you are Abram's wife, then you are Sarai, the priestess of Asherah who renounced her vow."

"I was never her priestess, I never made a vow."

"But you *are* the one they say this of."

Sarai nodded.

"Your god is right. For marriage to Milcah, the desert maiden, Pharaoh would pay your brother a handsome bride-price. But Pharaoh would kill ten thousand husbands to have as his wife the daughter of the ancient kings of Ur-of-the-South."

"My husband's future is in your hands."

"As my future is in yours," said Hagar.

So it would be a bargain. "How can I hold your future?"

"When you leave here and go home to the east, take me with you."

"But you belong to Pharaoh."

"I do not ask you to steal me," said Hagar. "He'll ask you what gift you want to take with you. I beg you, ask for me."

"But I live in the desert, where life is hard and we lack for water, for almost everything."

"What do I care? I own nothing, not even my body. I

have spent my childhood wishing I could die. But if I lived as your servant, my captivity would be bearable."

Sarai tried to figure out why Hagar might feel this way. And then gave up, for there was never a way to know why others felt as they felt or did what they did. "As long as you want, you will always have a place at my side."

"But you must ask for me, as a gift."

"I will ask," said Sarai. "When the time is right. I won't leave without asking, as long as you don't—"

"Don't what? This is not a bargain, not a trade. I will never tell your secrets."

Sarai blushed at having been caught in such a false judgment. "It's the same with me," she said. "Even if someone else guesses my secret as you did, I'll ask for you as my handmaiden. But on the day when the desert life is so hard that you wish you were still a slave in Egypt, remember that this was your own choice."

They clasped hands. Sarai wondered as she gazed into the eyes of this bold Arab girl: Might this child be a part of God's plan?

Or was Sarai merely part of Hagar's plan?

CHAPTER 9

For a woman who was used to being deeply involved in all the concerns of a large household, the sheer inactivity of Pharaoh's house was mindnumbing. No one came to her to make decisions. She could not even see any real work being done close by. Hagar helped her bathe that first day, teaching her the use of bathing tools that she had never seen before, and then it took two hours to do up her hair to Hagar's satisfaction. There were more hours spent searching for Egyptian clothes that Sarai was willing to wear, until at last she insisted that her own clothing be brought from the camp. Hagar looked at even her lightest frock in distaste, but when Sarai wore it she didn't feel naked as she did in the Egyptian linens. She ate supper, she went to bed, she tried to sleep, and for hours she drifted back and forth between fretting about Abram and dreaming about him.

Then, the next morning, Hagar was ready to start it all over again.

"Bathe *again?*"

"Every day," said Hagar.

"But I've gone nowhere, done nothing since I bathed yesterday. I've done no *work*."

Hagar looked faintly ill. "You expect to move through Pharaoh's house *unwashed? What if *he* sees you?"

"I won't do it. It would take hours to do my hair again."

"Not so long a time as yesterday, Mistress. I've done your hair once, and now I understand it better."

"There's nothing to understand. I'll bathe again when there's some reason to. Water is precious!"

"Begging your pardon, Mistress, but here it's not."

"That's still no reason to waste it!"

"You might as well use the water, Mistress. If you don't, it either dries up in the heat of the day or it flows back into the Nile."

"Forget the bath, and tell me where I'm to go."

"Go?"

"The work of the house," Sarai said. "I'm good with a needle, I'm excellent at cakes, sweet or hearty, and if I'm not up to the standards of the house I can always work the distaff."

Hagar looked baffled. "You're not a servant, Mistress. You're a guest."

"I should hope that I may still do something useful. What I don't know, I'll learn."

"But . . . there *is* no work in this house. Except hand-maid's work—and whose hair would *you* put up? Mine?"

In the days since then, Sarai had come to see that Hagar was right. When Sarai pitched in at any task, horrified servants backed away in fear, complaining that she'd get them beaten if anyone caught her doing their work. At last she found herself pacing her room like a lion in a pit. "What do the women of the house *do* all day?" she demanded.

"They visit each other, which you could certainly do."

"I don't know any of them."

"You can be introduced."

"I would have to lie to them."

"You have to lie to everyone."

"Each time I tell it, it becomes less convincing."

"If you won't visit, and you can't work, I suppose you'll have to lie on your bed and sleep."

"I've lain there long enough without sleeping," said Sarai. "I'll at least walk somewhere."

"I thought you were a captive."

"As long as they have Abram separated from me, I dare not go far. But I can walk by the river."

Which is what she was doing when a horn was sounded from the roof of the house. Sarai turned to face upriver, back toward the house, to see if there was some raid on the flocks by marauders or a lion. Of course there was no such thing. The horn had sounded in greeting—a barge was coming down the river, a throne in the center of it, and on the throne a splendid-looking man wearing the double crown of Egypt. It was Pharaoh.

"They'll be looking for you, Mistress."

"Why?" said Sarai. "I'm sure Pharaoh will keep them busy enough."

Hagar smiled knowingly. "I'm sure Pharaoh is here to keep *you* busy."

"Enough of that, I beg you."

"Why do you deny the very reason for a woman's life?"

"The reason for a woman's life," said Sarai, "is the same as the reason for a man's—so that she might have joy."

"Then most people have no reason to live," said Hagar.

"Most people try to find joy where joy is not to be found," said Sarai, thinking of her sister. Though Qira no doubt thought she *was* joyful. If you believe you have joy, Sarai wondered, then how can you be wrong? Certainly many people managed to be miserable in the midst of a life that others envied, and their misery was real enough. Didn't most of the household think she was a woman who should be happy, having every luxury they knew of, and the love of her husband? Why did she allow the one great lack of her life to blind her to the many great bounties?

As Hagar had predicted, a runner soon came to seek her—came straight toward her, without hesitation, which proved, if she had needed proof, that someone was always watching where she went. "If Great Lady Mistress will return to meet the god," said the girl.

"I told you," said Hagar.

With sick dread Sarai went to meet the man who held her life, and her husband's life, in his hands.

The regalia of the Pharaoh gave an overwhelming impression, but the man beneath the double crown did not. Sarai tried to be fair—what man could measure up to the majesty surrounding the king of Egypt?—but then realized that she knew dozens of men, including her husband and her father, whose personal dignity would easily match the costume and the pomp. As to Pharaoh being a god, no man could equal such a claim, and in Sarai's opinion calling a man a god did not elevate the man, it only diminished the idea of godhood. If this weak-chinned, flaccid, narrow-faced, cheery-looking fellow was a god, then why were gods worth worshiping?

But Sarai could not blame this man for the pretensions surrounding Pharaoh. He had inherited all of it, the stories and the costumes and the ludicrous claims. When Pharaoh was strong, with military might and political skill, no one would dare to question his claim to divinity. But this man . . . Sarai could see at once the contempt that powerful men in Egypt would feel for him. As long as it was in their interest to keep the office of Pharaoh strong, then they would tolerate a weak man on the throne. And, of course, it was quite possible that Pharaoh's physical appearance was deceiving. He might be an extremely clever man.

For that matter, though, he might be merely a figurehead, occupying the office while others wielded the power. Sarai thought back to Sehtipibre, the man who, according to Eshut, managed the kingdom of Egypt for

Pharaoh, while Eshut herself managed his household. Two loyal stewards in such offices would naturally confer with each other. But it might just as easily be the case that they conspired with each other to keep the reins of power in their own hands.

Suddenly the life of a pastoral household seemed very simple and clean to Sarai, while here, where the palace was kept free of dirt, nothing was simple and there might be many a dirty secret hiding in plain sight. She felt sorry for Pharaoh. He had once been a little child in a king's house, as she had been. The formalities of royalty came easily enough to one who grew up with them. But because her own father was without power, Sarai did not have to grow up suspicious of everyone and unsure whether anything said to her was true. She had learned much about political maneuvering from her father, with his tales of past political struggles in Ur-of-Sumeria and his analysis of the politics of Ur-of-the-North. But the worst that she ever saw for herself was the idle flattery that is the cheap coin spent by everyone who speaks to a king, even one who is in exile. Since her father had no power, no one was trying to steal it; since he was already off his throne, no one was trying to topple him from it. Pharaoh, though—from boyhood on, whom had he ever been able to trust?

Well, he certainly can't trust *me*, thought Sarai. I come to him with lies on my lips from the start, and whether he himself directed that I be separated from Abram or that was the plotting of his underlings, the fact remained that everything she said to him would be calculated to keep Abram safe and this king out of her bedchamber.

The first step in her deception was, of course, to flatter him, and so she greeted him, not as the daughter of another monarch, for that she could never admit to being, but as the daughter of a noble house. To her knees, then, but no farther, her eyes cast down, but her forehead never coming near the stone steps by the water. Hagar, of course, was bowed like a broken reed, fairly pressing herself into the stone. But that's what it meant to be a slave. You were lower than everyone.

"This is the sister of my good friend Abram! Arise, Lady Milcah, and walk with me into the house of my wives!"

Good friend Abram. The words gave Sarai hope. Not that they couldn't be said by a king planning to murder Abram—but the fact that he bothered to say them at all suggested that he was still trying to win whatever it was he wanted by flattery and persuasion rather than by force or threat.

"I am grateful to the mighty Pharaoh Montuhotpe for his kindness in bringing me into his own house, where I have been so well treated that it takes half the sting from being separated from my dear brother Abram."

"Only half?" said Pharaoh, with a wink. So he knew that she and Abram were being kept apart, and understood that she did not like it. "I suppose it was too much to hope that the graceful life in Pharaoh's house would make you forget your brother completely."

"Would Pharaoh deign to offer hospitality to a guest who could so easily forget her own brother?"

There it was—her challenge. She called herself a guest and asserted that Pharaoh was offering her hospitality. It was a claim to the privileges and rights of a guest. Not that such rules could not be broken, but to break them would be a crime before the gods, and would do Pharaoh's reputation harm.

He smiled more broadly and cheerfully. "Must we think of ourselves as host and guest? I would so much rather think of you as kin."

An ambiguous answer. A marriage proposal? An evasion of guest-right?

"I am glad if the ruler of Egypt has come to think of my brother as his kin. Am I to think of mighty Pharaoh as my father? Or my brother?" And there was her answer: She was not going to play flirtatious games. If he wanted to claim kinship, he was welcome to do so—but not as her husband.

"I think of Abram as my brother," said Pharaoh. "But Lady Milcah, I am unsure yet how I might think of her."

"As your guest, first," said Milcah, "for that is how I arrived in your house, as a lonely traveler separated from her family and friends."

"But how can that be?" said Pharaoh. "Have you not been visited by your people?"

"I have had no visitors, nor even a servant from my brother's household."

Pharaoh glanced at Hagar, who was tagging along behind them. "Is this not your handmaid?"

"She is a servant of Pharaoh's own house, assigned to me by the Lady Eshut, to my great pleasure."

"Well, let's solve that problem right now. I give her to you. She *is* your handmaid now. So you do have someone from your household with you—and not from your brother's household, either. She is your own."

Just like that. As a grand gesture. And a sneaky one. For he had easily sidestepped the whole question of hospitality and guest-right, and by making Hagar a member of Sarai's household, he had made it unnecessary to admit anyone from Abram's household.

They were indoors now, and Pharaoh seated himself, not on the throne in the main hall, but rather on a bench beside a pool of water. He patted the seat beside him, but Sarai had no intention of playing that game. She knelt beside the pool, not even touching the bench where he sat. "Your kindness and generosity are legendary," said Sarai.

"I have no doubt," said Pharaoh dryly. He understood what she meant by not sitting beside him.

"I am glad that my brother has found favor in your sight."

"More than favor," said Pharaoh, and now his expression warmed. "Your brother is precisely what I had wished for. All my life I have sought the learning of the

East. Here in Egypt we claim to be the most ancient kingdom, but I have studied the oldest books, and I know that the first Pharaohs of upper and lower Egypt were conquerors from the East. Rulers of the ancient lineage of Utnapishtim, whom your brother calls Noah. It is the might of the East that first established the kingdom of Egypt, and Pharaohs who forget the source of their ancient authority grow weak through their ignorance."

Sarai tried to see if anyone in Pharaoh's retinue seemed to chafe at this idea, but of course they would long since have learned to hear Pharaoh's attitudes without visible response. Any resentment she could see, Pharaoh could also see. Still, she knew at once that if Pharaoh often talked like this, it would surely provoke many of the nobles of Egypt, who, despite the eastern origins of the original Pharaohs, thought of themselves as pure Egyptian and despised the Hsy who came now to Egypt as refugees from the drought. To them, the idea that Egypt had anything to gain from these impoverished wanderers must seem either laughable or offensive.

And it also meant that the more Pharaoh liked Abram and Sarai, the more the nobles of Egypt would detest them. As long as Pharaoh was powerful, he was the greatest danger to them; but if he slipped from power, then those who took it from him would almost certainly be filled with resentment toward any of the Hsy whom Pharaoh had preferred. Danger from every quarter. Hagar remained her only friend here—and there was always the possibility that Hagar had been assigned to her as a spy.

She hated that—the fact that she could not trust anyone completely.

"My brother has always spoken of Egypt as the repository of great and ancient knowledge," said Sarai.

Pharaoh laughed. "I know exactly what your brother says. My father knew of his ideas before I redeemed him from death. Pharaohs as usurpers of a priesthood that only he and his family—your family—possess. We have agreed to politely disagree on this point, and to learn from each other on every other subject. I'm afraid I'm getting the best of the bargain, however. Abram is opening my eyes to many things in heaven and earth."

"My brother is known for his wisdom and learning. But I am sure that if he were here with us, he would insist that he was learning more from Pharaoh than Pharaoh could ever learn from him."

"Oh, I doubt your brother has ever spoken to you of the things he has been teaching me. For instance, did you know that the sun is a star?"

Sarai was taken aback. What an absurd thing to say. "I would be sorry if I could not tell the difference between sunlight and starlight, since it is the very difference between day and night."

"Ah, there, you see? He has not taught you. But just as a candle grows dimmer the farther away you are, so also are the stars dimmed to our sight by great distance. They seem to us to be smaller than the sun because the sun is so very close, and the stars very far away. But Abram assures me that our sun is not even the greatest of the stars. As the sun governs the Earth, so are there greater stars that govern the sun, until you come to the one star that governs them all, and there, he says, is the place where God dwells."

"He speaks to you of God?" asked Sarai.

"The one he worships, yes," said Pharaoh. "He does not mention to me that he thinks his god is the only one that exists, and I pretend to him that I do not know that he thinks so, and so we do not argue. It is enough for me to try to imagine the heavens as he sees them. Instead of the great dome of the sky, pierced to let starlight shine through when the sun is not present to blind us to their faint light, he shows me a heaven in which the Earth is a ball whirling around the sun, and the sun but a star among many stars that are governed by a far greater one. The River of the Sky, he says, is really millions upon millions of stars, so many that their light flows together. Ah, but he sees a wondrous vision of the heavens! The priests

think him mad, of course, but I see that many of them—
the younger ones especially—grow thoughtful when he
speaks, and I suspect many of them go home and write
down the things he said. They will remember. He is our
teacher. And the god that teaches him to see such things,
that god is a mighty one indeed, even if he is jealous of
any rivals."

Sarai heard these ideas with some interest, yes, but
mostly she felt a sharp pang of jealousy, for Abram had
never spoken to her of the stars. She thought he spoke to
her of everything, that he shared his life with her as if
they were equals, but now she realized that he excluded
her from his loftiest ideas. It was fine for her to learn
about the household and help with the governance of his
flocks and herds, his servants and his possessions. But
when he wanted to talk about how God had ordered the
universe, he could not speak of this to a mere woman. To
this weak-chinned narrow-faced man, top-heavy with the
double crown, he could confide these great mysteries. But
to his wife, not a word.

She tried to quell her resentment, but she could not will
away her hurt feelings. Abram thinks me foolish after all.
He still has great secrets that I will never know.

"He told me," said Pharaoh, "that he tells his wife
everything, so that I'm surprised that his sister did not know
of them. He says God sees men and women as having
equal value. But perhaps you were busy with the distaff
when he would have taught you these things."

Was he goading her? Did he suspect that Abram's wife
and this woman kneeling at Pharaoh's feet were the same
person, so that these words were meant to taunt her, or to
show her that he did not hold her in high esteem?

"In truth," said Pharaoh, "I speak of such things to none
of my women, because they would not understand me or,
if they did, they would not care. Indeed, few men care—
certainly not Sehtepibre, whose eyes glaze over whenever
I try to discuss heavenly things with him. His eyes are
only on provisioning the troops, collecting the taxes—all

the concerns that are for servants, not kings."

This comment did what the earlier comments did not—it caused several people in Pharaoh's retinue to shift their position, to breathe differently, showing their discomfort. Was Sehtepibre here himself to hear Pharaoh's criticism of him? No, Sarai would have recognized him if he had been among these men. But she had no doubt that Pharaoh's words would be relayed to him. It was a foolish thing, for Pharaoh to denigrate his chief steward before his household. Unless this was an assertion of Pharaoh's supremacy after winning a power struggle between them. She would have to find out something of the history of this household. She hated being ignorant of the context in which such things were said.

"The king's house does not run itself," said Sarai. "I know that Eshut labors mightily in the king's service, and I have no doubt that outside these walls, Sehtepibre does the same."

There. If the king wanted to cause bad blood between himself and his most powerful servants, that was his affair. She would not be part of his goading. Not that they would be grateful that she spoke up for them. All she hoped was that they would not become hungry for her or Abram's death. Let us be the enemies of no man or woman in this dangerous place.

"Oh yes, they work very hard," said Pharaoh. "But their labors all have to be done over again the next day. It is the work of the mortal world, which is never completed and undone every moment. But the work of Pharaoh is to learn truth and cause it to be written, for learning is work that, once done, remains done as long as scrolls can be read and copied and read again. Sehtipibre feeds soldiers, who are never grateful and are hungry again in the morning. But I feed the mind, which keeps everything that is fed to it and builds upon it, even in sleep, for the gods teach us in dreams as surely as men teach us in the light."

"Pharaoh's works are mighty indeed," said Sarai.

She thought of Abram, and the hours he spent in his

tent, reading the books that most certainly held some of these very ideas he was teaching Pharaoh. He would agree with Pharaoh that truth was important, and that as long as you had someone to receive what you wrote, your learning would never be lost. Still, Abram emerged from his tent and saw to the feeding of his household, for even though he relied on Sarai and others to do that work, he made sure he knew of every lamb and kid in his flocks, and every child of every servant in his household, and nothing happened that was not according to his will.

Pharaoh, you love wisdom, but how wise are you to leave the daily power of your kingdom in the hands of others, and to let them know that you disdain them even as they make your life possible?

"By the way," said Pharaoh, and his voice sank to a whisper, though she was quite sure that everyone in the room could still hear every word he said, "I have given your brother permission to call me by my personal name. I am Neb-Towi-Re, but you, like him, may call me Neb when we are alone."

"A generous gift, such confidence," said Sarai. "But I cannot imagine when it would be proper for us to be alone, and so Pharaoh's personal name is a treasure I shall guard in secret, and never utter aloud."

Pharaoh glowered. "I see that you are a stubborn woman," he said.

"My brother has often said so," said Sarai, "and so I'm sure it must be true. However, what you see as stubbornness, I see as obedience to God and respect for the dignity of your crown. Even the lowliest shepherd would never expose to scandal a girl that he claims to love."

Pharaoh rose abruptly. "When your brother told me that it was his sister's decision what man she would marry, I can see that he knew her well indeed. What seemed to be generous permission was actually a warning from a friend. I can see why Milcah has no husband, for if she can turn away Pharaoh, what other man can possibly be worthy of her hand?"

Frightened at the suddenness of his anger, Sarai bowed her head. "Forgive me, mighty Pharaoh. I do not know how I gave offense, or what was being asked of me. Is it the custom in Egypt that a woman is given no choice, nor time to think? Or that she is condemned for having refused an offer that was never made?"

Pharaoh stood there for a moment, his fingers drumming on his thigh. "Perhaps I have blamed you for a fault caused only by your ignorance and humility," he said. "There is no hurry. But I must tell you—I would be cheating Egypt if I gave my kingdom an heir who did not have the true priest-right. Knowing now the great knowledge and power that come from that priesthood, I will have it for my people and my house."

"But I have no such power," said Sarai.

"You have it in your power to give it to my sons," said Pharaoh. "I know the value of that, even if you do not. A man who does not hope for his sons to surpass him in excellence is not a good father."

"Does Pharaoh not have sons already?" asked Sarai.

"Seven women in my house carry my children in them," said Pharaoh, "and of that number, surely some will be sons when they are born. But it matters not to me, for they will be born without the ancient priesthood of Abram your brother, and so they will not be sons that can come to me when I am dead and raise me into heaven. What Egypt needs, that will I do."

"Everyone knows the devotion and magnanimity of Pharaoh," said Sarai.

"And I know now of the willfulness and stinginess of the woman I love," said Pharaoh.

The woman you love! The very words made Sarai burn with outrage. He had said nothing to her of love, and dared to call her stingy for not having given in to his suit before he even bothered to make it.

"I know not what woman you refer to," said Sarai. "For myself, I know that it is impossible for a man to love a woman or a woman to love a man if they do not know each other well. One cannot love a stranger."

Pharaoh almost lashed back with a quick retort. Then his face softened, and that cheerful smile returned. "If I am to regain the ancient knowledge of the land of Retenu, where the first Pharaohs came from, then I must also learn to respect the customs of that land. What Lady Milcah asks for is not a burden, for any man, even a god-in-making like Pharaoh, is only blessed when he takes the time to know a lady like Milcah, and to let her know him."

"Pharaoh's condescension is remarkable," said Sarai, "and I pray that he will find me worthy of it."

"I have plenty of time," said Pharaoh, "but not an infinite supply." He turned to his retinue. "Tell the Lady Eshut that I will see the pregnant ones first." Then Pharaoh walked to his throne and sat down. "Lady Milcah may remain, so she can see the gentle way that Pharaoh deals with the women who bear him children."

Never mind that it seemed far from gentle to Sarai that the women were brought to him instead of him going to them. Pharaoh could not know that the cruelest thing he could have done to Sarai was to make her sit there by the pool and watch as these fertile women were brought in, one by one, to be petted by Pharaoh as he asked about their health and commiserated with them on their discomforts and promised them the favors that they asked of him. If he had such gentle ways with the women who bore him children, what ways did he have with the women who bore him none? Somehow she doubted that Pharaoh would have the same unconcern with her barrenness that Abram had always shown. Even if she wanted to marry Neb-Towi-Re, even if she were free to do so, she would not dare. Such a marriage would be a double fraud—for not only could she bear no children at all, but also, even if she could, they would not have the priest-right through *her* lineage. All she had to offer was the king-right of the ancient house of Ur. What Pharaoh wanted, or at least said he wanted, was Abram's to give, not hers.

Though if Pharaoh knew who she really was, he might just as easily decide that the ancient king-right of Ur was good enough, and he would happily marry Abram's widow.

O God, she prayed silently, over and over, as the women came in and went out, keep Abram safe, and me also, from the wrath of this Pharaoh, and from his love, both equally dangerous to us.

PART IV

MA'AT

❧ CHAPTER 10 ❧

Pharaoh stayed the night in the House of Women, and the next night, and the next—but he did not see Sarai again. Nor did anyone else pay much attention to her, which she did not mind, except for the endless boredom of having nothing worthwhile to do.

Of course it was no secret why Pharaoh had visited there. Besides the wives and concubines who were with child, there were others who were not, and Pharaoh had come to alleviate their loneliness. Hagar was full of stories about Montuhotpe's virility, but Sarai did not care to hear them. "He may not look like a god," said Hagar, "but he—"

"Please," said Sarai. "Enough."

"A king—no, a god desires you, he is known for being able to put babies into any womb, and you don't even want to hear about it?"

"I don't," said Sarai.

"You don't believe he *is* a god."

"In Pharaoh's house, you expect me even to listen to such a thing?"

"You don't believe his seed could grow in you."

"I believe that my barrenness is caused by God."

"So let a god take it away!"

Sarai shook her head. "Hagar, I don't want to talk about this again."

Miffed, Hagar continued dressing Sarai's hair, but now was sullen and jerky in her movements.

"If you're trying to hurt me by pulling my hair," said Sarai, "you have succeeded a dozen times already."

"I'm sorry, Mistress."

"Hagar, do you really want to be my friend?"

"You know that I do, Mistress—am I not your true handmaid?"

"Find me something useful to do."

Hagar laughed. "Useful? To whom? Pharaoh has something useful for you to do, but you won't do it. What else can a woman do that's of use?"

"All my life, whenever I wasn't doing something else I had a distaff in my hand. Surely I may spin."

"Have you ever spun linen?"

"No."

"It's not the same as wool."

"So teach me."

"And the weaving is different, too."

"That I don't need to learn."

"Why not?"

"Because I will never weave linen in the Egyptian fashion."

"Why not?"

"Because you can see through it as if it weren't there."

Hagar was baffled. "But don't you like to intrigue your husband?"

"Eshut manages to intrigue every man in this house— that's what such fine linens do. Modesty is right for a woman, not brazenly showing her breasts to everyone."

Hagar looked down at her own bosom. "But I have nice breasts."

"They are for *your* husband to see, and no one else."

"Are you trying to hurt me, Mistress? For you have succeeded, six times sixty, with those words."

Sarai was startled at the grief in Hagar's voice. "What have I said?"

"I will never have a husband, Mistress! I am your handmaid!"

"But of course you will find a husband, when we return to Canaan, or wherever the Lord leads us when we get free of this place."

"How can I be your handmaid then, with a husband?"

"At that time, you'll cease to be my handmaid and I'll find another."

"You would send me away?"

"No, I would permit you to go away! What are you talking about?"

"I have been raised up to be handmaid to a princess of Ur, and you would turn me away and force me to be with a mere slave and bear slave children?"

"But you said it broke your heart that you would never marry, and I told you that you could!"

"No, it broke my heart that you thought so little of me that you would deny me the pleasure of showing my body while I'm still young and I can take pride in the way men look at me, and pleasure in the knowledge that they cannot have me. But I never want to leave your side, Mistress. There is no man who could tempt me to want to fall from this elevated station and go back to carrying night soil from the House of Women."

Sarai blushed to realize how Eshut had insulted her. "You were the servant who emptied the chamber pots?"

"I was, Mistress. Didn't you know that?"

"All I know is what I'm told, and no one told me."

"I washed many times before I ever touched you, Mistress."

"I'm sure you did. If there's one thing they do in this house, it's wash."

Hagar was silent.

"Hagar," said Sarai. "Find me something useful to do."

Hagar stepped back and looked at Sarai, at first petulantly, but then slyly. "You could teach me curses from the temple of Asherah."

"Hagar, there *are* no curses in the worship of Asherah! And if there were, I would not have learned them. And if I had, I would not teach them to you."

Hagar shrugged. "I was going to offer to teach you some good curses in return. There's one that can make a baby cry all night." Hagar giggled. "Oh, that's a nice one! That one makes them crazy!"

"I don't understand you, Hagar," said Sarai.

"Why should you?" said Hagar. "I obey. Isn't that enough?"

"It's never enough," said Sarai. "What do you want? What do you dream of?"

"I dream terrible dreams, Mistress, of being taken into slavery, of losing my family. It makes me hate to sleep. Does that help you understand me?"

"Do you grieve all the time, then?"

"Grieve? I never grieve."

"But I thought . . . when you think of being taken into slavery, that you . . ."

"It fills me with hate. And anger. I hold it in, because if I ever let it out, blood would flow all through this house, and they would torture me to death."

If Hagar had said this with virulence, Sarai would have understood. It might have frightened her, but she would not have been surprised by that. Instead, though, Hagar said it coolly, with a touch of amusement.

"You're joking?" asked Sarai.

"No, Mistress."

"But you're smiling."

"I am holding my rage in a little pot, with the lid fastened tightly on. It never shows in my face." Hagar turned around and pulled her gown over her head, showing her naked back to Sarai. There were scars from her thighs to her shoulders. Hundreds of them. "That is how I learned to keep my face from showing what I feel."

"Just a little smile," said Sarai, "to keep off the whips."

"And the reeds. And the rods. And the open hand, and the fist, and the bare foot, and the shod foot, and the hands that push down into water, and the hands that push down steps, and the hands that push off roofs, and—"

"No, please," said Sarai. "Surely you were never pushed off a roof!"

"I saw it done. To a boy who was impish but meant no harm. He walked crooked from then on, but the overseer made him run everywhere, knowing the pain it caused him, and knowing how he was ridiculed for his camelish walk. Emptying the chamber pots in the House of Women was a great improvement over working for that overseer."

Sarai ducked her head to brush tears from her cheeks.

"My mistress has a tender heart," said Hagar.

But there was something in her tone that made Sarai look sharply at her. "What did you mean?"

"I saw your tears of pity, and I praised you for them."

"That was not praise," said Sarai.

Hagar's face wore that little smile. "If you thought I did not mean my words, then you may slap me, Mistress. I am yours."

"Why are you trying to provoke me?"

"Mistress, I am trying desperately not to provoke you."

"You were not praising me! You were mocking me, and I want to know why."

"Mistress, if I knew what you were talking about, I'd answer you."

"Did you think my tears were false?"

"I could see that they were real."

"Is it wrong for me to feel pity?"

"Compared to a king's daughter, all men and women are slaves."

"Oh," said Sarai. "So that's it. You don't believe that I can possibly understand suffering, is that it?"

"Mistress understands whatever she sets her mind to," said Hagar. With that little smile.

"I will not quarrel with you," said Sarai. "I have many

faults, but punishing someone for misjudging me is not something I do. The longer you're with me, the better you'll know me. And someday you'll realize that there is suffering in every life."

Hagar said nothing. But wore that smile.

"Say it," said Sarai. "I command you, and I will not punish you for it."

"Mistress," said Hagar, "if you take off your dress, what scars will I see?"

"I do not say that our suffering has been equal. But your suffering was yours, and mine is mine—so you know yours, and I know mine. The only way I can hope to understand yours is to think of my own fears or sadnesses, my own angers and resentments, and then magnify them as best I can. Imagining such suffering as you told of, such heartlessness, that brought tears to my eyes. I did not cry because I thought I had suffered as much. I cried because I had *not* suffered so much, and pitied those who did."

"Mistress does not need to explain herself to me."

Either Hagar was not capable of believing that Sarai could possibly understand suffering, or she was deliberately trying to provoke her. Either way, it was maddening, and Sarai put an end to the discussion. "I must have something to take my mind off Abram's and my situation. Thinking of how much greater is the suffering of others does not help. I need *work*. Until I came here I helped manage a great household, and my hands were never idle. I must have work to do or go mad."

"I will think on this, Mistress. But in the end, you will have no work unless Eshut gives it to you."

"I don't like Eshut."

"Eshut is not likable," said Hagar. "But she rules this house, and if you are maddened by inactivity, it is because she has chosen for you to feel that way."

That had not occurred to Sarai. But of course it was true. The other women here were not inactive, doing nothing. Eshut was keeping Sarai utterly unoccupied on purpose.

"Why?" asked Sarai.

"Maybe she is waiting for you to come to her and ask."

Was that all this is? Eshut's desire to compel Sarai to humble herself before the mistress of this house? "Well of course I'll ask. I don't know why I didn't think of it before."

"Then I have done well to suggest it?" asked Hagar.

"Yes, child, you've done well," said Sarai.

"Even when I . . . provoked you?"

"Did you provoke me?"

"You said I did."

"I said it seemed that way. Or that's what I meant to say. Hagar, do you want me to humble myself before you? Because I'm glad to say I'm sorry, if I misjudged you somehow. I'm not ashamed to admit mistakes, if I know I've made them. But at this moment, I can't remember who said what in our conversation. It's all mixed up together. I only know I meant no harm, and if I offended you, I'm sorry."

Hagar stood there in silence—but wore no smile on her face.

"Please put your gown back on."

Hagar silently pulled the linen over her head again, and tied the sash.

"We *will* get used to each other," said Sarai.

Hagar nodded.

"Someday you may even trust me," said Sarai.

Hagar nodded again.

"But for now, would you kindly go to Lady Eshut and ask her when I might come to see her?"

Hagar walked briskly to the door. If Sarai had not been watching her closely, she might not have noticed how Hagar's hand flicked up to wipe something from her cheek. And then again, to wipe the other cheek.

So the saucy handmaid was not untouchable by kindness after all. If that was, in fact, what her tears implied.

❧ CHAPTER 11 ❧

And what work," said Eshut, "do you wish to do?"
A cat preened on the bench beside her. Eshut
ignored the cat—the animals were sacred to
Egyptians, and no one interfered with them as they wandered about, doing what they wanted. Sarai, for her part,
had no use for them, and she had noticed that when cats
were near, her nose began to run, but Hagar had warned
her never to be seen shooing them away.

"I'm experienced in many things," said Sarai. "I can
card and spin wool and weave it in my sleep."

"We work in linen here, and flax is very different from
wool."

"I also managed a large household."

"That," said Eshut dryly, "is my job. I hope you do not
plan to displace me."

Displace her? What could possibly prompt her to suggest such an impossible thing? "I could be of help."

"Knowing no one? Having no notion of what tasks are
required, what flows in and goes out, or who does the

jobs well and who badly? Nor are royal protocols second nature to you, as to the people trained to the service of this house. You would only get in the way, Lady Milcah."

Of course this was not true. While Sarai did not know the particular people who did each task, she knew perfectly well what the work of a king's house entailed, and she was quite sure she knew at least as much about protocol as Lady Eshut. But she could not explain this to Eshut without revealing that she was not Milcah at all, but Sarai, daughter of the exiled king of Ur-of-Sumeria.

"I can see that you are right."

"And while I could have you trained in some lesser task, you must understand that it would shame Pharaoh for a visitor of your stature to be set to servants' work."

"My days are empty," said Sarai.

"Among Pharaoh's women are several from Retenu." The Egyptian name for Canaan. "And others who are Fekhenu." The polite word, Sarai was learning, for those more commonly called Hsy—people who tended flocks and herds. "Go and visit with them. Surely they would delight in news from home."

"Am I here as entertainment, then, Lady Eshut?"

"I don't know why you're here," said Eshut. "I did not bring you."

"I am a woman of ability and experience," said Sarai, "and I offer my service in whatever small ways I might be useful. With a little thought, you can find something for me to do that will not interfere with your work, but will, in some small way, ease your burden. Since I do not plan to stay, I will not seek to accumulate power or influence."

"If you're right, and you do not stay, then the time I spend training you will be wasted, and I'll have to put someone else to do your work the moment you leave. And if you're wrong, and you do stay, you will doubtless be in a position where Pharaoh would not be happy to have you working under me."

There it was, as directly stated as it could be: Eshut

knew that Pharaoh intended to marry Sarai, and not just as another concubine, but as a wife whose children might inherit the throne. Quite possibly as his queen, whose children would be first in line. Eshut had to make sure she had done nothing to demean the queen of Egypt, if Sarai should ever ascend to that position. And if she did not, then Sarai was indeed worthless to her.

"My hands are tied," said Eshut, with a sweet and sympathetic smile. Her eyes also smiled, but there was no sympathy there.

Sarai left, sure then that her boredom would have no ease. As usual, she walked at evening by the river, and in a secluded stand of trees she knelt and prayed. Hagar knelt beside her; whether she prayed or not, Sarai did not know and did not ask.

O God, she said, what am I to do with these empty hours? I have nothing to study, nothing to do. How can I serve Thee or serve my husband?

What have I done to deserve this maddening punishment? The sword of Pharaoh's marital ambitions hangs over me and my husband, and I have nothing to take my mind from this danger. Am I meant to live in fear?

Abram has answers from thee, but to me the heavens are a curtain of brass. Do my words reach whatever star shines upon the world where Thou livest? Hast Thou no words for me?

Thus her prayer began, step by step descending from humble request to ardent complaint until, finally, she was once again pouring out the darkest doubts of her heart:

O Lord God of Abram, I see nothing of Thy hand in my life. All that happens to me points to my being under the rule of Asherah. My womb is dry. I am to be taken from the man I love and given to a king, just as if I still lived in my father's house. Did I dare to love Abram more than Asherah? Then she will have him killed. Did I dare to refuse to live in her house? Then I will live in the house of a god all the same, only instead of being pure, singing to the goddess all day, I will be in the bed of Pharaoh,

bearing him children if Asherah deigns to forgive me, or
being rejected in the end for my barrenness, if she does
not. O God of Abram, why dost Thou hide from me, while
Asherah shows me her angry face everywhere I turn?
How can I believe in Thee, and disbelieve in her? Nevertheless I do believe in Thee, and obey Thee. Only help
me, God of Abram! Give me the strength to conquer my
doubts. Give me hope!

"Mistress," said Hagar softly, "I have not seen such
weeping in many years. Please don't cry so much."

Sarai was startled, roused from a prayer that had become nothing but a litany of grief. "I was praying," she
murmured as she wiped her eyes with her skirt.

"What god is heartless enough not to hear such a
prayer?"

Sarai shook her head. She had no answer to that, except
the bitterest one: A god who hates me, if he exists at all.

"God loves me," she said insistently, more to reassure
herself than to convince Hagar.

"As does your husband," said Hagar. "Maybe your god
is being kept from you the way your husband is."

"Speak not of husbands," Sarai said mildly. "We are
not always alone, even when we think we are."

"I have walked around and around this place while you
prayed, Mistress, and I assure you that no one is listening."

Not even God, Sarai thought. And then, hurriedly: Forgive me for that unworthy thought, O Lord! "It's a good
thing I'm incapable of real misery," said Sarai.

"Oh, Mistress, forgive me for my false and ungrateful
words last night!" cried Hagar. "I know that your suffering is greater than mine. Because your mind is so much
wiser than mine, your heart so much loftier, the pains you
suffer must be exquisite compared to the poor dull suffering of a slave!"

"No, no, Hagar, don't be foolish. You spoke the truth
to me last night, and gave me more wisdom than I had
before. I weep because I'm helpless, not because my suf-

fering is so terrible. I weep because there is nothing I can do, of my own will, to help either Abram or myself. I have no choice but to rely on God, and yet I can't bear to rely on Him because . . ."

"Because he has never shown you that you *can* rely on him," said Hagar.

"I have seen His hand, but always in Abram's life. He only touches me to bring about Abram's work. I am nothing of myself, and that is hard to bear. I'm a proud woman, that's what I'm learning, and the silence of God is a constant lesson that I am nothing."

"If that god of your husband's thinks you're nothing, then *he's* nothing. How could a god be so foolish as not to know that you're a great woman?"

"The greatness of this world is like a broken pot to God. It might have bright paint on it, but it's good for nothing."

"I don't mean your greatness as a rich woman or a princess or anything like that," said Hagar. "You kept your word to me and asked to keep me as your handmaid, so I could leave Egypt when you go."

"I did you no favor. The lies we've told may lead to our destruction. What would happen to you then?"

"Mistress, why do you argue with me? You're a woman with a noble heart, not just a noble bearing. If your god is God of gods, as you say, then he knows that. And for all you know, Mistress, he is planning great things for you if you only have the patience to wait for them."

Sarai opened her mouth to argue once again, but then realized: I asked God for an answer. Whose mouth did I think his answer would come from? Could Hagar's words not be God's answer to me? Be patient and wait. God is planning great things. "Once again, Hagar, you have taught me wisdom." Sarai rose to her feet. "Come, let's return to the house. The sun has set and soon the desert cold will settle in."

When they reached the house, there were many torches burning in the dusky light, and boats drawn up at the dock. Pharaoh's boat was not among them—he had not returned. So what was this gathering? Sarai knew that as a shy and modest lady, she should stand away from the men's work that was going on, as slaves loaded the boats with foodstuffs and tools. But she could not master her curiosity, and so she descended the steps to the water's edge and asked the man who seemed to be directing the loading, "Who will use these boats?"

"Sehtepibre goes to the quarry for more stone tomorrow," said the man. "The sarcophagus of Pharaoh is being built with great fineness, and Sehtepibre is not happy with the quality of the blocks most recently brought. So he will go and show the stonecutters where to find flawless stone that can be worked without crumbling or shattering."

"Is the quarry far?" asked Sarai.

"Across the river and up into the mountain. It's a journey of several days, Lady."

From behind her came another voice. "Does the Lady Milcah wish to come with me?"

She turned to find that Sehtepibre had apparently followed her down the steps and listened to her question. She knew that if this wily steward was asking her to come with him, it was because he saw some advantage in it for himself. But she also knew that he was offering her a chance to get away from this house and see something of the land and hear conversation that was not the empty chat of bored women. She had never had anything to do with stone cutting, and so she had a chance to learn something new to her. She hesitated only a moment before saying, "Lord Sehtepibre is gracious, and unless it would displease mighty Pharaoh, Lady Milcah will make haste to be ready for the journey."

"We leave as soon as the boats are loaded," said Sehtepibre. "And your desert clothing will be useful to you, since the sun will shine brightly where we're going."

"I don't have that clothing, sir," said Sarai.

"I'll have it sent to you," said Sehtepibre, thus sweeping away in a moment the claim of Eshut that she did not know where that clothing was.

When the boats pulled away from the dock, Sarai sat on the largest barge, Hagar at her feet, Sehtepibre at her side. This was no procession. It was a working journey, and Sehtepibre did not bother to explain anything to her. Instead, once he saw that the boats were going where he had commanded, he lay down upon the deck of the barge and fell asleep almost at once.

"I can't sleep on a chair," Sarai murmured to Hagar. And in moments she, too, lay upon the deck. But she made sure that Hagar lay between her and Sehtepibre, so no tongues would wag and no scandal would endanger either her or Pharaoh's steward.

Sarai had never slept on a boat before. Unlike the Nile, the Euphrates was not reliable for transportation, varying from flood to mud at different seasons of the year, and while traders sometimes floated their cargoes down the river, no one used it for ordinary travel. So she had never had the experience of being rocked gently by the current of a river. She slept as peacefully as she had used to sleep in her father's house, when as a child her future seemed secure and no fretting kept her awake at night or invaded her dreams.

When she woke, though, she had lain too still, it seemed, for her neck was stiff. Like an old woman, she thought, as Hagar kneaded her shoulders to try to work the pain to the surface and away. "Not so old," said Hagar, trying to be comforting and failing. Old enough that before long her natural child-bearing years would be behind her, and then all hope would be gone. Every joint that did not bend the way it used to bend, every muscle that ached where once there had been no pain, every breath hard-drawn where once she would not even have noticed the exertion, all were warning signs that her life as a woman would soon end in futility. And there was young Hagar, her buoyant breasts dancing under her translucent linen gown, telling her that she was not so old. How ignorant

was youth! How devoid of understanding! And yet that
was why youth was so precious, for most of its sins were
sins of innocence.

Sehtepibre must have risen before them—and properly
so, since the expedition was his responsibility. He had
docked their boat well upstream of the others, so that the
noise of offloading did not waken them. Even now it was
still not dawn—no light shone yet in the east. Sarai
watched the last of the unloading with a practiced eye:
dozens of men working in torchlight, yet almost silent in
their order and vigorous obedience. Sehtepibre was not
one of those fools who ruled through fear—none of these
men cowered from him, and none malingered. They
obeyed him willingly, because . . . why? Had he enlisted
them willingly in his work? Was there some higher cause
they shared? Or was it simply himself they served, for
love of him, or admiration, or hope of his future?

The latter seemed more likely, though she did not put
the first beyond him. Eshut was easy enough to understand—a person of some authority, jealously guarding it
and contemptuous of those who were not of her own degree. But Sehtepibre was different. A clever man, that was
obvious, but perhaps a subtle one as well. Where Eshut,
by her very jealousy, revealed her fear that she might not
keep her place, Sehtepibre seemed perfectly confident, as
if he could not be removed, as if his authority came from
himself alone, and not from Pharaoh after all.

Whom did he remind her of? Abram, of course. Only
Abram's serenity did not come from confidence in himself, but rather trust in God. He feared nothing because
all that he was and all that he had belonged to God, and
he believed that God would protect what He wanted protected. Was there a god that Sehtepibre trusted in that
same way? Or was he the god of his own idolatry? It
would be interesting to understand the man. And interesting indeed to see how long he lasted in the service of
a Pharaoh who, for all that he seemed more interested in
heaven than in earth, and more a student of the East than

of Egypt, held the reigns of power. The priests obeyed him. The soldiers obeyed him. And if Pharaoh decided one day that Sehtepibre was no longer useful to him, Sehtepibre would be gone, and with him all his authority.

A man in such a place had to be something of a fool to be too confident. Yet Sehtepibre seemed not to be a fool.

A young officer came toward her boat, carrying a torch. To her surprise, it was Kay, the very one who had met them at the border. She greeted him by name, and he also greeted her. "Have you been reassigned from duty at the border?" she asked him.

"When I brought you here," said Kay, "it was decided that I should remain."

Interesting, thought Sarai. "A reward for your initiative?"

Kay shrugged. "The decision of my superiors." But she could see that her words had made him both proud and nervous. He preened a little, but was also just a little furtive. He was still too young to be as subtle as Sehtepibre. She could read this boy. "I hope you'll be traveling with us today."

"I will," said Kay. "This is a land of robbers. The Hsy come among us and we feed them, but still they slip away and become bandits in the hills. It is a shame that a stone-cutting expedition should need military escort here in the heart of Egypt, so close to the Nile." He caught himself being too heated. "Of course my Lady Milcah is not of the sort I referred to."

"It never crossed my mind that you might think of me as Hsy," said Sarai. "And I understand your concern. In all the land from the Euphrates to Sinai, it has become like that, farmers turn to wanderers and wanderers to bandits, all in a month or a week or even a single day. Civilization only lasts as long as the citizens trust that they will have food tomorrow."

"But in Egypt, there is always food," said Kay. "Why then do they turn to robbery?"

"Because the food is not theirs," said Sarai. "It's a gift, which can be withdrawn at any time. What will the Hsy do then?"

"But the gift has *not* been withdrawn, and therefore it is a shameful thing for the guest to rob the host."

"With that I agree. The world turns upside down, when host-right and guest-right are so casually disregarded."

He looked at her for a moment before replying. Did he guess the double meaning of her words?

"We call it Ma'at," he said. "The good order of the land. When all is right, when all is as the gods ordain, then we live in Ma'at. But when Ma'at is lost, then no one can trust in the future until it is all set right again."

"And that is the work of Pharaoh," said Sarai.

Kay sniffed. "It should be," he said. And then, perhaps realizing that his irony betrayed too much, he added, "And so Pharaoh does his best."

Sarai was no fool, however. She had studied at her father's feet, and heard his commentary on all that happened in Ur-of-the-North. Here was a young officer who believed that Ma'at was the most important work of Pharaoh. And what had caused the breakdown in Ma'at? The Hsy—the nomads from the East who had entered Egypt in such numbers. Pharaoh's duty, then, was to control them, but instead Pharaoh was fascinated with the Fenekhu, seeking a wife from their number, spending his days learning religion from a man of Retenu who claimed to be a great priest. If there was dissatisfaction like this in the army, it meant that Pharaoh might not have all the authority he thought he had, for a king's power lasts only as long as he is obeyed.

And the resentment of the Hsy is bound to center around Abram, Sarai realized. Yet it was Kay who brought us straight to the people who put us in the king's presence. He passed us to Khnumhotpe, who separated us and made sure Abram went straight to Pharaoh's presence and I went into the House of Women. And someone then rewarded Kay by keeping him close at hand. Or was it, instead of a reward, simply a matter of putting resentful young officers in command of soldiers near the king? Where they could see firsthand how Montuhotpe was enthralled to this desert prophet?

So why had Kay let slip his resentments to Sarai? If he truly saw her as the enemy, then he'd have no reason to speak to her at all. Instead he had, in effect, given her a warning. This was all too arcane and confusing for her. She would have to learn more in order to sort out how much of this was a plot, and how much mere chance, and who posed the greatest threat to her and Abram.

Just as the first light appeared in the east, Kay helped Sarai into his own chariot. They would ride next behind Sehtepibre. "You can't have much fear of bandits, to put a woman in your chariot," said Sarai.

Kay laughed. "Because we're here at all, the bandits will leave us alone."

"But then, if the bandits can be frightened by so small a number of troops, they can't be much of a threat."

"When Egypt has Ma'at," said Kay, solemn again, "a lone man can travel from one end of the kingdom to another and none will harm him or cheat him."

"Then there has never been a kingdom in the world that had this Ma'at. Because there are always thieves and cheaters."

"In Retenu, perhaps," said Kay. "But in Egypt, there used to be Ma'at."

Such a fantasy, thought Sarai. She had heard people talking of the golden age of Ur-of-Sumeria, too, when the wealth of nations flowed to that city and there was no crime and all men were noble and all women virtuous. But her father had told her afterward that past times are always held to be a golden age, compared to now. Old men who say that once there was a golden age are liars, Father said, and young men who believe their tales are fools.

Kay was just such a fool. Who was the old man who had been lying to him?

It was slow going up the stonecutters' road into the mountains. It was not steep, really—a steep road would never do for transporting stone—but it wound around and around, so that they seemed to make no progress.

The sun was well up from the horizon when Sehtepibre called a temporary halt. Before them was an old quarry which had not been used for some time. Several large blocks of damaged stone lay where they had been abandoned. And a half-dozen were in various stages of being cut away from the mountain.

Sehtepibre jumped lightly from his chariot and walked back to where Sarai stood in Kay's chariot. He patted Kay's lead horse as he approached, and returned Kay's salute. "My Lady Milcah," said Sehtepibre, "I thought you might like to see the quarry where we used to draw good stone."

"What happened?" asked Sarai. "How can good stone fail?"

"The stone did not fail, Lady," said Sehtepibre. "The water did. You can't cut stone without an ample supply of water, and when the nearby spring went dry, they either had to haul water a long way or search for a quarry closer to the water they still had. So because of the failure of the spring, we had to leave the best stone behind."

Sarai listened with interest, but she also wondered: Why is Sehtepibre himself telling me this? And why stop the whole expedition to tell it? Perhaps the men needed a rest—many of them had stepped aside to urinate beside the road—but Sehtepibre still lingered with her. "In the old days, all this mountain was thick with grass. You still find tufts of it, dried up like an old man's hair, tucked into corners where the wind has not yet ripped it away."

"Before the drought," said Sarai.

"Oh, this is just the latest drought of many," said Sehtepibre.

"My brother Abram says that all these little droughts are really part of one great long drought that has been uprooting kingdoms and turning pasture into desert for a century."

"If your brother Abram says it, then how can I doubt?" said Sehtepibre. "If he were not wise, he would not have Pharaoh's attention for hour after hour every day."

The words were so innocent, on the surface at least. But they were said loudly enough for many soldiers besides Kay to hear. Pharaoh spends hours and hours listening to a Hsy, that was the message.

At that moment Kay saw something and spoke in urgent, hushed tones.

"A gazelle, my Lord Sehtepibre," he said.

Sure enough, a lone gazelle—a female, and from the look of her, a pregnant one—was picking her way through the quarry. She showed no fear of the humans gathered there—she walked right toward them, among them, past them until she bounded awkwardly onto the most nearly finished of the blocks that had been abandoned in place. Once there, she stood on trembling legs, facing the sun.

"She is sent by Horus," whispered Kay. "See how she worships the sun!" But it was a loud enough whisper that nearby soldiers heard him, and murmured their assent.

The gazelle braced herself, shuddered, and began to give birth. Sarai's first instinct was to start directing the men on how to help, for she had been involved in many a birthing of calf, kid, lamb, or foal in the years since joining Abram's household. But this wild creature would not want help anyway. So Sarai watched as the newborn was squeezed out onto the stone. All the while, the mother did not take her eyes from the sun.

The baby gazelle stirred as the mother finally turned to it and began to lick the mucus of birth from its small body. In doing so, it seemed to stop and stare right at the three of them—Sarai, Sehtepibre, and Kay.

Hagar by now was standing on the ground beside the chariot. She reached up and touched Sarai and whispered, "Perhaps your brother's god sends a promise of fertility."

Sarai laid a finger on Hagar's lips. She knew Hagar

meant no harm, but Kay had definitely heard, and Sehtepibre probably as well. Since it was not known that Sarai was married already, to speak of an omen of fertility could only mean that she expected to be married, and there could be no candidate for her husband-to-be but Montuhotpe himself. If Kay was part of a conspiracy, or later joined one, this would surely not bode well for Sarai's future, to be seen as planning on a marriage to Pharaoh.

"It was not to me that God sent this creature to give birth," said Sarai. "It is not my quarry and not my mission here."

Kay whispered to her—again loudly enough that all the nearby soldiers and workmen could hear him, "Are you saying that this gazelle was sent to Sehtepibre, then?"

"I only know that it was not sent to me," said Sarai. And, in a much softer voice, she added, "as easily might it be said to have come to you."

"Come," said Sehtepibre. "We've rested enough. I know not what the gods meant by sending us this omen, except that clearly it is not an ill one. Let us rejoice in that and go on!"

Sehtepibre's speech surprised Sarai. Normally the duty of a steward would be to proclaim such an omen as a sign of heaven's favor on the king, for having sent forth this expedition. If the gods of Egypt send an omen, it is sent to Pharaoh, and Sehtepibre should have said so. By specifically *not* saying so, he left room for much idle speculation.

Or perhaps not so idle.

"Mark this stone," said Sehtepibre to the foreman of the stonecutters. "When the gazelle leaves here of her own accord, mark the stone as the place where Horus sent a gazelle to greet my expedition."

"I will leave a man to do that, sir."

My expedition. There it was. Sehtepibre was claiming this omen as a sign given, not to Pharaoh, but to him. And not one person gasped at the sheer audacity of it.

And in that moment, Sarai understood it all. It was Sehtepibre who had decided to rebel against Montuhotpe and take the double crown. By claiming this miracle for himself, as word of it spread so also would spread the other implied message—the gods had chosen to show favor to Sehtepibre at a time when all other omens, including the drought, seemed to show their disfavor toward Montuhotpe.

The expedition began to move again, but as they crested a rise in the road, Sehtepibre turned his face to the right and said, "Let us leave the chariots and walk this way."

There was a murmur from the men. There was no reason to stop again so soon, and everyone knew it.

"We came in search of a source of better stone. Yet here, in this old quarry, is some of the finest stone ever found in Egypt. What we should be searching for is not stone, but water so we can cut the blocks for the sarcophagus. The old spring was up here, wasn't it?"

"No, my lord," said the chief stonecutter. "The old spring was farther down."

"And yet the gazelle came from here. How could she live in this mountain without water?" Sehtepibre strode forward boldly, making some show of searching, but in fact moving quite relentlessly toward a place where, Sarai was quite certain, he already knew that water would be flowing.

More than flowing. A spring spilled over and trickled rapidly down to where it filled a natural basin with a small lake of clear and perfect water. Sehtepibre lay down at once, saying loudly, "I will taste first this gift from the gods."

Sarai shuddered. This was even more blatant than before. To drink first from a new spring was a king's duty and privilege. Sehtepibre was laying claim to this miracle of finding water. When word spread of this, there would be some who would demand that he be stripped of office for having acted as if he thought he were Pharaoh himself.

But there would be many others who would spread abroad the story that the gods had surely chosen Sehtepibre. Horus sent a gazelle to him, and she gave birth before him on an uncut block of sarcophagus stone. And then Sehtepibre found water where it had not been before. A waterfinder! Surely if the gods had chosen Sehtepibre, did that not mean that they had rejected that disloyal Montuhotpe—no, that would not be his name in the eyes of those who saw him as a fallen Pharaoh. To them he would be nothing more than Neb-Towi-Re, whom the gods rejected and who now occupied Pharaoh's place unworthily.

To those who had ears to hear and eyes to see, Sehtepibre had declared himself Pharaoh, chosen to take the place of his nominal master, Montuhotpe. And yet Sehtepibre had said nothing to declare himself in rebellion, and it would take some time before Pharaoh began to see the danger that today's events put him in.

Sehtepibre drank from the pool. Then, dipping his helmet into the water, he brought it dripping back to Sarai and offered it to her.

When she took it from his hands, she almost laughed aloud. "I'm afraid, Lord Sehtepibre," she said, "that the water has all drained out."

His dismay seemed real enough as he hurried back for more, this time using Kay's helmet, which was watertight. But the symbolic statement had been made. This holy, godgiven water had been offered to this noblewoman of the Hsy, only when she went to drink of it, it was gone. Egypt had no more hospitality for the Hsy, that's what he was saying. And that's why she had been brought along— to be both the witness and the butt of the joke.

Later, when they were back at the dock, tediously alone while Sehtepibre oversaw the loading of chariots back onto barges, Sarai assumed that Hagar had understood it all, too.

"What are you talking about?" said Hagar.

"Sehtepibre has declared himself," said Sarai. "Today.

This whole trip was designed to announce that the gods have chosen a new Pharaoh."

"But my lady," said Hagar, "how could he have planned it when he didn't know the gods would speak to him like this?"

"I was raised in a king's house, Hagar," said Sarai. "Things like this don't happen by accident. It was the purpose of the expedition. The gazelle was tame—she had no fear of man—and no doubt the spring was dug out weeks ago and then covered over and kept under guard so no one would hear of it until Sehtepibre could discover it."

"If Sehtepibre can make gazelles give birth," said Hagar, "he *should* be Pharaoh."

"Whoever tamed the gazelle knew when its time had come. Sehtepibre chose the day for this expedition, didn't he? The hand that cut a hole in Sehtepibre's helmet also caused the spring to be opened and that little pond to be filled. And that same hand caused the gazelle to be trained and the whole expedition to be in place when her time came to be delivered."

"You are wickedly suspicious, Mistress," said Hagar. But she smiled, for now she understood how the trick had been set up, and she admired it as much as Sarai did. "Did your father play tricks like that?" she asked.

"My father knew how to make a gesture that the people would understand," said Sarai.

"And your 'brother,' does he help his god along?"

"The true and living God does not give signs to advance the political ambitions of disloyal servants," said Sarai. "And if he did give a sign, he wouldn't need Abram to set it up for him."

Hagar giggled. "It's like teasing children," she said. "But it's only funny to those who know the joke."

Hagar did not know enough to fear the coming political turmoil the way Sarai did—though in truth what did Hagar have to fear? She had already lost everything, her family and her freedom. Slaves could afford to be amused at how the powerful jockeyed for position, for it would make little difference in their lives. And even if it would make their lives even worse, there was nothing they could do to prevent it.

How long now? Sarai wondered. How long before Sehtepibre puts it in plain language instead of declaring himself in signs and portents? He must have time for word of this manifestation to spread to many ears. Yet he must also strike before Pharaoh has time to recognize the danger.

What is my best part in this? Sarai wondered. Should I keep silence, and so serve the purpose of the conspirators? Or should I give warning, and give Neb-Towi-Re a chance to thwart this revolt before it's well started?

She doubted the conspirators would know or care if she held her tongue—they would assume that she had not warned Pharaoh because she was an ignorant desert woman and did not realize how she had been used in this little drama. So the only possible advantage would come from warning Pharaoh. But this would ensure the white-hot hatred of Sehtepibre's people. Did Pharaoh have enough power left to protect her and Abram?

O Lord, is this how you answer my prayer? By putting in my hand the power to save our lives—or end them—without telling me which the result will be?

Silently speaking this inward prayer made her think of something else. If Sehtepibre was in the business of faking omens from the gods, it must mean that he does not believe in any god at all. And if he feared no god, then what would restrain him from any crime he wanted to commit? A man without a god was a man without decency, for he would fear no divine retribution.

Abram, I have to speak to you! How else can I know what I should do!

❧ CHAPTER 12 ❧

A few weeks later, Pharaoh returned for another round of conjugal conversation, and in the midst of his busy days and nights, he met with Sarai again. With Hagar just behind her, Sarai again avoided the place he offered her beside him, and sat humbly—but unaffectionately—at his feet.

"Your brother sends his greetings," said Neb-Towi-Re.

"I'd like to see him."

"He wishes he were not so busy, but he hasn't time to come."

Sarai knew Abram would come to her if he could, so Pharaoh's answer meant he was still determined to keep them separated. Still, she couldn't resist pushing a little. "Then I would gladly go to him."

"And interrupt the work he's doing?"

"I certainly wouldn't want to do that."

"He reads our most ancient documents and finds meanings in them that were long since lost. For instance, we have long identified the god Seth with the Fenekhu god

Ba'al, but Abram shows us clearly that in the beginning, both our Osiris and the Fenekhu Ba'al represented the same being, whom Abram calls . . . well, he won't tell us the actual name, but the one he calls 'the Lord,' which is what Ba'al means. And Seth represents the one Abram calls 'the Enemy,' and is not really a god at all, with no power over the living except to lie."

"I'm so happy that my brother is bringing you such enlightenment," said Sarai.

"I would be glad to have your brother always with me," said Neb-Towi-Re. "I would be glad if your brother could also be my brother."

"The bonds of friendship can be as strong as the bonds of brotherhood," said Sarai. And then, without quite deciding to do it, she added, "Just as the bonds of stewardship can be as false as the promises of Satan."

Neb-Towi-Re blinked. "Why don't we walk in the garden?"

So he wanted to hear her message, and knew better than to converse openly indoors. The trouble was that she had never decided to *give* the message. And yet, at the moment she spoke, she knew that it was right to speak. How had she known? And why did she know even now that she was going to warn Pharaoh of everything she had seen and everything she knew was coming?

Once outside, Sarai was surprised that he allowed his guards to remain within earshot. When she said so, Neb-Towi-Re scoffed. "They're all Fenekhu. They have no friends among my enemies."

"The dangerous spy is the one that you trust," said Sarai—a lesson her father had often repeated.

Pharaoh waved a hand at Hagar.

"She is only one, and she already knows anything I would tell you," said Sarai.

"But she doesn't know what I will say in reply," said Neb-Towi-Re, with a smile.

Sarai turned to Hagar. "While I speak with mighty

Pharaoh, please stay as far away from me as Pharaoh's guards stay from him."

Hagar bowed and stepped back to stand beside one of the soldiers. With Hagar standing by him, Sarai noticed that while the man's hair was clean, he still kept it at an Amorite's length, and he wore more clothing than an Egyptian soldier ever would, though less than Amorites normally wore. The others also showed signs of being Amorite or Canaanite, or from some other land. Not one Egyptian.

"That must please your army, that the soldiers you trust the most are not Egyptian."

"You had something to tell me?" said Neb-Towi-Re.

It was time. She knew it was dangerous to speak; she couldn't guess what the consequences would be for her and Abram. Yet she didn't even hesitate, because in a place deeper than language, deeper than thought, deeper than fear or even hope, she simply knew that this was what she ought to do. And in a place even deeper, the place where her true self dwelt, she wanted with all her heart to do what was right. Her confidence was perfect. And so she spoke. "Perhaps you've already heard the story of Sehtepibre's expedition to find better stones for your sarcophagus."

"The gazelle that gave birth on a stone was regarded as a very favorable omen, and the priests tell me that the discovery of a new spring nearby is even more so."

"I was there," said Sarai. "And these omens were not presented in your favor."

"It was an expedition for my sarcophagus, in my name," said Pharaoh.

"These omens seemed to me to have been carefully planned. Sehtepibre knew where to stop to rest and chat with me until the gazelle appeared. She had no fear of humans, which means that she had already been tamed. The expedition was no doubt timed to coincide with her time of bearing. And as for the new spring, it had been flowing for some time. I believe Sehtepibre had a channel dug to connect with a known spring. It was in place for some time, ready for him to discover it after the gazelle gave birth."

"Sometimes my servants feel that it is helpful to give the gods a little push when there's a need for an omen."

"These omens were not intended for your benefit, but rather for your harm."

Neb-Towi-Re sighed and looked away.

"I was there. Your name was not mentioned. The gazelle was viewed as coming from Horus in order to show favor to Sehtepibre. And it was Sehtepibre who was led by the gods to 'discover' the new water source. He could easily have named these omens as being in your favor, but instead he laid claim to them himself, in a roundabout way, so he could not be accused of anything. But it was his announcement, all the same, that the gods had chosen him."

"How very clever of Sehtepibre," said Neb-Towi-Re.

"The word is already spreading through the army and among the nobility, I'm quite certain," said Sarai. "He is preparing to move against you."

"Yes, I'm not surprised."

"You knew already that he was your enemy?"

"I choose to keep my enemies close to me, so I can watch them."

Sarai shook her head. "But you don't watch him."

"I have many eyes, Fair Milcah, not just yours."

"Don't you see how they manipulate you? Even my presence here, and Abram's with you—the very thought that you might make me, a Hsy, queen of Egypt, and that you let a Hsy prophet speak his strange ideas about the gods—it must enrage them, frighten them."

"Yes, your presence is meant as a provocation," said Pharaoh.

"And yet you keep us here!"

"Because I know what is good for Egypt. The land is weak and decaying. The gods have dried up all the lands around us, and the Nile floods grow weaker over time, giving us lean harvests in too many years. Why? Because we have become corrupt and ignorant. We have lost the ancient knowledge that once gave us power to unite and rule this land. We need to go back to our roots in the east and reinvigorate Egypt from the house of Pharaoh on down to the poorest farmer and the humblest beggar. Of course those who love the weakness of Egypt, who profit from her corruption, of course *they* resent what I'm doing, and of course they mean to oppose me. I would have to be blind not to know that, and a fool not to make sure I know who is plotting against me. When the time comes, I will destroy them completely. But in the meantime, I will continue to do what is needed to bring back the vigor and wisdom that once made Egypt great."

His eyes flashed and for the first time, Sarai understood that this man was not weak at all, that he was a bold man with the courage to try to change the kingdom he had inherited.

The trouble was, he was utterly, hopelessly wrong about one key fact. "Neb-Towi-Re," she said. "Your love of Egypt is clear, and your plans for Egypt are good. But you cannot do this if the people do not follow you."

"The people? They care only for their families and their farms, for bread and beer and babies."

"All power in this kingdom comes from the obedience of the people."

"Which comes from the granary and the whip," said Pharaoh. "I control the supply of grain, and I have the power to punish those who rebel."

"Mighty Pharaoh, you have that control and that power only as long as you are obeyed. But when the people—from the highest to the lowest—come to wonder whether the gods have left you and chosen someone else, how quick will be their obedience? How energetically will they act to defend you, to obey you?"

"Which is why I have so carefully built up an army of Fenekhu soldiers," said Pharaoh. "Their loyalty is to me alone, and Sehtepibre's little show of miracles will have no effect on them."

"A whole army? Of foreigners? Outsiders?" Sarai was horrified.

"Not one of whom will pay the slightest attention to Sehtepibre."

"But . . . if it comes to war, that means that *you* are the one who will be sending foreign soldiers to kill Egyptians, and Sehtepibre is the one who will be defended by true Egyptians!"

Pharaoh glared at her. "Why are you concerning yourself with such things?"

"Neb-Towi-Re, I believe you are a good man who means well. But you have set yourself up to be destroyed, and everything you're trying to do will come to nothing."

"I am not a good man," said Neb-Towi-Re. "I am a god, the god who rules Egypt, and I will restore this kingdom to its ancient greatness."

"You can still save yourself," said Sarai. "Send me and my brother away. Repudiate what Abram has taught you. Declare that you were merely trying to find out what lies the Hsy were telling about the gods, and now you are expelling them from Egypt. Disperse your Fenekhu army, disarm them, and declare that only true Egyptians will be your soldiers from now on."

"Are you insane?" said Pharaoh. "Do you think that *I'm* insane? There's not an Egyptian soldier I can trust!"

"You can trust them if you become the Pharaoh Sehtepibre has been teaching them to want."

"In other words, I should become the kind of Pharaoh Sehtepibre would be."

"You can't do anything for Egypt when you're dead."

"When Pharaoh dies, he rises again."

"Only if his son comes after him, like Osiris, to raise him up," said Sarai.

"I know you're lying to me because Abram has told me that neither he nor you believes that story. *You* believe that it is the father who raises up the son, though of course that makes no sense at all. If you would lie to me about that, why should I believe anything you say?"

Sarai despaired. "I have told you the truth—I have told you the only path you can take that will keep you alive with the double crown upon your head. The path you're following will lead to your death. Your name will be stricken from the history of Egypt as if you had never lived. Your body will not be in a sarcophagus, it will be fed to the dogs of the street."

"To prophesy against Pharaoh is treason," he said, his face growing dark with anger.

"I'm not prophesying, I'm telling you the natural consequence of making your own people hate you. Everything you're doing is playing into the hands of Sehtepibre. And the fact that he now openly claims these omens for himself as signs of the gods' favor, while you do nothing to punish him or stop him, only makes you seem helpless and his victory seem inevitable to his supporters."

Neb-Towi-Re looked away from her, his body tense with rage, his fists clenched tight. "By law I should have you killed on the spot for what you've dared to say to me."

Sarai trembled with fear, and yet the fear was nothing compared to the white-hot certainty that burned within her. "If you did, it might save your life," said Sarai. "Certainly you should send me away. Me and my brother. Expel us from Egypt. Do it. Don't you see that my brother and I have been sent by God to warn you? To show you how to save yourself?"

"Since when do the gods speak to Pharaoh through a woman?"

"Ask my brother if the things I've said are true! He'll tell you just what I've told you."

"I wouldn't waste his time with such foolish womanly concerns. Leave these matters to men. What can a shepherd girl know of affairs of state?" Pharaoh turned from her and stalked away. His soldiers jumped into action, following him, surrounding him.

Hagar rushed to Sarai. "What did you say to make him so angry?"

"As if you didn't hear, with our voices raised like that."

"But you as much as invited him to kill you!"

"God will protect *me* if he wishes. But who will protect poor Neb-Towi-Re?"

"Poor Pharaoh? You say *poor* Pharaoh?"

"He has such good intentions."

"Let his gods take care of him as your God takes care of you."

"That's the trouble," said Sarai. "Only the one God is real. Gods that don't exist can't give much help to the men who serve them. Sehtepibre knows that—why else would he manufacture omens instead of waiting for the gods to show him real ones? My fear is that when Neb-Towi-Re Montuhotpe falls, he'll drag me and Abram down with him."

"I promise I'll kill you myself before I let Sehtepibre's men have you," said Hagar.

Sarai looked at her, appalled. "You'll do no such thing! What a terrible thought!"

"Don't you know what they would do to you?" said Hagar. "You'd die from it in the end, but you'd wish a thousand times for death before it finally came."

"What happens to me is in God's hands."

"Then why is God keeping you here so long? And why hasn't God given you the babies you want so much? As far as I can tell, your God isn't helping you any more than his gods are helping him."

Hagar's words stabbed at Sarai's soul. Yet she knew that Hagar was wrong. Knew it because . . . because . . . "No," said Sarai. "While I was talking to Pharaoh, I felt the power of God within me. I hadn't planned to say all that I said. Once I gave him the warning about Sehtepibre, I was finished with my message. But new words came into my heart, into my mouth. I was on fire with those words. Yes, some of it came from things I had learned in my father's house, growing up. But if I were speaking only as my father's daughter, I would have kept my mouth shut because to speak was so dangerous to me. But along with the words that came to my mind there came also a certainty that I must speak, that it was right for me to speak."

"You mean your God promised to keep you safe?"

"No, there was no promise. God doesn't take away fear. Pharaoh might have ordered one of his soldiers to strike me down on the spot. What I knew was that if I did *not* speak, I would be in the wrong. That to serve God in that moment, I had to open my mouth."

"Well, you certainly did open it."

"And yet Pharaoh did not hear me."

"Oh, he heard you. And he didn't kill you, either."

"Yet."

"If he didn't kill you then, he never will, Mistress," said Hagar.

"All these years that I've been praying for myself, let me bear a child, and the weeks and months that I've been praying, free me from this captivity and reunite me with my husband, I've received not a single breath of a response from God. But in this moment, when I hadn't prayed at all, God fills me with words in order to tell *Pharaoh* what he needs to hear?"

"Maybe God cares more about kings than mere women."

"Abram says God cares about all his children the same."

"Look around," said Hagar. "If he did, why are there slaves? Why is there such hunger? No, the gods have favorites. And if there's only one god, then all the blame for this misery is his."

"No, no," said Sarai. "The misery is nothing, in the end. The scars on your back, my barren womb—"

"They are not nothing," said Hagar hotly.

"They are what we make them," said Sarai. "We make them good or bad depending on how we respond to them. Your pain has hurt you, but you refused to let it destroy you. My barrenness—I have been tormented by doubts and fears, but in the end, God was still able to use my mouth to speak through. Oh, Hagar, he knows that I exist!"

Unable to contain the joy she felt, Sarai threw her arms around Hagar.

"He wouldn't be much of a god if he didn't know *that*," said Hagar. And then she added, "Pharaoh knows that you exist, too."

Sarai pulled away, laughing now. "Yes, I suppose so," said Sarai. "After that little scene, you don't suppose he still wants to marry me, do you?"

Hagar laughed, too, and with light steps they took a walk along the river, deeming it wiser to let plenty of time pass before they returned to the House of Women. Sarai did not see Pharaoh again before he left the House of Women and returned upriver.

The days and weeks now passed more lightly for Sarai, which should have made no sense to her, for if anything her situation was even more dangerous than before. But having felt that spark of God's fire within her, she faced each day with greater confidence. And now, at last, she did go among the other women and talk to them and join in their gossip. They were shy with her at first, for of course they had all been talking about her for weeks and they feared and resented the possibility that she might be raised above them and made queen. But in due time many of them—the Fenekhu among them, especially, but some Egyptians, too—began to speak more candidly with her, and in time she came to know their stories, their hopes and fears. She also came to know their children, and though her heart sometimes seemed about to break with her own yearning, she still took joy in watching their little ones play and quarrel and cry and laugh and, above all, learn more with each moment that passed in their headlong lives.

But as months passed, she began to hear something else, as well—the worries of women who had been visited by Pharaoh, but had not conceived children. At first she scoffed at their fears—it had been such a short time, not *every* visit from Pharaoh had to have results, did it? Because she was supposedly not married, she could hardly tell them that if they wanted to see *barren*, they should look at *her*, but she still found it difficult to take their misery seriously.

Then came the flood season, and Sarai joined in the move to higher ground while the river rose and covered the land in mud. Hagar told her then that several times the flood rose high enough to cover the floor of the House of Women with mud. "And they couldn't clean it out until the planting was done," she said. Which made sense to Sarai—the survival of Egypt depended on planting seeds in the fresh mud, so the plants could grow roots that would keep finding ever deeper moisture until the grain was ripe. This year, though, the flood was a scant one, and they moved back into the palace sooner than anyone had hoped. "It will be a poor harvest this year," said Hagar.

A poor harvest. In the year that Pharaoh had taken to spending so much time with Abram and courting Sarai. For he did return, every few weeks, and without ever referring back to their argument in the garden, he made it a point to speak to her genially and it was plain that he still wanted to make a queen of her, despite all she had said to him, despite all the dangers that it would pose. This was no secret to anyone, of course, and so the weakness of the Nile flood would be used as proof that the gods were outraged at the supposed influence of this desert prophet and his sister over Pharaoh. Sehtepibre would have to be a fool not to make his move soon.

Now Sarai began to take the complaints of the women seriously. She had been here almost a year, and the last of the women who had already been pregnant when she arrived had given birth. Not one woman in the house of Pharaoh was with child. Their barrenness was complete.

This, too, would be taken as a sign of the gods' rejection of Pharaoh.

And, more to the point, it was the one sign that Pharaoh himself could not ignore or explain away. If there was one thing he prided himself on, it was the fact that when he planted, there was a harvest. He might not be willing to see how this endangered his crown, but it certainly endangered his pride.

Which was why, a year to the day after Sarai had been separated from Abram at the dock, Pharaoh's barge arrived at the House of Women bearing not only him, but also that outrageous desert prophet who had been causing so much controversy among the priests.

It was all Sarai could do to keep from rushing to Abram and throwing her arms around him in a very unsisterly way. But she restrained herself, and tried to keep even from gazing at him, for she knew her expression would surely give away their secret.

Abram came to her and with geniality, not love, he put his arms around her in a hearty embrace. But in her ear he whispered, "This has been the worst year of my life. I've missed you desperately."

No words could have made her gladder. She did not have to pretend to smile when he broke off the embrace. "Let me look at you," he said. "Neb keeps telling me how beautiful you are, and I refused to believe him, but I suppose it's almost true."

She laughed—she hoped the way a sister would laugh at a teasing brother—and turned to Pharaoh. "At last you were able to persuade my brother to leave his studies and come see his poor sister."

"I had to threaten him," said Pharaoh. "I told him I'd burn the book he's been writing if he didn't come."

"You've been writing a book?" asked Sarai.

Abram shrugged. "Pharaoh asked me to write an account of my life, and of God's dealings with me."

"And of the place where God lives and which stars rule

over other stars and all that," added Pharaoh. "It should be in writing, so it won't be lost."

"Truth is never lost," said Abram mildly. "Merely forgotten."

Pharaoh led them inside, showing off the place to Abram, and it became clear that Pharaoh's affection for Abram was genuine. He really did think of Abram as his brother and treated him almost as an equal. How it must gall the priests to see this friendship.

But after Abram had seen the sights and met Pharaoh's wives and had Eshut presented to him, there came a time when Pharaoh once again went out into the garden, this time with both Abram and Sarai. No one had to ask him to make his guards stand off a little way, and Hagar with them.

"My Lady Milcah, you'll be happy to know that Sehtepibre has begun his revolt. He has declared that I have been rejected by the gods and they have chosen him to be Pharaoh Amenemhet."

"I am not happy to hear this," said Sarai. "Is the revolt widespread?"

"Most of the noble houses are waiting to see which way the wind blows. They don't rally to him. They send messages to me about how they pray to all the gods for my success. No doubt he has his share of messages, too. A few houses, though, Nehry, the monarch of the fifteenth township of Upper Egypt has declared for Sehtepibre, along with his two sons, Kay and Thutnakht. I think you warned me about Kay, but I did not expect the father to revolt. I raised him to his position—he was a commoner, a tradesman."

"There is little gratitude," said Abram.

"He has no idea what he should be grateful for," said Sarai. "I imagine that by now he believes that he was born to his high position."

Pharaoh chuckled, but he seemed concerned.

"This revolt doesn't trouble me," said Neb-Towi-Re. "My armies will subdue these men. And I've sent Khnumhotpe south with a flotilla of boats to supply my army there."

"You trust Khnumhotpe?"

"He and Sehtepibre have never gotten along."

"It was Khnumhotpe to whom Kay delivered us when we arrived," said Sarai.

"Your sister still believes that this conspiracy reaches everywhere," said Neb-Towi-Re to Abram. "It was *my* command that you be brought to me."

"Was it your command that we be separated?" asked Sarai.

Pharaoh shrugged. "That's not an interesting subject," he said. "What I need to talk to you about is this. Here in my house, some evil influence is at work. My wives and women have conceived no children for a year. The very same year when I try to learn about the God whose priesthood you hold, Abram—and this is what happens to me! I have married as the Fenekhu marry, many women, none of them a sister of mine, and I must know—is it your God that I have offended?"

"I don't know," said Abram. "Have you?"

"If I have, I don't know it. How can I lead my troops in confidence, when I myself wonder if the gods have forsaken me?"

"So you must think," said Abram, "and see if you have sinned against God."

Pharaoh shook his head. "Do you think I haven't already pondered this? I beg you to pray to your God and find out. Or you, Milcah, you will speak boldly to me, tell me what my sin is! Or tell me if some enemy has poisoned my women so they can't conceive!"

They sat in silence, all of them thinking. But Sarai doubted Pharaoh could guess the thoughts going through her head, or Abram's either, if she was any judge. Not that her thoughts were all that clear. To be near Abram and yet unable to speak to him, unable to touch him—a year of being imprisoned without him, and now he was still out of reach. How could she think of anything?

So it was Abram who spoke first. "Mighty Pharaoh, have you dealt justly with God's servants?"

"What do you mean? Who serves God in Egypt, except you and your sister?"

Abram said nothing.

"Do you have some complaint?" said Pharaoh. "Is there any favor I haven't granted you? No, the only person with a complaint is *me*, a complaint against *you!* Haven't I given you great herds of cattle that I received from Fenekhu who came to buy grain? Flocks and herds, riches beyond measure I have offered you, all for the hand of your sister, and yet you tell me that she must decide, she must tell me her will—knowing that she is a woman who will never say yes to a man!"

"But that is not so, Pharaoh," said Abram. "She is a woman who would say yes to a man and wait ten years for him without ever hearing a word from him, trusting him to come and marry her. She is a woman who, for love, would give up every aspect of the life she knew, of the future she was raised for, in order to follow her husband wherever he takes her, and into any danger."

"These things are easy to say, but when the king of all Egypt woos her, she—no, I will not waste more time discussing this. You have both been wickedly ungrateful to me. You will not marry me, the most powerful man in the most ancient kingdom in the world, and *you* will not give me your priesthood. Do you not know the peril you are in? Do you now see how I have restrained myself in not avenging these insults you have given me?"

The rage that flashed in his eyes, that stiffened the muscles of his body—yes, Sarai was afraid of him. He had never let her see this before, not even when they argued.

Abram, however, only smiled sadly. "Neb-Towi-Re," he said, "did you not declare yourself my friend?"

"Many times, much good it did me."

"And each time, did I not tell you that your friend would like very much to see his sister?"

"And each time I told you that on the day that either

you or she agreed to the marriage, you would see her!"

So Abram *had* been trying to get to her this whole miserable year.

"I asked you to let me pass a message to her, and you refused," said Abram.

"I said I would pass a message if it was your command for her to marry me. It's not *my* fault if you refused."

"And did I not tell you that I would never give her such a message."

"You did! And I wanted to strike you down for it, but I was patient! I was kind and loving! I did not kill you!"

"For a year, you have kept me and my sister apart, despite our many requests. We have both tried to help you in every way we could. Milcah warned you of conspiracy, and I have taught you everything I know about the heavens and God who dwells there. You have kept us prisoner, because you were so determined to have her as your wife that you could not treat either of us as your guests."

Neb-Towi-Re seemed dumfounded. "But I'm Pharaoh. There is nothing more important than my having an heir to succeed the throne. An Osiris to come and raise me from the dead. No, no, don't correct me, I know that you don't believe the son raises the father, but I'm Pharaoh! How could I invigorate that throne without a worthy queen from the East?"

"But Milcah is only the sister of a desert priest," said Abram. "Why didn't you treat with one of the kings of the East and marry a princess?"

"The kings of the old cities of Mesopotamia are usurpers. The true and ancient kings are gone, and all that's left are desert upstarts or the kings of new cities that have nothing to offer me. The only princess I wanted was the one Suwertu wrote to me about—before your God struck him dead. The girl who had been promised to Asherah but chose to marry instead. Who but she was fit to be the queen of Egypt? Only she was taken by another man." He pointed his finger at Abram as if this were a terrible accusation. "Why didn't you bring her with you! Why did you travel with your sister when you came to Egypt!"

"I thought you wanted to marry my sister," said Abram. "I did. I do."

Abram shook his head sadly. "You can lie to me and you can lie to her. You can lie to your kingdom. But you can't lie to God. You know why your women are barren, Neb-Towi-Re. And I can promise you that they will remain barren until you tell the truth and repent of your sin before God."

Abram's words were strong, but Neb-Towi-Re's reaction was out of all proportion. At first his face turned red, and he seemed about to burst with rage. Then he burst into tears and flung himself to the ground at Abram's feet, weeping and howling. "Oh, the God of Abram is mighty! You have known all along, you have known the truth!"

"I hoped," said Abram mildly, "that you would repent on your own."

"What sin?" asked Sarai quietly. "What lie?"

"I will not say it," said Abram. "Only Pharaoh can say it, because only his own tongue will accuse him."

Pharaoh got some control of himself and sat crosslegged, miserably bowed, his face in his hands. "I would marry you, Milcah, and then demand that Abram bring his wife to the wedding."

"That doesn't seem so terrible," said Sarai.

Abram put his fingers to his lips to still her.

"Once she was here, I would have taken her in marriage as well, and raised her to the throne of Egypt. No one would have murmured against me then—a queen of the ancient lineage of Ur! It would have been a perfect uniting of Egypt and Sumeria. Our children would have been a new dynasty."

"But you couldn't have married Abram's wife."

Pharaoh took his hands from his face and rolled his eyes in exasperation. "Do I have to *say* what is so obvious?"

"From your own lips," said Abram.

"I would have married Abram's widow. It would have been a quick and painless death, no bloodshed, merely a poison that they say has no flavor and causes only a deep sleep. I'm not a cruel man!"

"This is why he never called us his guests," said Abram to Sarai. "Because if he did, then to kill me would have been a terrible offense against every god he ever heard of."

"Is this why God has stricken me so? What did I do that was so wrong? To kill one man—Pharaohs kill ten thousand men when the need arises!"

"In war, defending Egypt, there would be no sin in that."

"I *was* defending Egypt, against decay, collapse, chaos!"

"Murder is murder," said Abram. "Coldly planned, to get from me what God had given me, the one I love above all others, the most precious part of my life, you would have killed me to take her for yourself, and you say there is no sin in it?"

"She was meant to marry a king!"

"She was meant to serve God, like every other man and woman born upon the earth. Even you. God is giving you a chance to repent. A chance to restore your house."

"What chance! I have already waited too long."

"Repent and see."

"How can I repent? What hope is there for me?"

"A good beginning," said Abram, "is to welcome me as your guest, with your soldiers as witnesses."

"My soldiers? What do they know of guest-right?"

"They're Amorites and Canaanites, Hittites and Nubians and Jebuzites. To them guest-right is sacred. They would never violate it or follow any man who did. There could be no better witnesses than that."

"And this will lift the curse of God that rests upon my house?"

"I don't know," said Abram. "There may be more tests to follow. But it's a beginning."

Pharaoh got to his feet and called out to his soldiers to listen and watch. "I accept this man, Abram, as my guest and my friend! He is under my protection, and cursed be any man who lifts a hand against him in my kingdom! You are witnesses!" Then Pharaoh embraced Abram and kissed his cheek.

The soldiers nodded. Some saluted. Some knelt. It was done.

Pharaoh sat on a bench, exhausted. "Pray to your God now. Get him to lift the curse."

"Not yet," said Abram.

"You dare to demand more?"

"I demand nothing," said Abram. "I merely want you to meet my wife, Sarai, daughter of the King of Ur-of-the-South."

"What!" cried Pharaoh. "She is here in Egypt? This whole time you have kept her concealed from me? Where is she! Send for her!" And then, as the truth dawned on him, his face grew red again, and his rage was so terrible that he trembled with it. "You lied to me! From the very beginning you lied to me!"

"God told me to tell the soldiers who met us that Sarai was my sister and not my wife. I did not understand the reason for it, except that if I did not, you would surely kill me. It made no sense to me, but I obeyed God. If I had told you who she really was, how long would it have taken for you to kill me?"

"I should kill you now," said Pharaoh, his voice choked with fury.

"What Hsy would follow a faithless killer of a guest?"

"How are you my guest, when you lied to me!"

"My lie saved my life, and kept my wife from being forced to marry you against her will. Your lies were meant to deceive me so you could kill me and take from me all that gave me joy in life. Which of us has reason to complain?"

Pharaoh again threw himself to the ground, and this time sobbed like a child, deep body-wracking sobs that made Sarai want to run to him, to comfort him like a baby. But she did not move. This was between him and God. She had no part in it now.

When the sobbing grew still, Abram began to speak. But it was not to Pharaoh that he spoke, and not to Sarai. "Thou knowest his heart, O Father. If there is still murder in his heart, then do not forgive him, for the law must stand. But if he has truly repented, then take the curse from his house, I pray. Thou art the judge."

"I *have* repented," Pharaoh whispered.

"Then the curse will be lifted," said Abram simply. "It is entirely in your hands."

"All my dreams are nothing," said Pharaoh. "The year I wasted on you . . . I should have been tending to my kingdom."

"All your choosing," said Abram. "If you had not plotted my death—"

"I know, I know," said Pharaoh miserably. "But marrying . . . Sarai . . . that was supposed to cure all these woes. Now I go to battle empty-handed and alone."

"Pray to God and honor him as the only true and living God, and he will protect you from your enemies as he protected me and my beloved from ours."

"I didn't want to be your enemy," said Pharaoh, weeping again. "I loved you. It broke my heart to think of losing you as my friend!"

"Set us free, Pharaoh. Let us go from this place. I'll return to you all the flocks and herds you gave me. I know they were meant to be a bride-price, and you have no bride from me."

"No," said Pharaoh. "Keep all I gave you. I will give you more. Let me show God that I am not his enemy. I will give you gold and precious stones to take with you back to Retenu. I will give you servants and soldiers, horses and—"

"God's love is not to be bought with gold," said Abram. "It is bought with obedience, and paid for with humble service to God's children. No one has it in his power to serve more people than Pharaoh. Even now, God has the power to save your crown."

"I will," said Pharaoh. "Stay with me!"

"No," said Abram. "It is the beginning of wisdom for you to send us away. As long as we're here, your enemies will use us as a cause against you."

"Go then," said Pharaoh. "Go at once. Your household awaits you. And the gifts I declared will still be yours."

"May I take with me the handmaid you gave me?" asked Sarai.

Pharaoh turned away from her, covering his ears as though her voice caused him pain. "Yes, she's yours, only don't shame me by making me hear your voice or see your face again."

They walked away from him. As they approached the nearest of the soldiers, the man glanced at Pharaoh and spoke to Abram. "What is all this?"

"A man is only great when he humbles himself before the Lord," said Abram.

"They say there's going to be fighting," said the soldier.

"Have you given your oath to Pharaoh?" asked Abram.

"I have," said the soldier. "But they say half of Egypt is in revolt."

"Keep your oath," said Abram. "You came to Egypt hungry, and he fed you."

"What about you?" asked the soldier. "Are you going to fight for him?"

"I was never a soldier and I took no oath," said Abram. "But I will pray for him."

Hagar ran to Sarai as soon as they were beyond the circle of soldiers. "Is there anything you need to bring with you?" Sarai asked her.

"Nothing, Mistress," said Hagar. "I own nothing, not even my own body."

"That's true of all of us," said Abram. "This is the servant you asked about?"

"Hagar, this is my husband. Abram, this is my hand-maiden. She knew my secret almost from the start, and did not betray me, even though she would have been well rewarded if she had."

"Welcome to my household," said Abram. "We'll get you decent clothing when we reach my tent. You can keep that gown to show your husband on your wedding night." He walked ahead of them, leading the way to the river.

Hagar leaned close to Sarai as they walked, so she could speak softly and still be heard. "I can never wear linens again?"

"You can wear them all the time," said Sarai. "Under your clothing."

"It'll be like wearing a house," said Hagar. She laughed at her own jest, but her hands trembled where they held Sarai's arm.

"Don't be afraid," said Sarai. "We all work hard, but life is good for everyone, servant and master."

"I have put my life in your hands," said Hagar.

"As I put mine in yours," said Sarai.

Abram commanded the pilot of the king's own barge to take them down the river to where his herds were pastured and his household tents were pitched. The pilot obeyed him with only a glance at Pharaoh, who was visible in the distance, walking slowly to the House of Women.

"Don't worry," said Sarai. "Pharaoh has much to do in the House of Women before he'll need this boat again."

It was sunset when they reached shore, and only torchlight showed them the glad faces of their friends and servants when they reached the tents. Sarai was gratified to see that all was in order in the camp, everything in good repair and all at peace. Abram's steward, Bethuel, had been ill, but had delegated everything to a young Damascene named Eliezer. Neither Sarai nor Abram knew him. It was an alarming thing, that Bethuel had reached outside Abram's household to choose his second. What had he promised this Eliezer? Could he be trusted? Sarai was ready to be angry at Bethuel for such a dangerous decision.

But Eliezer took the initiative. "Abram," he said, "Bethuel first gave me hospitality in your name, but I insisted that I serve for my bread. He would not take me as a servant, but he did allow me to labor, and he found my work pleasing. I did not seek the trust that he gave me when he became ill, and I have no expectation of keeping such a position. I only ask that you confirm the hospitality your steward gave me in your name."

"I confirm you as my guest," said Abram. "But we leave Egypt tomorrow."

"Abram," said Eliezer again. Sarai wasn't sure she liked the way he called Abram by his name, though as a guest, and not a servant, that was technically correct. The man was young—scarcely twenty, by her estimation—but he carried himself with assurance, like a master or a host, and not a servant. She wondered if there had been resentment or even conflict when an outsider was given authority over many who were older than he, or who had been born into service to Abram's family.

"Eliezer," said Abram as mildly as if he had no such suspicions. Sarai was never quite sure whether Abram's mildness represented great self-control or dangerous naivete.

"I came to Egypt because the drought had devastated my father's household. Our wealth died with our cattle. I valued my father's honor more than his wealth, but he was ashamed of having lost my inheritance, and when he dismissed our servants he left me and commanded me not to follow after him. Whether he died in the desert or begs in the streets of Damascus or serves in another man's house, I do not know because he does not want me to know. What knowledge I have I learned from my father. It is my whole inheritance, and I now offer it in your service. Take me into your household forever, and I will serve you well."

"Bethuel is my steward," said Abram.

"I will do whatever task you find me suited for," said Eliezer.

"And if I give you work to which you are not well suited?"

"Then I will learn the work until I do it as well as you need or wish me to."

"It's a solemn thing to give up your freedom to another man," said Abram.

"It is no more than you have done, Abram," said Eliezer.

Sarai gasped before she could stop herself. It was an outrageous thing to say. Abram was master of a house, a great lord of the desert, and no servant to any man.

"I think my wife wishes to know in what sense you meant those words," said Abram—again, showing no annoyance at either his words or her gasp.

"You have given your life to God's service, and God is your master in all things," said Eliezer. "How then can I better serve God than to enter into obedience to his steward?"

Now Sarai's suspicions were fully aroused. If a man wished to deceive Abram he could choose no more devious path than to pretend to serve God. Did Abram see this? Or would he simply take Eliezer's protestations of faith as if they must be true?

"God is little spoken of these days, at least not with his true name. It is only Ba'al that I hear of now," said Abram. "In Damascus as in any other city of Syria."

"Not everyone forgets that Ba'al was simply a term of respect for the true God. My name is the one my father gave me. He taught me of Father El, and he told me also of the priestly family in which at last a new prophet had arisen—Abram son of Terah. He rejoiced when the priest of Pharaoh was slain by the hand of the true and living God. I have known your name from my childhood."

If the man was a flatterer, he was better at it than any Sarai had seen in her father's house, though that was partly because the best flatterers would not have wasted their talent on a king who had lost his city. Still, his words and manner were so simple that Sarai could not help but believe him, or at least wish to believe him.

Abram took Eliezer's hands. "You stand here as my guest, and I offer you guest-right on the journey back to Canaan. I will teach you what I know of God during the journey."

Eliezer shook his head. "I have no desire to be your guest, and I wish to learn about God, not just from your words, but from your life, and not just by hearing and watching, but by taking part in your works wherever and whenever you have need of me. Accept me as your servant, or I will not go with you."

"You know, of course, that only a child born in my house can inherit from me," said Abram.

So Abram was not naive. He knew that a man of his wealth who had no children could look like an opportunity to an enterprising young man. Abram's people were not like the Egyptians, adopting adults as sons or daughters in order to circumvent the inheritance laws. Nothing of Abram's would ever belong to Eliezer. A practical concern that had to be dealt with—though if Sarai were not barren, the question would never have come up.

"I know the law," said Eliezer. "I want not to have what is yours, but to *be* yours."

"For a term of five years I take you," said Abram.

"An oath that ends is no oath at all. I do not wish to be your hireling."

"Let all here be my witnesses that I offered to take you with me as a guest and as a bondservant. It is at your insistence that I take you as a servant in my household, you and all the children who might be born to you."

Eliezer knelt before Abram and stretched out a hand. Abram raised his foot and stepped on Eliezer's hand, symbolically taking him as if he had been captured in war. Then he reached down and raised Eliezer by the hand.

"Eliezer," said Abram.

"Yes, master," said Eliezer. Sarai was pleased to see that he used the term of respect as soon as he was officially Abram's servant.

"Please continue to help Bethuel as you have been do-ing. There will be time enough tomorrow for you and he to tell me all that I need to know. In due time I'll decide where you fit into this camp."

So quickly had they slipped from the sophisticated manners of Egypt to the more earthy ways of the herd-keeping household. Sehtepibre had taken solemn oaths to Pharaoh, but they did not keep him from plotting his mas-ter's overthrow. Nothing that anyone said in Egypt meant what it seemed to mean. Everything was layered and dis-guised and distorted and, above all, expendable. But these words and actions of Abram's and Eliezer's would bind them both for life—Abram to provide a place and suste-nance for Eliezer, and Eliezer to serve Abram in any way he might direct.

There might be turmoil in Egypt, but in Abram's house-hold, there was Ma'at.

The only sadness was that Sarai's old servant Bitute had died months before. Her last words had been of Sarai, calling her "my good little girl, my best little child." Sarai wept in gratitude for the love of the old woman that had been part of her life from the start, and in sorrow that she had not been with her when she died. But her body had been embalmed and they would take it with them and bury her in Canaan. "As I must be buried," said Sarai. "I was born in exile, Abram, but when I die, bury me in the land God has given you. Not in Ur-of-the-North. I was born there, but it was never my home. I'm done with cities."

"If you die before me, which I doubt, I'll bury you in Canaan," said Abram. "But only if I have your promise that if I die first, you will see to it we lie beside each other. We had a year of our marriage stolen from us. From now on, even in death I'll never be away from you for long." He turned to the others who were gathered round. "You've done well, my friends. You've kept everything ready for travel. Tomorrow we set out for home."

That night, Abram slept in Sarai's tent and held her

close to him far into the night. They dozed and woke and dozed again, and in one of their wakings, she thought of something. "What about the book you wrote? Did you bring it with you?"

"No," he said. "Everything that's in the book is in my memory."

"What if Sehtepibre wins the war? Won't his people destroy your book?"

"They will if they find it," said Abram. "But where I've hidden it, I doubt it will be found for a century."

"Where did you hide it? Did you bury it?"

"No. I rolled it up within the scroll of a very boring book of the exploits of a long-dead king. Someday someone will open it and copy it out because they'll think it's part of the royal archive. By then no one will remember my name. The scribe will simply copy what I wrote because that's what scribes are paid to do."

"So you might as well not have written it at all."

"If God has a use for it, God will get it into the hands of those who need it. In due time."

"I need *you*," said Sarai.

"And after only a year, look whose hands I'm in."

"*Only* a year!"

"Hush," he said, and kissed her. "You'll wake the camp."

They were both very quiet after that, and woke no one.

✿ PART V ✿

DIVISION

❧ CHAPTER 13 ❧

Qira tried not to be angry at Sarai. It was not the wife's fault when the husband was selfish and cruel. But when she saw how Sarai made such a point of acting *happy* about living in a tent surrounded by the stink of animals, a life without grace or pleasure, well, it just made Qira too angry to hold her tongue sometimes. Sarai carried this business of wifely subservience much too far. Sometimes a wife had to let her husband know that she was unhappy. How else could he possibly realize how important it was for him to change?

And it was all Abram's fault, anyway. When he and Sarai came back from Egypt, they had so many cows and sheep and goats that their servants couldn't tend them all. The obvious solution, as far as Qira could see, was to either sell the animals or turn them loose. If the beasts were too stupid to find food on their own they didn't deserve to live. But when she said so, Lot actually sent her out of the room to fetch wine—like a servant!

She left the room all right, and just kept on walking until she was at the home of her friend Jashi, who understood completely that there's only so much humiliation a woman can bear. Qira had rather expected Lot to come looking for her, but he never did, and then it was so late at night that Qira had to impose on Jashi's hospitality. Even the next morning, there wasn't a sign that Lot was looking for her, so she finally went home as if nothing had happened. To her fury, Lot didn't say anything about it, either. And then she realized that the servants were packing up all of Lot's clothing and putting cloths over the furniture—in every room but hers.

"Where are you going?" she demanded.

"I'm closing the house," he said. "Abram has given me half his herd."

"I fail to see how a gift can cause us to lose our house."

"We aren't losing it. We're just closing it up and leaving a caretaker while we join Abram and Sarai."

"Join them? Why don't they join us? All they have is a few tents, and we have a fine house, with plenty of room for them."

"Oh. I thought you found the house too small."

"Too small? Well, indeed it is too small to make the impression that the daughter of a king should make in this city, but it is certainly not too small to offer hospitality to my sister and her husband. I'll go and tell the servants to uncover the furniture."

"No you won't," said Lot cheerfully. "You're coming with me to Abram's camp."

This stunned her. He had never tried to boss her around before. But she was hardly going to start putting up with that now. If you let men push you at all, they thought they could do it as much as they wanted. So she put her foot down. "I do not go to camps," she said. "I am a woman of the city. I told you that when we married."

"And I'm a man of the open sky," said Lot. "We've had a good many years of useless city life. It's time to spend a while doing something worthwhile."

It was unbelievable that he could treat her years of service to him as if they counted for nothing. "I have worked endlessly to improve your position in this city, to win you more influence, to—"

"To get me invited to even more boring banquets with even more stupid and worthless people."

"You are talking about my friends! Who are, I might point out, your friends as well!"

"They are not my friends," said Lot, "and they are not your friends either. It's only your royal birth and my wealth that win you entry into their homes. Otherwise they'd despise you. They certainly despise *me*."

"You are simply too sensitive. And my birth is who I *am*, so it is hardly inappropriate that my birth should entitle me to respect. We have been perfectly happy in Sodom for our entire marriage, and suddenly Abram comes home from Egypt stinking of goats and you want to leave everything I've built here—"

"Qira, my dear, the decision is made. You'll find that you enjoy spending time with Sarai and hearing from her about what women wear in Egypt."

In fact, that was an intriguing thought, but it wouldn't do to let Lot see that. "Women can go about naked in Egypt for all I care," said Qira.

"We're leaving in an hour," said Lot. "If you want to bring anything with you, you can take what fits in two bags. You won't need most of your clothing, since it's not suitable for camp life. Sarai will have plenty of clothing to share with you. So I've already ordered your servants to pack most of your fine gowns away till we need them again."

He had actually given orders to *her* servants. This was intolerable. "I'm not going," she said.

"I won't force you," said Lot. "You are free to stay with any of your friends who'll have you as a longterm guest. Write to me often."

"I will stay in this house," said Qira.

"This house will be closed," said Lot. "No food will be

brought here, no servants will serve here, and no guests will be admitted here. I fear you would die very quickly in such a house. But Jashi is such a good friend that you could spend the night with her last night—see if she'll have you for a year."

"I wouldn't even ask such a thing."

"I leave in an hour. I certainly hope you'll come with me."

Qira did not believe him. She went to her room and ordered her servants to stop putting things away. They were obviously very upset at receiving contradictory orders from her and Lot, and stood there fluttering their hands and looking miserable. Finally she took pity on them and allowed them to continue. "But we won't be putting them into storage. They'll simply be transferred to whatever house I live in next."

Relieved, the servants continued their packing. But Qira knew that when Lot saw that she was simply not going to leave, he would relent.

She had not counted on the way that Abram's return from Egypt had transformed her husband. She could just imagine their conversation after she left the room. Lot must have explained how important it was for her to live in the city, but Abram no doubt answered, "You've got to show a woman who's in command! Be a man! Not like these weakling city men with their pretty clothes and their vanity! God will punish them for being so wicked!" With Abram everything was always about God. He was really quite tedious on the subject. "If she won't go, you drag her! That's what I do to Sarai, and if she doesn't like it, I show her a stout stick!" Oh, Qira was sure he filled Lot with all sorts of false images of manliness and guilt about city life. These shepherds had the most foolish notions about what went on in the city. Even Lot persisted in his belief that the reason her friends had so few children was because their husbands were somehow sinning against God.

Still, Lot was bound to see reason when he realized that

she simply would not budge on this matter.

Only he didn't. In fact, he didn't even come to bid her good-bye. She heard him call out several times, as if she were a dog to be summoned by a shout. And then the house was still. After an hour or so, she decided to go in search of something to drink. She was shocked to find that he was so petty as to take her servants with him. The house was quite empty. There was not so much as a jug of wine or a rind of cheese. Nor could she even find where the bags of clothing and boxes of jewelry had been put. It never occurred to her that he would store them anywhere but in the house.

So he was being stubborn. Trying to teach her a lesson. She'd see who learned a lesson first!

She stayed that whole night without a bite to eat and nothing to drink, either. She thought of simply going to one of her friends' houses, but then realized that she was wearing the same dress she had worn to Jashi's yesterday, and besides, it was simply too humiliating—people must have seen Lot departing with all the servants, and they would ask questions. So she slept that night in the empty house, frightened half out of her wits at the noises of the city and of the empty house. She kept thinking she heard rats scrabbling around, or thieves trying to break in.

In the morning, her mouth so dry she could not even swallow, her eyes sore from weeping, she went to the front door and opened it. And there, sitting on a stool right in the doorway, sat, not a servant of hers or of Lot's, but that obnoxious Eliezer, a young Damascene servant that Abram had taken into his service in Egypt. Eliezer had apparently spent the night there, and no doubt made half the noises she had heard that so frightened her in the darkness!

"If my lady would like to join her husband, I have two horses."

"What do I care how many horses you have?" she asked. "I'm not going out to the desert. Your master might be able to impose his will on my husband, but he'll soon find that Lot's love for me is greater than his enthrallment with Abram."

"My lady seems misinformed," said Eliezer—the impudence, a servant speaking in such a way to a king's daughter! "My master begged Lot to wait until he could persuade you. Lot declined to leave a servant to guide you. But Abram knew he would regret that, and so he sent me back with two horses."

He might have sent back a little food and wine for me while he was at it, thought Qira. But she did not deign to answer Abram's slave, who was no doubt telling whatever lies would best serve Abram's plot to destroy her life. She walked past him and out into the street.

She fully intended to go to the house of a friend, but halfway there she was suddenly seized with doubt. Was Lot right? Did they only value her because of her royal birth and his wealth? Oh, it was vile of him to put such a wedge between her and her friends! Yet she remembered how they talked about Nabeleth when her husband simply disappeared one day and left her deeply in debt. She was quite ruined and fled the city before she could be sold into slavery by their creditors. There were all sorts of rumors, including the truly nasty story that she had killed him and buried his body in the garden, as if she would ever have done such manual labor as to dig a grave. But Qira knew that they would tell stories about her, too. And even though she was not faced with debt—Lot was very good about lending money to others, but never borrowed from anyone—the scandal would be unbearable.

The reality was that wives were as much slaves to their husbands as any of the actual servants were. That's the horrible injustice of the world, she told herself as she walked miserably through the city. A woman has no voice in what happens to her. Husbands just do whatever they want, and run roughshod over their wives, and women are supposed to bow down and thank them for the privilege of bearing their children and . . .

The girls! Lot had taken the girls with him! Oh, that

was intolerable. What lie was he telling them about why she wasn't with them? Or was he telling the truth? "That's what happens when a wife doesn't obey her husband! She gets left alone in an empty house, without food or drink or protection of any kind. Remember that when you think you might ever disobey a single one of your husband's brutal commandments!" Inculcating them with the doctrine that women exist only to please men!

That's why she had to go to the desert and join Lot, despite his heartless treatment of her—because if she did not, he would raise her girls to be absolute slaves to whatever husband he chose to sell them to. I will tell my girls I made this sacrifice only for them. I'll tell them how I could hardly sleep for worrying about them all night. Let them see how their father made me suffer. He'll be sorry he mistreated me this way when he sees how his daughters hate him. And it won't even be a lie, because I really *did* lie awake all night, and I'm sure now it was because I was missing them so deeply. It's not *my* fault that I had to have my bedroom at the opposite end of the house— they were forever waking up for the morning just when I was getting to bed after a party, and I couldn't sleep with all the noise of the servants feeding them and Lot playing with them—he could never seem to understand that a truly civilized man of Sodom did *not* get down on the floor and play with his children, especially not his *daughters*. The only reason I didn't notice they had been taken from me was because Lot's noisy disregard for propriety forced me to sleep away from my precious girls. Just one more example of how my life has been distorted and my daughters have suffered because of my husband's perversity and selfishness. Was there no respite for women in this world?

It was nearly dark when she got back to the house. There was Eliezer, of course—Abram apparently valued relentlessness in his slaves. He had the gall to offer her wine straight from his own flagon, and if she had not been so bitterly thirsty after a whole night and day in the dust and heat, she would have flung it in his face for the insult of expecting her to touch with her lips the very vessel that a slave's lips had touched. As it was, she held it above her lips and dribbled the wine into her mouth until she realized that any splashing drop might stain her dress. She forced herself then to put the goathide bottle to her mouth, and she only gagged twice. She did have the courage to refuse the bread and cheese he offered her with his bare and not terribly clean hands.

He expected her to go with him to the stable where the horses were kept! When she expressed her intention to remain at the house until he brought the animals to her, the poor fool actually said, "But will you be safe here alone?"

"I have been out all day in this city, and spent all night alone last night," she said disdainfully. "A lady has nothing to fear in Sodom."

He got this odd smile on his face and said, "My lady is probably right."

Of course she was right. He left her and came back after an unconscionably long time—no doubt he stopped for dinner!—with two horses. It was obvious from the saddlery that she was expected to ride the beast astride. She had expected the two horses to bear her in a chair, but *he*, no doubt as part of Abram's plan to humiliate her completely, considered himself equally entitled to ride! When he offered to help her mount, she at first refused— she was not about to let a slave have an excuse to handle her body!—and it was only after she fell twice that she impatiently ordered him to get her into the saddle. He was very strong and liked showing off, practically tossing her like a doll.

Qira had expected the ride to be only a few minutes— Lot was bound to be waiting for her just outside the city, ready to gloat over his victory. But no. When they passed through the city gate, there was no one to meet them. And they almost immediately left the road and headed east into open grassland without a path or track. It was so dark that she could not tell how he was able to discern where they were going.

He laughed at her! "My lady," he said, "the moon is full. The night is not dark, it's very bright. And I don't need to find a path. I know which star they were using as their guide."

Of course he did. Lot was always talking about how knowledgeable Abram was about the stars. But then, Lot thought Abram was the sun in the morning. *You should have married him and left me to find a husband who actually knew how a princess should be treated!*

She could smell the camp before they reached it—indeed, it was the stench, not a star, that led them. And the snorting and snuffling of animals and the barking of dogs gave her all the proof she needed that she had truly left civilization behind her. Not that dogs didn't bark in the city. But here there was no one to kick them to shut them up.

"I'll stay in my sister's tent," said Qira as the little village of tents became visible down in the hollow between two hills.

Eliezer seemed not to hear her. Instead, he led her horse to the pen where other horses were nickering to greet them—which was considerably more courtesy than any humans were showing tonight. When he lifted her from her mount, her legs were so sore she almost fell over, but then decided not to, since it would only get her dress dirtier than it already was.

Wordlessly a boy appeared and started brushing the horse, as if good grooming were more important to animals than sleep or food or drink.

"Where is my sister's tent?" she asked Eliezer.

"My lady is to have her own tent, where her servants await her," said Eliezer.

"No, I will sleep in my sister's tent," said Qira. Was the man obtuse? Or merely disobedient? Either way, a beating would help him to hear instructions when they were first given. Naturally, Abram trained his servants to be insolent.

"My lady," said Eliezer softly, "you have not been invited to share the Lady Sarai's tent. Nor have you been invited to enter any tent but the one where your servants await you."

"Is this what passes for hospitality here in this beast-ridden place?" she said with contempt.

"Food and drink await you there," said Eliezer.

"So I was expected? And yet no one greets me?"

"They could not know the hour you would decide to begin the journey, and so they could not know when you would arrive. But whether you arrive or not, the same work will need to be done tomorrow, and so they will sleep undisturbed."

"And if I choose to raise my voice and waken them?" asked Qira.

Eliezer loomed over her then, lowering his face so he stared directly into her eyes. "My lady may do what she wishes." But there was something in his face that frightened her. He was very large, and she was small. She hated him then, more than she had hated anyone in her life, more than she hated the Amorite usurpers who had deprived her father of his throne, more than she hated Abram.

Qira did not like being frightened. It made her want to frighten him back. "What if I scream and say you were taking liberties with me?" she said, making sure she knew from her intonation that this was a serious threat.

"I am known here," said Eliezer, "and my lady would not be believed by anyone. But my lady may do as she wishes."

A servant with so much pride would never last a moment in any noble house on Sodom. But she was tired and hungry, and it wasn't worth the bother of proving that her sister, at least, would believe her. "I am *not* your lady," she said coldly.

"Would my lady please follow me to her tent?" he said.

Filled with rage, she followed him to a tent that was, she was sure, a seedy old thing that would stink of animals and where her servants would bump into each other dressing her in the morning. To her surprise, when he pulled aside a flap and she stepped into the tent, several lamps were burning, and one of her servants immediately gave a soft cry. "The Lady Qira is with us!"

The other servants awoke immediately and fussed over her, helping her take off her filthy clothing and giving her wine and fruit and bread and finally covering her upon a bed of soft hides and blankets that was surprisingly soft. It was good to be surrounded by servants who knew how to treat a lady. Tomorrow Lot would pay for how he had aggrieved her, but tonight she would sleep the deepest sleep of her life.

In the morning, though, Lot was nowhere to be found. Sarai was there, greeting her and fussing over her as if she had no idea how Qira had been forced into coming out to the desert. And when Qira asked where Lot was, Sarai seemed unaware of the deep injury that Lot had caused her. "Oh, he didn't want to wake you before he went with Abram to divide the goats. Yesterday they got back well before dark, and the goats aren't as far as the sheep were."

"Divide the goats?"

"Didn't you know? When we left Egypt, Pharaoh gave us a very large herd as a parting gift."

"Pharaoh?" asked Qira. "Pharaoh *himself?*"

"Well, he didn't actually drive the cattle, but he gave the order for the herds to be brought to us."

"You *met* Pharaoh?"

"A few times," said Sarai. "It was an awkward business."

"Since my husband has seen fit to force me out of my home and into the desert where he has abandoned me without a word," said Qira, "I suppose I have nothing better to do than hear your tales about Egypt." She yawned.

"Oh, I'll try to tell you what I remember," said Sarai.

It had taken all afternoon to get what Qira suspected was only a small fraction of the story, for Sarai was constantly being interrupted to solve stupid problems that Qira neither understood nor cared about. It quite offended her that Sarai had not cleared her schedule to make time for her own sister whom she had not seen in years. But she bore the insult with great patience, only mentioning it a few times during the afternoon.

When Lot came home that night, he greeted her with a hug, which she did *not* return. Indeed, she said not a word to him, but he seemed not to notice. Well, when he came to her tent that night, he'd find out exactly how welcome he was.

Only he did not come.

And so it had gone for all these weeks. Lot spoke to her cheerfully during the day and never mentioned or even seemed to notice that she did not answer him or utter a single word in his presence. And at night, he made no effort to come to her. Nor did Sarai ever say a word about the coldness between Qira and Lot, and when Qira tried to talk about how badly Lot had treated her, Sarai would immediately think of something that required her immediate attention. It was the same when Qira spoke of men in general, not mentioning names. Poor Sarai was so intimidated by her husband that she couldn't even allow herself to hear even the vaguest criticism of the man. Qira hoped she would *never* be so frightened of a man that she would refuse to listen to the truth.

What disgusted her most, though, was the way Sarai fawned over Abram. Instead of having a life of her own and friends of her own, Sarai's whole life was entirely centered on her husband. All she wanted to talk about was his work—either what he had done apart from her, or the portion of his work she had done for him while he was gone. She seemed to hang on every word he said, and of course he listened to her quite avidly, since she talked about nothing but him and his work! Sarai had obviously lost herself here, forgetting she was a daughter of a king. She was nothing but a glorified servant. A concubine. It broke Qira's heart to see it. Especially because Sarai put such a brave face on it, laughing with a false merriment to mask the pain she must surely be feeling inside. Unless her soul had been so deadened by Abram's long domination that she didn't even realize the pain she was in.

Well, Qira was not about to try to save her from this abasement. She might have tried, if Sarai had not been such a busybody about Qira's girls. It was the second day in camp that Qira happened to see the younger girls running like little hoydens, shouting their heads off and screaming with laughter when they caught some filthy little slave girl and all of them fell in a heap in the grass at the top of a hill.

"Girls!" cried Qira. "Come down here right now!" Of course they were making so much noise that they didn't hear her—she had to send a servant to fetch them.

"Oh, let them play," said Sarai. "I used to play like that when I was little. It did me no harm."

"No harm?" said Qira. It was such an absurd thing to say that Qira forgot courtesy for a moment. "You live like *this* and you don't call it harm? I want my daughters to grow up with grace and culture, so they can marry a man who will provide them with a *home*."

Sarai got her stony face then—she had always had that look when she was angry but didn't want to say anything. Qira laughed when she saw it. "Sarai, you used to make that same face when you were a baby. Nothing changes about you!"

"It does a child no harm to play," said Sarai. "Shouldn't they have any memories of happiness from their childhood?"

Oh, that was intolerable. "Before you give advice about child-rearing," said Qira pointedly, "perhaps you should have a child or two so you have some idea of what you're talking about."

Sarai turned her back and walked away without a word,

thereby proving Qira's exact point about how ill-mannered she was. If a barren woman does not wish to have her barrenness pointed out, she ought to refrain from offering advice about motherhood. If Sarai expected Qira to apologize for pointing out such an obvious truth, she would have a long wait. Qira did her best to tolerate the insults offered by everyone in this camp, but sometimes one had to draw a line.

She could see that her servant was bringing her daughters, who already looked chastened. When she turned back toward the shade of the tent door, she saw Sarai's handmaid, an insolent-looking Egyptian girl named Hagar, looking at her with a scornful smile.

"Did your mistress give you something to say to me?" asked Qira, attempting to remind Hagar that the only reason for her to look at Qira was if she had an errand that required it.

Of course the girl was oblivious to the implied criticism, since Sarai had picked up her husband's bad habit of permitting insolence in the servants.

"I used to carry out the night soil in the house of Pharaoh," said the girl.

A disgusting confession, and Qira was about to tell her to keep her little tidbits of personal information to herself, but the girl went on before she could say a thing.

"I never once threw any of it at anyone, not even my enemies," said Hagar. "But you—you throw it in the faces of those who love you most."

Qira could not believe the girl had said something so outrageous. It left her speechless.

In her own house, Qira would have ordered the girl flogged till she had more blood outside her than in, but she had no doubt that Sarai would take the girl's side. It wasn't worth reporting what she had said. Imagine, talking about night soil to the daughter of a king.

❧ CHAPTER 14 ❧

Sarai saw how Hagar had watched young Eliezer from the moment she became aware of him. In Pharaoh's house, Hagar the nightsoil-carrier would never have bothered to look at a servant at Eliezer's level. But in Abram's camp, Hagar was handmaid to the mistress of the house. She could look at any servant in the camp as an equal, and since Eliezer was a fine-looking young man without a wife, it was no surprise that Hagar found reasons to be near Sarai whenever she had business with Eliezer.

Which was often, for as Eliezer's regular duties evolved, he seemed to make a special point of bringing many questions to Sarai. "You know the ways of this house," said Eliezer. "If you have the patience to teach me, I can perhaps avoid giving offense to anyone."

"Bethuel knows as much as I do," said Sarai.

"If I show my ignorance to him, he'll have constant reminders that I don't know all that I should, and he'll not feel he can use me for sensitive tasks."

"But showing your ignorance to me makes no difference?" It annoyed her when people thought that it didn't matter what a woman thought.

"No difference at all," said Eliezer, "since my lady is already suspicious of me and never forgets for a moment that I'm an outsider."

Courtesy demanded that she protest. But since his words were true, she could only laugh. "Come to me with any questions or problems you have, Eliezer, and I'll tell you all that I can to help guide you in your dealings with the other servants."

He had taken advantage of that invitation quite often, but Sarai had naturally thought that part of the reason for his frequent visits to her in the doorway of her tent was so he could see Hagar. Certainly Hagar thought so, and sometimes spoke quite openly of him when she and Sarai were alone. Yet when Eliezer conversed with her, Sarai could never catch him seeking even the briefest glimpse of Hagar. Either he could see remarkably well out of the side or back of his head, or he was paying Hagar no attention at all.

So when he came to her with yet another account of conflict between Lot's herdsmen and Abram's, she found her attention wandering as she tried to figure out whether the fact that he never looked at Hagar meant that he was extremely interested in her or had no interest whatsoever.

"My lady," said Eliezer, "will you or won't you?"

"Forgive me," said Sarai. "My attention wandered for a moment."

"I have come at an inconvenient time," said Eliezer. "I'll take it up with Bethuel, my lady, forgive me for—"

"Don't be absurd, these quarrels are a serious business and getting more serious," said Sarai. "Truly, my attention only wandered for a moment."

"My lady," said Eliezer, "Bethuel refuses to lay the matter before the master because Abram loves Lot so much that he is likely to give in to him on every point without giving Lot a chance even to *offer* to compromise on any issue."

Sarai chuckled. "Thus does Bethuel try to save my husband from his own better nature. But you were laying a proposition before me. Will I or won't I do what?"

"Decide whether we dare suggest a division."

"But the herds are already divided."

"That's the problem. The herds are divided, but Lot's household and your household are hopelessly intermingled. No one wants conflict, but naturally Lot's people look out for his interest and take every tiny preference for Abram as a slight to Lot. I think this has something to do with the fact that Lot's entire herd came to him as a gift from the master."

"As it was a gift to Abram from Pharaoh, and ultimately, of course, from God."

"It puts Lot in the position of receiving his worthship as Abram's gift rather than by his right as heir of Terah's eldest son."

"You are suggesting that we divide the households," said Sarai.

"The quarrels grow more rancorous. Good servants doing their best to serve good masters, yet when there is only one well, the first water must be drawn either by a servant of Lot or a servant of Abram, and whichever happens, the other takes umbrage."

"Tell the truth now," said Sarai. "The quarrel isn't over who should go first, but who should magnanimously grant the other the first use of the water."

Eliezer grinned. "Actually, we've had both arguments. Either way, the other side has to get into the competition."

"Abram has missed Lot for many years. He won't want to part."

"And Lot seems happy to be with Abram," said Eliezer dryly. "I don't think he cared for the life of the city."

Sarai knew the message encoded within those innocent words: Lot was grateful to have Abram's company so he could get away from Qira. Since his absences with Abram forced Sarai to be in company with Qira for hours every day—only a few hours, but each seemed very long—she well knew how mind-numbing Qira's constant complaining could be, especially because Qira always seemed to think she was being very subtle about her chafing.

In order to continue the conversation, Sarai would need to speak rather candidly about Qira, and she didn't want to do so in front of Hagar, because if Hagar thought it was permitted, she would be sniping at Qira in her inimitable way whenever she and Sarai were alone. And while every bit of japery would be well deserved, Sarai could not be so disloyal as to permit even her most intimate servant to speak ill of her sister. "Hagar," said Sarai, "I need to know what fruits were brought back from the orchards of Ai, the exact count."

Hagar was annoyed at being sent away—she knew exactly what was happening, of course—but sending her on such an errand allowed her to save face in front of Eliezer, and so she should also be grateful that Sarai had handled it so delicately. Ah, the politics of keeping ma'at within the camp, within the household, and even within the tent.

As soon as Hagar was out of earshot, Eliezer said quietly, "Of course my lady knows that I have the exact count of today's purchases by heart."

"And yesterday's and last week's too, I'm sure," said Sarai. "But it was of Qira that we were speaking. I love my sister, Eliezer, and Lot loves his wife."

"I'm sure of that, my lady."

"But I also am quite ready to begin praying for Qira to be stricken with a disease that leaves her mute, if I thought there were any hope of God granting such a prayer."

Eliezer nodded gravely.

"And Lot no doubt feels the same."

"It occurred to Bethuel that one reason Lot might not wish to divide the camps is because he would then be under constant pressure to return to Sodom. At least for part of the year."

"And part of the year would soon become all of the

year," said Sarai. "He really hates the city."

"Any city?"

"Well, he dislikes city life, but he hates Sodom. Abram and I have had a hard time believing some of the tales he tells."

"My lady," said Eliezer, "the real problem is this: It is as hard to stop the quarreling between the servants of the two households as it is to stop your sister from saying the . . . things she says."

"The ridiculous and provocative things she says, you mean," said Sarai.

"I would not dream of ridiculing her," said Eliezer, "and since few of her barbs are aimed at me, I am not provoked by them either. What I am is . . . embarrassed."

"Qira never should have married Lot," said Sarai. "That much is obvious to all of us—including Qira and Lot."

"And one does not put away the daughter of a king," said Eliezer.

Sarai blushed, with both anger and shame. "Eliezer, Lot does not keep my sister as his wife because he fears losing his connection with the erstwhile royal family of Ur-of-Sumeria. Lot keeps my sister because he took an oath and he's a man of honor."

"My lady, I did not mean to imply otherwise."

But Sarai was not done. "Because if my husband and Lot were not men who kept such oaths, it is I, not Qira, who would have been sent back to my father's house long ago. I am the one who has borne no children."

"My lady," said Eliezer, his mouth twisting in the effort to keep from smiling. What did he find so amusing?

"I don't know that I want to hear what you have to say now."

"My lady," said Eliezer again, insisting. "Qira has borne only daughters, in case you've forgotten. There are no heirs in either house. And even if my master were not a man of perfect honor, he would remain married to you because you are so deeply entwined in his life and his heart that he could not imagine a day without you. There is not a servant in his household, nor Lot's either, who does not see that."

Sarai blushed even more deeply, for he had spoken extravagantly out of turn, and yet his words were so reassuring that she could not bring herself to rebuke him for it. "Eliezer, I was not asking for reassurance."

"My lady, I report a simple observation. Your lack of children is mentioned among the servants only with regret. No one ever speaks scornfully of you, and when your sister has been heard making some of her slighting comments, it causes outrage among the servants. I know that as the mistress of this household, you do not concern yourself with the opinions of the servants. But as a woman among women, I thought you would want to know that you are loved and respected here for your own words and deeds, and not merely because you are of a royal house, or because you are married to our loved and honored master."

"You have acted out of kindness, but this discussion should close now," said Sarai.

"Of course, my lady," said Eliezer.

On impulse, though, as long as they were speaking so personally, Sarai went on. "But speaking of marriage, I want to know why you so constantly ignore Hagar? You are driving the poor girl mad with frustration."

The look of dismay on Eliezer's face was comical. "Mistress, I'm not aware of ignoring Hagar."

"You ignore her so completely that you don't even notice that she feels ignored?"

"She is of your tent, mistress, so I have no dealings with her."

"I'm speaking of love and marriage, Eliezer," said Sarai. "She longs for you to court her. I break no confidence in telling you this, because it is shouted so loudly by the way she looks and speaks to you that you are the only person in camp who doesn't know it already."

It was Eliezer's turn to blush. "Mistress," he said, "do

you remember when the master first took me into his service?"

"Very clearly."

"And he pointed out to me that only a child born in his house might inherit?"

"He meant no offense, Eliezer. We did not know you then."

"I wasn't offended. But I did take a vow. No one would ever be able to say that I joined Abram's household in order to win any portion of his wealth for myself or my sons. Therefore I took a solemn oath before God that I would father no child to be born in Abram's household until Abram had a son and heir born of his own seed."

As it dawned on her what this implied, and her own part in it, Sarai was aghast. "Eliezer, that cuts me to the heart, to think that my barrenness will also leave you without the joy of fathering children."

"Mistress, you misunderstand."

"No, I understand completely. My husband is too loyal to me to divorce me because of my barrenness. Because of his honor, not only is he left childless, but you also, a young man, are cut off from the joys of marriage."

"Mistress," said Eliezer, rather sharply, "you have not heard the truth of my words."

"I know your words are true! I face them every morning and every night," Sarai said. She was surprised at her own bitterness. She had never spoken of this to anyone but Abram, not in terms so heartfelt and therefore so wounding. It was all she could do to keep from bursting into tears and fleeing into the tent. "Now let's have done with this conversation."

"Mistress, you are too just and too merciful to forbid me to explain my words, because if you understood me you would not be suffering such pain."

"I understand better than you do what you have sacrificed because of my barrenness!"

"You do not understand me at all," said Eliezer, and though he lowered his voice, he spoke with a harshness that could only exist between equals, and not between servant and mistress. For a moment she glimpsed the authority that he must have had in his father's household, and how readily he could have stepped into that role, if it had existed for him when he came of age.

"Mistress," said Eliezer, taking her silence as permission to proceed, "I took that vow for many reasons. First, I was born heir to a family that once was respectable if not as great as Abram's. I saw how it devastated my father to have no inheritance to give his son. I feared that if I had a son before Abram does, I would become a father before I was a servant, and I would find myself hoping and, yes, praying that you and your husband would never have children, so that my son might have some portion of this house as his inheritance."

"If you're trying to make me feel better, it isn't working. It still comes down to my barrenness."

"It comes down to the will of God," said Eliezer sharply. "Do you think that God lacks the power to open your womb at any time?"

Chastened, Sarai looked away. "I know God has that power."

"Then when I make a solemn vow to God not to have children until Abram has an heir, I am making my vow to the same God who will decide when that heir will be born. I am putting my future in the hands of God, just as you and Abram have done. Nothing depends on you. Everything depends on God."

She could not stop tears from spilling from her eyes and tickling their way down her cheeks. "Now you have truly shamed me," she said.

"Mistress," he said, bowing his head submissively. "All my words come out wrong."

"You shamed me at last because you reminded me of my own lack of faith. It *is* in the hands of God. Abram never forgets that. Neither do you. But I can never seem to remember it. Sometimes I even. . . ."

But no, she could not confess *that* to any man.

"Sometimes," said Eliezer, "you even wonder if it might not be Asherah punishing you for leaving her service."

Sarai burst into tears in earnest now, covering her face in her apron. "I can't help it—that thought comes to me all the time."

He said nothing.

When she gathered herself together enough to speak without weeping, she had to ask him, "How did you know my most terrible secret? Is my lack of faith in God so obvious?"

"My lady, I assumed that you would have such thoughts simply because any human being in your position would *have* to have them. You give no outward sign of it. And it is not a lack of faith. You can't stop thoughts like that from entering your head. Faith doesn't mean that you never doubt. It only means that you never act upon your doubts."

"Abram never doubts," said Sarai.

"First, I don't believe that," said Eliezer. "He, too, is human. And second, if he has fewer doubts than you, it might be because God speaks to him more often than to you or to anyone else in this world. So it's easier for him to drive out of his mind any questions about how many more years you'll be young enough to bear children at all, and when it is that God is going to get around to granting you a son."

"God doesn't speak to him constantly, you know. He goes months and sometimes years without a word from heaven."

"But I have never heard the voice of God at all," said Eliezer.

"But you *have*," said Sarai.

He looked puzzled and perhaps a little angry. Apparently it mattered to him that he had not heard God's voice himself. "When?" he demanded.

"Coming from the mouth of the prophet." She grinned

at him. "There, I caught you being less than perfectly faithful."

A smile slowly came to his face, too. "Now we're even," he said.

Hagar was coming back—and not alone. Qira and three servants were with her. It made Sarai tired just to see them coming.

"Eliezer, you know that I can't speak to you like this again," said Sarai.

"We both stepped outside our roles as mistress and servant," said Eliezer. "We spoke for a few moments as brother and sister—children of God. It will happen again if it needs to, and not if it doesn't."

"Yes," said Sarai, "that's right."

"But we both know that while we must treat each other properly, to maintain the good order of the camp, in the eyes of God there is no master and slave, but only men and women trying, with varying degrees of success, to be good. That is truth, my lady, but you never need to fear that I will treat you with anything other than the proper respect that the world requires of one who is in my position when dealing with someone who is in yours." He bowed his head.

Qira and Hagar were nearly within earshot, and Sarai could see now that Hagar's face was rigid with anger.

"About your original business," said Sarai to Eliezer. "I will speak to Abram and make it clear that in your judgment, Bethuel's, and mine, something must be done."

"Thank you, Mistress," said Eliezer. "And I hope you will also tell Hagar that because of a vow I have taken, she must not hope to marry me, but must look for love somewhere else."

"I will," said Sarai.

And then Qira was upon them. "Did you deliberately humiliate me, Sarai, or is your envy of me so ingrained that you don't even notice when you insult me?"

"It's hard to know which answer is right," said Sarai,

"until you tell me what it is that I apparently did that caused you to be embarrassed."

"Oh, you'd like *that*, wouldn't you, for me to repeat the whole humiliating experience in front of that gossipy little dirty-mouth Egyptian servant that you spoil so shamelessly."

"Hagar," said Sarai mildly, "my sister feels uncomfortable speaking candidly in front of you. Perhaps you can find a shepherd within walking distance and stand near him until he makes an indecent suggestion so you can give him a good, solid slap across the face."

The anger on Hagar's face gave way just enough for Sarai to see the corners of her mouth twitch toward a smile.

"I must also take my leave, Mistress," said Eliezer. "Bethuel will want an accounting."

"Of course," said Sarai. "Thank you for calling the problem to my attention."

In moments, Eliezer and Hagar were both gone, leaving Sarai alone to face the lioness.

"Now we're alone," said Sarai. "What is it that I—"

To her shock, Qira lashed out with her right hand to try to slap her across the face. Sarai's reflexes were quick, and she ducked in time to catch the blow glancingly across the top of her head. Even at that angle, the blow was painful. Qira had not intended the slap to be symbolic.

And she meant to try again. Sarai had to catch her by both wrists to stop her, and when Qira tried to kick her, Sarai had no choice but to twist her around and hold her from behind.

"Let go of me!" howled Qira. "How dare you!"

"It was you who hit *me*," said Sarai.

"Get your filthy sheep-covered hands off me!"

"First give me your word that you won't hit me or kick me again."

"I promise!" said Qira.

Sarai let go. Immediately Qira whirled around and

kicked at Sarai. It was like their fights when they were little children—and, just like then, Qira got clumsier in exact proportion to her rage. It took little skill for Sarai to catch Qira's foot and raise it high, upending Qira and leaving her flat on her back in the dust and grass. Qira rolled onto her side and curled up into a ball, sobbing dejectedly. Nowadays, though, Father wouldn't come into the room and see Qira sobbing like that and demand to know what Sarai had done to her. Some plays worked only in front of a select audience.

"Now you really *are* humiliated," Sarai said. "How much better it might have been if you had merely told me your message instead of trying to deliver it physically."

"Don't play the princess with me," snarled Qira. She went back to sobbing at once, but it was even less convincing now that she had shown the rancor that underlay the tears.

"I'm going into my tent," said Sarai. "If you wish to speak to me, you may enter and we can have privacy. But if you raise your hand against me again—or your foot—I will forbid you to come near me again, and the servants will be happy to see to it that I am obeyed."

As Sarai expected, Qira's crying ended the moment Sarai went inside the tent. And it took very little time for her to compose herself enough to enter with a shy little smile. "I was so very upset, I didn't know what I was doing," said Qira.

This was as close to an apology as Qira was likely to produce. But Sarai wasn't inclined to be forgiving. She and Qira had never been close, but they had stopped exchanging blows by the time Qira was twelve. And there had been times, in Qira's teens, that the two of them had almost been friends. All that was gone now. Qira had somehow reverted to the worst aspects of her childhood. Was it Lot who had done this to her? Or Sodom? Or . . . was this Qira's true character and she had merely stopped concealing it?

"I don't expect you to forgive me right away," said Qira.

Good thing. "Have a seat," Sarai said aloud.

Qira lowered herself daintily to the carpets. She was not young anymore, but she still had the grace that had once made Sarai so envious. "To look at you, you're still a girl," said Sarai.

"After all those babies, it's a miracle I'm not a cow," said Qira. "But you wouldn't know what a battle it is to recover from being pregnant."

Sarai sighed inwardly. Was it truly impossible for Qira to respond to any overture of friendship without saying something hurtful?

"I believe you said that I somehow humiliated you earlier," said Sarai. "Since I was obviously not present for the event, I will need to have you explain to me which of the many traps I've set for you happened to be sprung."

Qira looked at her in wide-eyed surprise. Then her eyes narrowed. "Oh, I see, you're mocking me."

"Make your accusation, Qira."

"Yes, and that weary tone in your voice. I've heard quite enough of *that*, I can tell you."

"Have you forgotten what was bothering you? I can always go ask the servants to remind you."

Sitting there on the cushions, Qira drew herself up into her most regal posture. "You are destroying my daughters," said Qira, "and teaching them to hate me."

I'm sure they'll come up with their own reasons for hating you, if you treat them the way you treat everyone else. "Qira, just tell me what made you angry, will you?"

"I have devoted my life to making sure they do *not* become shepherdesses, thank you very much, and now you've given them a sheep."

At once everything became clear. "I haven't given them anything," said Sarai. "They saw a ewe with its lamb only moments after the birthing. They asked if they could have it—an absurd idea, of course, and I told them that the lamb needed to stay with its mother or it would starve to death. But that made them cry, so I told them they could visit the lamb every day and they could give it a name."

"Yes, and thank you for *that*, too. They are now arguing bitterly about that, which gives me a headache."

"What I don't understand," said Sarai, "is how any of this could possibly have humiliated you."

"Oh, no, of course not. You interfere with the way I raise my children, and there I am in front of everybody, not even knowing what my girls were talking about. Come away from that sheep, I tell them, and they answer me by saying, 'Aunt Sarai gave us this lamb and she's in charge!' "

"I'm sure they meant that I'm in charge of the lamb, which I am, since it was one of our ewes."

"I'm sure I couldn't tell one sheep from another."

"The lamb is the little one. The ewe is the big one."

"You made me look as though I had no authority at all over my own girls!"

You always look as though you have no authority over them, Qira, because you barely notice they're alive most of the time and whenever you do, you clearly have no idea who they are, beyond their names. "My dear sister, everyone understands that children leap to wrong conclusions. All you needed to do was remind them that you're their mother and they must obey you."

"I don't need lessons in child-rearing from *you*," said Qira.

Well, you need them from *someone*. "Of course not, Qira," said Sarai.

"And there you are, sounding weary and put-upon again."

"I don't think I sounded that way at all, except that I am, in fact, weary. But that has nothing to do with you and everything to do with getting little sleep last night."

"Oh, and there you go with the other thing, telling me for only the ten thousandth time how *busy* you are while I, apparently, do nothing at all."

Apparently. "Qira, it appears that whatever happens is

going to be my fault, and whatever answer I give you will only make it worse. So before you accuse me of murder and declare a blood-feud between us, let's have done with this conversation. You go to your tent and I'll stay in mine, and we'll both calm down and realize that neither of us is trying to harm the other."

"Well, I know *I'm* not trying to harm *you*."

You were the one with the slapping and kicking. But never mind. "I'll explain to your girls that the lamb is not theirs, and that even if I had intended to give it to them, you're the one with the final say."

"Indeed I am," said Qira.

"Yes, and so I will say."

"I don't need *you* to tell my daughters that I'm in charge. I already explained to them that Uncle Abram would no doubt take their little lamb and kill it and burn it up on that altar of his, so you couldn't possibly give the lamb to anyone."

"I'm sure they were happy to hear that tale."

"They cried, but they obeyed," said Qira.

"So everything's all right."

"Nothing's all right," said Qira. And she burst into tears.

All Sarai wanted was to lie down and sleep long enough that when she woke up, Qira would not be there. Instead, she moved over to sit beside Qira and hug her and pat her hand. To see us, thought Sarai, no one would imagine that I'm the younger sister.

"Lot hates me," Qira wailed.

"I have it on very good authority that he loves you."

"Do you think so?" said Qira. "Well, what kind of love is it when he hasn't come near me since Ajiah was born?"

Sarai tried to conceal her disgust. She already knew through Abram that it was Qira who banned Lot from her bed after her fifth daughter was born. It had been the cause of great grief to Lot, and not just because he had no son yet. "Every day she lives in that city," Abram had said, "she becomes more and more like the other women of

Sodom. Except that her husband is not at all like the *men* of Sodom. He actually loves his wife, and she's breaking his heart." That was even before this last quarrel, when Lot decided that as long as he was going to live like a bachelor, there was no reason for him to do it in a city that he hated. He could be a bachelor out with his herds and live the life he was born for. Twice before, Sarai had tried to explain this to Qira, but when Sarai used words that were gentle enough not to provoke a rage, Qira did not understand what she was trying to say.

"Qira," said Sarai, "I know how you can set everything right between you and Lot."

"Oh, of course, all I have to do is treat his every whim like a commandment from God and bow down to him like a slave, the way you do with Abram."

It took all Sarai's strength of will not to make some cruel retort. But she knew that despite the obnoxious way that Qira had of expressing it, her misery was real, and even if she had caused most of it by her own choices, she was not yet ready to understand that. You have to speak to people in a language they can understand. "I believe, Qira, that you and Lot are at cross-purposes right now. I believe that he is quite sure that you don't love him."

"I don't," said Qira.

The words stunned her. "Then I don't know what to say," said Sarai.

"Well, how can I love a man so selfish that he turns me out of my home and takes my children off to make shepherdesses out of them and ignores me completely when I come to the desert to join him!"

"I believe," said Sarai, "that he did those things because he already thought you hated him."

"I didn't hate him," said Qira. "I thought he was boring and rude to my friends and utterly lacking in ambition. I thought he needed to dress better and let himself take part in the life of the city."

Do you still not understand precisely what that would require of Lot, to become a man of Sodom?

"Perhaps he needed to hear an occasional word of love from you."

"I gave him five girls, didn't I? And if he had been a true husband to me, and helped me take my proper place in the city, he would have heard whatever words of love he wanted."

The whole idea Qira had of marriage—that you were nice to your husband only to the degree that he obeyed you—appalled Sarai. Again, it took all her strength not to speak bluntly.

"Lot kept his promise to you—for all these years, you've lived in the city. But he never promised you that he would become a man of the city himself."

"Well, I don't see the distinction. Without a husband I can be proud of, I'm completely on my own in society. I do rather well, but still, it cripples me, and it's not *that* many years until the girls will need husbands so I can have grandchildren. *Someone* needs to keep alive the blood of the true kings of Ur. He should be thinking of *that*, not of his own petty desires."

To answer this completely idiotic statement would have been pointless—if Qira couldn't see how unlikely it was that her daughters would ever bear children to men of Sodom, it was because she chose to be blind.

"You see, Qira? You have only to talk reasonably to him, and listen to his words when he answers you."

"But he *doesn't* answer me. He hasn't spoken ten words to me since I came here!"

"I'm not talking about now," said Sarai. "Back in Sodom, when you said these things to him, didn't he answer you?"

"Oh, of course he did. He nattered on and on about things he would *never* do and how I was asking too much and on and on."

"Qira, listen to yourself. You're telling me that you didn't listen to him."

"I *did* listen. I just didn't agree."

"Well, he listened to you, too—and didn't agree."

"But he *didn't* listen, or he would have understood just how impossible he was being!"

It was too maddening to continue. Qira simply could not see her own actions from Lot's point of view.

"Well, Qira, what can I say? It looks to me as though you won't be going back to Sodom until you convince your husband that you intend things to be different between you."

"Oh, indeed I do! No more of his foolish refusal to take part in society! No more of his—"

"It's that kind of talk that got you here to this camp, with your house closed up and your daughters playing with sheep," said Sarai. "*Keep* talking that way and you'll find yourself growing old and dying in a camp somewhere."

"So that's it. I have to lie to my husband and pretend I don't wish him to become a better man, and if I'm a convincing enough liar, he'll return me to my home, is that it?"

"I said nothing about lying," said Sarai. "I merely suggest that you refrain from insisting he change. Give him the freedom to be himself, and he'll give you the same freedom. Isn't that what you want? All you have to do is give him the same thing."

"Men *have* freedom. They don't get it from women." But this time Qira's response was half-hearted, a mere reflex, parroting the ideas of the women of Sodom. Even as she spoke, she seemed to be contemplating what Sarai had said.

"Surely there's some way," Sarai said, "for you and Lot to share the city *and* the camp. A season of one, a season of the other, each of you rejoicing that you can make the other happy."

Qira sighed and rose to her feet. "I can see that you have nothing to suggest except that I become the kind of brainless please-your-husband-no-matter-what-it-costs-you kind of wife that *you* are."

Sarai held very still until Qira left the tent.

When she finally unclenched her hands, Sarai found that two of her fingernails had cut into her palms. Blood seeped from the shallow wounds.

Well, it would be worth the pain if this conversation led to Qira making amends with Lot. For she *had* listened, at the end. It was what she had always done in childhood—if someone made a suggestion that she intended to follow, she had to lash out and insult the person whose idea she was planning to use. That way she could maintain the illusion that she had come up with the idea herself.

It was an illusion that only Qira herself believed. Indeed, it was quite likely that the only person in the camp who did not see through Qira's pretenses was Qira herself.

Hurry home, Abram. It's time to find a way to get Qira out of this camp before someone kills her.

❧ CHAPTER 15 ❧

Abram came to her tent that night, but Sarai could see that it was conversation he wanted more than affection. Emboldened by Sarai's agreement, Bethuel and Eliezer had apparently laid before him their desire for a separation of the camps, and Abram was dismayed. "Before you say more," said Sarai, "I must tell you that Eliezer came to me already to see what I thought. I already told him that I think it's the right thing to do, and for more reasons than the quarrels between herdsmen loyal to different masters."

Abram looked glum. "So I'm alone in wanting Lot to stay with me."

"My love, you're so happy to be with Lot during your daily work that it would be a cruel wife indeed who did not wish you to keep your brother beside you."

"And yet you lend your voice to the forces of division."

"You and Lot are together during the day, doing the labor that you love, roaming this beautiful land, talking with men who know the beasts as well as you do, caring for animals that you understand better than people. You have the wind and the sun and the stars, the bleating and lowing and braying—of animals and of people."

Abram chuckled. "You almost make it into a song."

"The joy that you know in the field with Lot is not matched by any pleasure here in the camp."

Abram gave that a little thought before he answered. "Lot speaks little of Qira. But I know that he was not happy when she followed him to the camp. It shocked me, in fact—that he left her in the city in the first place, and that he wasn't relieved to have her prove her love for him by coming."

"If he really wanted her to stay in the city," said Sarai, "he would not have closed up the house that provided her position in society."

"Yes, well, there you are. I think he doesn't know how to feel about her. But . . . I know she causes ill feeling. I hear about it from Eliezer and Bethuel—in fact, Bethuel told me that the one thing Lot's herdsmen and mine agree on is that my wife is the queen of women, and Lot's wife is . . . not."

"She's in a constant rage here," said Sarai. "I think her fury is completely unjustified, but it doesn't change the fact that she's decided to feel this way."

"Decided?"

"It's her choice to dwell on these feelings and not make the best of it. It's her choice to lash out at everyone. She sprays insults like a dog shaking off water—no one around her stays dry."

Abram chuckled again. "She's always had a temper."

"Everyone has a temper," said Sarai. "But Qira was never taught to control hers. If my mother had lived, she might have raised Qira differently. But then sometimes I think that it is Qira's deepest nature to behave as she does. Whatever she wants is the only thing that matters, and the desires of others are either obstacles or steppingstones. She's always been that way. She won't change, Abram."

"Lot does love her, though," said Abram. "So she can't be entirely awful."

"Yes she can," said Sarai. "My own sister, so this is

disloyal of me, but then, Lot is my brother now, too, isn't he? And who knows Qira better than the sister who had to grow up dealing with her? She knows how to be charming—how to make alliances in order to achieve her goals. But she also knows how to punish those who don't give in to her charms. As long as Lot did what she wanted, she was lovely to him, and so he loved her."

"Lot said to me a few days ago, 'How could my wife and yours come from the same house?' Qira sees nothing, Sarai, and you see everything."

"Qira sees as much as I do. The difference is that I care about the people around me."

"Harsh," said Abram.

"I've put the best face on it up to now, Abram, because I could bear my sister's petulance and nastiness for the sake of your happiness with your brother. In truth, I've been happy with Lot here, too—I'm used to Qira and I can shed her cruelties without noticing them. But she's growing impatient. She's not content merely to insult me and criticize me. She's accusing me now of plotting against her. Even though everyone detests her, when she accuses me openly it weakens my place in the camp."

"Nothing could weaken your place here," said Abram. "If she attacks you, your patience with her only makes you seem more of a saint in the eyes of all."

"A saint, but a weak one," said Sarai. "You know that even a beloved leader is weakened if he tolerates insolence. You would never put up with it, and neither would I, except that when it's my sister *and* my guest, my ability to control her is limited. And today it came to blows."

"You gave her a beating?"

He sounded so delighted that it shocked her. "I did not!" she said. "I don't even beat the servants! I would hardly beat my sister."

He laughed. He'd been teasing her.

"Abram, this is serious. She hit me. Only a glancing blow, but she meant it to hurt. I had to throw her to the ground before she finally stopped. And this was outside my tent, where all could see. I'm surprised you didn't already know."

"There are some things that people are reluctant to tell me," said Abram. "You've said enough. Qira has to go."

"Easily said."

"I'll get Lot to reopen the house in Sodom and send her back to it."

"And keep him here with us? I think not."

"He's done with her, Sarai. She makes his life unbearable in Sodom, constantly pressing him to take part in a society that makes him sick at heart and sick to his stomach. He can't live there again."

"He's not tempted by their sins, is he?"

"Of course not. But from the king on down, the men of Sodom are entirely given to debauchery and cruelty, and they don't have much tolerance for men who don't join in. When he stands aloof, they accuse him of judging them. Apparently the only sin that Sodom doesn't embrace is the sin of choosing not to sin. And they're right, of course. The fact that a man like Lot even exists is a constant affront to them. Because he's there, all can see what a man of honor and decency acts like, and the contrast is clear."

"When I ask her about Sodom, Qira says that all men are like that in their hearts, and that it's hypocritical to pretend otherwise. When I tell her that you're not like that at all, nor are any of the others in this camp, she just rolls her eyes and says, 'They spend weeks and months on end away from their women, with only the sheep and each other for company. Don't fool yourself, my dear.' As if that somehow proved her point."

Abram's face reddened. "She accuses even me?"

"She's repeating the story that the women of Sodom tell each other in order to make their lives bearable."

"But she needs no such story—*her* husband is not like that."

"If she said that to them, then wouldn't they mock her for her blindness? Besides, she's weak, she'll believe whatever her friends believe, or say that they believe. Abram, I know that Lot's life in Sodom is unhappy. But if he sends her back and doesn't return at all, it's an insult to Qira, to me, and to my father's house."

"Less of an insult than if he sent her back to your father's house."

So Lot *had* talked about divorce. "Abram, all I ask is that Lot keep up appearances. Spend enough time in the city to keep a good face on things. Then he can return to his herds. A few days in each month should be enough."

Abram sighed. "Until Qira decides that he needs to be in attendance on her at a banquet or a feast day."

"If Lot can be forceful enough to close up the house and come here—"

"Sarai, Lot was not *forceful* when he did those things. He *fled*. He hides from her even now. The only way he can have peace in his life is not to see her at all."

"And what does that do to the girls? To have their father gone all the time?"

"What does it do to them to have their mother constantly criticize him and demean him?"

"She does that whether he's there or not," said Sarai. "But if they see him, they can make their own judgment and realize that their mother is wrong. Abram, there's no happy solution to the problem. If Lot decides not to live with Qira, I'll try to make my father understand. Certainly *I'll* understand. But the trouble is that my father may end up paying the highest price."

"Your father! If Lot sent Qira home to him, *then* he'd pay dearly."

"When Qira and I both married into the greatest of the herding houses, it gave my father prestige—which gave the king of Ur-of-the-North a reason to continue to support my father's pretensions to royalty. But if that same great family repudiates the marriage and treats the daughter of the deposed King of Ur-of-Sumeria as worthless, then my father is weakened. Enough that the king of Ur will turn him out? Probably not."

"But it's the beginning of the end for him," said Abram. "I didn't think of that."

"If Sodom is truly dangerous for Lot, then don't send Qira back, either. We'll make things work."

"What if we divide the camps and Lot simply takes Qira with him and deals with the problem on his own?"

"No!" cried Sarai.

"Why not? It's his problem, ultimately. He said as much to me."

"Because she would turn all his men against him, Abram. Some would become her tools in undercutting his authority and giving her whatever she wants, and the rest would turn against him because they despise a man who can't control his wife."

"So let him control her."

"How?" said Sarai. "She doesn't respond to reason— she doesn't hear it. She always has an answer, a foolish one, but it's an answer. So what does he do, beat her? Is Lot the kind of man who can beat his wife bloody and call it love?"

"If he were, she'd already be crippled by beatings."

"Or *he'd* be dead—after the first time he beat her. Abram, if Qira does not return to Sodom, she has to stay here with us—in a place where she has no authority."

"No," said Abram. "Because what you don't know is that the quarrels between Lot's herdsmen and mine seem to be Qira's idea."

"What?"

"She's constantly at his steward and his most trusted men, making snide remarks about how Lot's herds aren't really his, they're just a gift from me. She says things like, Be careful how you treat those sheep; Abram may want them back someday. Or, Don't get in the way of Abram's men; they have *real* work to do; herding isn't just a hobby for them."

"I had no idea," said Sarai. "Though why not? She's so angry that if she thinks of something nasty, she'll say it."

"She knows what she's doing," said Abram. "She never says such things in front of you or me. Or Bethuel or Eliezer, either, for that matter. But she shames Lot's men.

Makes them feel second-rate. Naturally they're more belligerent."

"The only reason she has the power to do so much evil," said Sarai, "is because you and Lot are so good. Lot is too patient with her, and you're both too loyal to me to do anything that would insult my sister."

Abram laughed. "Don't call it virtue, my love," he said. "If I were *really* loyal to you, I'd have thrust her out of the camp into the desert the first time she made one of her vicious little remarks about how *she* is a mother and *you* don't know anything."

Tears leaped to Sarai's eyes. "I didn't know you heard those things."

"She never says them in front of me, if that's what you mean," said Abram. "But the men and women of this camp love you to distraction. Do you really think that I don't hear an outraged report of every insult she offers you? Don't you understand that if anyone but your sister had said such things in this camp, his life would be forfeit?"

Sarai pressed her face into Abram's chest and wept. "If only her insults weren't the truth," she said.

"You are more of a mother to every child in this camp, and every grown man and woman, too, for that matter, than Qira is or ever can be. All she did was what any cow or cat can do—give birth."

"The one thing I *can't* do."

"I only told you that so you'd understand that our loyalty to you is a reason for getting her *out* of the camp, not keeping her here. No, Sarai, they love you, they honor you—not as much as I do, but only because they don't know you quite as well. No one thinks ill of you. We all know that you'll have my children when God wills, and not sooner. And in the meantime, we all rejoice in the great blessing of having you as my wife, as the mistress of this camp. And they have never loved you *more* than since Qira has been here to show them just how awful life could be if you were a different kind of woman."

Sarai laughed through her weeping. "So Qira's doing wonders for my reputation."

Abram held her tighter. "You are the wise one, as usual. I'll lay your suggestion before Lot, and I think he'll do it. A few days in Sodom, a few weeks in the field—and he can visit here, too, without bringing Qira. It wasn't a mere coincidence that his defiance of Qira finally came just after we returned from Egypt. The time we spent there was very hard on him. He had nowhere to go then. But if he knows that he can come to see us, then he can visit Sodom, too, and spend most of his time there with his daughters. It's still not a happy life, but sometimes happiness consists of nothing more than finding the right balance of misery."

"And is love, then, finding the right balance of loneliness?"

"Love is you," said Abram. "Love is finding that the things you like best about yourself are not in you at all, but in the person who completes you."

"Oh, Abram, that's how I feel about you, but I have no idea what I have that you could ever need."

"And one of the things I love best about you is that you are completely oblivious to your own virtue." He kissed her. "And back on the subject of having children, do we intend God to give us sons by miracle alone, or shall we do what we can to help?"

That was the end of conversation for the night. And the next day, Abram and Lot walked for a few hours in the first light of day. When they came back, the plan was set. The herds would be divided. The long drought had ruined most of the great herding houses. Now rain had returned, the great grassy plains and hilly pasturages were almost empty. Abram gave Lot the choice, and he decided to keep his herds here, east of the Jordan. It was farther from most cities, but closer to Sodom, so he could more easily stay in touch with his men when he was in the city.

Qira's reaction was just what Sarai expected. She immediately became cheerful and charming to everyone. But her sweetness was still laced with poison—for she could not resist barbs at Lot. "I hate to leave my dear sister," said Qira, "but when a man decides to move his household, his wife has to bite her tongue and obey." It was Sarai, however, who bit her tongue and said nothing. Let Qira spin the story however she wished. Everyone in camp knew the truth.

Lot and Qira and the girls left first, with their household servants in train. No tears were shed, though Qira looked for a moment as though she was trying to work up a nice little flurry of them. Sarai put a stop to that by pulling her close, hugging her, and whispering, "Don't bother crying, Qira, everyone knows you wanted to return to Sodom, and this move represents your victory. You can put on the tears for the women of Sodom."

Qira flashed her one sharp glare as she pulled away from the embrace, but the smiles returned at once, and she put on a show of graciousness and charm until they rode away. Her departure lifted such a burden from everyone, Sarai especially, that even the work of packing up the camp for a move was like a holiday.

For it was Abram's camp that would move, leaving Lot's men in possession of this place. It was no hardship to Abram, though, except for the loss of Lot's company. The hills of Canaan had always spoken to his heart in a way that the great flatlands to the east never had. The drought had almost emptied Canaan, so that Abram could tear down the idolatrous high places and cut down the groves of Asherah, and no one was there to complain. Wherever Abram went, Canaan became a land where only God was worshiped. It was the land of promise, after all, and never had it been more beautiful than in this year of plenty after so many years of desolation.

PART VI

KINGS AND JUDGES

❧ CHAPTER 16 ❧

They lived on the plain of Mamre, near Hebron. The town had stood empty for many years, but it was one of the first villages to come back to life as the rains returned. Most of the old houses were still empty, since the new villagers, not wanting to live in a house that had been unlucky for the previous owners, simply took stones from the old dwellings and built new ones.

Sarai did not envy them the dwellings of stone. Once she had thought of a tent as flimsy and impermanent, but now her tent was home. In a dust storm, the tent could be sealed much more tightly than any house of stone, yet it could also be opened to catch every breath of a breeze. When they moved from place to place, she gloried in the new scenery, regretting nothing about the move because she knew that she would sleep each night in her familiar chamber. Now she looked at the builders of stone houses and wondered why they would want to be so rooted to one piece of ground.

A piece of ground—that's what the villagers settled for.

But to Abram, God had given the whole land of Canaan. It would have been absurd for God to give a whole land to a town dweller. Only a wandering herdkeeper would know how to use the grassy hills and valleys in this land between the Jordan and the sea.

The people who had lived here before the drought were all Canaanites, speaking one language. But the people who moved here now were of every nation—Amorites, of course, those perpetual wanderers who sneaked like dust through every crevice, and also Hittites, Perizzites, Jebusites, and even a few Hebrews who called Abram kinsman, though none of them knew his genealogy back to Abram's ancestor Heber. There were a few whose families had dwelt in Hebron before, but their memories of the old city were distant at best, and second- or third-hand in most cases. It was a new people they were making here, a new nation in an old land, like the new city being built out of the stones of the old.

And on the hills, Abram's flocks and herds looked over all. He sold wools and cheeses, beef and mutton, and bought tools and pots from smiths and potters, wines and oils from vintners and orcharders up and down the land, making contact with each new village that sprang up in the ruins of old cities. The name of Abram the Hebrew was known everywhere in Canaan. But except for the people of Salem, who still remembered the true religion, not one soul knew that God had made him keeper of this land. He watched over his kingdom with a sharp eye, but ruled it so lightly that no one noticed the touch of his authority. Yet he was the link between villages, and his language became the common tongue that strangers adopted so they could live together in peace. Ma'at prevailed in northern Canaan in those days.

Not so in Egypt. Word reached them that Neb-Towi-Re was dead, his name expunged from the monument. Sehtepibre now ruled as Pharaoh Amenemhet, and he waged war against the Hsy, driving them out of every enclave in Egypt where they still lingered. The history, as

Sehtepibre was now writing it, told of the Hsy usurpers
who almost succeeded in ruling Egypt, defiling the holy
places and worshiping strange gods in abominable cere-
monies, burying their dead in the ground, wrapped only
in sheepskin. It was Amenemhet who saved Egypt from
these invaders.

The Hsy who could, fled from Egypt, back across Sinai.
Those with connections in Arabia went south, but many
tried to find a living in Sodom or one of the other cities
of the Valley of Siddim southeast of the Dead Sea, or else
wandered up into the southern part of Canaan.

And many made their way east to Mesopotamia, to Akkad and Babylon, Ur and Sumer, and even as far as Elam.
The men who made such a long trek were not the settled
or settling kind. They had heard that the Amorite kings
who now ruled the ancient cities of Mesopotamia would
pay for soldiers. Many of these men had fought for Neb-
Towi-Re. There was no one now to hire their swords in
Egypt, but swordskill was all they had to sell.

The most ambitious of the Amorite warrior kings was
Chedorlaomer, who ruled in Elam. During the worst of
the drought, when Abram and Sarai were in Egypt, he had
brought an army and raided Sodom and the other cities
of Siddim—Gomorrah, Admah, Zebolim, and Zoar. Surprised and unprepared, the five kings of the cities of Siddim were easily defeated and agreed to pay tribute to
Chedorlaomer.

Now, in these more prosperous times, with refugees
returning from Egypt to swell the population of Sodom
and the other cities, the people of Siddim became complacent. A raiding party like the one Chedorlaomer had
brought in his surprise attack would never defeat them
now. Their armies were strong and well-trained. They
needed no longer pay tribute to the king of such a far-off
city as Elam.

Lot and Abram talked about these matters many times,
often when Sarai was part of the conversation. Lot and
Abram were sure this was a foolish mistake. Chedor-

laomer was of Amorite origin, and he clung to the old ways. To him it was nothing to bring an army across hundreds of miles of grassland—the desert was no more a barrier to him than was the sea to a sailor. "They've provoked him," said Abram, "when they could have paid his tribute out of what falls from the king's table."

"Do you think I haven't told them, again and again?" said Lot. "But no one listens to me. They call me 'the shepherd' and claim that wandering herdsmen know nothing of the strength of cities."

"It was wandering herdsmen called Amorites who conquered Ur-of-Sumeria and drove my father into exile," said Sarai. "Have they forgotten that?"

"People have short memories," said Abram. "This year's prosperity is all they remember. There has been no war in a few years, so they will always have peace. There has been no drought for a few years, so they will always have rain."

"But you remember," said Lot.

"I have the books," said Abram. "It has all happened before, over and over again. A city begins to think that it is great. But to a rival king or to a tribe of hungry strangers, that great city looks like a prize to be taken, not a trap to be feared. And suddenly those proud citizens who boasted of their greatness are sold into slavery."

"Those that aren't put to the sword," said Lot.

"But when they came before, all they demanded was tribute," said Sarai.

"Tribute is a tax without the trouble of governing the taxpayers," said Abram. "They regard these cities as conquered, and to them the decision to withhold the tribute is a revolt. Treason. When they come back, someone will pay for the crime."

"Well, I hope you're planning to move out of Sodom before they come!" said Sarai to Lot.

The silence that greeted her outburst made her feel like a fool.

Lot smiled and patted her hand. "Don't think the subject hasn't come up," he said. "I think the most common answer in my house is, 'I don't see any soldiers. Where are these armies you fear so much? Do you run from every shadow?' Much of the reason I'm scoffed at in the council and the market is because my wife is mocking my warnings in the homes of all the leading citizens of Sodom."

"Ah, Qira," sighed Sarai.

So it was that when Chedorlaomer came again, everyone was surprised, despite the warnings.

Chedorlaomer came with allies, King Amraphel of Shinar, King Arioch of Eliasar, and Tidal, a tribal leader who styled himself King of Nations. They brought such a large host that their supplies had failed them—they struck first at some of the small new villages, slaughtering everyone who had not had the sense to run away and taking all their food and animals to feed their soldiers. Replenished, they turned to Siddim and the great cities that gleamed like precious stones amid the orchards and grasslands east of the Dead Sea. There were traitors to punish and overdue tribute to collect.

The first word of the coming of these armies came from Abram's shepherds in the southern hills. Obeying a standing instruction, a messenger had headed for Lot at the same time to give him warning. Abram gave orders for all his herds to be driven up to the high valleys, where they would be invisible to armies coming up the Jordan Valley. And beyond the minimum number needed to keep the herds together, all his men were to gather to Abram in the plain of Mamre.

Even before they had all assembled, another messenger arrived, this time one of Lot's men. The armies of the five kings of Siddim were outnumbered and undertrained. They fled almost before the first attack had begun, and the kings of Sodom and Gomorrah fell in the slimepits that blocked their retreat. But the worst was yet to come.

Sodom and Gomorrah had been taken, but not sacked. Chedorlaomer meant for these cities to continue paying him tribute for many years to come. But they would not rebel again. He took all five kings as captives, to be displayed back in Elam before they were executed. He also took the richest citizens of Sodom and Gomorrah with him as hostages, to make sure the heavy tribute was paid. Whether they would return alive was doubtful. The other three cities were relatively untouched, but the warning was clear. Obey or pay dearly.

"Lot is taken," said the messenger. "All the wealth of his house. His herds and flocks are safe, but to get him back will take more gold than we can ever get for selling them all. Master Abram, I beg you to help pay the tribute so we can free my master before he is taken all the way to Elam!"

The news filled Sarai with fury. If the fools in Sodom and Gomorrah had listened to Lot and Abram instead of mocking them, they would still be paying a negligible tribute and prospering in peace. And now, because of their stupidity, not only had they lost everything, but Lot, too, would be impoverished, and Abram too, to save him.

Abram said nothing, as they all waited to hear what he would say. He raised his eyes to heaven, as if calling upon God, but he said nothing with his lips. Then he looked at the messenger and smiled. "I'll pay a tribute to Chedorlaomer that is beyond his wildest dreams."

There was something in his tone that sent a chill through Sarai's heart. It was the voice of a man making ready for war. She had never heard it before, but she recognized it at once. Ever since the human race had existed on the earth, that voice had echoes in the deepest places in the soul. Sarai was afraid, yes, but she was also filled with a strange exaltation. The arm of her husband and his men would fall upon their enemies.

By the next morning, Abram's men had assembled. He inspected them all, and while Bethuel and Eliezer took them through the battle exercises they practiced every month, to make sure their fighting skills were honed, Abram and Sarai rode on horseback to a vantage point from which they could look down over the valley of Jordan.

They got there almost at noon, and Sarai could see at once the great cloud of dust that rose from the huge host coming up the valley from the south. It took only a glance for all the exaltation of war to vanish and rank fear to take its place.

"Abram," she said. "Even with our friends Mamre and Eshcol and Aner joining us with their servants, you have only three hundred and eighteen men. There are tens of thousands in that army."

He smiled, a slight and menacing smile. "I have three hundred and eighteen men strengthened by the hand of God, coming upon an army that is burdened with treasure and drunk with wine every night. They think no enemy will dare to attack them. Triumph has made them careless and stupid. God has delivered them into our hands. God will bring Lot back to us, and restore the kings of the five cities of Siddim, and their treasures."

"God will give them back their treasure?"

"What else would he do with them? Such things have no value to God. It's the life of Lot that I asked for. But if God wants also to give these foolish kings a chance to learn from their mistakes, who am I to be a sterner judge than the Lord? It's Chedorlaomer who is marked for destruction today."

Then he turned his horse and started back down to Mamre. Sarai lingered only a moment, trying hard to find a way to believe that any of Abram's little host could come home alive from a battle with such an army. Abram waited for her without a hint of impatience, and it annoyed her a little that he seemed to feel no urgency as their horses walked slowly down the path back to Mamre.

"Abram," she said, "why aren't you hurrying?"

"God may be on our side," said Abram, "but that doesn't mean I can act foolishly. Chedorlaomer may be overconfident, but he's not blind. I can't bring my men down out of the hills while the enemy is marching up the

Jordan Valley—they'd have hours to prepare to meet us when we reached the valley. We have to come on them unaware, which means we'll pursue them but keep our distance, so they never know we're there. In the mountains of the north, they'll camp in a place where their army is divided among several small valleys. The hostages and prisoners will all be kept close to Chedorlaomer. We'll have the victory almost before they know the battle has begun."

"How can you be so sure of this? Has God shown it to you in a vision?"

"Did God have to show you in a vision that Sehtepibre was maneuvering to usurp the crown of Egypt?"

"No, of course not, I was trained in statecraft all my life," said Sarai. "But you and your men have never fought a war; you've only skirmished with raiding parties and driven away robbers."

"What do you think is written in those books I study?" asked Abram. "Prophecies and revelations, yes, but also the stories of the lives of my ancestors, including the wars of the righteous and the wars of the wicked. Just because I've never fought a war against kings doesn't mean I don't know how. After all, you never saw your father ruling over a city, either."

"Abram, I have faith in God's power to bring you victory," said Sarai. "But I also know that God does not think of the deaths of men as a terrible calamity."

"Sarai, I know we'll have a victory, but I don't know which of my men will return home alive, only that God wants me to take them into battle. One man, though, will *have* to return alive."

"And who is that?"

"Me," said Abram. "Because I don't have any children yet, and the Lord promised me that my descendants would fill this land like dust—every corner of it."

"Oh, so now I'm supposed to take my barrenness as a sign that God can't let you die? What if I take it as a sign that God doesn't always keep his promises?"

Abram's face darkened. Sarai hadn't seen him angry very often, but she remembered it all the more because of that. "I wish you wouldn't say things like that," said Abram. "God keeps his word, Sarai. Heaven and earth can pass away, but his word will still stand."

"It's easier for you to be sure of that," said Sarai. "You've *heard* his word."

"And so have you. When you spoke to Neb-Towi-Re and the words came to you with such certainty that you couldn't doubt them. Have you already forgotten?"

"No, but . . . this doesn't feel like that."

"It doesn't have to feel that way to you," said Abram. "You're not leading these men into battle. It only has to feel that way to *me*."

"Then don't get angry with me for not having the same certainty you have."

"I wasn't angry," said Abram.

"You were something," said Sarai. "Disappointed in me? That's worse. Worried that I might be falling into unbelief? Ashamed of me?"

"Not disappointed, not worried, not ashamed."

"What then?"

"All right, I was angry, but I see now that I was being unfair to expect you to have the same confidence I feel when you haven't received the same assurance God gave me. I can't help how I feel, anyway."

"I just don't want you to go away from me into battle with anger in your heart."

"The only thing I'll be feeling is dread."

"But you said that God had assured you of victory!"

"Many men will die," said Abram. "Some of them at my hand. Only an evil man could head joyfully into battle, even when the cause is just. And God does not fight the battles of evil men."

"Except for the kings of Sodom and Gomorrah," said Sarai.

"They'll just be spectators. In *their* battle, God did nothing for them."

"Send me word, Abram, that's all I ask. Send me word of your victory."

"I'll ride home to you myself, faster than any messenger could come."

"No you won't," said Sarai. "That's very sweet of you to say and it made my heart jump when you said it, but you'll have a thousand decisions to make and tasks to do and it will take you days to get home and I want to know as fast as possible. So will all the wives and children of the other men. Send us word."

"I will send a messenger," Abram promised. "With a list of all the men who have been killed or injured. You're right that no one should worry for a moment longer than necessary."

They rode in silence for a while. Then they talked of other things—plans for weddings of several of the young men of the household who had found wives, supplies that were running short and would need replenishing, the need to acquire a servant who knew metal-working at a higher level than any of the men now in the household, the need for a new loom. Only as they came in sight of the camp did they speak again of the battle to come.

"I used to think," said Sarai, "that it was good that I didn't marry a king, because kings have to lead soldiers into war, to defend the city or drive off enemies. Kings have to bloody their hands with the judging of criminals. I was glad that I was married to a man who had no such painful memories, none of the wounds that such things can cause to a man with a gentle heart. But now, Abram, now I see that I did marry a king after all."

"Only the servant of a king," said Abram.

"No, Abram. All kings are servants of God and servants of their people, or they're not worthy to be kings at all."

"Melchizedek in Salem, *he's* a king. A whole city of people who live in holiness, whose every possession is consecrated to the service of God. I'm just a shepherd."

"You are king over the land God has given you, Abram. Don't argue with me on this. I'm right, and it's only because you take such pride in your humility that you're even arguing with me."

Abram laughed at that, laughed loud and long. "Pride in my humility," he said, and laughed again.

But he didn't argue with her anymore.

They rode off that morning, Abram at their head, quite a formidable looking army to anyone who hadn't seen the horde in the Jordan Valley. At least they didn't leave with jesting and boasting, as Sarai had seen soldiers do back in Ur-of-the-North. Abram offered sacrifice on the altar at dawn, and the soldiers left with solemnity, knowing that if they succeeded, they would be sending many of the enemy back to God, and probably some of their own number would make that journey, too. It was with grim determination to be a fit weapon in the hands of God that they went, and not with any pride in their own strength. They well knew that they were armed shepherds, not soldiers who also tended sheep.

And when they were gone, the camp was Sarai's to command. There were boys to send as runners to the various flocks and herds scattered throughout Canaan, making sure that all was well with them. There were women to keep busy in the work of the camp and in the spinning and weaving that occupied them always. And through it all, Sarai could not show her own fears and doubts, for she had to set an example of cheerful confidence and faith.

Faith. She felt hypocritical, pretending to a confidence she did not feel. Of course, she could hear Abram's voice in her head, saying that to give the appearance of confidence *was* an attribute of faith, for to behave as if you were certain when you had no certainty was to throw yourself into the hands of God, and encourage others to make the same leap. But if she could not be certain in the first place, it was hard to then be certain of the rightness of her pretense of certainty. It was like the way four-legged creatures moved across ragged ground. Having three legs to stand on while the fourth found a new step, their bodies remained steady and their forward progress smooth. But Sarai was a two-legged creature, and so when she walked the same ragged ground, she lurched back and forth like a drunk. She just didn't have as many legs to balance on, when it came to faith.

And yet she did what needed doing, day after day, until a girl started shouting, "A rider! A rider!"

Sarai arose from her place at the door of her tent and walked toward where she could see what the girl saw. Hagar trotted after her, and soon all the other women and children and old men of the camp had left their work to watch the rider approach. He did not have his horse at a gallop—he was not giving a warning, and it was not worth the life of a horse just to deliver news, good or bad. Still, it was maddening to watch as the horse varied from canter to trot to walk, depending on the path. Finally, as the horse came nearer, the rider himself became impatient. He leapt from the back of the beast and ran on light feet toward the camp, leaving the horse to follow at its own leisurely pace. That was when Sarai knew that the news was good, for no man would have run on his own feet to deliver news of grief.

"Victory!" cried the man. "And not one of ours is dead!"

"Bring him food and drink before he says another word," said Sarai. "And make sure all the runners are here to listen to his tale, so they can carry the same word to all the herdsmen. You may tell the rest of the tale without me." Then she returned to her tent.

She could hear them murmuring behind her. Why didn't she want to hear the tale herself?

Hagar reluctantly followed her toward her tent, but Sarai sent her back. "I can do this work for myself, and you'll want to hear the whole story."

"But don't you want to hear it?"

"In due time," said Sarai.

Hagar went back to the group gathered around the messenger, who was gratefully drinking from a carafe and gobbling bread. Sarai went inside her tent and quickly

packed some extra clothing into a bag for herself and for
Hagar. Then she made her way to the tent by the cookfires
where food was kept and put traveling food into another
bag. Only when she started loading these things onto the
back of a horse did anyone come to help her. And then
they understood why she hadn't bothered to listen to the
details of the story—she was going to have the messenger
lead her back to Abram.

Soon she, Hagar, and the messenger were mounted and,
leading a single pack horse, set off across the same country the messenger had just traveled. Then at last she heard
the tale. Abram's little army had remained out of sight in
the hills as Chedorlaomer's host journeyed up the broad
valley of the Jordan. The invaders were not in a hurry
now, and so instead of hurrying across the desert they
were taking the great circling route through the well-
watered lands, to join the Euphrates somewhere in Syria
and then use the river to carry their spoils down to the
cities that they ruled. Knowing their plan, Abram did not
have to remain close enough to be detected.

Even when the enemy began to make their way up the
narrow roads into the hills on the road to Damascus,
Abram kept his men back, and the messenger was candid
about how some of them began to wonder if Abram was
afraid of the battle to come. But no, he simply knew that
the right opportunity had not yet presented itself. It was
not until the enemy camped near Hoban, not far from
Damascus, that the circumstances were right. The enemy
camp was divided among several small valleys, and steep-
walled hills made them complacent. The mercenary soldiers drank and ate copiously, and Abram waited until the
camp was still.

Then he led his men quietly on foot down the steep
slope. The plan was simple—to move swiftly and quietly
toward the tents of the four kings, and Abram divided his
men into five groups—four to attack the kings where they
slept, and the other group to free the prisoners and keep
them safe in the ensuing battle. Abram's men did not stop

to kill drunken soldiers in their sleep, but rather passed them by—passed by the sleeping sentinels supposedly on watch, passed by even the guards at the doors of the kings' tents. Only inside the tents did the shouting—and the killing—begin.

The shouts of those who were wakened by swords, the clash of weapons, and the screams of the dying finally roused the camp, but by the time the soldiers had found their weapons and staggered out in search of an enemy, they saw the tents of the four kings already burning and their erstwhile prisoners now free and armed, joining in the battle against them. Since most of these soldiers had entered this army for the pay and the spoils of war, they had no reason to stand and fight once their paymasters were defeated. Their only hope was to try to run away with as much of their booty as they could carry.

So the actual fighting did not last long. Three of the kings died in their tents. Chedorlaomer himself managed to get out and, with a few of his retainers, fled on horseback. Abram was not content, however, to let them or any of the soldiers get away. The men he had left with his horses brought the herd down to the valley and his soldiers were soon mounted. Leaving the former captives to guard the camp with all the treasure that had been abandoned there, Abram led some of his men in pursuit of Chedorlaomer and rode him down in the valley of Shaveh, where he and all his men were killed from horseback. Meanwhile, other parties of Abram's soldiers gave chase to the escaping soldiers, killing or capturing any who stood to fight—though there were few of those. Most of the soldiers understood what was happening, and dropped their heavy spoils and stripped off their outer clothing so they could run faster—and so Abram's men could see that they had abandoned what had been stolen from Sodom.

By dawn, the fighting was done. Abram's men directed the few captives in gathering up the abandoned treasures. Beyond that, the messenger knew nothing, for Abram had paused only to be sure none of his men had been lost before sending him to give word to Sarai.

On the way to Hobah, they met another messenger, this time bearing the news that Lot and all the other hostages and captives from Sodom and Gomorrah and the other towns of Siddim were unharmed and free. Sarai shared food and water with him and sent him on his way, first to the camp and then on to Sodom itself, where rejoicing would immediately take the place of mourning.

When Sarai reached Hobah, where the cookfires of the camp were a beacon that drew her through the gathering darkness of the evening, she was surprised that it was not Abram or Abram's men who greeted her, nor Lot, nor any of the kings or citizens of the cities of Siddim, but rather Melchizedek, the king of Salem, who recognized her and welcomed her. Sarai was bewildered to find him there—had he been captured, too?—but Melchizedek cheerfully explained: "The Lord sent Abram to do the fighting, but I and some of my people came also, not to fight, but to provide supplies and beasts of burden for the return. We're not fighters in Salem, you see—our protection is God alone. But we have been blessed with plenty of food and drink to share, and beasts to bear, and strong arms to labor and legs to travel. And so we journeyed in the path of destruction left by Chedorlaomer's army, feeding people who were returning to their ruined and despoiled homes, sending them to Salem and the other hill towns for succor." It was just what Sarai should have expected, and she embraced the young king of Salem and let him lead her to where the former captives now feasted on the supplies left by Chedorlaomer's vanquished army.

Lot greeted her with a shout and an embrace, and told them all that this was Sarai, the wife of Abram, who had delivered them. She was made welcome, and listened to each of the five kings of the cities of Siddim as they told their own account, in which, not surprisingly, they turned out to have been heroic, too—at least in the awfulness of the suffering which they endured during their captivity.

But Abram was not there. He had not yet returned from Shaveh, where the labor of gathering up the abandoned treasure was still not finished. Already his men had made several trips back to Hobah with fully laden animals, only to return for another load.

So it was that Sarai was there in Hobah when Abram himself returned at last. The place of honor was given to him at the feast, and Melchizedek gave him the formal hero's greeting: "Blessed be Abram of the most high God, possessor of heaven and earth!" cried Melchizedek, and even though few of the former captives cared much for Abram's God, they joined in the shout of acclamation that came from Abram's and Melchizedek's men. "And blessed be the most high God," Melchizedek went on, "who has delivered your enemies into your hand!"

Abram arose then, and everyone fell silent to hear him speak. "The victory truly did come from God, at whose word I came and by whose strength we conquered. Melchizedek was also sent by God to help us, and to comfort all who suffered from the passing of Chedorlaomer's army. Therefore of all this great treasure that God has delivered from the hands of our enemies, let us give a tithe to God's high priest Melchizedek, and the people of Salem, so they can use it to do God's work and help the many poor and innocent villagers who have lost all their goods and cattle."

At once the kings agreed, and the former hostages as well, but Sarai well knew how the generous promises made in the moment of deliverance could shrink day by day as memories faded and treasure grew more precious. So she was not surprised to hear Abram say, "I was sure that you would agree, so I have already caused my men to divide out one-tenth of all the treasure we have recovered. It is ready to load onto the beasts of burden at dawn, and Melchizedek will take it with him to do God's work with it."

Sarai could see that there was noticeably less rejoicing at this news—it was always disappointing to the makers

of empty promises when they were compelled to keep
them. Still, no one was angry or even displeased. They
had thought they had lost everything, including their freedom, and to give up a tenth of what had been recovered
seemed trivial by comparison to what had been returned
to them. By taking care of this business at once, Abram
had brought it off. There would be no disputing it in the
morning.

Then Bera, the king of Sodom, rose to his feet. Since
generous gestures were the order of the evening, he spoke
in praise of Abram's courage and the bravery of his soldiers, and then said, "I ask of Abram only that he return
my captive people to me. All the gold and treasure he
may keep as my gift to him!"

Sarai heard this and understood at once that Bera
thought Abram was nothing more than an Amorite ad-
venturer. It was an easy enough mistake to make. If
Abram were nothing but a bold raider, then as far as Bera
was concerned, Chedorlaomer's captives and hostages
would now be his captives and hostages, and all the treasure his as well. Indeed, by any law of any city, that was
Abram's right. From the moment they were captured, all
these hostages had been transformed into slaves—or dead
men, depending on the will of their captors. Abram had
just disposed of a tenth of the booty by giving it to the
king of a hilltop city who had apparently been following
along to scavenge what he could—or so it would seem to
Bera, who could only assume that others were motivated
by the same desires that controlled his life.

Abram treated Bera's insulting misjudgment of him
with the contempt that it deserved. "I lift up my hand to
the most high God, who owns all things in heaven and
earth, in a solemn oath to you that I will not take so much
as a thread or a shoelace from you, nor anything else that
is yours or that belongs to any king or man of Siddim.
None of you will be able to say, I made Abram rich. The
only thing I'll keep is what my young men have eaten
here at this feast. And of the freemen who rode with me,

my friends Aner and Eshcol and Mamre, they should keep their portion. But of the portion that by law belongs to me and my house, I return it all to you. What I already had before this war, God gave to me, and it is enough."

Bera and the other kings were obviously surprised and relieved. They would not only be returning to their cities, they would still be rich. The devastating defeat that was caused by their own foolishness in ceasing to pay tribute had turned to victory, for Chedorlaomer would never again come back to demand payment of them. In the end, thanks to Abram, they were getting out of it without serious consequence. And, Sarai well knew, it would not take long for them to forget their gratitude to Abram; as for God, they clearly paid no attention to Abram's and Melchizedek's words attributing the victory to Him. An experience that should have taught them the danger of pride and gratitude to God for His mercy was instead teaching them nothing, because they were men who were not disposed to learn.

Sarai understood, though, that Abram had acted wisely. For if he *had* kept the treasure that rightfully belonged to him and his men, the kings of the cities of Siddim would soon have come to resent him as a profiteer, and before long there would have been hostility between them, even bloodshed. And certainly it would have gone badly for Abram's brother Lot if he stayed in Sodom. Abram's generosity would instead make Lot one of the great men of Sodom, and would earn him a place in the highest councils. After all, hadn't Lot's warnings all been borne out? And hadn't everyone been saved by Lot's brother, Abram, a man so rich and powerful that he could defeat great armies and yet refuse the spoils of war?

You've done well today, my husband.

That night, though, as she embraced Abram in the opulence of a captured enemy tent, she felt him trembling. "What's wrong?" she asked. "Lot is free, and all your men are safe."

"I don't like killing," said Abram. "So much blood was shed."

"You killed as few as possible," said Sarai. "They came to kill and rob and enslave—there was not one whose death was not well deserved by law."

"Let justice come," said Abram, "but not by my hand."

"And yet it *was* by your hand."

"Only because I have given my hand to God, to use as he sees fit."

The idea of giving his hand to God made her think of what he had said at the banquet, about how he didn't want anyone to think Bera had made him a rich man. Abram gave his hand to God, and yet it was still Abram's hand. If Bera had given his treasure to Abram, it would still have been Bera's treasure in everyone's mind—even though Bera had already lost the treasure, and Abram had taken it from someone else.

If I could give a child to Abram, it would still be my child, because it would be my gift, even if the child came from someone else.

The thought frightened her, because it meant surrendering to the barrenness of her body, admitting that she would never have a child. Still, what mattered was that Abram have seed in order to fulfill the promises of God. And if Sarai gave him another body, a body that belonged to her also, the body of her handmaiden, to receive his seed and bear him a child, then that child would come to him from Sarai as surely as if her own body had borne it.

O God, is this the sacrifice that I must make? To forswear my own child-bearing as I give my husband his son? No, please, Lord. Let my own body bear the child of Abram's promise. Don't leave the gates of my womb locked forever. Let life grow within me!

But she knew even as she prayed this silent prayer that she already had the answer when God gave her the thought of giving her handmaid to her husband to bear him a child. Now everything made sense to her—why

God had placed her in the House of Women in Egypt, so she could meet Hagar and take her out of Egypt and bring her here to be her husband's concubine. I was sent there only to bring Hagar's young body to my husband.

It was with a bitter heart that she made her vow to God, to obey him in this. For only despair could make her let another woman take this place within her husband's arms.

❧ CHAPTER 17 ❧

Abram did not answer. They had been at home in Mamre for a week before Sarai worked up the courage to say what she knew she had to say. All the rejoicing was over. The kings of the cities of Siddim had left, and Lot with them. Aner, Eshcol, and Mamre had gone home. Life was back to normal.

And Abram came to her one morning and sitting there in the door of her tent, he said, "Why are you unhappy? The Lord gave us the victory. Not one of our men lost his life. Lot has returned to his family. Melchizedek left his blessing with us and went back to Salem. All is as it should be. And yet through it all, whenever I look at you I see something terrible in your eyes. And it isn't the old sorrow that I always see. It's a fresh pain, and it frightens you, and so it frightens me. But you have to tell me. I have to know. You can't bear this alone, whatever it is."

His words came in a rush, or so it seemed to her; and yet it also seemed to her that it took him forever to say it, and after every sentence she thought a thousand sentences of her own, long explanations and longer pleadings, discourses, volumes, libraries were in her heart and yet she said nothing, she barely breathed until he was through and then, in the silence, she said, "Abram, you must lie with my handmaiden Hagar. She will bear you the son you have been promised."

He did not answer.

The silence grew very long. So she found the courage to speak again. "It was to find her that we went to Egypt, and all we have been waiting for is for my heart to be ready to hear the Lord and do what must be done."

Still he did not answer.

"That is what we've been waiting for," said Sarai. "For me to humble myself, and to realize that a man does not have to bear children only through the body of his wife. Hagar's body also belongs to me, and that is the body you must use to get your children from the Lord."

And still he said nothing.

So she fell silent, and looked out over the camp, and beyond it, to the brown hills of autumn, to the thin skiff of dust being raised by the passing of a small flock of goats and the boy who was herding them with his long stick.

Her heart leapt within her. He is silent because he will refuse the gift. It was enough that I offered. He will hold me in his arms and tell me that he would rather have no child at all than to break my heart by accepting this gift. He will tell me that the Lord forbids it, and so he will not do it. He will tell me that all the children of this camp are his children. He will comfort me and we will never speak of this again.

O God, she cried silently. What am I thinking? In my heart I deny the gift. I make myself a liar by taking it back again, by hoping that he will say no. But that is not what I hope. I want him to say yes. I want the promise to be fulfilled. O Lord, let him take Hagar into his bed and let her give him a son that I can love and raise as my own.

My own, but he will look like her, he will have her eyes, and I will hate him for that, I will hate him for her mouth, for every word he says, and I will hate myself for having stolen her son from her and for trying to raise him in a lie.

O God, forgive me once again, for pretending to myself that the boy can be mine. No, he will be Hagar's. Abram's and Hagar's, *their* son, not mine. She will be his mother. I will not steal her child from her.

But please, Lord, do not make me give up my place beside Abram!

A strange new peace came into her heart. As if a kind voice said to her, You have given all that I ask. The child will be Hagar's, but I will not take Abram from you. She did not hear the voice, she did not know the words, but she felt the peace that could only come from having heard that voice, and understood those words, and so she knew they had been spoken, and by whom.

"Abram," she whispered. "Now I truly mean it. Lie with Hagar."

She turned to face him.

Tears streaked the dust on his cheeks. "I know what that cost you, my love," he whispered, "but I will never do that."

"You will if the Lord tells you to," said Sarai. "It is God who has restrained me from bearing. Go to her as a husband, and get children from her. I would never say it if God had not given it to me."

"Have you spoken of this to Hagar?"

"No," said Sarai.

"She has to agree, freely. Work we can command from a servant, but not this."

"I couldn't ask her till now," said Sarai.

"How could you ask me without asking her first?"

"Because until a few moments ago I hoped you would say no," said Sarai.

"And you no longer hope I'll say that?"

"I want you to have a child," said Sarai, "more than I want it to be mine."

Abram leaned to her, put an arm around her shoulder, kissed her cheek. "You ask Hagar," he said, "and I will ask the Lord."

He got up and walked to his tent.

Sarai went nowhere at all. She just sat there. Sure enough, Hagar, who had been waiting not far away, saw that Sarai was alone, that she was doing nothing, not even spinning with the distaff that was always at her hand.

"Mistress," said Hagar, "are you ill?"

Sick at heart, said Sarai silently. But with her lips she smiled. With her hand she beckoned, then patted the cushion beside her, where only moments ago Abram had been sitting. Such a coincidence would never have mattered to her, but now, knowing that her husband's warmth was still on the fabric, she cringed as Hagar sat on it.

Hagar, still so young of body, so beautiful. I'm an old woman, and Abram will find her so sweet that he will never want me again. O Lord, must I do this?

And having decided to do it, must I keep deciding to do it each step of the way? Will I ever stop wishing for thy word in my heart to tell me that I need not do it after all?

"Hagar," said Sarai, "you know that I have borne my husband no children."

"Mistress," said Hagar, "you will bear him a child someday."

Sarai laughed mirthlessly. "Hagar, this is a good time for you to listen instead of trying to reassure me."

"I'm listening, Mistress."

"The body I was born with has grown old. Too old to bear a child, I fear. The Lord has shown me another way to give my husband the son who will inherit all that God has given him and through whom God will fulfil all his promises."

"How will it be done?" asked Hagar. Sarai knew that Hagar expected some kind of magic. In fact, now that

Sarai looked at her, she could see that Hagar was steeling herself for something terrible. She was afraid.

"Girl," said Sarai, "why are you afraid?"

"I've known for years that it would come to this," said Hagar. "Mistress, I will submit to your will."

"Submit to what?" said Sarai. "I haven't even asked you yet."

"The sacrifice," said Hagar. "So Asherah will let you have a child."

It took a moment for Sarai to realize that Hagar meant a human sacrifice, and thought that she would be the victim. "Are you out of your mind, child?" said Sarai. "Have you lived with us all this time and yet you still think that Abram would ever, ever sacrifice a human being? Asherah is nothing but statues and empty words. The true God does not ask for human blood! You *know* that. We've taught you that."

Hagar searched Sarai's face, trying to see if there was some lie in what she was saying. And when she found no lie, she burst into tears and clung to Sarai in relief, in gratitude.

"What were you thinking?" said Sarai. "What *were* you thinking of us?"

"You were so long without a child, Mistress," said Hagar. "It had to be Asherah punishing you."

Sarai petted her hair. "You poor confused child."

At that moment, Sarai looked up to see Abram standing in the door of his tent, looking at them, appalled. It took a moment, but then she realized how it must look to him. He must think Sarai had asked Hagar to lie with him, and that at the thought of it, Hagar had burst into tears and was clinging to Sarai to plead with her not to require her to do it.

For a moment she thought, Serves him right!

But she knew at once how unjust it was for her to think that. This wasn't *his* idea, after all.

So she shook her head, so he'd realize that it wasn't what he was thinking, and then with her fingers she made a little dismissing gesture. Go inside your tent. Pray to God. Leave me to my business with this girl.

He understood. Maybe not all of it, but at least the part about going away—or maybe he understood nothing at all, but it didn't matter the reason. He went inside the tent, and Sarai got back to the task of giving her husband to her handmaiden.

"Hagar," said Sarai, "do you want to hear what I was actually going to ask you?"

"Yes, Mistress."

"I have asked my husband to lie with you and get you with child for me."

Hagar nodded. "Of course," she said.

"Just like that?" asked Sarai. "You don't need to think about it?"

Hagar pulled away a little, so she could look at Sarai. "Mistress," said Hagar, "your husband is the only master I've ever heard of who did *not* lie with every servant girl who wasn't actually deformed or sick. I wondered at first what was wrong with me that he never came to me, until I found out from the other women that he didn't lie with any of them. And then I thought, perhaps he has the curse on him, so he can't lie with anyone. But some things you said . . . well, you kept thinking that perhaps you might be with child this month, or the next, and you wouldn't have thought such a thing if . . . I simply didn't understand. But if you want him to lie with me, then of course I will. And if you want me to bear a child, I'll do it. I am yours. The child will be yours."

"All right, then," said Sarai. "Now we have only to wait for Abram to get his answer from . . . no, wait." She had just understood what Hagar's words really meant. "No, you don't understand yet. The child you bear will not be a servant in this house. The child you bear will be Abram's son."

Now it was Hagar's turn to stare at her in silence, trying to understand. "You mean . . . a son who inherits?"

"That is the only kind of son that Abram will ever have."

Hagar's eyes grew wide, and she sat very still, staring at nothing.

"I will still be Abram's wife," said Sarai, wanting that to be very clear.

"Of course," said Hagar. And then, "This was *your* idea?"

"It was given me by God. I think."

Hagar nodded. "Yes, I'll do it." She turned to Sarai and searched her face as she said, "Mistress, will you hate me if I bear him a child?"

"I will rejoice for you," said Sarai. "And I will rejoice for my husband. And I will rejoice for the child, and for the land of Canaan that will be blessed by him."

"But you will also hate me," said Hagar.

"I will never hate you for obeying me, for serving me as I ask you to."

"You will," said Hagar.

"I will not," said Sarai. "Please don't accuse me of being an oathbreaker."

"You have to hate me for it," said Hagar, sounding as if she were desperate to make sense of this thing that was happening. "You have to."

"Why do I have to, when I say I will not?"

"Because I would hate *you* for it, if I were in your place. To have another woman bear a child for my husband, when my own body could not? How could any woman endure that, Mistress?"

"A woman can endure it," said Sarai, "for love."

When she said it, she meant it. But later, she realized it was not true. She had loved Abram all along, and yet never thought of this solution to her barrenness. It was only for faith that she did this, to offer a way for God's promises to come true.

Abram got his answer from the Lord. He went into Sarai's own tent with Hagar, and lay with her. Two weeks he lay with her every night, while Sarai went with Eliezer to visit Qira and Lot in Sodom. It was the nicest visit that Sarai had ever had with her sister. Not that Qira was not as awful as usual—she was in her finest form. But it all washed over Sarai like a gentle breeze with no sting in it. Qira had no power to cause her pain, now that she knew what pain was. Instead, Qira was a kind of antidote, for she carried Sarai back so many years, to a time when they were girls in Father's house, before either of them had married, before Sarai had met the man from the desert who promised to come back and marry her. They promised me to a goddess then, but now I belong to God. He is using me as he sees fit. It is hard to bear, but I have this much more than I would ever have had, serving Asherah: I have known the love of a man. And such a man. He will love Hagar now, as a man must love the mother of his child. I have lost everything. But I have everything, because my husband will have a son at last, and his joy will be my joy.

After three weeks, Eliezer took Sarai back to Mamre. Life returned to normal. No one spoke to her of what had passed between her husband and her maidservant. Everyone acted as if nothing had happened at all.

But no one was fooled. Everything had changed. What had once been real was now a play, everyone acting an old part, going through the motions, saying the speeches, but knowing that no one was, any longer, what they still pretended to be.

And the pretense finally ended when Hagar said to her one night, "Mistress, five days have passed since it should have been my time."

That was when Sarai's last hope died. "I'm so glad," she said to Hagar. "Let's go tell Abram." She held the girl's hand as they crossed the continent between the tents.

❧ CHAPTER 18 ❧

The first time, Sarai did not think it amounted to anything. Hagar was feeling ill in the morning, as women often did when they were with child. So when Hagar's voice awoke her, croaking, "Sarai, Sarai," all she could think was, Something's wrong with the baby she's carrying.

"Bring me a jar," whispered Hagar.

Sarai rose from the carpets she slept on and hurried to fetch an empty jar and carry it to Hagar, who promptly vomited into it. When, exhausted, Hagar collapsed back onto her pillows, Sarai took the foul jar outside and left it for one of the women to empty it and clean it later.

It did not even cross her mind at the time that Hagar had not called her Mistress, but had addressed her by name, as an equal. Nor did she take it amiss that Hagar ordered her to bring a jar. She would have to be a fool not to realize that such breaches arose out of the need of the moment—Hagar was sick and could not rise; she had to wake her mistress because there was no other woman in the tent.

All Sarai thought of was that they would need to bring another woman into the tent, so Hagar would always have someone to take care of her. And so she brought Ptahmet, a Cushite girl that Abram had bought only the year before from Amorites who had captured her in a raid on Egypt. Ptahmet would sleep at Hagar's feet and attend to her in her sickness.

A few days later, as Sarai sat in the door of the tent and dealt with a dispute between two women, one of whom was accusing the other of trying to seduce her husband, Hagar called out angrily from inside the tent, "Can't I have peace here! Can't you take that somewhere else!"

"Oh, we're disturbing poor Hagar," said Sarai. She led the two women away from the tent to work out some sort of peace between them. Only later did it annoy her that Hagar had shouted so impatiently instead of sending Ptahmet to request that the discussion be taken away from the tent door.

But when she suggested this to Hagar, the girl looked away angrily.

"Why are you angry?" said Sarai.

"I shouldn't have had to shout *or* send Ptahmet," said Hagar. "You should have thought of it yourself."

"Perhaps I should," said Sarai, "but in the future, if you wish me to do something, send Ptahmet to ask me quietly, instead of shouting at me as if I were a disobedient servant."

"Oh, I see," said Hagar. "It's not enough that I'm carrying your husband's baby and have to endure this sickness and take care every moment that I do nothing to cause the baby harm, now I have to make sure I don't hurt your feelings somehow. I'm sorry I'm causing you so much difficulty."

Sarai was dumfounded by her tone, by her words. What Sarai had asked for was nothing more than to help maintain good order in the camp. "Hagar, you *are* my servant, and I never yelled at you the way you yelled at me," said

Sarai. "I always either came to you or sent another servant to deliver my message."

"Yes, well, that's because you were never lying here suffering the misery of being childsick."

There it was, the taunt that Sarai had been dreading. But she had never expected it to come from Hagar herself.

"I would have given anything, including my life, to be where you are, and as you are," said Sarai.

"Well, you're not, and I am," said Hagar, "and I can't get any rest because you keep this tent so busy with things that are apparently more important than whether this baby is healthy or not."

"How can you say that to me?"

"Because it's true and you need to see what you're doing to me."

"I'm doing nothing to you," said Sarai. "I'm going about my life while I try to see to it that all the baby's needs are met."

"Yes, the *baby's* needs. But right now the baby is inside *me* and that means *my* needs matter, too."

"Hagar," said Sarai. "I've done nothing to deserve these cruel things you're saying to me."

"Yes, you've done *nothing*. Except that here I am bearing a child for Abram and all *you* can think about is that I'm still your slave. Well, I wasn't born a slave, you know!"

"I didn't take you into captivity," said Sarai. "I brought you out of Egypt, and you've been treated well."

"Oh, yes, you're treating me *so* well, standing here railing at me when all I asked for was a little peace." Hagar started to weep. Loudly.

Too loudly. Sarai knew what was happening here. Hagar's weeping would be heard outside the tent. People would wonder what had been said and done here. And if they asked, what would Hagar tell them?

Sarai walked out of the tent and stood alone, thinking.

A boy, passing, stopped and asked her, "Mistress, is something wrong?"

"No, no," said Sarai. "Go about your business, I'm all right."

"No," said the boy. "I meant with Mistress Hagar."

His words stabbed her almost more than Hagar's had. Mistress Hagar. The boy was but a child and no one had explained to him that just because Hagar had the master's baby in her did not make her the equal of Sarai.

The equal of Sarai? That wasn't how Hagar had spoken back in the tent. No, she had despised Sarai, treated her as if she had become nothing compared to Hagar.

I will disappear, thought Sarai. I will become nothing; I will turn to dust without even having to go through the step of dying first.

Is this what God intended for me? Then why did he bring Abram to marry me in the first place? Better to have let me die a lonely old virgin priestess in the temple of Asherah than to give me a prophet for a husband and then make me nothing in the eyes of his servants.

Nothing in my own eyes, too.

For the worst of it was that Sarai agreed with Hagar. It really was the mother-to-be who mattered, and nothing Sarai was doing amounted to anything compared to that great task.

It got no better over the next few days. Every time Sarai and Hagar were in the tent together and awake at the same time, Hagar was full of snide remarks with stinging little innuendoes. "I know you're busy, Mistress, but would you send for a servant to mop the sweat from my face?"

"Ptahmet will be back in a few moments," said Sarai, "but I'd be glad to do it myself."

"Oh, no, it wouldn't do for the mistress to wipe the face of the slave girl."

Sarai wanted to scream at her. I've done nothing to deserve your cruel remarks! But she held her tongue and went to mop the girl's brow.

Hagar turned her head away and would not permit it.

At that moment Ptahmet returned with the figs she had gone for, and Hagar at once said, "Ptahmet, please, if you don't wipe the sweat from my eyes I swear I'll go mad from the stinging in my eyes." And Ptahmet came to her, glancing at Sarai as she passed, at the cloth Sarai was holding, and Sarai knew how it must look—that Hagar had asked Sarai for relief, and Sarai had refused her.

It could not be an accident. Especially because Hagar was not that ill. She could have mopped her own brow. She could have gotten up and fetched her own cloth. She wasn't crippled, she was just pregnant.

But Sarai learned that it was easiest simply to stay away from the tent during the day, and do her business elsewhere—near the kitchen fires, usually. And at night she'd come in and ask Hagar how she was feeling and Hagar would rebuff her questions. "Ptahmet does her best," Hagar would say, or, "not that it matters, but I was sick all day," or, "Can't I get *any* rest without having to report on how many times I threw up today?"

Sarai could hardly sleep. Until finally she had Eliezer order that the guest tent be put up, and Sarai moved into it, so she could sleep without lying awake enraged at Hagar's spitefulness.

It didn't work. For she still lay awake, wondering whether Hagar had hated her all along, and it was only the pregnancy that had made the girl bold enough to show Sarai how she really felt.

And then, when she was finally about to sleep, Abram burst into the tent. "What is this?" he demanded.

"What is what?" asked Sarai, too sleepy to know at once what he was talking about.

"Leaving Hagar alone in your tent!"

"Ptahmet is with her," said Sarai.

"Well, that's small comfort," said Abram. "Hagar is crying her eyes out because you've treated her so unkindly and now you've left the tent because she displeased you. What can the girl possibly have done wrong? All she does is lie around and throw up, and she can't help *that*."

The injustice of Abram's words were the final blow. Sarai burst into tears.

"Oh, good," said Abram. "Now I have two tents' worth of crying women."

It isn't Hagar, Sarai realized. It's something about *me*, for Abram has never spoken to me so impatiently, like a disobedient child. What have I done to turn these two against me? Maybe they have only just begun to show what Qira has shown openly all my life—that I'm haughty or annoying or . . . something that makes it impossible to love me or respect me. All these years, has Abram been hiding his real feelings?

Why doesn't he come to me and put his arm around me as he has always done on those rare occasions when I cry?

Instead Abram was pacing back and forth. "It's causing gossip all through the camp, the way you've been getting more and more hostile to Hagar ever since she got pregnant," said Abram. "And now to reject her completely by moving out of the tent—do you have any idea how it makes you look in the camp?"

"Yes," said Sarai. "It makes me look like whatever Hagar tells people to see."

"What do you mean by that?" said Abram. "Is this somehow Hagar's fault?"

"No," said Sarai. "I'm sure it's mine. Only I don't know what I'm doing to make her hate me."

"Nothing she does is right," said Abram. "It's all over camp that you complain about everything she says and does."

"If it's all over camp," said Sarai, "how do you think it *got* there? Things that are said between me and Hagar when we're alone, how could they possibly become known?"

"I . . . suppose you were overheard."

"Yes, I'm such a shouter," said Sarai. "Always screaming at people. You've seen how cruel I am with all the servants."

"I don't think I deserve your sarcasm," said Abram.

"Why not?" said Sarai. "You thought I deserved *yours*."

"I wasn't sarcastic with you," said Abram.

" 'Oh good, now I have two tents' worth of crying women.' "

"You can't pretend that my exasperation is an excuse for you to—"

"Did you come here to condemn me without having bothered to judge me first?" said Sarai. "Is that the justice that Abram's own wife receives from him?"

"I haven't condemned you," said Abram.

"Your first words when you came into this tent were accusations. Hagar is crying her eyes out because *I've* treated her so unkindly, what can the girl have possibly done wrong. You start with the assumption that she's the poor wronged innocent, and why is that?"

"I didn't assume anything," said Abram, "I came in here to ask you for your side of things."

"No you didn't," said Sarai. "In all the years I've known you, I've never seen you be unjust to anyone. But you have been unjust tonight, Abram. Your questions were accusations, and you spoke to me without respect."

"And are you speaking to *me* with respect?"

"Yes, I am," said Sarai.

"When is it respectful for a wife to rebuke her husband?"

"If I'm rebuking you, Abram, at least it's not for something someone else told me about you, but for what I have heard you say to my face. I have been driven from my own tent and treated with despite by a servant who has had nothing but kindness and trust from me. The same servant is spreading lies about me, and even though everyone in camp has known me for years, they all believe her accusations readily. And *you* believe her accusations without so much as asking me whether anything that Hagar says is true."

"But why would I think she was lying?"

"Because she accuses me of acting in a way that I've

never acted in my life!" said Sarai. "At least it ought to make you wonder, shouldn't it?"

"But of course you're acting differently," said Abram. "You've never had another woman pregnant with your husband's child before."

It was just too ridiculous. Angry and hurt as she was, Sarai could not help herself. She laughed bitterly.

"This is *funny?*" asked Abram.

"Doesn't it occur to you," said Sarai, "that maybe I'm the one person who has *not* changed? But that everything I do and say is now *seen* differently because everybody *else* assumes I'm so terribly bothered because Hagar is pregnant with your baby?"

"Everybody's wrong but you?" said Abram dryly.

"It's happened before," said Sarai. "In fact, I'd say you've spent most of your life knowing that everybody was wrong but you. And in this case, Abram, I can give you my solemn oath that I have done nothing unkind to Hagar, no, not one thing. Everything I've done has been designed to help her and the baby she's carrying to stay healthy and at peace, and yet no matter what I do or say, Hagar has treated me with spite and has interpreted my every word and deed as some horrible mistreatment."

"And it's not even slightly possible that your words might have been unkind without your meaning it?"

Sarai shook her head. "All right, Abram, of course it's possible, I might easily be wrong. So if it displeases you to have me go to a separate tent, and it displeases Hagar to have me there in my own tent, what choices are left? I know, Abram. Why don't you divorce me and send me back to Ur-of-the-North. I'm sure they'll find me a place to sleep in the temple of Asherah, and you can stay here and be happy with the woman you love."

Abram looked as if he had been lashed across the face. "The only woman I have ever loved is you," he said.

"Not at this moment," said Sarai. "Because the woman you believe without question is Hagar, and the woman you disbelieve no matter what she says is me."

"I don't disbelieve you, I just suggested other interpretations."

"Did you suggest other interpretations of *my* behavior to Hagar?"

He started to answer, but then fell silent.

"No, you didn't," said Sarai. "You simply told her— let me guess the words—'Don't worry about a thing, Hagar, I'll take care of it.' Am I right?"

He looked away, his mouth set.

"And now you're angry at me, Abram. But I've told you the truth. I haven't lied. And I'm not wrong. Hagar has been insolent with me almost from the first moment she was sure she had a child in her. She has been giving me orders and shouting at me in front of the other servants. She has refused to let me help her and then has made others think that I refused to help. She is telling lies about me and everyone believes them, including my husband. Every time I went into my own tent I was accused of the most awful things so I could hardly sleep for the unfairness of it. And even when I fled from my own tent, she had to lie to you so that you'd think I was somehow mistreating her by coming here. Yes, I can see why you'd be angry with me."

Silence fell between them, and lingered.

Finally Abram spoke. "I'm glad we've never quarreled before," he said. "Because you're a terrifying opponent in a war of words."

So he was going to ignore what she said, and accuse her of simply bandying words. Despair sent tears from her eyes again. But she turned her face away from him so he couldn't see. She had been humiliated enough.

"Don't turn away from me, Sarai, I beg you," said Abram.

She turned to face him, letting him see the tears, but saying nothing.

"I *have* been unjust to you. It's as you said—I came here intending to reassure you that I loved you so you'd stop being so resentful of Hagar and would treat her better. It never crossed my mind that she might be lying, that all the gossip in the camp might have come from her. But of course it did—where else could it have come from, considering that every bit of it paints you in the most distasteful color. I should at least have asked for your side of things."

"I have no side of things," said Sarai. "I only want to be left alone while you and Hagar have your baby and go on with your lives."

"That's childish to talk like that," said Abram.

"No, Abram, you mustn't spare my feelings. Rebuke me plainly."

"I'm sorry, I'm doing it again," he said. "But you know that you don't want to be left alone."

"Abram, at this moment, that's all I want. To be allowed to lie down and cry myself to sleep because I, who a few weeks ago had a loving husband and the respect and honor of my household now have lost it all, without having done a single thing to deserve it."

"That's the thing that makes it so hard for me to believe you, Sarai," said Abram. "When you talk as though *none* of the blame for this problem falls on you—when is a problem like this ever the fault of just one person?"

"Is that a question, or a lesson you're trying to teach me?" asked Sarai.

"I suppose it was a lesson, but why don't you go ahead and treat it like a question," said Abram.

"Problems are often the fault of just one person," said Sarai. "And you know it. And you also know that when two people come to you with opposite stories, sometimes they're both exaggerating or both mistaken, but sometimes one of them is telling you the complete truth and the other one is lying or misinterpreting everything. Sometimes, one side has all the right and the other side is completely wrong. Sometimes."

"Yes," said Abram. "Sometimes."

"And when you consider that everything Hagar has accused me of has only two witnesses, her and me, I think it's pretty astonishing that you would believe her completely and me not at all."

"It is astonishing," said Abram. "Because that's what we've all been doing. Maybe just because we all expected you to be hurt by all this, and so anything that happened, we assumed was caused by the pain you were going through."

"Well, the pain is real enough," said Sarai. "And maybe that *has* changed the tone of my voice or the look on my face without my knowing it. But it hasn't made me forget to treat the servants with courtesy. It hasn't made me so disloyal as to do anything that would interfere with the health of the baby that's growing in Hagar's womb."

"But Sarai, we had some idea of why you might be unkind to Hagar. What no one can figure out is why Hagar would be unkind to you. That's why no one even imagined that she was lying."

"I can't figure it out myself," said Sarai. "The best I can come up with is that after all her years in slavery, she's learned to take advantage of any opportunity that comes up, no matter how much she has to lie. In Egypt, she was assigned to me—as a way of showing the contempt they had for me, she knew that. But she acted like my friend, treating me with complete loyalty because she was betting on my ability to get her out of the shameful place she occupied in the House of Women. And here, she acted like my friend because that kept her in the most advantageous position of any of the servants in the camp. She slept in the finest tent, she had the easiest labor, she had the greatest prestige among the servants. But she never was my friend, in her heart. That was just an act she put on. That's what I think now. Because the moment she had your child in her, she had the upper hand over me. Now *she* was the mother of your heir-to-be. And all her hatred can finally come out. Now the way for her to gain the most from this situation is to weaken me, so that she can rise above me in your eyes and the eyes of everyone else in camp. And . . . it worked."

"You really think she's that evil?" asked Abram.

"No, I don't think she's evil," said Sarai. "I think she's a girl who had everything stolen from her as a child, and thinks that's how the world works—you take everything you can the moment you can get it. She hears us talking about God and his commandments, but she doesn't listen in order to find out the truth, she listens to us talk about God in order to find out how to use our belief in God to her own advantage. It's not evil, it's survival. She's still struggling to survive."

"Even if it means crushing you to do it."

To hear Abram speak as if he believed her was such a relief that she could hardly answer. "Yes," she said. "But if you believe in me, she can never crush me."

"I do believe in you," said Abram. "I love you with my whole heart, you're the best gift God has ever given me."

"Until Hagar's son is born," said Sarai.

He had no answer to that.

"And that's why you believed her, Abram," said Sarai. "Not just because you expected me to be upset. You believed her because she has your baby in her and your loyalty is with her, with the mother of your baby. And that's why I need to leave here. I need to go back to Qira until the baby is born. And maybe forever. What I said about Asherah, that was my anger speaking. I would never turn my back on the Lord. But the Lord has turned his back on me. I have displeased him somehow, and so I've lost the respect of my husband and his people. I can't live here without that respect. It would be wrong of you to ask me to."

"It *would* be wrong, Sarai. But you do have my respect. I've been blinded, just as you say. But I'm not blinded now. You are my wife and my friend, closer to me than my brother Lot. I've lived all these years without children, and it caused me grief that only you could understand because you felt the same grief. But if I had to choose between you, without children, and any other woman in the world, with a dozen children, I would choose you."

He had said it before. And she had always believed it. But she didn't believe it now. It was sweet of him to say it, and she wouldn't argue, but it was obviously untrue.

"Sarai," said Abram, "I am with you on this. I put Hagar into your hands. You are her judge. Whatever you say, I will do."

Sarai was filled with despair. "I don't want to do anything to Hagar," she said. "I don't want to judge her. I just want to go on with my life as it was before. Let her be the pregnant woman with everyone pampering her, and let me go on being mistress of the camp and helping you with your work as I always have."

"But that isn't happening," said Abram.

"Because Hagar won't let it happen."

"So something must be done," said Abram.

"Yes," said Sarai. "And it's your job, not mine, to do it."

"And I will," said Abram. "But as you said, I'm not able to see what's happening. So I have to rely on you to judge and tell me what to do to solve the problem."

She wanted to throw a pillow at him to wake him up to what he was doing. Because she knew what his words meant. He still didn't believe her. He still thought she was misjudging Hagar and being unfair to the girl. By giving her such power over Hagar, he was hoping that she would feel more confident and less resentful and so, by being kinder to Hagar, allow peace to return to the camp. He was, in other words, "handling" the situation.

"As you say," said Sarai, knowing she would not use the power Abram had given her. Instead she would stay away from the business of the camp, keep some servant child near her and work with distaff, needle, or loom. She would become, in other words, a servant in her husband's house, and leave the wifely position to the woman who coveted it so.

And then, as soon as she decently could, she'd arrange to go visit Qira in Sodom and then delay her return. She would think back on her marriage to Abram as the brightest, most beautiful part of her life, as treasured memories. But it was all over now. Hagar had that place. And that's how Abram wanted it, even if he didn't realize that's how he was arranging things.

"May I sleep now?" asked Sarai.

"Not here, please," said Abram. "Come to my tent."

"You're very kind, Abram," she said, "but I'm so tired. I beg you, please let me sleep here."

His face grew hard again. "As you say," he said, and then arose and left the tent without another word.

To her surprise, Sarai only brooded for a little while before she slept.

And in the morning, she was almost happy, to wake up without dreading what Hagar would say. And—just as everyone suspected—Sarai also enjoyed not having to look at a woman pregnant with her husband's child. As long as everyone believes I'm cruelly jealous, I might as well admit it to myself—it cuts me to the heart that she's the one with his baby, and not me. The Lord knows that I feel that envy. But the Lord also knows that I never treated Hagar unkindly because of it. Abram was wrong. I'm not Hagar's judge. God is, as He is my judge, and Abram's, too.

Sarai arose and dressed herself and then sat and prayed, murmuring the words of her heart, pouring out her feelings to the Lord. And by the end of her long prayer, she was able to say, with an honest heart, "I thank thee for granting the prayers of my husband and me, and giving him the child that Hagar carries. Please let the baby be born healthy and live long, for my husband's sake."

At peace with herself, she got up and left the tent and stood blinking in the bright light of midmorning. The life of the camp had gone on without her—of course it had. The cookfires were burning, the normal work and bustle of the camp caused all the familiar noises and smells and movements.

And then Sarai turned to face her own tent, where Hagar had slept last night, and a chill ran through her heart.

For there was Hagar—who supposedly could not lift a finger to stir from her bed, she was so sick with her pregnancy—there was Hagar, sitting in Sarai's place in the door of Sarai's tent, and there was Eliezer sitting beside her, conferring with her just as he used to do with Sarai.

It is complete now, thought Sarai. She has moved entirely into my place.

Almost she returned to the guest tent, to spend the rest of the day weeping or brooding.

Almost she fled the camp, to wander in the hills until, blinded with tears, she fell into some ravine and mercifully broke a leg or arm to take her mind off the pain in her heart.

Almost she screamed aloud and condemned everyone in camp for being so blind as not to see how monstrously this servant girl had usurped her place.

But she did none of these things. Not even knowing what she was going to do, she walked across the yard between tents and stood before Hagar, who looked up at her sullenly from heavy-lidded eyes.

"Good morning, Hagar," said Sarai, and to her own surprise she was able to make her voice sound perfectly cheerful. "I'm so glad you're well enough to come out and see the day."

Sarai carefully avoided looking at Eliezer, for his betrayal, by conferring with Hagar in Sarai's place, was almost unbearable, and she might break down and cry if she actually had to speak to him.

"Good morning . . . Mistress," said Hagar. The contempt in the word *mistress* was subtle. Sarai knew that no one would hear it but herself. Hagar was so careful in front of witnesses.

"Do you mind if I sit beside you here this morning?" Sarai asked.

Hagar immediately sighed and began to get up, making a great show of how hard it was for her. "Help me, will you, Eliezer? My mistress needs her place back, and so I'd better go inside."

"No, not at all," said Sarai. "I only asked if I might sit beside you. Please, sit down."

"Never mind, Eliezer," said Hagar. "My mistress commands me to sit. My back is so tired, though. Is it all right, Mistress, if I have some pillows to lean on, since I can't go in and lie down?"

"But of course you can go in," said Sarai, "if you need to lie down. Whatever you wish is fine with me."

Hagar's eyes filled with tears. "Oh, Mistress, I wish you'd decide what you want from me. Sit here, go in and lie down—I'll do whatever you ask of me, if only you'd make up your mind." And Hagar began, softly, to weep. But her body arched over and she put her hands to her face so it was obvious to anyone within sight of them that somehow Sarai had made Hagar cry.

"Forgive me, child," said Sarai, somehow containing her rage at the way Hagar had manipulated everything to make her look monstrous once again. Indeed, despite her fury at the unfairness of it, she couldn't help but admire how skillfully she had done it, right under Eliezer's nose—and Eliezer, all solicitude as he helped Hagar get up to go inside, no doubt believed completely that somehow Sarai had been cruel to Hagar.

He'll never even realize that every word I said was courteous and kind. He'll only see that I somehow distressed the mother of Abram's child, no doubt because of my envy of the girl.

When Eliezer returned from helping Hagar go back into the tent, Sarai spoke to him—in a businesslike way, without looking at him. "Eliezer, would you see that a horse is prepared for me? And a few servants to accompany me? I'm going to visit my sister in Sodom."

"I will, Mistress," said Eliezer. But then, before he left to obey her, he hesitated, and leaned a little closer. "Mistress, I think the master wishes to speak to you."

"Oh, is he in his tent?" asked Sarai.

"No," said Eliezer. He looked over her shoulder.

Sarai turned and gasped to see that Abram was standing

directly behind her. "You startled me," she said. "I didn't hear you come from your tent."

"Because I didn't," said Abram. "I've spent the morning sitting on the other side of your tent, waiting to hear for myself what passed between you and Hagar."

She felt her heart sink within her. Hagar's victory was complete. Abram was now convinced that he had proof that his wife was being cruel to the girl in whose body he had placed his child.

But to her surprise, he wrapped his arms around her and held her close. "You poor thing, to have borne such insolence and deception all these weeks, and to have none of us believe in you even though you did no wrong."

He believed her! He had not been fooled by Hagar's manipulation! Tears of relief flowed—even though she had thought last night that she could never cry again. "Oh, Abram," she murmured.

They stood like that a few moments longer. Then Abram spoke to Eliezer. "You heard what I heard, and saw with your own eyes, didn't you?"

"As you asked me, Abram, I'm your witness."

"Since someone has been trying hard to slander my wife in front of my whole household, I want you to take great care to make sure everyone knows exactly what you saw today," said Abram. "Make sure they know I stand with Sarai."

"I will, Master."

"But stay here for now, Eliezer," said Abram. He drew Sarai within the circle of his arm, so they stood side by side facing the door of the tent. "I want you to witness this, too."

Eliezer stood then on the other side of Abram.

"Hagar," called Abram. "Come out of your mistress's tent." There was no anger in his voice, but no tenderness, either. And he spoke loudly enough that the heads of many nearby women turned to see what was happening.

"I'm coming, my love!" called Hagar from inside the tent.

My love. The words galled Sarai. But she felt Abram's arm tighten around her. To reassure her, she hoped. Though it was just as possible that he was gripping her more tightly to keep her from leaping on Hagar and clawing at her.

The girl emerged from the tent, a blanket gathered around her. She was padding out with an air of deshabille, perhaps designed to be seductive—but the moment she saw that Abram stood with Sarai on one side and Eliezer on the other, she knew that this was not a tete-a-tete with the father of her baby.

"Hagar," said Abram, "you will be sleeping in the guest tent from now on, and not in my wife's tent."

Hagar's eyes went heavy-lidded, and she glanced briefly at Sarai. "As you command, Master."

"This morning I heard with my own ears the insolent, dishonest way you spoke to Sarai. It will never happen again, Hagar."

For only a heartbeat, Hagar seemed to be starting to act contrite. But apparently she changed her mind and decided on a different course of conduct, for all of a sudden she began to wail loudly as if she had just been beaten. "What have I done to you, Mistress, that you turn the face of your husband against me! Please don't drive me away! Please don't turn me out of the only home I know."

Abram's body stiffened with anger. "Stop that at once," he said to Hagar.

"Don't beat me!" Hagar wailed. "Please, I beg you, for the baby's sake if not for mine! Don't beat me!"

"You fool," said Abram softly. "Don't you know that now that I see the truth, it doesn't matter whether you deceive the rest of the world? I know my wife has been honest with me and with you, and everything you've been saying and doing is a lie."

But Hagar was apparently incapable of giving up the deception. She spoke directly to Sarai, pitching her voice loud enough that many others could hear her. "This is what you've been trying for ever since I got a baby from him when you couldn't. You've set your face against me, to get rid of me *and* my baby. Well, it's worked! I won't let you beat me! I'll die in the desert before I let you beat me!"

With that, Hagar cast away the blanket and, wearing only a thin, semi-transparent linen shift, she scampered away, running past the tents, out into the grass. Only once did she look behind to see if she was being pursued. Even though she must have seen that no one was chasing after her, she screamed anyway, and ran as if a lion had just leapt toward her.

"Shall I go fetch her, Master?" said Eliezer.

"No," said Abram.

"You have to," said Sarai. "What about the baby?"

"If the Lord means that baby to be the one through whom His promises to me will be fulfilled, then the Lord will protect her and lead her where He will. I did not send her away, or mistreat her in any way. Neither did you, Sarai, and neither did anyone else. Her leaving was part of her own lie. Apparently she still believes it."

"What if she comes back?" asked Eliezer.

"Then welcome her kindly," said Abram, "and escort her to the tent I assigned to her." He turned to face Sarai, and stroked her hair possessively as he said to Eliezer, "This is my wife. This is her tent. Whoever shows disrespect to her is not mine, and has no claim on me. But whoever shows honor to my wife, then I will be his friend and protector."

"Thank you," murmured Sarai.

Then she sat down in the door of her tent. "Sit with me, husband," she said. "In the door of my tent, please sit with me today."

Abram sat down beside her, and for the rest of the day, whoever came to him saw how he included her in every discussion and every decision, and how he heard her advice with great respect and did whatever she suggested and granted her whatever she asked. By nightfall there was no doubt in the camp that whatever struggle had gone on between Hagar and Sarai, it was over now, and Sarai was more firmly than ever in the good graces of the master of the household.

At the end of the day, Abram came inside her tent with her. They prayed together, Abram first, then Sarai. Abram did not mention Hagar. Sarai did, though, begging the Lord to watch over her and keep her and the baby safe. "Bring her home to us, O Lord, so we can show her that we forgive her and love her and that she does not need to lie to anyone in order to have a sure place in this household."

When the prayer was over, Abram said to her, "You are more virtuous than I am."

"That is not true at all," said Sarai.

"To pray so generously for Hagar, after what she tried to do to you?"

"Of course I can be forgiving," said Sarai. "Because she failed."

The next morning Hagar returned to camp and was ushered into the guest tent. Abram spoke with her for a little while. Sarai did not ask what was said, and Abram did not tell her. Every day, Sarai visited Hagar and told her the news of the camp. Hagar always seemed glad to see her, and chatted away as if nothing had ever been wrong between them.

Sarai did not believe in her for a moment. But there was peace in the camp, Abram's baby was thriving in the womb, and for now, that was enough.

❧ PART VII ❧

FIRE FROM HEAVEN

❧ CHAPTER 19 ❧

The boy Ishmael was born in Hagar's tent. All the camp rejoiced, and Sarai led the rejoicing. Hagar reared the boy, but Sarai also watched over him, and delighted in him. And the boy's father saw that he was strong and clever, and when Abram taught him of God, the boy learned and obeyed. He took no pleasure in learning to read, so Abram waited, hoping that as he grew older he would grow curious about the ancient books. And the boy seemed to pray only when Abram bade him, but Sarai had seen that few boys were quick to pray, and reassured her husband.

Between Hagar and Sarai, there was a strange kind of peace, each giving place to the other. Sarai was careful never to intrude on the rearing of Ishmael, and not just because she wanted never to have to imagine another person thinking, Who are you to give advice about children? No, she recognized that even though Hagar's pregnancy began as a gift to Abram from Sarai, it was still Hagar who lay with Abram, and Hagar who bore the boy, and

Hagar whose eyes could be seen looking out of Ishmael's face. The child was Sarai's gift, but Hagar's son. So Sarai never intruded.

Nor did Sarai ever treat Hagar as a servant, after that night Hagar spent alone in the desert. For she realized that even though Hagar had lied and betrayed her and tried to take her place, it was partly because slavery had taught her to lie and scrabble for advantage and feel loyalty to no one. Sarai had never questioned the practice of slavery, believing, as most people believed, that if God did not want people to be slaves, He would not allow them to be captured in battle. But, having known Hagar, having seen how slavery poisoned a girl who had such quickness and beauty, such a gift for laughter and such understanding of other people, Sarai saw all the servants of Abram's house differently.

She had admired Abram from the beginning for the way he treated his servants with courtesy. Gradually she had realized that Abram really believed that his servants were also children of God, worthy of dignity, and so Sarai had followed her own natural inclination to be gentle and courteous even with the lowliest and least reliable of the servants. She did this believing that it was good to be kind to those who already bore the heavy punishment of God's disfavor.

Hagar had taught her, however, that every slave longs for mastery and resents having to submit. All of Sarai's kindness and gentleness was no replacement for freedom and respect. It was in the nature of their relationship that despite all the friendship that Sarai believed they shared, Sarai had never forgotten who was slave and who was master. Neither had Hagar. There was not and could never be friendship between them as long as Hagar was a slave.

That is why Sarai insisted to Abram that the tent where Hagar slept should no longer be called the guest tent, but should be called Hagar's tent. "As if she were a wife?" asked Abram.

"Will her son inherit?"

"Sarai, I will not raise up Hagar as my wife. I lay with your handmaiden, under the law that made her a substitute for your body."

"And if I free her?"

"It doesn't matter. I won't marry her," said Abram. "I won't lie with her again. You are my wife."

"I will free her," said Sarai, "and you will call that tent Hagar's, not because she is your wife, but because she is the mother of your son, and your son will not be reared in a slave's tent."

"Are you commanding me?" said Abram.

"I'm predicting the wise course that you will choose because of your wisdom."

He didn't like it, but he agreed because she was, in fact, right. Whether Abram told Hagar that it was Sarai's idea or not didn't matter. Neither of them ever mentioned it. But in the camp each woman had her sphere. No one came to Hagar to settle any business of the camp—Sarai was the judge who ruled under Abram. But Hagar was the mother of Ishmael, and all the fussing and flattery that came to the baby and, as he grew, to the boy, was done under Hagar's watchful eyes. All delighted in the boy, but only Hagar and Abram had the right to be proud of him, for he was theirs.

Of course this did nothing to ease Sarai's grief that her age of bearing had passed without her womb ever quickening with the life of a child. But at least she was eased of the burden of guilt for never having borne a son to Abram. He had his son as a gift from Sarai, and so she might still have the pity of others, but not their resentment or scorn. And when she felt envy for Hagar stir within her, she channeled it into the envy she felt for every mother, instead of allowing it to fester as resentment that Sarai's husband had known Hagar's body in order to make the boy Ishmael.

And so, because Sarai willed it, there was peace in the camp.

Only one question remained in Sarai's heart concerning

Hagar. That night when Hagar fled from the camp and spent the night in the desert, something had happened that sent the girl home transformed. It was more than just having spent a night alone, because Hagar did not seem to have been broken by the experience. She was not docile—far from it. She took command of her tent and later took command of the raising of Ishmael, without the slightest sign of deference to Sarai. She did not leave Sarai in peace out of fear. It was something else. A transformation that had happened that night.

Sarai asked Abram once, and Abram said, "It's not for me to tell what she saw and heard that night." With that he dropped the matter and made it clear he was never going to say more than that.

But what he had said was perhaps more than he realized. What Hagar saw and heard? Not for him to tell? Well, he wouldn't have said that if Hagar saw a scorpion or a serpent or a bramble bush or sand or rock—the ordinary things one sees in the desert. He would only have said such a thing if what she saw and heard was miraculous. A sign from God.

That explained everything, of course. Especially it explained why Hagar no longer prayed only when the whole camp prayed. Now she prayed on her own, without prompting, and sometimes even when she thought no one could see. Sarai could only conclude that Hagar prayed because she believed in God. And, to Sarai, this meant that now, despite what had happened between them, Hagar could be trusted. She was no longer lawless, seizing advantage wherever she could. She knew that God lived, that Abram was not just pretending to know God the way that Sehtepibre had faked the signs of divine favor. That's what had humbled her and given her courage, both at once.

God can make of anyone what He wishes, thought Sarai.

She even said this to Abram once, but Abram disagreed. "God can make of anyone exactly what they are willing to become, and nothing better, just as the Enemy can make of us only as wicked a creature as we are willing to become."

"Then Hagar has a good heart," said Sarai, "because look what she has allowed God to make of her."

Abram smiled at that, and embraced her, but said nothing. And sometimes Sarai wondered what he meant by that silence.

No matter. There was peace in the camp.

For thirteen years, peace. Sarai thought she could see the end of her life. She would watch as Ishmael grew to manhood. She would continue helping in the camp as long as she had strength. She would live in the light of Abram's love, as part of him, and with him as part of her. If God willed, she would die before Abram, and she would consider herself the most fortunate of women.

Every now and then she wondered what would happen if Abram died first. Especially if he died before Ishmael came of age. The boy did not know Sarai very well. He knew only his mother. Sarai would be at Hagar's mercy then. If Hagar was truly converted to God and his law, then Sarai would be allowed to spend the rest of her life in Qira's household; if Qira died first, then surely Lot would take her in. But one thing was certain—if Abram died, Sarai would have no future here. The servants might wish to serve her well, but they would belong to Ishmael, and Ishmael would obey Hagar. Sarai could not believe that Hagar had changed so deeply that she would keep Sarai here to grow old. And even if she did, it would be a useless life for her. Lonely without her husband, her days meaningless, she would pray for death.

Indeed, she prayed for death already. Not immediate death. Just for priority. Let me die first, O Lord, if thou lovest me. My life has been good. Let my life end well, asleep in the arms of my husband. And then let my body be lowered into a deep cave and laid out with respect, whole and unbroken, to await his coming to join me.

It was all she had to look forward to. But it was enough. Her life had been interesting in her youth, but in her old age she did not want it to be interesting. She wanted it to drift on, day after day, unchanging.

Excitement was much overrated by the young.

Abram went one day into his tent to work with his books and to pray. It made her feel good to see him go there, for on days when he prayed he often came and spoke to her, not about the business of the camp, but about God or the stars or the history of tribes and nations or the words of ancient prophets. He was happiest then, and spoke to her of things he spoke of to no one else. That was when Sarai was happiest. Even happier than when Abram so joyfully worked with his son beside him, teaching him the ways of a herdmaster—for despite her pleasure at how glad he was to have a son, there was always just that little twinge of sadness. There was no sadness when Abram sat and talked with her, filled with understanding and peace and the love of God.

But today, as she worked the distaff, waiting for him to emerge, she felt something strange. She kept looking to see if someone was coming. Several times she arose— not as easy a task as it used to be, though she was still hale for her age—and walked out beyond the tents, to scan the horizon in all directions.

"What does my mistress look for?" Eliezer asked her.

"I feel as though someone is coming," she said. "Or as if someone just arrived."

"No one but runners from the distant camps," said Eliezer. "And a wagon with a load of melons from Hebron."

"It isn't melons I'm looking for," said Sarai. She laughed as if it were nothing, but she was still uneasy. She could see that Eliezer was worried by her words, and seemed extra vigilant, as if he feared some enemy might be presaged by her warning. She wanted to tell him, No, Eliezer, you need fear no enemy. It's a friend that I'm looking for, or a kinsman. But since she couldn't be sure that her feeling meant anything at all, how could she be sure that it meant something good? No, she was just growing feeble-minded. She'd seen it happen to many a woman who had outlived her mind.

Only she knew she was not feeble-minded. Something was happening, and she wanted to run into Abram's tent and beg him to ask the Lord what it was.

Instead, not long after noon, the door of Abram's tent parted. But he did not emerge. He stood there, in the darkness inside, only his hand protruding from the gap in the cloth. As if he were reaching for something, or someone.

Sarai arose and walked across the yard between the tents and, not knowing why she did it, or what he would think when she did it, she reached out and took hold of his hand. "Abram," she said. "Abram, are you all right?"

"I'm not Abram," he said.

But she knew his hand. She knew his voice. What could he mean?

"I am not Abram," he said again. "God has visited me, and He gave me another name."

"Come out, then," she said, "and tell me who you are."

"No," he said.

"Then let me come in," she said. "Let me see you."

"First," he said, "I must tell you the name that God has given you."

She felt a thrill run through her. God had spoken to Abram and mentioned her? God knows me? God has given me a new name?

"You are no longer Sarai," said Abram. "God has named you in Hebrew this time. Sarah."

She was vaguely disappointed. The word *sarah*, "princess," was close enough to her Sumerian name that more than one Hebrew had thought Sarai was a title and not a name. And why princess instead of queen? It was a name for a daughter, not for a wife. Yet . . . she did not know what this new name might mean. And Abram also had a new name.

"May I come in?" asked Sarai.

"What is your name?" asked Abram.

She understood. He wanted her to call herself by the new name, to show that she accepted it.

"Sarah," she said.

"The Lord has been in this tent today," said Abram. "Enter the place where the Lord has been." He drew her inside.

She came in and saw nothing changed about the tent. But Abram was changed, she could see that. His face glowed, or so it seemed. She could not take her eyes from his face.

"My name," he said to her, "is no longer Abram." *Abram* meant "exalted father." What new name could the Lord have given him?

"My name is Abraham," he said.

Father of multitudes.

Another disappointment, though Sarai—no, Sarah—tried to stifle the feeling. Still, it hurt that God named her *princess*—a daughter, albeit of a king—and named her husband *father of multitudes*. The difference between them could not have been plainer.

It was as if he saw into her heart. "No, Sarah, you don't understand. You are named princess because you are the beloved daughter of the king of heaven. And I am named father of multitudes because Ishmael and his children will not be my only descendants."

She closed her eyes. He was going to take Hagar as a wife after all. He was going to have more children by her.

"The Lord came to me and made a covenant with me. Not just a prophecy, but a solemn vow. A covenant, not just with me, but with all my seed after me. Giving us this land as an everlasting inheritance as long as we keep our part of the covenant. And you, Sarah, you will also be the mother of nations."

"Me!" She couldn't keep a derisive laugh from escaping with the word.

"Yes, I laughed, too," said Abraham. "It was such a strange thought, at our age."

My age, you mean.

"And I prayed to him that Ishmael would live righteously before God, for obviously he is the only one through whom the covenant can be fulfilled. But the Lord said, Sarah thy wife shall bear thee a son indeed, and thou shalt call his name Isaac. And I will establish my covenant with him for an everlasting covenant and with his seed after him."

"God came to you?" said Sarah. "To promise you that I would bear a son?" Immediately she thought of what such a thing would mean to Hagar. "But what about Ishmael?"

"He confirmed great blessings on Ishmael. That he would be the father of twelve kings. But Sarah, he said that you would be a mother of nations, that great kings would be your descendants. This very covenant will be passed down through your son, Isaac, and he'll be born at this time next year."

He gathered Sarah in his arms.

She wanted to be happy for him. She wanted to be happy for herself. But instead, all she felt was a great wracking misery, and she sank to the carpet and wept.

"I understand," said Abraham. "It's too wonderful to bear, isn't it?"

Wonderful? thought Sarah bitterly. How many times have I heard such promises before? Oh, now it was more specific. Now at least she'd have a date to mark the bitterness of disappointment. Abram, she wanted to say— no, Abraham—Abraham, your love for me has misled you. You think this will make me glad. But it only wounds me anew.

She said nothing of her real feelings to Abraham, however. She let him hold her there on the floor of his tent. Then he arose. "I won't let the sun set without making sure that every man in my household takes on him the mark of the covenant."

"A mark?" she asked.

"A cut in the flesh," he said, "where it won't grow back, marking us all as fathers of children consecrated to the worship of God. Today every man of us will bear that cut, and every new manchild born to my house will receive the mark of the covenant when he reaches his eighth day, so that his whole life he will see in his own flesh that he belongs to God, and so will all who come after him."

By sunset, every man in the camp had received the cut. Sarah stood with the other women, watching from a distance as the men came, their faces full of misgivings as they arrived, their walk speaking of considerable discomfort as they went away. At first some of the women had been terrified—they had seen the castration of too many rams and bulls not to fear what was being done to their husbands or sons. But Abraham reassured them that after the pain subsided, their manly functions would not be impaired. "The Lord means to make a great nation of us," said Abraham. "He wouldn't require us to do anything that interfered with conceiving children."

To Sarah's relief, he said nothing to the others about the promise God had made concerning her. The last thing she needed was to have everyone else watching as, once again, the promised day passed by. She knew that like all God's promises, this one depended on her worthiness before the Lord. And since she didn't know what had made her unworthy during all the years when she might have borne children, it was hard to imagine that she'd be able to repent of it now. This promise, like all the others pertaining to her, would be rescinded. Only this time, because she never believed it, she wouldn't be half so disappointed.

Most of the men who had been circumcised were miserable all night, and few of them were worth much at their tasks the next day. Abraham, though, insisted on traveling to the other camps to cut the mark into the men there. He was in as much pain as anyone, so if he insisted on going, Eliezer had to get a party of men together to give him safe escort. At least Abraham didn't insist on walking. They mounted donkeys for this journey—no one wanted to be astride a horse if it should break into a trot.

Days later, it was finished, and life was back to normal. The women, of course, were full of talk, as the mothers talked about what the cutting had done to their sons, and then the wives began discussing, with some crude humor, how it affected their husbands.

Only Hagar and Sarah remained aloof from these discussions, Sarah because it would be undignified to speak of the master of the house in such a way, Hagar because there was no man's mark that she would see. She had no husband, and Ishmael, at thirteen, was much too old ever to allow his mother to see how he had been injured. She had too much pride to make a point of looking at one of the little children, though she was bound to see eventually. Once again it struck Sarah how much Hagar had lost by accepting Abraham's son within her body. She couldn't marry someone else, and therefore could have no more children. Ishmael was everything to her. But now that he was old enough to learn a man's duties, he was more and more often away from her tent for days on end. Hagar had a son, yes, but he was no longer a baby. For the first time Sarah realized that despite the great joy that child-bearing could bring a woman, it was a great disappointment, too. For the years when a boychild was close to his mother were not that many, and then he became a man among men, and the mother was alone again.

I'm sorry for all this has cost you, Hagar. But surely it's better than it would have been if you had stayed in Egypt. You can't hate me for this.

If Hagar felt any pain, she never mentioned it to Sarah—nor to anyone else, as far as Sarah knew. Hagar could laugh and jest as well as anyone, but what went on inside her heart no one knew or ever had known.

❧ CHAPTER 20 ❧

Abraham had never stopped lying with Sarah in her tent from time to time—but the times had become rarer over the years, and more often than not they would lie together and talk until one of them fell asleep. Now that he had the Lord's promise to inspire him, though, Abraham became, if not youthful, then at least persistent in his efforts.

But he was too old. The time for this had passed. "A younger woman would waken your desire," said Sarah.

"A younger woman has no promise of a son to be named Isaac," said Abraham impatiently.

"Abraham, if the Lord wants you to have a son, then He'll simply have to do something about this."

"None of the other men has had any problems like this after receiving the mark of the covenant," said Abraham.

"Abraham, you're not a young man, and my old body shows few signs of the girl that used to waken you," said Sarah. "It has nothing to do with the knife."

Abraham muttered and went to sleep, then came back

the next night, and the next. He had never spent *every* night with her even when they were younger, but he made sure not to travel to any of the other camps.

But when three and a half months had passed after the day of the covenant, even Abraham had to admit that it simply wasn't going to happen. "I don't understand it," he said. "How could I have misunderstood the Lord's promise? It's not as if I wasn't listening closely."

She comforted him for his embarrassment, but because she had not really believed in the promise, her own disappointment wasn't all that grave.

He slept beside her that night, enfolding her in his arms the way he did as a young husband, and she found that she enjoyed his company more now that he had given up on conceiving the promised child. "Love outlasts desire, I'm glad to say," she said. "It's just as well, you know. Can you imagine me chasing after a toddler at my age? Or getting milk to flow from these old breasts?"

"Apparently there are a lot of things that can *only* be imagined," said Abraham.

And, just to prove the point, his arm fell asleep and his joints got quite painful and he had to draw away from her after only a few minutes of nestling. "How did this happen to us?" Abraham said. "I never noticed getting old."

"It's the only job we've ever done so faithfully, never missing a day."

"Well, I didn't know I was so effective at it. You're still beautiful."

"And now the eyes are going," said Sarah.

"I think I can see well enough to get back to my tent," he said.

"Stay," she said. "Let me at least hear your breathing all night."

"From what I've been told, you can hear it from *my* tent."

"Oh, that was *snoring*?" asked Sarah. "I thought it was a sledge being dragged across stones."

"Now I have to stay, just to punish you for that remark."

So he spent the night. She slept well, despite his snoring, which had indeed grown much louder in the past year or so.

They each woke the other several times in the night when they had to take trips outside the tent.

And in the morning, they laughed ruefully over how little they had slept.

"Well, we're done with *that*," said Abraham. "But I liked spending so much time with you. Come to my tent this morning. Read aloud for me while I do my work."

It was the story of Enoch she read, the great miracles of those days before Zion was taken up into heaven. While she read, he did calculations in a box of sand, growing more and more concerned as he did. Finally he interrupted her. "I'm not wrong," he said. "I hoped I was."

"What?" she asked.

"I saw a new star last night," said Abraham. "A returning star, I thought. I consulted the records to see if such a star was due to appear. There were two that might be coming at about this time. One wears a great sword, and it seems to mark the coming of wars. But the other is a star that has no sword, only a slight beard. But whenever this star returns, fiery stones fall from heaven and cause terror and destruction. Sometimes it has caused brightness in the heavens all through the night. Sometimes it has made the earth quake, or great fires that sweep away forests or grassland. Well, I did the calculations and it is most likely that this is the bearded star, the one that causes stones to fall from the sky."

"Are we in danger?" asked Sarah.

"I don't know. Someone is. The Lord will decide."

"You really watch the skies for this?" asked Sarah.

"All priests watch the sky. That's how we keep the calendars, marking which day the shadows are shortest and which day they're longest, every year. And we watch the sky for signs like these, and keep the record for generations. No one has records older than mine, for I have the book in which Adam wrote, and before him, what man was there to watch the heavens and write down what he saw? Every star and wonder that men have seen, I have in my books."

"Does anyone else have copies of these books?" asked Sarah.

"Melchizedek does," said Abraham.

It was as if the mention of the name of the high priest and king of Salem had summoned him. For only moments later, a tumult could be heard outside. Abraham arose and went to the tent door, and he returned with a sense of urgency. "Three visitors have come, common travelers asking for food and drink."

"Then why are you so worried?"

"Eliezer says he's sure one of them is Melchizedek."

"Dressed as a common traveler?"

"Maybe he's in disguise so that he doesn't have to bring soldiers with him to ward off robbers."

"But we're not ready to entertain a king!"

"We're always ready," said Abraham. "Take three measures of the fine flour and with your own hands make cakes on the hearth. I'll have the men butcher a calf."

They hurried about their business. As she and the baker women kneaded the dough, she could see Abraham select a calf and set the butchers to work. Then he fairly ran to meet Melchizedek and his companions and escorted them to his tent. They went inside. Sarah fretted at having to make bread instead of being part of the conversation. But Abraham had been very clear—he wanted her to be doing the baking herself, which meant that she was not to be part of this conversation. This was not uncommon with distinguished visitors—most would be insulted to have Abraham expect them to converse in the presence of a woman. But surely Melchizedek was not such a man as that. Still, it was Abraham's decision to make. So Sarah formed the cakes and watched as one of the women braved the oven's heat and slid the cakes onto the hot tiles with her paddle.

It didn't take long for the cakes to be ready. At least Abraham had not expected her to make bread and wait for it to rise! The first strips of tender veal were carved from the spit at the same time, and Sarah insisted on carrying the cakes and veal to Abraham's tent herself.

She stopped outside the tent, taking care not to stand close enough to eavesdrop, and laid out the basket of cakes, the pot of butter, a jar of milk, and the bowl of veal. Then she clapped her hands to announce that the food was ready.

Abraham emerged almost at once, followed by Melchizedek and his companions. Sarah immediately backed away as Abraham sat by the food and offered the cakes and butter and milk to his visitors. He gave her a smile of thanks, and then turned back to the guests in order to pray over the food. Sarah quickly returned to her tent.

What could this mean, this visit from Melchizedek just as the bearded star returned? Sarah could not concentrate on anything. She finally set down the distaff after making a tangle of the yarn and simply sat by the door of the tent. She could hear their voices and now and then catch a phrase or two. They were talking of numbers and years, comparing calculations and arguing, though only mildly, and with rueful laughter now and then as someone's calculations were found wanting.

Then, to her surprise, Melchizedek spoke more loudly and said, "Where is Sarah, your wife?"

What does he want with me? thought Sarah. Or is he only making sure that I'm not listening? Well . . . I *am* listening! Have I been caught?

"In her tent," said Abraham.

"Abraham," said Melchizedek, "the way of a man with a woman is not finished for you. It will return to you despite your age, and Sarah your wife *will* have a son."

Oh, no, not again, thought Sarah. Just when we have finally come to our senses, we have to have another go at it because Melchizedek is too young to understand what happens to old men and old women? Even if Abraham's natural force returns to him, what good is that? My womb couldn't do the job even when we were both young.

"Why is Sarah laughing?" said Melchizedek.

At once Sarah grew frightened. Had she actually laughed aloud? She didn't think so—but apparently she had embarrassed herself and shamed her husband by being caught eavesdropping.

"I didn't hear her laugh," said Abraham.

"She was saying in her heart, 'Oh really, will I bear a child, as old as I am?' "

She was relieved to know that if he was reading her mind, at least he wasn't getting it word for word.

She got up and emerged from the tent to find Melchizedek and Abraham and the others all looking at her. To Abraham's credit, he was the only one not smiling smugly.

"Is anything too hard for the Lord?" asked Melchizedek. "At the time appointed the Lord will make you as if you were young again, and Sarah will have a son."

"I didn't laugh," said Sarah.

"No, you laughed," said Melchizedek. "Maybe not with your voice, but the Lord can hear your heart." Then he smiled, so she knew he was not angry with her for listening.

One of the other men said, "Shall I hide from Abraham the thing that I'm doing?"

"Not from Abraham," said the other stranger. "Not from the man who will found nations. Not from the man of the covenant, whose children's children's children will still bear the mark of the covenant a hundred and fifty generations from now."

So the first man spoke again, and now Melchizedek and Abraham listened with equal intensity. Melchizedek did not know what was coming, either. "Because the complaint against Sodom and Gomorrah is great, and because their sin is terrible, I will go down now and see whether they are as wicked as I've heard."

At those words, Melchizedek and the other man arose at once, but not the man who had spoken them. Abraham arose to embrace Melchizedek and the other man, urging the last of the cakes on them to eat along the way. Soon they were walking down the hill, heading southeast, their faces set toward Sodom.

But the one traveler remained with Abraham, and because he didn't send Sarah away, she waited to hear what he would say.

It was Abraham who spoke first. "Will the Lord destroy the righteous along with the wicked?" he asked.

So that's why they were talking about Sodom. Apparently some of the conversation Sarah had overheard but had not quite understood was about some danger to Sodom. She could only assume that it meant the fiery stones that came with the bearded star would strike the city, and that it had something to do with the wickedness of the place.

To her shame, her first thought was, It's about time He did something about that cesspool, after the way it ruined Qira as a human being.

Only then did she realize that when Abraham asked about destroying the righteous with the wicked, he was talking about Lot and Qira, who lived in the city. Abraham was thinking about the danger to them, while all Sarah could do was condemn the city. What kind of sister am I?

Why, the kind who's going to have a baby.

She almost laughed aloud again.

"What if there are fifty righteous people in the city?" said Abraham. "Will the Lord not spare the place for the sake of the fifty righteous? That's not the way of the Lord, is it, to destroy the righteous with the wicked?"

"If I find fifty righteous souls in Sodom, I'll spare the whole place for their sakes."

Sarah had visited Sodom often enough and stayed with

Qira long enough to have her doubts about whether there *were* fifty righteous people there. It's not as if she could count her own sister among that number.

Nor did Abraham believe there would be fifty. "I know I don't have the right to ask, being nothing but dust and ashes before the Lord, but what if the city comes only five short of fifty righteous men? Wilt thou destroy the city for lack of five?"

"If I find forty-five righteous souls, I won't destroy it."

"Please don't be angry," said Abraham, "but . . . what about forty?"

And so it went, until Abraham had bargained all the way down to ten. And the visitor said, "I will stay my hand and spare the city for the sake of ten."

With that, the visitor arose. Abraham offered him no food, nor did they embrace. But Abraham looked long after the man as he walked away.

"Was that the Lord?" asked Sarah, not wishing to disturb Abraham's reverie, but less able to wait a moment longer without asking.

"A messenger," said Abraham. "But he spoke with the authority of God."

"Will he find ten righteous souls in Sodom?" asked Sarah.

"Let's pray, for Sodom's sake, that he does."

"When will we know?" asked Sarah.

"If the city is destroyed, it will be no secret," said Abraham.

"And while we wait," said Sarah, "when is this other miracle supposed to happen?"

Abraham came and took her by the hand. "I don't know," he said. "But if we're going to have a son a year after the covenant, there's no time to lose."

❧ CHAPTER 21 ❧

Qira normally paid no attention to what Lot did, since he was always more concerned with the flocks and herds outside the city than with anything going on inside. But this was hardly the time to receive visitors.

"You know how dangerous it is on the streets after dark," said Qira. "If your visitors are foolish enough not to arrive in daylight, then let them take their chances outside the city."

Lot only looked at her with the cool, distant expression he might use to gaze at a recently stepped-on roach. She saw that face so often these days that she avoided speaking to him at all, when she could. But Lot *was* her husband, and if he was so disconnected from the city that he didn't know what had been happening lately, she had to warn him. Not that Lot himself was in any danger—everyone knew that he was under the protection of the king. But that protection meant less and less these days.

The war with Chedorlaomer had changed everything.

During the time when the king and the richest men had been in captivity, the worst sort of men had ruled in the city, and those days had been terrible, with all sorts of vengeance-taking that left many men dead in the streets. And as the riotousness in the streets went on, the murders began to include more and more women—most of them killed, it was rumored, by their husbands or their husbands' friends, which struck terror in the hearts of many wives. Not Qira, of course. Lot had no reason to wish her dead. The wives who were murdered during those days of chaos were rumored to be the ones who had tried to interfere with their husbands' friendships. Since Lot had no friends in the city, Qira had nothing to worry about.

When the king and the leading citizens returned, they found it impossible to get the streets back under control. The king came up with the bright idea of creating bands of citizen-soldiers to patrol the streets by night, and this became quite a popular idea—there was hardly a man of any stature in the city who did not join one of the patrols. Lot, of course, refused to take part, saying that the patrols were not going to be much help to public safety.

Which turned out to be the case, to Qira's surprise. The patrols looked so fine when they paraded by day, each group with its own costume, competing with each other in their finery. But by night, the killings did not stop, though the choice of victims changed. The victims now seemed to be foreigners or low-class men who ventured out after dark. Word soon spread that the killings had been done by the patrols themselves in their effort to keep the streets "safe," but the victims were hardly dangerous. And darker rumors began to spread. "The patrols chase them," said Qira's friend Jashi. "For sport."

"Sport?" said Qira. "Like hunting gazelles?"

"And when they catch them," said Jashi, curling her mouth in disgust, "they use them up."

Qira had no idea what that meant, but she didn't want to ask and appear foolish. So she nodded knowingly and then, later, asked her handmaid what such a thing might mean—for she knew that the servants talked among themselves.

"Mistress, they use them for pleasure," said the girl, "and then for pain."

This was hardly more information than Jashi had given. But when Qira pressed for more information, the girl became so frightened and upset that Qira gave up. Servants were useless for anything really important.

Whatever they were doing, the patrols were getting bolder every day. Naturally, men who were not in the patrols had stopped venturing out after dark, so the patrols had begun going to the homes of foreigners and dragging the men out in order to chase them. But when the king demanded an accounting, the leaders of the patrols denied any knowledge of the event, even when the women of the house identified them by name. The members of each patrol simply gave their oaths to the king that they had been patrolling in a different part of the city and had seen nothing like what the women described. What could be done? Apart from the king's bodyguard, he had no army except for the very men who were in the patrols. And each patrol was sponsored by a leading citizen. There was hardly a man of any stature in Sodom who was not involved with one patrol or another.

"My husband hates it," said Jashi. "But when I tell him that he should quit, he looks at me as if I were stupid and says, 'In this city, you're either a hunter or the prey.' Well, *I'm* not either one, that's what I tell him, and he says, 'You don't even exist in this city,' which I find offensive, I must say. Didn't I push him into the friendships that led him to membership in the most prestigious of the patrols? Some of the patrols may do nasty things, but the streets *are* safe by night, and no more women are being killed. And boys will be boys. We women have to look the other way, that's all there is to it."

Qira knew well that Jashi was right. Just like tonight. Qira could warn Lot that it would not do to bring visitors into the city, but if he was so vain as to think that his personal prestige in the city would protect them if he flaunted them right out in the open, well, what could Qira do about it?

How did he know these visitors were coming, anyway? As far as she knew, there had been no messenger. He just seemed to know, suddenly, that travelers were coming and that he had to go meet them at the gate of the city.

Lot had been gone for hours, and the sun was just setting, when a servant called Qira to the door. It was a man in the costume of the same patrol that Jashi's husband was in, though he was a young man, and Qira didn't know him.

"Mistress Qira," said the young man, "they'd kill me if they knew I came here, please tell no one."

"How could I? I don't know who you are."

"Everyone's very angry at your husband. He says he's waiting for visitors to come to him, but he won't say who they are. There's a lot of talk about how Lot is flouting the authority of the king's patrols, and it's time to show him that he doesn't rule in Sodom."

"What can I do? He doesn't listen to me."

"Don't let him bring these visitors here tonight. There's talk of taking them, if he doesn't give them up."

"But . . . we're citizens!"

"There's talk about how you aren't really citizens. You're from Ur-of-the-North, and he's a Hebrew."

"But it was because of Lot that Sodom was saved from Chedorlaomer!"

"That was thirteen years ago," said the young man. "When I was four. The men don't care about that now. They don't like the way Lot thinks he's better than everybody else. They aren't grateful, they hate him."

This was worse than Qira had feared. "But if everyone hates him, why are *you* here?"

The young man wanted to leave, she could see that. And he didn't want to tell her. But still he stayed, and with his face twisted as if the words hurt to speak them, the young man said, "When I was a boy and the patrols were just starting, my father used to share me with the other men. It hurt but I couldn't even cry because my father would beat me if I didn't smile and say I liked it. And then one day Lot and some of his servants came to my father's house. I don't know what he said or did, but my father stopped lending me to his friends. In fact, he left me alone himself after that. Tell your husband the warning came from a boy he saved once."

Qira watched as the boy darted away from the house, then closed the door and had a servant bar it. Moments later she thought better of that. She called the servant back to the door and made him open it. "Leave it standing open," said Qira, "and stand here to watch for the master." Then Qira went through the house and sent several more servants to the door to stand watch there. "Be ready to close and bar the door behind him."

All the while, Qira pondered what the young man had said. She had heard that young boys often were included in the men's parties, but it had never occurred to her that they might not be there willingly. And Lot, who seemed oblivious to what went on in the city—he had found out, somehow, and intervened to protect a boy whose family Qira didn't even know. Surely Qira would have heard a rumor about such an event. Unless the boy's father simply never talked about what had passed between them.

But Lot should have told her. She *was* his wife, after all. Besides, it was a foolish thing for Lot to be doing. What if he tried such a thing with someone who was dangerously powerful? It might have had repercussions for Qira and for their two youngest daughters, did Lot think of that? It was bad enough that he would not allow the girls to entertain any suitors. "I won't allow any more of my girls to marry men of Sodom or any of the cities of Siddim," he said. Qira had wept and howled and vilified him for that. "The older girls have married perfectly respectable young men of good families!" she cried, but that did no good—Lot had taken it into his head to hate his sons-in-law, even though they were always perfectly respectful to him. He was so judgmental, condemning perfectly nice people just because they went to parties and didn't bring their wives. Arguing had done no good. Lot remained adamant—his youngest girls were going to marry Hebrew men, or perhaps men of Salem. Well, Qira wouldn't hear of *that*, either—she hadn't raised these girls to be the wives of shepherds, or to live in some mountain village. They were still in the midst of that particular war, and the poor girls cried themselves to sleep as often as not. They were getting old enough that it was a little scandalous they weren't yet married.

The sky was almost dark when, finally, she heard the servants at the door speak in greeting. Qira rushed to the door, meaning to tell Lot at once about the young man's warning, but Lot had no interest in talking to her. All he seemed to care about was the two visitors. Qira didn't know them, and they didn't look like anybody important—their clothing was very plain, the costume of poor men, not merchants at all. And when one of them stopped and looked at her for a moment, his eyes were very disturbing. He seemed to see right into her, and to pity her. Which made her furious. She tilted her chin in disdain and looked away from him.

Looked, in fact, right into Lot's face. There was no pity in *him*. He was looking at her, not with that distant who-stepped-on-this-bug expression, but with open contempt.

"Aren't you going to introduce me to your guests?" said Qira archly.

"You've never heard of them," said Lot, "and neither have your friends, so it wouldn't matter." He ushered the men into the room where he talked business, and closed the door.

Well, so much for the young man's warning. Qira couldn't help it if her husband was so rude to his wife that he didn't even give her a chance to speak. Let him find out the hard way.

Only a few moments later, however, Qira realized that the young man's warning was more important than her anger at the contemptuous way Lot had treated her. He had spoken of a patrol breaking into the house, and that put them all in danger. Even if Lot didn't care what danger he brought to the house, Qira did. She'd knock on his door and make him deal with her.

But as she passed the front door of the house, she heard a commotion outside, and something banged against the door. The old servant at the door opened the small viewport and turned back to her, shaking his head. "There's no one there," he said.

"Open it and see if someone left something," said Qira. "I heard something strike the door."

The servant unbarred the door. At once it fell open as if someone were pushing on it, and when the servant stepped back, a man fell partway into the entry hall. He was naked, and skin had been stripped away from his flesh on his arms and chest. His eyes were open and something bloody was in his mouth and Qira couldn't understand why he didn't spit it out and say something.

And then she understood after all. He was dead.

It was the young man who had warned her.

She screamed.

At once Lot and the visitors rushed out, and Lot ordered the servants to get the body out of the doorway. Qira started to tell him who it was, what the young man had said, but Lot cut her off. "I know him," he said. And then his eyes turned to the doorway. For there was someone there.

Qira stepped to where she could see what Lot was looking at.

It was the patrol that the young man had belonged to—the same costumes. But there were the costumes of at least two other patrols there, also, and Qira could see torches burning far enough away that it seemed as though all the men of Sodom had gathered in the street outside their house. The men nearest the door were smiling. Some were young, some middle-aged, some old—but their faces were all the same, their eyes glistening in the light of the torches some of them held, an intensity of expectation on their faces. Like hungry men looking at a feast. Like cats who have spotted a rat.

"We hear you have visitors," said one of the men. "Our job is to keep the peace here. Bring them out, so we can know them."

Qira looked up at Lot, to see what he would say. He seemed to be considering what the man had said, and he half-turned, as if to give an instruction to the servants. But instead, he slammed the door shut and dropped the heavy bar into place. His movement came suddenly enough that the men outside had no time to react before the bar was in place; but it terrified Qira, the force with which they slammed against the door and pounded on it. A great shout went up from the men in the street, and then the babble of many voices crying out.

Lot stood there looking at the visitors, who looked back at him wordlessly.

"That young man tried to warn us," said Qira. "I would have told you, but you didn't bother to give me a chance to speak."

Outside the door, snatches of the shouting could be distinguished from the general tumult.

"Letting spies into the city!"

"Hebrew traitor!"

"Too proud to let us court your daughters!"

"Never a true man of Sodom!"

Lot turned to Qira, but it was as if he hadn't heard a thing she said. "Bring the girls here," he said.

"What for?" said Qira.

Lot turned to one of the servants and repeated the order.

One of the visitors spoke. "We're in no danger, Lot."

"You don't know these patrols," said Lot. "This is a city of monsters now."

"No," said the man sadly. "It's a city of men."

"I will not let them take you," said Lot. "I'll die first, I and everyone in my house."

"I tell you, Lot, they can't hurt us."

The servant reappeared with the girls following.

Lot opened the viewport. "Stand away from the door," he shouted. "Let me come out to you."

There was more shouting outside the door, but after a few moments Lot was satisfied. He unbarred the door. "Close it and bar it after me, and don't open it unless I say. No matter what they do to me."

"Lot," said the visitor, "you don't need to—"

But Lot was already through the door, and it closed behind him.

Qira could hear him as the girls came close to her, frightened by the noise even though they hadn't seen the tortured body of the young man. Qira held their hands.

They could hear Lot speaking loudly to the crowd outside. "My brothers of Sodom, I beg you, don't do this terrible thing."

"We don't know what you're talking about," said the leader. "We only want to do our duty and find out whether these men are dangerous to the safety of Sodom."

Qira looked at the visitors. Whoever they were, if they had any decency they would go out themselves and answer whatever questions the patrols had. By staying here inside the house they were exposing the whole family to danger. Lot couldn't make them do it, because he had taken them as guests. But they could take the decision out of his hands, if they weren't so selfish and cowardly. She glared at them, but they looked at her as coolly as if she didn't exist.

"I have two virgin daughters," Lot said. "I know some of you have tried to court them. Let me bring them out to you now, and you decide among you which of you should have them to wife. You can have them tonight, with their dowries, whichever men you choose."

The girls clung to their mother.

"This is monstrous," Qira said.

One of the visitors spoke mildly. "Your daughters are safe."

"What do you know about it?" said Qira.

Outside, they had apparently considered Lot's offer. "If we wanted your daughters," said the spokesman, "we would have had them already."

"Bring out the spies," someone said.

"Let's see how fast they can run!" cried another.

"Let's see how many riders they can carry!" cried another, and there was much laughter.

"You can do as you see fit with my daughters!" cried Lot. "But you can't have my guests! I gave them the shelter of my roof!"

"We can have what we want!" shouted the spokesman. "Listen to how this Lot talks to us! He came here as a foreigner and we gave him the hospitality of our city, and now he thinks he can judge us! He thinks he rules in our city!"

The crowd roared its disapproval.

"Stand out of the way, Lot," cried the spokesman, "or we'll deal worse with you than we do with your precious guests!"

"The king won't tolerate you harming me or anyone in my house!"

"The king!" shouted the spokesman derisively. "The king knows our sport, you fool. He plays with us, and he's tired of you, just as we are! We're done with talking!"

Something slammed against the door.

"They've killed him!" cried Qira.

"No they haven't," said one of the visitors. "The Lord won't allow it."

"The Lord the Lord the Lord!" cried Qira. "I hear Him talked about, but He never does anything!"

Again and again the men outside slammed against the door. The bar couldn't hold much longer. It was meant to keep out a thief, not an army.

The visitors walked to the door and raised the bar.

"It's about time you gave yourselves up," said Qira angrily. "My husband could have been killed out there!"

They opened the door. The men outside looked hungrily at them.

"Come out and join the sport," said the spokesman. "We've been waiting for you."

The visitors said nothing as they stepped out.

Lot was being pressed against the wall by several men. One of the visitors reached out his hand toward Lot.

"Yes," said the spokesman, "let him go. The king likes him. It's the only reason we haven't used him up years ago."

They let go of Lot. He staggered to the visitors. "Don't do this," he said to them. "Please."

"I told you," said one of the visitors. "They have no power over us."

The other visitor ushered Lot inside.

The one who remained outside the door raised his hand. "You cannot harm what you cannot see," he said.

Qira could see the faces of some of the men outside. Could see how their expressions changed, how their eyes darted around, how they began to reach out as if they were in a fog, trying to feel their way toward the door. "Where is he!" "I can't see!" "Get them!" "Where are they!"

The visitor stepped inside and closed and barred the door behind him. The shouting in the street turned into wails and weeping and howling for help. There were arguments as blind men trod on each other or bumped each other, and curses as they fell, screams as they were trampled.

"You struck them blind," said Qira. It had never occurred to her that Lot's talk of God might actually mean something. These men really had power.

But the visitors ignored her. They spoke only to Lot. "Do you have any family besides these? Sons-in-law? Sons? You have time enough to warn them and bring them with you. But there's no time to take any of your possessions. Leave everything and flee this place. Don't come back for any reason."

"How far?" asked Lot.

"Into the hills southeast of the city," said the visitors. "God will not delay the destruction of this place. If you stop for any reason, you'll be destroyed along with Sodom."

Destroyed! The words sounded absurd to Qira. "If Chedorlaomer could not destroy Sodom, what makes you think—"

The man looked at her, saying nothing. But she fell silent all the same.

"Go find your family in the city," said the visitor. "Leave this city at the first light of dawn. Anyone who isn't with you then is lost."

"Thank you," said Lot. "The blessing of God upon you."

"And upon you and your family," said the visitor. "All of them who will accept it."

Lot unbarred the door.

"No!" cried Qira.

"There's no danger from blind men," said Lot. He went out into the darkness.

"You don't really think," said Qira to the visitors, "that we'll be gone long, do you? I mean, how much clothing should we take?"

They looked at her like she was crazy. "Take the clothes you're wearing, and enough wine or water for a few days. You'll have your lives. That's more than anyone else in Sodom will have."

Their words frightened her. "You really mean it? Everyone will *die?*"

"Has there ever been a city so wholly given over to evil?" asked the visitor. "There's not one man or woman here who is not complicit in the wickedness. There's not one child here who has a hope of growing up without being destroyed by the wickedness. The adults will die in order to face the judgment of God. The innocent children will be taken up in the mercy of the Lord."

"But why should *we* lose our home?" said Qira. "*We've* done nothing wrong!"

"It's for your husband's sake that the Lord offers to spare you, mistress," said one of the visitors.

"Are you saying I'm as wicked as—well, I don't think the city *is* that wicked! These patrols, they're out of hand, yes, we've got to put a stop to that, but the women of Sodom haven't done anything wrong!"

"None of you is innocent," said one of them.

"The fiery stones have already been flung from the heavens," said the other. "There is no stopping them now."

They turned away then and returned to the room where they had been closeted with Lot.

Qira took her daughters to their rooms. "Gather two gowns each, and your jewelry," she said. "I suppose we'll have room for nothing more than that. We can take one trunk, I'm sure."

She went to her room and busied herself choosing. She finally settled on four gowns, because she just couldn't limit herself to two.

Hours later, Lot came back alone. "They won't come," he said, dejected. "Our brilliant sons-in-law vilified me, and our daughters condemned me for not obeying the patrols tonight. They paid no attention at all to my warning."

"What did you expect?" said Qira. "It's not particularly believable. If I hadn't seen them strike those men blind I wouldn't believe anything they said."

"Well, they *did* see it," said Lot.

"They were watching?" asked Qira, surprised.

"Our sons-in-law are as blind as any of the others," said Lot.

"Oh, you're always saying that everyone in Sodom is blind, as if you're the only one who knows anything," said Qira.

"I mean," said Lot, "that our sons-in-law were among the men struck blind as they gathered at our door."

Qira was stunned. "They must have been passing by. Mere chance."

"Believe what you want," said Lot. "Why are you putting those dresses and jewels in that trunk?"

"You don't expect me to go naked, do you?"

"Who's going to carry the trunk?" asked Lot.

"The servants, of course," said Qira.

"I've already dismissed them all," said Lot. "With a warning to tell every other servant they know—be out of Sodom before dawn, and head for the hills southeast of the city. I don't know if any of them believed me. But there's no reason the slaves should die for the sins of the masters."

"You're—you're fomenting a revolt among the slaves!"

"They won't be slaves when God has slain their masters," said Lot. He slammed shut the lid of the trunk. "We're taking nothing with us but wine to drink. It will take all our strength to carry that, and still make good enough speed to reach the hills in time. Now go to sleep, so you can keep up with us in the morning."

Sleep! Oh, that was rich. She's supposed to sleep, when he's talking about leaving everything behind? The things these Hebrew men thought they could get away with, ordering women about as if they had no minds of their own. If he'd stupidly sent away the servants, then he'd have to carry the trunk himself, unless he wanted everyone to see the shameful spectacle of his wife and daughters carrying a trunk with their own hands through the city.

By the time she had packed her things, the girls were asleep. They had chosen their gowns and laid out their jewels before they went to bed—they knew which parent had their best interests at heart!—and it took a while longer for Qira to fit everything in the trunk. In the end, she had to settle for only two dresses for herself after all— she hoped her daughters would appreciate her sacrifice.

Nothing was going to happen anyway. These men might have the power to blind a crowd of half-drunken soldiers, but burning stones from heaven? Stones couldn't burn, and they didn't fall from the sky. How stupid did they think she was? Tales to frighten children. She'd go along with her husband's madness because what choice did a woman have? But then they'd have to come crawling back to town, humiliated. Well, she wouldn't have it. They'd have to stay away for at least a few weeks, to pretend they were visiting Sarai—no, Sarah, that stupid vanity of changing her name, what was that about, anyway?—they'd say they were visiting relatives and no one would know about this embarrassing delusion.

No, of course they'd know. Lot had sent the servants around to stir up trouble everywhere! That was a crime, didn't he know that? There were laws. What if they couldn't persuade the king to forgive him for that? Inciting slaves to run away, that was unforgivable.

Even after Qira finally got to bed, she could hardly sleep for worrying about how they might solve the problems that this madness of Lot's had caused. No one would be more hated in Sodom than they were. They could never come back. It was that simple. All was lost. Sodom might or might not be destroyed, but one thing was certain— Lot had destroyed her and her daughters! They'd have to start over again in another city, but who would have them anywhere? They'd be no better off than lepers.

She must have slept because Lot was shaking her awake. She could barely open her eyes. It was still dark outside.

"Go away," she said.

"It's first light," he said.

"Not to me," she said.

"Get up, woman," said Lot rudely. "Your daughters need you."

It was the most horrible morning. Lot was a tyrant. He refused to carry the trunk. She had to get the girls to carry one end while she carried the other, all the time making sure Lot knew how shameful it was that he allowed his womenfolk to do manual labor like this in the streets, it was a good thing it was so early in the morning that no decent person would see them doing it. Lot, who was burdened with carafes of wine for them to drink, ignored

her at first, but then turned back and took the trunk out
of their hands.

"It's about time," said Qira.

Lot raised the trunk above his head and dashed it into
the street. It broke open on the stones, spilling gowns and
jewelry.

Qira shrieked and knelt to pick up some of the fallen
pieces of jewelry. "Look what you've done, any thief
could come along and—"

But Lot dragged her to her feet, slapping the jewels she
was holding out of her hands. "We have no time for this."
Brutally he pulled her along. The girls were crying now
as they followed after. "You're hurting Mother!" they
cried. But Lot was merciless. The man had no pity for
anyone. His true nature was revealed now.

Right through the streets of Sodom he dragged them.
"We're poor now, did you think of that?" said Qira. "All
we have is those stupid sheep and cows out in the desert.
Nothing left to show that we ever lived in a city. Did you
ever think of that? How will the girls find a husband now?
What dowry will you offer? *Cows?*"

"Cows are what I paid for you," said Lot.

She wasn't sure what he meant by that.

They were outside the city now.

"You can let go of me now," she said. "You've made
your point."

But he dragged her along anyway. The girls joined in
her complaints. "Father, you're hurting her. There's no
reason to act like this. You're just being mean now."

He paid no attention. Not until they were in the foothills
did he finally let go. Her wrist hurt so badly that she cried
as she rubbed it. "I hate you," she said to Lot.

"Tell me something new," he said. He handed her a
carafe of wine. "Sling this over your shoulder and carry
it yourself now."

"I'm not a servant," said Qira.

Lot ignored her as he put carafes of wine on the girls.
It broke Qira's heart to see her beautiful daughters carry-

ing burdens as if they were beasts. But she took her own carafe of wine then, to show them that she, too, would submit to the rule of this cruel man. They were not alone—their mother was with them, and somehow she'd make this all right.

They hiked another hundred steps up into the hills when Qira stopped. "Enough of this. We're in the hills southeast of the city, just like they said. Let's not go any farther, so we don't have so far to go when we return."

"We're never going to return," said Lot.

"We did what they said," Qira responded patiently. "They told you we wouldn't have time to get this far if we delayed at all. Well, here we are. I don't see any destruction, do you?"

"It will begin at any moment," said Lot.

"We made very good time, with you dragging us. We have plenty of time. In fact," said Qira, "it's still early enough that I'll bet no one has found our trunk. It was foolish of you not to let me bring at least a few of the nicest pieces. Those are very expensive and it will take years to find others just as good."

"You're not going back," said Lot. "If you do, you'll die."

"Is that a threat?" said Qira. "Are you threatening to kill me?"

"I'm warning you again of what the Lord is going to do to anyone in Sodom."

"I can go and come back again in no time," said Qira.

"I forbid you."

Qira looked at him and assessed his intentions. He was talking very firmly, and yet he did not take a step toward her to restrain her. He had lost some of his resolve, she could see it. "You can forbid me all you like, but am I not a free woman?"

"Don't leave your daughters motherless," said Lot. "They're already going to lose three of their sisters."

"Pay no attention to your father," said Qira. "Come back with me, girls."

Now Lot moved—to grab hold of the girls. But with his hands occupied holding them, he couldn't possibly stop her now. He'd have to let go of someone.

"I'll be back soon," said Qira.

Then she turned back to the city.

"Mother!" cried her daughters, but when Qira glanced back, she could see that Lot was dragging the girls farther up into the hills. Finally he had come to his senses and realized that his wife was the daughter of a king, and not someone to be dragged about like a disobedient child.

If she hurried, she could surely reach the jewels. Even now, the sun was just beginning to cast light on the tallest buildings in Gomorrah, which was not so close to the hills in the east. No one was awake at this hour, surely. Though Qira couldn't be sure—she had never awoken so early in all the years she had lived in Sodom.

She was distressed to see how many servants were out on the streets already. Not crowds, but enough that someone was bound to have noticed the trunk. And slaves were such natural thieves that they were bound to steal at least one piece of jewelry. She began to run. She had to get there before it was all gone. She had to salvage *something* of her life in Sodom, didn't she?

A terrible roar sounded in her ears, and a hot wind blasted through the streets. The earth seemed to heave underneath her, and she fell sprawling in the hard-packed street. What was it? What had happened?

People were emerging from their houses, looking frightened. Someone climbed onto a roof and shouted down what he had seen. "Gomorrah is on fire!" he cried. "It's all smoke, and half the city is gone!"

Suddenly terror struck in Qira's heart. Half the city gone! And the earth shaking like that—the visitors had said nothing about earthquakes. This was worse than she had ever imagined. Why didn't they tell her it would be so bad that half of Gomorrah could be wiped out in an instant? Why didn't Lot stop her from going? She realized now—he *wanted* her to go. He dragged her and ordered her about just because he knew it would make her angry enough to make her run back to the city. This was what he planned from the start. He was trying to get her killed!

She started to run back the way she had come. Lot might want her dead, but her girls still needed her. And now that they knew it was real, her sons-in-law would surely not forbid her to bring her older daughters with her. The house of the eldest was just over this way—she could run past there and get her daughter and bring her out of the city and . . .

And a stone about two cubits across tore through the sky and exploded in the air just above the city of Sodom. The shock wave flattened every building. The fireball instantly burned everything within a half mile. The sound of it could be heard as far away as Hebron. Qira's sister Sarah heard it, and felt the trembling of the earth.

Later, there would be stories about how one of those pillars of salt near the dead sea was Qira, turned to salt by the power of God because she turned back to watch the destruction of Sodom. But the truth was what Sarah knew in her heart when she heard the sound of the explosion, and felt the shaking of the earth, and then saw the brightness in the sky that lasted all through the following night. Five great stones hit the earth or exploded above it, one for each of the cities of Siddim. No one was left alive except for the few slaves who had made their escape during the night. And Lot and two of his daughters.

Sarah grieved for her sister. For many days she grieved. Not because Qira had died—Qira was not young, and death was not the worst thing in the world. No, Sarah grieved because she knew how wasted her sister's life had been, and how pointless her death, and how empty the soul that she would have to show before the judgment bar of God.

O God, was there something I could have done to save her? Sarah prayed.

The answer came from her own heart, for she knew

that there was never a time in Qira's life when anything Sarah might have said or done could have reached past her pride and touched her heart. Qira controlled her own life, and so she had nothing at the end of it. While Sarah had given her life to others, and never controlled it at all—and so her heart was full of treasures, and if she died, she would die with little fear of seeing the face of God.

She had something else, too. For several months later, it was very plain that Sarah, old as she was, had a child in her. Conceived on the night before Sodom was destroyed. God had performed many wonders that day. Lives were taken. A life was given. In Sarah's womb, a great nation had been given its first moments of life. His name would be Isaac. Sarah's grief for her sister was lost in her joy at the stirring, finally, of life in her belly.

PART VIII

ISAAC

❧ CHAPTER 22 ❧

For all these years that she had been with Abraham, Sarah had cared for the smooth running of the camp. Abraham could leave when he needed to and stay away for weeks at a time, knowing that all would be in good order when he returned, for Sarah would deal with any problems that came up.

So it galled her that her pregnancy might cause the good order of the camp to be disrupted. Her plan was to live as she had always lived—to spend her days in the door of the tent until the morning of the day her son was born, and then, by evening of that day, to again be in the door of the tent, keeping her ear to the heartbeat of Abraham's household.

After all, Qira had not been ill with her pregnancies, not the way Hagar had been. Why shouldn't Sarah expect to be more like her sister than like her handmaid? And, in fact, despite some nausea, Sarah never did get particularly sick. But that didn't mean her life could go on as it normally did.

Because she was not young. As her belly grew, the joints of her hips began to feel loose and painful, as if they might dislocate at any time. Her back ached so that she could hardly rise in the morning or lie down at night. And one thing that was utterly out of the question was for her to sit, hour after hour, distaff in hand, at the door of the tent.

So because her body did not have the resiliency of youth, she ended up lying down in her tent. For three days she lay there, sending servants away because she wanted them to be about their regular duty, then having to call out for them because she needed help to do things that it shamed her not to be able to handle for herself.

Through it all, Abraham stayed close to the camp, even though Sarah urged him to go about his business. "*You* are my business," said Abraham, "and so staying by you is going about my business."

"I don't want anything to change because I'm having a baby," said Sarah.

"Everything has changed already," said Abraham. "You're the only one who refuses to see that."

Sarah understood exactly what he meant, but it didn't matter. She couldn't abide staying cooped up in her tent while the life of the camp went on around her. She told Abraham, "I don't want Eliezer to know that he doesn't need me."

"He knows he doesn't need *me*," said Abraham. "What makes you think he doesn't know the same about you?"

"He does need you," said Sarah. "You're the authority in whose name he makes all his decisions. The only thing that brings him to me is . . ."

And then she realized how foolish she had been. Eliezer did not come to her anymore because he did not know what to do without her wisdom. He came to her because of loyalty. Because she needed to be a part of everything.

She could stay in her tent and be pampered and it would make no difference.

But if that's true, I could die in my tent and it would

also make no difference. And when you come down to it, everyone eventually dies, and life goes on, so no one is needed for anything if that's the test. When I'm out there by the tent door, I do relieve Eliezer of much of his burden. He doesn't need me to tell him what to do—he needs me to settle petty problems so he can deal with more important ones. I serve him and I serve Abraham by easing their burden. I don't do these things because they can't do them, I do them so that they don't have to. And even though they're happy to take up the slack during my pregnancy, I will be far happier if they don't have any slack to take up.

So she ordered a litter to be made, and every morning had two maidservants lay her upon the litter and arrange her clothing around her. Then two men came in and carried her out into the shade at the door of her tent. Lying there, she could not use the distaff, but she could embroider so her fingers would be busy while she listened and talked to those who came to her. Several times during the day they would move her litter so it would stay in the shade, And by lying down so much, she conserved enough strength and flexibility that she was able sit up to deal with personal needs, shielded from view by the maids.

That was the compromise that allowed her to get through the months while the baby grew within her. It helped keep her mind off her fears for the baby. What if the child was deformed or feeble-minded? She had heard so many stories of what could go wrong. Of course she knew that it was a miracle for her to have the baby growing inside her at all, and that God, having done that much, would have no difficulty in protecting her child and making sure he was born hearty and strong. But she could not help but fret, all the same, and it was good to stay busy.

The one thing she never feared was to die in childbirth. As long as the child survived, she would have accomplished her purpose. Oh, if she were twenty or thirty years old, she would long for the years she might spend with her child and fear death greatly. But at her age she knew that the chance of her living long enough to see Isaac reach manhood was slim indeed. The rearing of this child would almost certainly be in other hands someday. He would most likely learn of his mother through the stories he was told. Let him be told that his mother worked to help his father until the day she died. And if that turned out to have been the day he was born, it made for all the better a tale around the fire.

Only one of her fears was real, and therefore that was the one she could not face. Hagar.

Ishmael was born to be the heir, but only because Sarah could not have a child of her own. Now that Sarah was pregnant, the child within her was the only one who could inherit when Abraham died, for only he was a child of Abraham's wife. Hagar was not even a concubine.

Abraham loved Ishmael. Everyone knew that, and knew as well that Abraham was a fair and generous man. Ishmael would be well taken care of. And Hagar, too.

Yet Sarah knew how this would look to Hagar. Though there had been peace between them for fourteen years, it was a peace based on balance. Sarah was the wife, with great authority and respect from all. But Hagar was the mother of the heir, and that also gave her an unassailable position.

Now that position was gone. Sarah was wife and mother, and Hagar was nothing except insofar as Abraham, out of charity, doled out favors to her in memory of her useful service some fourteen years ago. Or so it would seem to Hagar. The old hungers and fears were bound to return.

And yet if Sarah so much as mentioned any of this to Hagar, even if she was trying to reassure her, it would only make things worse, for Hagar would take it as confirmation that Sarah was plotting against her. How else could it look to someone who had already lost everything once before in her life? Oh, Sarah understood well. Her heart ached in sympathy for this young woman who, despite all the pain between them, had once been Sarah's closest woman-friend. Hagar was the one who had been Sarah's companion and comfort and, yes, guide in the Pharaoh's house. Hagar had given the use of her body in Sarah's service. The debt was great, and the love, however strained, was still strong for her in Sarah's heart. But she could not speak of this to Hagar. She could only watch, and dread.

For one thing was certain. No matter how the rest of the camp might long for the baby Isaac to be born, and dote on him after he appeared, there would be one woman who hated him because he had taken the place of her son.

What made this secret harder to bear was the fact that she was the only one who knew it. For only Sarah had grown up in a king's house, knowing all the family lore of dynastic struggles, assassinations, poisonings, maneuverings behind the curtains and under the sheets, all to secure a throne for this child instead of that one. The bitterest stories she learned from her father were the tales of fratricide and parricide. The sons who could not wait to inherit, and so rebelled against their fathers. The wives who feared their husbands would choose the wrong child, and so poisoned the rivals. The young men who, upon acceding to the throne, had their brothers murdered. The royal uncle who somehow "forgot" to feed his sickly nephews, the little princes, so that they passed away and the regent inherited the throne after all.

She tried to tell herself that only royal houses had such problems. Shepherd families did not kill each other to get control of some wells, some sheep, some tents.

But Abraham's house *was* a royal family. Kings were priests first, soldiers second, rulers third. Abraham was all three. And he had the promise of God that his descendants would rule the land of Canaan. Hagar would have to be a fool not to know what her son was going to be deprived of because of Isaac's birth.

She would not be in a hurry, though. She was still young. Abraham and Sarah both were old. How long could they live, after Isaac's birth? What if Sarah lived till Isaac was three? What if Abraham lived five years after that? Isaac would be eight years old, and Ishmael would be a man of twenty-two. By then he would have had time to make friends and gather followers. He wouldn't even have to lift a finger himself. One of the men would do it for him. Or perhaps Hagar would. Whoever it was, Ishmael could be outraged, could deny that he ever wanted such a thing. He could have the killer strangled over Isaac's grave. Whatever show he wanted to put on. All that mattered was that Isaac would not outlive Abraham by a week.

That was the fear that lived in the back of Sarah's mind. That was what she tried so desperately not to think of while she lay on the litter, her belly growing above her brittle bones. That was the one thing she never mentioned to Abraham during all those months until at last the child was born.

It was a terrible birth. The midwives commiserated with her and tried to comfort her, but she could see how frightened and frustrated they were. Her body was too old. She hadn't the strength in the muscles of her back and belly to push the child out. Nor could she give birth squatting: Her bones were too brittle, her joints too frail to sustain her in that position. For hours she lay in the pangs of birth, as the child waited in vain, unable even to show the crown of its head.

Of course Sarah prayed. For her baby, for herself. After all the years that she had been barren, her womb unused, the passages of her body closed, it was no surprise that the baby should have trouble being born. But if the Lord had done the miracle of letting these two old people conceive a baby, shouldn't He go ahead and finish the job? She prayed and complained and pleaded and, yes, demanded, for in the throes of pain she did not care about the protocols of addressing God, and instead spoke to Him as one would speak to a friend whose help was needed and who, for reasons known only to Him, was standing uselessly by.

Then there came the moment when, once again, she remembered that the goddess of childbirth was Asherah, the one that Sarah had repudiated by marrying Abraham. Was there some divine struggle going on over the baby in her womb, the God of her husband battling with the stubborn, angry, vengeful goddess of her childhood?

O God of Abraham, help me drive such thoughts from my mind! I know that Asherah is nothing, a misunderstanding, a memory of Mother Eve and not a god of any kind. I know that I sinned against no one when I broke the vow that gave me to her. And yet the fear and pain drive the thought of her through my body like a tent spike and I cannot pry her out. O God, deliver me of this baby, pull him out of my body and let me die, if that be Thy will, only let me die forgiven for having thought of Asherah again.

The baby suddenly slid down, and a midwife said, "Ah, there's the little one." Another pain. Another sensation of release, of sliding, of her body being pried open like a butchered sheep and all of her insides slopping out and she tried to scream at the pain and terror but all that came from her throat was a gurgling sound and she thought, This is death.

"A little man," said the midwife.

A baby cried.

"God is merciful to his daughter!" cried Sarah.

"She's whispering something," said someone.

"God watch over my son!" she shouted.

"Hush, sleep." A hand stroked her forehead. And as if the words had some power in them, she could not stay awake another moment, but slipped into the darkness of sleep, not knowing if it was the sleep from which the dreamer never wakens, and at that moment not caring either. The child was born. Her boy was alive.

She woke again and again, each time surprised to be alive at all, and then surprised by the pain that still gnawed at her. Hadn't the child come out after all? Was this going to go on forever? And then back down into the darkness of sleep.

Finally she awoke and did not feel so much pain. Nor did she collapse again. She saw only darkness around her. Then she realized that her eyes were not open. She parted her eyelids and saw that there was faint light coming from somewhere. She was thirsty. Her mouth was so dry that she could feel her lips split open like sun-dried mud.

"Water," she whispered.

Someone stirred beside her. Her handmaid, of course. She closed her eyes and waited. Soon water splashed over her lips. She licked with her tongue, drew water inside her mouth. More trickled in. She managed to swallow some through a throat that seemed to have been mortared shut. That was enough. Sleep reached for her again. "Thank you, Hagar," Sarah murmured.

At last, hours later, she woke to daylight. Her mouth was dry again, but this time she could see who lay beside her. Abraham. What was he thinking, to lie by a woman who was not yet purified? But then, why not? If she died, what would it matter then?

"Abraham," she whispered.

He woke, and almost at once reached for a flagon of water and offered it to her, just as Hagar had offered it last night, a splash over the lips, a trickle into the open mouth. "More?" he asked.

"It was you last night," she said.

"Not Hagar, no," said Abraham.

"Where's my baby?"

"He's with a wetnurse. A woman from Hebron and a shepherd's wife are taking turns with him."

"Is he whole?"

"Strong and healthy, all the right parts to his body," said Abraham. "As beautiful as if his mother had been a bride of only one year."

"How long have I been asleep?"

"Three days," said Abraham. "It was hard on you, that birth."

"I thought of Asherah," she confessed at once.

"You can think of Satan himself. What of that? Did you pray to her?"

"No, I prayed to God, but I feared her all the same."

"You were filled with fear, and Asherah was a name that came to mind." Abraham kissed her forehead. "Fear nothing, Princess. God knows you are worthy. Your heart turned to Him in your pain. And more than that, my love. When hands gave you water in the darkness, you called the waterbringer by the name of your friend."

She remembered last night, the water. "Hagar," said Sarah.

"It was only your husband," said Abraham.

"I'm sorry, I couldn't see."

"In your heart, you have forgiven her."

Sarah closed her eyes. "Have I?"

"You spoke her name so gratefully."

"I was in the madness of a dream," said Sarah. "All the years were fled, and it was she who slept at my feet. But no, Abraham, you judge me too kindly. I have not forgiven her. I fear her more than ever." And then she poured out her heart, all her fears for her son.

Abraham listened gravely. When she had finished explaining all and then explaining her explanations because he was so adamantly silent, showing nothing on his face, when she had no more words left to say, she concluded, "Now you know the evil in my heart, and how I judge the mother of your first son."

"My firstborn son, in the eyes of God and the law, is Isaac," said Abraham, "because only he was born of the body of my wife. And I am not as utterly innocent as you think me. Do you think I don't know the same tales that have haunted your nightmares? Hagar has shown no sign of resentment, but she's shown no great joy, either. But Eliezer keeps two men awake all night and watching through the day. I told myself that such a thing was foolishness, that no one would harm our son. But . . . who knows what dark thoughts might find purchase in some-one's heart?"

"What will we do about Ishmael?" asked Sarah.

"I love him," said Abraham. "He's a good boy, bright and happy, obedient, ready with animals, playful. How can I harm him, when he's done no wrong?"

"No, of course not," said Sarah. "Your love for him is right. I understand." But her heart cried out: Isaac!

"Let's see what Hagar does, what Ishmael does."

"It doesn't matter what they do," said Sarah. "You and I are old."

"I know how old we are," said Abraham. "Old enough to know how precious life is. How few the years we had with our parents, how fast the years pass while your children grow."

"I wouldn't know about that," said Sarah. "I may not live to know it."

"We'll see what happens," said Abraham. "I love Ishmael. And you love Hagar—I heard it in your voice last night. We'll wait and see."

She heard it in his voice: This discussion was over. He had heard her, and he had decided what he would do. And she knew that he was right, that it would be seen as a cruel thing to send Hagar and her son away. It would taint Isaac's childhood, a stain on him despite his innocence, for with his first step, everyone would remember the first step of another boy, and with his first word, everyone would remember another voice, now unheard.

Show us what to do, O Lord. Isaac will be in Thy hands, not ours. He is Thy gift. He was born to fulfill Thy covenant. Show us how to keep him safe.

❧ CHAPTER 23 ❧

All the flocks and herds were driven to nearby meadows, so that as many shepherds as possible could be at the feast for Isaac's weaning. Everyone wanted to see him, to be part of the celebration. Many friends were coming from Hebron, too. Several bullocks and kids and lambs had been roasting all night for the feast. The choicest lamb, however, was reserved for the Lord, to be offered as a sacrifice at dawn.

Sarah received the congratulations of the women. From time to time Isaac came toddling up, demanding to be fed. When Sarah offered him cheese and bread, he stamped his feet and reached again to be picked up and nursed. Sarah had been warned by many women that it was so hard on the mother not to give in to the child's pleading. But it wasn't hard for her at all. She had enjoyed nursing when Isaac was very little, but teeth had pretty much killed the pleasure for her. And she had wanted to wean him a year ago, when he started being able to ask for a breast with words instead of gestures. "He's ready to be a boy and not a baby," she had said, but the wetnurses acted as if Sarah were some sort of monster, not to keep the baby at the nipple until he was three, so she gave in.

Wetnurses. Hagar hadn't needed any help to nurse Ishmael. Well, Hagar wasn't an old woman with dried-up little dugs that had to practically be wrung out like damp clothes to get any milk from them. So two nursing mothers, one from Hebron, one from Abraham's household, had each given Isaac two nursings a day when he was little, one each day as he grew older and began eating solid food as well. Naturally, they felt they knew as much about mothering as Sarah, and offered their advice freely; and Sarah took their advice when she agreed with it, or when she didn't know. That's why Isaac was actually being weaned on the day of his weaning feast, instead of having been long since dining on bread and cheese and figs and dates, well-watered wine and chopped-up meat.

So today Isaac was being bratty, naturally. Everybody else was having a party, and *he* was getting ignored by his mother and his wetnurses. With all the strangers coming in from the town and the nearby villages, and all the men returning from the outlying flocks and herds, Isaac was afraid and wanted to be held, and to him, being held and protected meant suckling. Poor child.

Abraham was the proud host, which meant that he sat near the cookfires and talked to people who were lining up for food or whose flatbread was freshly covered with spicy meat or stewed beans and fruit. From time to time he'd call for the servants to bring Isaac to him, and Abraham—still remarkably strong and fit for a man his age—would hoist the boy high over his head for all to see. Naturally, Isaac, already out of sorts because he wasn't getting suckled, regarded this as an affront, and he yelled in protest, his face turning red. This provoked laughter and applause from the crowd, which only made Isaac angrier, and the moment Abraham set him down, Isaac would run off on his stubby little legs. The crowd parted for him and cheered him on.

Then, of course, Isaac would head for Sarah, needing the comfort of the breast. Soon he would learn that it was his mother he wanted, and not just one small part of her, but then, plenty of grown men had a similar problem, didn't they?

Feast days were tiring. Abraham seemed to thrive on them, getting so energized that he often could not fall asleep until late in the night. But Sarah could only take a few hours at a time before she had to withdraw to her tent. In her younger days, she would have lasted out the day and fallen exhausted into bed the moment the crowd broke up. But she simply couldn't do it now. And, because she was old, she didn't have to. People assumed her weariness was physical, that like many old people she needed frequent naps. Well, she didn't mind napping, but if that were her problem, she'd simply doze off where she sat. It was solitude she needed at times like this, not sleep.

So no one thought ill of her when she got up and doddered off to her tent. She hated the fact that her hip joints had never really recovered from the pregnancy, so that now she could walk only in fairly short steps. It made her look crippled, when in fact she was quite robust in most other ways. She could still outspin most of the women in the camp. Her eyes and her mind were sharp. Her hearing was acute. But, seeing her walk in that shuffling way, people assumed they had to speak slowly to her, and shout, and tell her who they were even though they were standing right in front of her. Oh, well. Let them assume what they assume. It only meant that when she revealed how keen her mind was they were pleasantly surprised. Or unpleasantly—depending on their own character.

It was hot inside her tent, but she didn't care. She drew the curtain closed all the same, so she would not be intruded upon. She lay on her bed, not intending to sleep, but soon she did doze off.

She slept only lightly, and not for long, for she heard noises outside her tent. A grunting sound, and soft laughter. Her first thought was to wonder if some young village

couple, wits dimmed by wine, had decided to have a tryst
behind her tent. But as she lay there listening, the sounds
began to make a different sort of sense. The grunting was
really not grunting at all. It was more like a sustained
scream, only so muffled that it could hardly be heard.

A muffled scream, she realized, from a little child's
throat.

She rose from her bed with an alacrity she had not
thought her body capable of. Heart pounding, she drew
apart the door of her tent enough to see a sight that chilled
her to the soul.

The soft laughter came from Ishmael. The screaming
came from little Isaac. Ishmael had bound a long scarf
around Isaac's open mouth, muffling his voice. And Ishmael held the end of the scarf like a tether, so that even
though Isaac strained against it with all his might, he
could not get away.

Isaac was desperately trying to get to Sarah's tent. It
was his mother he was calling for.

Was this not Sarah's worst nightmare, being acted out
in the flesh? All her fears of what would happen after she
died, with Isaac helpless in the hands of Ishmael, were
here before her eyes.

Isaac threw himself toward the tent so hard that his legs
flipped out from under him, and he fell on his back, still
tethered. The way his head was twisted by the scarf as he
fell sent panic through Sarah's heart. His neck! Ishmael
has broken his neck! But after a moment of lying there,
still and winded, Isaac scrambled back to his feet and ran
at Ishmael, pummeling him with his little fists. Ishmael
only laughed, holding his little half-brother by the head
so that his blows struck only air, or landed uselessly on
Ishmael's tight-muscled arm.

Grinning, Ishmael glanced up to share the joke with
someone standing off to the side. Obviously, he was still
unaware that Sarah was watching—but he had *some* audience that he was playing to.

Sarah parted her door wider, and now she could see

who it was that watched this miserable scene of torment
without intervening. It was Hagar of course, standing in
the door of *her* tent, smiling indulgently at the sight of
her son mocking Isaac's fear and rage.

Then Hagar glanced toward Sarah's tent and saw her.
At once the smile left her face. "Ishmael," she called
sternly. "Come here."

At first Ishmael simply ignored her, laughing as Isaac
tried to free himself by pulling the scarf from Ishmael's
grip. But when he glanced at her and saw her nod her
head toward Sarah's tent, it was Ishmael's turn to notice
Sarah standing there. For now she had the door fully open
and stood there in plain sight.

At once Ishmael started to untie the scarf around Isaac's
mouth. But all of Isaac's pulling had made the knot too
tight to undo easily.

"Let go of my son," said Sarah.

"I'm just untying the—"

"Let go of him now," said Sarah.

Ishmael, apparently realizing how bad this looked to
Isaac's mother, finally obeyed. At once Isaac ran to Sarah
and clung to her leg, sobbing, his voice still muffled by
the scarf. When he inhaled, his breath was a labored gasp,
for crying had plugged up his nose, so that the only breath
he could get was whatever air he could draw through the
gag. And since it was now soaked in saliva, there wasn't
much air getting through at all.

Sarah tried to get a finger between Isaac's cheek and
the cloth of the scarf, to open a passage for air to pass.
But it was so tight that she could not do it.

"I was trying to keep him quiet so you could sleep,"
said Ishmael.

"Go to your mother," said Sarah. "She thinks it's clever
for you to torture a baby." She couldn't undo the knot
either.

"I was just teasing him," said Ishmael. "I didn't hurt
him."

Sarah pulled the knife from the sheath at her waist.

Ishmael gasped. She looked at him, saw the horror on his face as he backed away from her. Stupid boy, to think she would take after him with a knife at her age. Carefully she worked the blade between the scarf and Isaac's cheek, then carefully sawed at the wet fabric, careful to keep the edge from touching Isaac's tender skin. Soon the scarf came apart, and Isaac gasped and sobbed and fell into her arms as she lowered herself to the ground to hold him close. She did not even bother to look to see where Ishmael was, beyond noticing that he was gone.

Finally one of the servants noticed her in the doorway and came to her. "Oh, is he crying again? Did he wake you?"

"Go get my husband," said Sarah.

"Let me take the baby and you go back to bed," said the servant.

"Go get my husband," said Sarah again. Perhaps because her intonation was exactly the same both times, flat and brooking no discussion, the servant realized that something quite serious must be going on. So she ran down the slope to where Abraham was regaling the company with some story or other. Soon he came up the hill, with far too many of the company coming with him, to see what was so urgent that Sarah would summon her husband, instead of going to him herself.

Well, let them wonder. They would see Isaac crying. They would see the stern look on Sarah's face. No doubt Hagar would be spreading the story through the camp that Ishmael was just teasing the baby as boys will do, and Sarah was making something out of nothing. Let her say what she would. It was Hagar's indulgent smile more than Ishmael's cruel teasing that condemned them both. Hagar had shown that rather than being a restraint on Ishmael's worst impulses toward Isaac, she would be an encouragement to him. Today she allowed petty cruelties and mocking contempt. What would she allow in a year or two? What would she allow when Sarah and Abraham were dead?

I have kept still for the first years of Isaac's life, because Abraham asked me to be patient and see how things turned out between Hagar's son and my own. But now I will be patient no longer. I saw this from before the baby's birth, and my husband did not hear me. He will hear me now.

Abraham looked puzzled and, perhaps, a little annoyed as he approached her. Sarah rose up, parting Isaac from his grip on her. "Your father will carry you inside the tent," she said.

Isaac turned his tear-streaked, saliva-soaked face toward Abraham and reached up his arms. Abraham lifted him as Sarah bent over and picked up the scarf. She led the way inside the tent, and when Abraham had also entered with Isaac at his shoulder, she closed the door behind her. She knew that Eliezer would soon have would-be eavesdroppers dispersed from around the tent.

She held up the scarf. "This was tied around Isaac's mouth so tightly that I could only get it off by cutting it. He could hardly breathe."

Abraham looked properly horrified. "Who did it, do you know?"

"The other end of the scarf was held by Hagar's son. Isaac was screaming for me and trying to run to my tent. He could have broken his neck when he outran the tether and flipped over on his back. Ishmael laughed at his screams and his fear and his rage."

"Surely he meant no harm by it," said Abraham.

"His mother stood at her tent door and smiled at him while he did it."

"Perhaps you're making too much of this."

"No, Abraham. You're making too little of it. I saw Ishmael's face, and Hagar's. You did not. There was no pity in them. Only malicious delight."

"You've been so sure that they would hate Isaac," said Abraham. "How can you be an impartial judge?"

"You've been so sure that your Ishmael could not do any wrong," said Sarah, "how can you claim to be impartial? I saw. You did not. Here is the scarf. It happened."

"The baby is not harmed."

"When will you die, Abraham? Has the Lord promised that you will outlive Ishmael? Because if he hasn't, the day will come when it won't be childish pranks. If Ishmael has no mercy now, when Isaac is a baby, and if Hagar has no pity when you and I are both alive to protect our son, what will happen when we're dead?"

"What do you want me to do?" said Abraham. "In all those family histories of yours, the only solution that seemed to work was to kill the rival son. Is that what you want? For me to sacrifice Ishmael for your son?"

"What do you want, to sacrifice my son for Hagar's? Because that is the choice you face, as God is my witness."

"Do you claim that God tells you this?" demanded Abraham.

"I didn't need God to tell me this, because I saw with my eyes what is obvious to anyone with any wisdom. But you have blinded yourself, so you can't see it. Look at how the scarf chafed against Isaac's cheeks!"

Abraham looked. Isaac's face showed two bands of red.

"He could hardly breathe," said Sarah. "He could have suffocated. His neck could have been broken. And Ishmael had the gall to tell me he did this so that Isaac wouldn't wake me. He's a liar as well as a tormentor. That's your precious firstborn. Well, Abraham, it's not really your choice. Isaac will not dwell with Ishmael, nor I with Hagar. They will not inherit together—that is not possible, no matter how you delude yourself. One will inherit, or the other. They will share nothing. They will not grow up to be friends. They will grow up to be enemies. So if you choose to keep Hagar and her son here with you, then I will take Isaac somewhere else with me, and if you try to stop me, I will sneak away in the night. And don't imagine that you can get your servants to stop me. They are not blind to the truth. They will help me save Isaac's life."

"Save your threats," said Abraham. "I can hear you without your having to bludgeon me."

"No, you can't hear me, or we wouldn't have reached this day."

"But we *have* reached it, haven't we?" said Abraham. He turned from her and headed toward the tent door.

Sarah ran toward him at once, ignoring the pain in her hips, though the bone ground painfully on bone with each bound. She blocked the door. "Where are you taking my son?"

"I'm keeping him with me, of course," said Abraham. "You just threatened to run away with him."

"So you'll steal him from me? You, the one who sees no danger, will steal him from me, the one who would keep him alive? That makes you a murderer."

Abraham was even more horrified by Sarah's words than she was. "You say this to me? After all these years together, you believe I could kill my own son?"

"I believe you can blind yourself to the truth and leave him exposed so that others will kill him, yes."

"And you say this in front of the boy."

"What choice do I have, since you're about to steal him from me. I gave you a choice. You merely take him. You who have two sons, when I have only one."

Grimly Abraham lowered Isaac to the ground. "Stay with your mother," he said.

Isaac, comforted at last, wandered toward the cushions that he loved to play on.

"I will never forget the terrible things you said to me," said Abraham.

"Nor will I forget that you valued Ishmael more than Isaac, and Hagar more than me."

"Put it in words, Sarah. What would you have me do? Kill them because of a boyish prank that went too far?"

"Send them away," said Sarah. "I wanted to give Hagar her freedom years ago. Free her and send her away. Give her a tent and put herds and herdsmen under her control. Let her raise Ishmael in plenty, but give him his inheritance now, and make it plain that he will have no more at your hands. And you will never see him again, you will never visit them, or he'll start to think himself the equal of Isaac, and seek to take what Isaac has out of his hands when you're dead."

"You would cut off a son from his father, and a father from his son?"

"You keep blaming me," said Sarah. "But I'm not the one who gagged and tethered your son Isaac, and then mocked his screams of terror. I will see that sight in my nightmares for the rest of my life, if you don't send them away. I did not cause this. And if you loved Isaac, you would see that I am the one who is wise, and you're the one who lets love for one son kill another."

"If you ever say again, to me or anyone, that I would consent to the killing of my son, you will never see my face again, woman."

"Ah. I see. I have become nothing but some 'woman' to you. This is how you hear wise counsel. Abraham, the father of multitudes. You condemn me out of your own pride. You accuse me of malice yet refuse to believe in the malice of those who have actually shown it." Sarah flung the wet, knotted scarf across his chest and shoulder. "Wear it with pride," she said. "Your precious Ishmael made it for you."

Sarah stepped aside and opened the tent flap so he could leave.

Abraham's face was terrible with anger as he left the tent. Perversely, Sarah stood in the door and watched how the crowd looked at him. She knew how the story would be told. Whatever came of this, the tales would make Sarah look bad. So be it, as long as Isaac lived.

Sarah stayed in her tent, playing with Isaac. And even though Isaac tried several more times to suckle, thinking perhaps that his mother would now relent, she remained firm with him. As firm as she had been with Abraham.

What my child needs, I will do. And foolish is the father who thinks he can stop his wife from protecting their baby—even from him. God gave us this child by a miracle. But in a world where Cain slew Abel, how dimwitted did Abraham have to be to deny that God's miracle could be undone because Abraham didn't have the courage to hear his wife's warning?

As for the crowds at the feast, let them chatter among themselves. Eliezer would see to it that food continued to be served until it ran out, and then he would send them all home with the blessings of the household. This quarrel between Abraham and Sarah would be the talk of Hebron . . . for a day. Let them have their entertainment.

An hour later, someone clapped outside her tent. Thinking it was a servant inquiring about her needs, she called out, "Please bring food for Isaac, but none for me."

She assumed that she was being obeyed when no one answered her. But then, a few moments later, someone clapped again.

"What is it? Come in."

It was not a servant at all. It was Abraham.

Wordlessly he came and sat down on the rug before her.

If he expected her to speak first, perhaps with an apology, he would have a long, long wait.

"I told someone to bring food for Isaac," he finally said.

"Thank you," she answered.

Isaac toddled over and began playing with his father's beard.

"I went to the Lord and complained about you," Abraham said. "I asked him what I should do to get you to stop being so angry and fearful and suspicious and jealous."

She bit back the stinging reply that came to her lips. Instead she tried to turn it into a wry joke at her own expense. "You aren't the first to utter such a prayer to one god or another."

"Yes, well, God hears our prayers," said Abraham, "but He answers more wisely than we ask."

"What did God tell you?" asked Sarah.

"He told me not to grieve because of Ishmael or Hagar. Because I should have hearkened to everything you told me. The Lord's promise is to come through Isaac, and the only way that can happen is if Ishmael and Hagar leave us now and never come near us again."

All Sarah's fear and anger disappeared in a rush of gratitude and relief. She put her face in her hands and wept. Isaac came to her at once and patted her arm and her ear. "Don't cry, Mama," he said. "It's all right, Mama. You'll feel better soon."

"He's right," said Abraham. "We'll all feel better soon. The Lord promised that Ishmael will thrive. That because he is of my seed, he will also become a great nation. But the covenant is with Isaac. Isaac must remain with me and you. Just as you said. Everything as you said."

And then, to Sarah's surprise, Abraham also wept.

Isaac turned to his father, then looked back and forth between his parents. "Papa," he said. "Mama was crying first."

"Yes, Abraham," said Sarah. "You must wait your turn."

Abraham laughed through his tears and reached for his little son and held him close. "I wanted to hold both my sons to my heart all the days I have left to me," said Abraham. "I wanted it too much, I refused to see that it could not happen. That to hold them both would mean that, in the end, I would lose them both. I will not let my one son destroy his soul by harming my other son. I will send him away as much to save his life as to save Isaac's."

"When will you do it?" asked Sarah.

"In the morning," said Abraham. "But now let's dry our eyes and wash our faces and come out to celebrate with our friends and our household. Today my son was weaned from his mother's breast, and now comes under the protection of his father."

He leaned forward to kiss her. She also leaned toward him, but her back could not take the strain, and she ended up having to catch herself on her hands and her forehead bumped his lips.

"Ow," he said. "You've lost your aim, old woman."

Laughing, they finally kissed.

"Good!" cried Isaac, clapping his hands. "All better now!"

They washed and dried their faces, then walked from the tent, each holding one of Isaac's hands, bound together by the son between them. The feast continued, and even though Sarah knew perfectly well that everyone was gossiping madly behind their backs, and that Sarah would get the worst of it, she was at peace. When it was out of her power to protect her son, God had intervened and wakened Abraham from his complacency. That assured her more than if Abraham had simply agreed with her from the start. For this day's events showed that God was truly watching over Isaac. He would continue even after Sarah died, and Abraham as well. Other mothers had to live with the dread that their children might die before them. But Sarah had no such fear now. God had shown his hand in her son's life.

In the morning, Sarah rose early. She refused to hide in her tent, pretending that what was happening today had nothing to do with her. The gossip would blame her for it no matter what she did, but she would show no shame. She would stand there openly and let it be seen that she knew that she was acting justly.

Hagar made a terrible scene, hurling accusations at Sarah, saying that she lied, then that she exaggerated, then that Ishmael was innocent of malice, and finally that Isaac was such a brat that someone needed to teach him a lesson because his parents were too old and feeble to raise him properly. By the end, it was obvious that she had years of malice pent up in her heart, and if Abraham had still harbored doubts about this course of action, Hagar's vituperation must have settled the last of them. This woman could never be allowed near Isaac again, nor could the son she had poisoned with her resentments.

"I'm a man now," Ishmael said to Abraham. "I don't need you or anyone."

"Nevertheless," said Abraham, "I will provide you with herds and servants."

"I'm good with a bow," said Ishmael. "I'll live by hunting. I don't need so much as a lamb from you."

"You are my son," said Abraham, "and I'll provide for you."

"If I were your son," said Ishmael, "you would not let that old woman poison your heart against me and send me away. What is that stupid baby to me? I would never bother to harm him."

And those words condemned him, too, as Hagar's had condemned her, without Ishmael even understanding how much he had confessed by saying them.

Abraham longed to embrace his son and reassure him, Sarah knew that, but Ishmael's and Hagar's rage had made that impossible. Instead he stood with his arm around Sarah, holding Isaac with his other hand, and watched silently as Ishmael and Hagar were mounted on sturdy donkeys for the journey.

Eliezer and three trusted men rode with Hagar and Ishmael, leading pack animals that held a tent and supplies to last them for weeks. Once the new camp was established, far to the south, they would return and lead the herds and servants of Ishmael's inheritance to join them.

That was the plan.

But by noon Eliezer was back. Sarah sat with Abraham in her tent door when he came to tell what happened. "They ran off," he said. "Hagar kept saying that she knew my job was to kill them in their sleep, that you would never allow Ishmael to live. It didn't matter how I denied it. When we stopped to rest in the heat of the day, she went to relieve herself and apparently she and Ishmael had planned something, because neither of them returned and by the time we realized it, we couldn't find them in the rocks."

"That's dry land," said Abraham, "and Ishmael has never learned the wells in that part of the country."

"I know," said Eliezer. "I came back to get help in searching for them. In that country we could come within ten paces of them and never know they were there. They could fall from a cliff and cry for help and we'd never hear them. And they could pass ten paces from a spring and never know it was there."

Abraham nodded.

"How many men should I take with me?" asked Eliezer.

"None," said Abraham.

"But they will surely die," said Eliezer.

"No they won't," said Abraham. "When Hagar ran off into the desert, before Ishmael was even born, the Lord sent an angel to look out for her. I have God's promise that Ishmael will be the father of a great nation. I will trust God to take care of my son in the desert."

Eliezer loved Ishmael, and couldn't help the tears that came to his eyes. "Father Abraham," he said, "may I search by myself?"

"Eliezer," said Abraham, "this is what you will do. In all your wanderings on my behalf, you will someday hear rumors of where Hagar and her son are living. And you will go to them and take the herds that belong to them, and the tents and implements of their household. They will be kept separate from that which Isaac will inherit, and when the time comes, you will deliver into Ishmael's hands all that we have kept in trust for him."

"And if I never find them?" asked Eliezer.

"But you will," said Abraham. "Because Ishmael is my son, and you are my true steward, and you will do for my son Ishmael all that I would do for him. Just as you will watch over my son Isaac and help him grow into a strong and good man who serves God, even if I die before he is grown, even if Sarah dies while he is young."

Eliezer bowed his head, and two tears dropped from his

eyes onto the ground. "I will do all that you command, Father Abraham."

"I tell you, it is three sons I have had in my life, and not two," said Abraham.

Then he took Sarah into his embrace, while Isaac played with straw soldiers beside them.

❧ CHAPTER 24 ❧

Sarah lived longer than she ever thought she would. She saw her baby Isaac turn into a boy, and then a stripling man with the first touch of beard upon his chin, and then put on the strength of a man, his arms more massive than Abraham's had ever been, his legs sturdy as young tree trunks, and Sarah remembered then how her father had looked when he was still a young man, and she was his daughter in their house of exile in Ur-of-the-North. See how my father is alive in my son, how the blood of the kings of Ur-of-Sumeria is mingled with the blood of the Hebrews. The two men I loved most in my life, the two who taught me all that I know that is worth knowing, and my son shows me the body of my father and the face of my young husband.

For Isaac's face had become the face of the desert traveler who stood filthy in her father's courtyard, for whom Sarah drew water so he could wash his feet. The young man who had come to entreat for Qira to marry Lot, and who ended up promising to marry Qira's little sister, a child promised to the goddess, without even asking her if she wanted him to come back for her.

That was the man that Isaac had become, a quiet man, who studied all that Abraham had to teach him out of books, and learned from Abraham's wisdom all there was to know about the care of animals and the leadership of a great house. There was no task so heavy that Isaac could not do it, once he set his back to it; no idea so difficult that Isaac could not grasp it, once he set his mind to it. From the body of an old woman like me came a man like this, Sarah thought in wonder. And from the loins of that old man, Abraham. And she laughed again to think of it, just as she had laughed when the holy men came to tell Abraham that he and Sarah would yet have the child of promise.

If God himself had a son, thought Sarah, surely he would be like Isaac.

"Why are you laughing, old woman?" said Abraham.

"Why do you begrudge me, old man?" said Sarah.

"I keep checking, to see if you've gone dotty on me," said Abraham. "There are signs, you know."

"The first sign is that you keep checking for signs of dotage in other people," said Sarah.

"Ah, that's what I've always loved about you, the way you show such unfailing respect for your masterful husband."

"Everyone says so," said Sarah. "It's my best remaining quality. Now that my breasts hang like empty sacks."

"Your breasts were never your best quality," said Abraham.

"There were other opinions than yours," said Sarah, wondering if she should be a little hurt.

"Oh, your bosom was a marvel, the servants could hardly work for the thought of what must be there beneath your gowns, but it was never your best quality because nothing of the body could ever compare to the glory of your mind, and nothing of the mind could compare to the beauty of your soul."

"Why, I believe you're flirting with me, old man."

"And I believe it's working, old woman," said Abraham. Abraham shouldered the bag of bread and cheese and carried it to where the asses waited to be loaded. Sarah walked with him, though her pace slowed him.

She followed because, through all this banter, Sarah could see that his face was sad. "You don't want to take this journey today, do you?" said Sarah.

"No. In solemn truth, I would give my life rather than go."

Well, that was a little dramatic. But then, he was in something of a flamboyant mood. "Why not stay, then?"

"Because it's not my life, but my soul that depends on going," said Abraham.

"Your soul? Because you're checking the wells and pasturage in Moriah, and offering sacrifice there?"

"When the Lord commands a sacrifice upon a hill in Moriah," said Abraham, "a wise man forgets what he might wish, and goes to Moriah with wood to burn and a knife for the kill." Abraham shuddered as if he were cold.

"Dress warmly! That's high country, and it's still winter."

"I'll be warm enough. God wouldn't be so merciful as to let me get too sick to travel."

He really was bothered. It wasn't just part of his flirtatious chatter with her, to pretend to want to stay at home. He really dreaded this trip. Why? Did he know something that he wasn't telling her?

"Abraham," said Sarah, "something *is* wrong, and you must tell me."

"What could be wrong," said Abraham, "if a man obeys the Lord?"

"Nothing," said Sarah. "If he's truly obedient, he gets a wife like me. And then, if he's a man of extraordinary righteousness, he gets a son like Isaac."

Abraham bent his head and leaned against the load he had just fastened onto the donkey's back. "What a man is given, sometimes he doesn't get to keep as long as he'd like."

"Well, you've got me, like it or not," said Sarah. "But why don't you just send Isaac with Eliezer? The two of them can offer sacrifice for you. Isaac has the same priesthood as you, and Eliezer sees with your eyes."

"When the Lord gives a man a cup to drink, the man drinks. He doesn't pass it to his son, or his servant."

"Abraham, you frighten me. Has the Lord told you that you're going to die on this journey? Is this the last time I'll ever see you?"

"No," said Abraham. "You'll see me again, if you want to."

"I want to. Come home to me, and with more cheer than you have now."

"And if I come home with even less cheer?"

"Why, I'll be cheerful enough for both of us," said Sarah. "I'll squeeze one last grin out of those parchment cheeks of yours."

In answer, he smiled, and she stood on tip-toe and kissed him without waiting for him to bend to her. "I think I know why you're so grim about this trip," said Sarah.

"You do?" said Abraham.

"You know where Ishmael is. You'll be passing near him. You're afraid you might see him and want to visit him. It's all right with me if you do. I just want you to know that."

Abraham laughed. "I don't know where Ishmael is, but I know he was last seen so far to the south that I'd have to take three journeys just like this one and I'd only be halfway there."

"He still loves you, I know he does," said Sarah. "He accepted the herds and gifts you sent him. Even if Hagar tried to poison him against you, he was already sixteen when they left here, he already knew you for himself."

"Yes," said Abraham. "I'm sure my son loves me."

"And it's all right with me that you love him, too," said Sarah. "I never hated him; I loved and admired him. I loved Hagar, too, as much as she let me. It was for Isaac's sake they left."

"I know it," said Abraham. "Believe me, Sarah, I blame you for nothing. In all our lives together, you have done nothing but good to me and for me, and you've been a blessing to everyone we've met. Even Lot, before he died, told me that the one good thing about marrying Qira was that he got to know one good woman in his life."

"I *knew* he loved her . . . somehow."

"Don't play the fool. He meant *you*."

Isaac came bounding up, a load of wood on his back that he carried as easily as if it were a sack of smoke. "Here's the last of it, Father," he said. "I think we're ready to go, and about time, we don't want to waste any more of the warmth of the day."

"Yes, we wouldn't want to waste daylight on mere conversation with my wife," said Abraham.

Isaac turned to Sarah and rolled his eyes. "Father's been in a perverse mood ever since he announced we were going to make this trip."

"I know," said Sarah. "So please be extraordinarily funny on this trip so he won't be so grim."

"No," said Isaac, "I'll be extraordinarily dull so that he'll be all the more eager to get it over with and get back to *you*. He's always happy when he's coming home to you."

This was not Abraham's playful banter. "Why Isaac. That's the sweetest thing you could have said to me."

"It's only the simple truth. I thought you knew." Isaac finished tying the last donkey to the one before, so they couldn't stray apart during the journey. He whistled for the young men who were traveling with them.

Sarah took one last opportunity to speak to Abraham alone. "Be happy to come home to me, Abraham," she said. "For the greatest joy in my life is to see you. And Isaac, of course. Tell me you'll be glad to see me when you come back."

In answer, Abraham took her in his arms and kissed

her. Not the passionate kiss of youth—that sort of thing he had always kept in private, where none could see. No, this was a kiss of simple love. It lingered because both of them were loath for the kiss to end. It was good to be connected, body to body, just as their hearts were joined.

Sarah watched them as Abraham mounted the first donkey and Isaac and the other young men took their places, leading the animals down to the road. Here the road was wide, but in the mountains it would grow narrow, with many a passage between the rocks so strait that they might have to unload the animals just to pass. But they would reach the place the Lord had commanded Abraham to go, just as they had reached every other place that was promised them.

As Sarah watched them move briskly along, she thought of the whole journey behind her. Her childhood in Ur-of-the-North, the temple of Asherah, her father's house, the Euphrates in flood and in a dry season. She thought of Abraham arriving with his extravagant dowry of impossibly large herds, and then of those early years as they watched the drought deplete their animals and their hope. The journey to Egypt, and the fear she felt when they were told to lie about who she was. She thought of Pharaoh and of Sehtepibre, of the great game they were playing on the magnificent stage of the most ancient and lofty kingdom in the world—and how petty and mean it turned out to be. She thought of Hagar in those early years together, when Sarah thought of her as almost a friend, they grew so close. The nastiness she set aside; there was no reason to dwell on that. But two sons had been born to Abraham, one by each of these women. That made them sisters, of a kind, even if they could not be friends. And thinking of sisters reminded her of Qira, and her tragic blindness to anything that mattered. Qira was almost as blessed as I was, thought Sarah, but she never knew it, and kept trying to get joy from those who had none to give, and rejecting it from the only ones who knew how it could be obtained. And she died because she couldn't let go of the very things that the dead always leave behind, and couldn't hold to the only things that the dead can carry with them.

The love of a good man for a good woman. The love of good friends for each other. The love of parents for children, and children for parents. The love of brothers and sisters. The memory of joy and grief, which all becomes joy when enough time has passed. This is the treasure that I have won through all the years of my journey through this life, thought Sarah. And every bit of it I'll take with me beyond the grave. I'll meet God then, Abraham promises I will, and I will take all these treasures and lay them out before his feet, for God can see them easily even if mortal men cannot. And I'll kneel before the treasures and say, "O God, I thank thee for giving these to me during my life on Earth. No daughter has been better loved than I, nor any wife, nor any mother. I never deserved them. They were not mine by right. But I hope that, having been given such gifts so undeservingly, I used them well, and gave back to thee a life that was worthy."

She had the thought of saying these things to God just as Abraham went out of sight, with Isaac walking beside him. They carry my treasures in their hearts, too, small treasures I suppose, but the best I had to give them.

The stars are great hot fires in a distant sky, so bright a gift from God that they can be seen by everyone on Earth. But when you take my love out of your secret hiding place, my husband, my son, and look at it, you'll see that even though it's as small and dull as a pebble compared to the stars, I have polished my love so long and fervently, and you hold it now so close, that surely, surely it must shine.

AFTERWORD

I n dealing with scripture, particularly stories from Genesis, it is a source of both freedom and frustration that the scripture is our only source. Archaeology and contemporary documents from other cultures and languages can be of great help in clarifying points of confusion—but they can also be annoying distractions, because to a nonscholar like me, such information is available only in secondary sources, filtered through the mindset of scholars and translators.

And therein lies the rub, for biblical scholarship and translation seem to come in only two varieties: apologist and rejectionist. The rejectionists' writings are poisoned by their fierce determination to deny that Abraham or Sarah or practically anybody else ever existed, let alone did any of the things that are claimed for them. While the apologists are unreliable because, almost without exception, they grimly set about gathering and bending every shred of evidence to form "proofs" that are usually specious and often downright fraudulent and aggrandizing.

That's why the story of Moses is always dated to the time of Ramses, even though culturally and historically the account makes no sense in that period—because Ramses built really fancy monuments that later Israelites wanted to claim as having been built by their ancestors. And with Moses dated so impossibly late, Abraham is also usually pushed forward as well, when in fact the Genesis account clearly belongs in the period of devastating climatic change that left Canaan virtually depopulated, flooded Egypt with Asiatic refugees, and fits, over and over again—the little details that can so easily go unnoticed but that could not have been invented by later writers.

(Contrast the story of Abraham in Genesis with the story of Joseph. Abraham's tale fits in the period from 2100 to 1900 B.C., reflecting information that no scribe from, say, 800 B.C., could possibly know. By contrast, Joseph's story is filled with "just-so" suppositions and poetic flourishes, and is filled with evidence of the cultural expectations of a much later time. This doesn't imply that Joseph did not exist or his story did not happen. What it most likely suggests is that a truer, simpler account, just as tied to its own time as Abraham's is, was replaced by a much more poetic treatment that had become popular in part because of those flourishes that gave Joseph credit for, among other things, inventing a system of grain storage that had actually existed generations before the first Pharaohs united Upper and Lower Egypt. The scribes who decided on the "fuller" account had no idea that its very fullness made it of doubtful authenticity—and besides, they loved the "cool stuff" that the account we now have is filled with.)

There is a middle ground between hostile skeptics who refuse to accept any evidence that suggests the biblical account is real and the fervent apologists who have never found a "proof" they didn't love. The virtue of this middle ground is not that it somehow averages the errors of both extremes, but rather that it fits the evidence far better and is less likely to lead to foolish self-blindedness. The middle ground is this: The biblical accounts are all authentic in that those who wrote them, those who copied them, and those who included them in later compilations all believed them to be true and sacred.

This isn't a very hard concept to swallow. After all, Homer's account of the Trojan War and its aftermath, while obviously embellished, nevertheless faithfully records the culture of the era when the tale was first told—which may be very near to the epoch in which the events the tale was based on first happened. And when those details were checked, they were found to be echoed in the archaeological record. It's easy to forget now that the same sort of critic who today claims that the biblical stories were all made up by scribes after 1000 B.C. and usually far later have their roots in the same scholarly tradition that insisted that all of Homer was a work of fiction barely older than the first plays of Aeschylus.

As a Mormon, I take the Bible very seriously, as a vehicle for giving us, with varying degrees of accuracy, true stories of God's dealings with human beings. But I believe in the Bible so seriously that I think it really is what it claims to be—a record, written by men, of stories that seemed important and truthful to them at the time of writing, using the standards of truth available to them at the time. This means that the idea of inerrancy of biblical scripture is silly on its face. It was written by human beings, limited by our finite understanding and subject to all the errors of transmission that inevitably corrupt all manuscripts. Our task, in reading the scriptures, is not to read it blindly as if God were dictating it to his secretary, but to read it faithfully, trying to understand what truths are being shown to us by means of, or in spite of, the words used to tell the tale.

In short, my purpose is pious—I believe there really was a woman named Sarai who married a man named Abram and that they very probably did all the things, or almost all the things, attributed to them. I believe that Abraham was a prophet and received the word of God, and that Sarah was also obedient to the same God.

But when we have two very similar events happening to Sarah and Abraham at different times—passing Sarah off as Abraham's sister in order to keep a king they're visiting from killing Abraham to get at his wife—I have no problem remaining completely ambivalent. Hugh Nibley has shown quite convincingly that the same thing might well have happened twice—three times, if you count the identical events happening to Isaac and Rebecca, and with one of the same kings, no less! At the same time, I think it's at least as likely that the story was orally transmitted and got attributed to two different patriarchs and two different kings, but it really happened only once. I won't be upset whichever one turns out to be true, on that happy day when we get independent evidence beyond the scripture itself. But for the purpose of this story, including two nearly identical incidents would have been bad fiction, and so I went with Plan B and had the event happen only once, in Egypt. Some would say I chose wrong, because having Abimelech as the king is much more plausible than the idea that a Pharaoh would care two hoots about a desert wanderer; but I say that having Sarah at age 90 or older, as she is in the Abimelech account, strains credulity far more. And I think Hugh Nibley is right in pointing us to a picture of Abraham as a very important man in the culture of the Middle East at that time. He would quite possibly have a very important wife as well.

Sarah means "princess." Her original name, Sarai, is deemed to be merely a variant of the same name—but that makes the name change meaningless. What if *Sarai* is merely a false cognate from another language? Perhaps even an unrelated one—perhaps even Sumerian. My guess is as good as anyone's. But to make Sarah a real princess of a historical royal house is not much of a stretch, given her name and the high prestige that Abraham obviously has in the culture depicted in the Genesis account.

There are a few other points where some readers might quibble with my choices. I didn't like the idea of Abram having his earliest adventures in "Ur of the Chaldees." The name is obviously spurious, having been inserted much later for the obvious reason that at the time of Abraham and for many centuries afterward, the people who gave Chaldea its name did not even live in the area or, if they did, were apparently unnoticed by any of the people who did live there. Furthermore, Ur "of the Chaldees"— in this book called Ur-of-Sumeria, the original Ur—was ruled in that period by conquering Amorite kings who had invaded Mesopotamia during the period of devastating drought and had toppled and supplanted the old kingly lines in many or most of the great cities of the area.

Ur-of-the-North, however, founded quite probably as a colony by the original Ur, was not very far from Haran, where Abram's father and brothers came to live. Furthermore, the cities in that area were, in exactly this period, susceptible to much Egyptian influence. Abram could more easily have become acquainted with—and butted heads with—priests of the Pharaonic religion who were doing what Christian missionaries did in Africa and the Pacific, spreading the "true" culture and opening the door to control by imperial merchants and soldiers coming behind them. The road from Ur-of-Sumeria to Egypt is strewn with historical and archaeological obstacles; the road from Ur-of-the-North to Egypt is smooth sailing. Again, if I turn out to be wrong, so what? I have done my best with the information that we have.

Now we come to the problem of Sarah as Abram's "sister." An astonishing number of apologist scholars have come to believe that Genesis actually says that Sarai was the daughter of Abram's older brother Haran, who was also the father of Lot, who was Abram's business partner. The King James version introduces Sarai in this way: "Terah begat Abram, Nahor, and Haran; and Haran begat Lot. And Haran died before his father Terah in the land of his nativity, in Ur of the Chaldees. And Abram and

Nahor took them wives: the name of Abram's wife was Sarai; and the name of Nahor's wife, Milcah, the daughter of Haran, the father of Milcah, and the father of Iscah" (Genesis 11:27–29).

(Here is Ur of the Chaldees, of course, and Terah and his sons could easily have been refugees from the Amorite invasion—except that Ur was a Sumerian city that did not speak a Semitic language, while Abram and his family presumably spoke an early form of Hebrew, which was probably similar to the language of the Amorites and definitely similar to the languages most commonly spoken in the region of Haran and Ur-of-the-North. That proves nothing, but disproves nothing about my suppositions, either, once you throw out "of the Chaldees" as an anachronism.)

Let's see what this passage actually says about the people named. We know that Nahor's wife was Milcah, and Milcah was the daughter of Haran, and that Haran was (redundantly) the father of Milcah and the father of Iscah. But we also know that Lot's father, Haran, was the brother of Abram and the son of Terah. So apparently Abram's brother Nahor married the daughter of his brother Haran. So, since a man could marry his niece, say the apologists, why couldn't Sarai also have been a daughter of Haran, and therefore, since Abram regarded Lot as his brother, couldn't he also have regarded Sarai as his sister, besides being his wife and his niece, and thus when he told both Pharaoh and Abimelech that Sarai was his sister, *he wasn't lying*.

And there you have the whole reason why the apologists go on this silly guessing expedition—they are desperate to show that Abram didn't lie when he called Sarai his sister. Which absolutely baffles me. Why *shouldn't* he lie if the Lord told him to, or even if the Lord didn't tell him to, if it was necessary to save his life? There is such a thing as a pious lie—the opposite of bearing false witness against your neighbor, it is the lie told to save the righteous from destruction by the wicked.

But setting aside the question of whether all lies are sins (they aren't, necessarily, but let's not argue), the fact remains that there is nothing in the text, at least as translated in the King James version, that even implies that Abram married his niece. For one thing, the text specifically identifies Milcah, Nahor's wife, as the daughter of Haran, and never says a thing about Sarai's parentage. And for another thing, it seems plain to me that this passage is speaking of two different Harans. There is Haran, the son of Terah and father of Lot—the Haran, in other words, who died. And then the scripture mentions that Nahor married Milcah, the daughter of a *different* Haran, who is identified as "Haran the father of Milcah and the father of Iscah." I mean, if the writer or oral storyteller wanted us to know that the same Haran who was the father of Lot was also the father of Milcah, why would he tag him without referring to Lot at all, and instead bring up "Iscah," whoever that is? No, the intent seems obvious to me—the storyteller wants us to know that Haran the father of Milcah is a different Haran from the other one already named.

Nobody married his niece. Not Nahor, and not Abram. Marrying siblings and other near relations was not unheard of in some places, and was very common in Egypt's ruling class, but it is certainly not the rule in the culture of Abraham and his descendants. They could marry cousins, but no one closer. So if the text does not require us to believe in consanguineous marriage of this degree, our predisposition should not be to accuse Abram of incest in order to excuse him from a lifesaving lie.

That's why, in this book, Sarai is born a princess but named in a non-Semitic language, and she is not Abram's niece and she is not Lot's sister. I believe the text permits and even encourages my decisions.

Of course, I'm not above flat-out manipulation for fictional purposes. There isn't the slightest reason, in the text, to suppose that Abram's wife and Lot's wife were related in any way. I made them sisters because it was useful and interesting to me in telling the tale to give them a connection that allowed us to see Lot's wife through her own eyes and also through the eyes of a sister who didn't like her much, but still cared about her.

Speaking of Lot's wife—Qira, in this novel—it's worth noting that the "pillar of salt" story is one that I take as a later interpolation. Why? Because there really are a whole bunch of salty deposits not all that far from Sodom's probable location to the southeast of the Dead Sea. Some of them rather resemble very small people. It's so easy to imagine a group of people passing through there, getting spooked by the weird humanoid forms of some of the salt pillars, and then around the fire that night, one of the travelers saying, "You know, one of those pillars really *is* a person. Lot's wife. Yep, she was forbidden to look back when God destroyed the city, and when she did it anyway, she was turned into a pillar of salt." In short, it seems likely to be a "just-so" story, like the tale of Elisha and the bears, and Joseph and the Egyptian practice of storing grain in fat years to provide for the lean years. But I might be wrong. Because I also have a personal preference for the idea of an omnipotent but parsimonious God. If he warns the righteous to get out of Sodom because it's going to be hit by a meteor shower, he lets the meteors have their effect on the disobedient, and doesn't fuss with a whole separate miracle just to get one woman for daring to look back—especially since the punished-for-looking-back story is such a common one in world folklore. That doesn't prove anything. It's just my preference. If I'm wrong, it's not like I erased the Bible. The story is still there, intact, as written. All I've written here is a novel, one view of how things might have happened, and what kind of people they might have happened to.

Which is not to say that I take my own work lightly. On the contrary, I take it very seriously, and I wrestled with these issues so long and researched the surrounding information so seriously that I ended up turning in the manuscript one very inconvenient year late. And after all that work, I know I've undoubtedly still made mistakes and missed out on important information that would have made the novel better had I gotten it right. But I can only tell the story that seems right and true to me at the time I wrote it, using the information that I had available. One of my goals was to give the story a plausible setting, but that was only to support my main purpose: To tell the story of Sarah in such a way as to make her come to life as a real person in the mind of my readers. The research was all undertaken in support of that purpose. And I'd like to think that, by bringing my understanding of the surrounding culture to bear on this story, I will have been able to help readers understand how Sarah might have come to make the choices she made in her life, and why Abraham loved her, and why Isaac honored her so much that when his wife Rebecca came to live with him, it was said that she dwelt in Sarah's tent—years after Sarah died.

This woman was remarkable, desirable to kings, seemingly harsh and yet also chosen by God. I think the harshness she showed toward Hagar was not only justified, it was probably overdue—just on the evidence already visible in the Genesis account, in which Hagar is already shown to be in conflict with Sarah almost as soon as Hagar conceives a child with Abraham. So in a sense I suppose I'm an apologist, too. But instead of being an apologist for God or Abraham, who need no defense from me, I'm an apologist for Sarah, a tough, smart, strong, bright woman in an era when women did not show up much in historical records. It's one of the things that's so remarkable about the book of Genesis. There aren't many other writings from that period that give women so much stage time as the chapters about Abraham, Isaac, and Jacob. Of course, the whole of Israelite scripture has this remarkable trait—Eve, Deborah, Jael, Naomi, Ruth, Esther, Bathsheba, Abigail, Tamar, and even Shiphrah and Puah—the Hebrew scriptures are, by the standards of the day, practically bursting with women, *named* women, who are often the heroes of the story.

The writers of the Old Testament took women very seriously. But nowhere are women more centrally involved in the lives of great and holy men than in the accounts of Abraham, Isaac, and Jacob. In some senses the women can be seen as driving the story; certainly the storytellers want us to see that marrying these women so they can be the mothers of the next generation of holy men is one of the most important things that these prophets can do. And sometimes the will of God is first discovered by or best protected by the wife, and not the husband—as we will see in the next book in this series, about Rebecca, the wife of Isaac.

For now, though, I hope only that the reader will grant me, if not agreement with my choices, then indulgence. I did not whimsically discard anything from the story. Every important omission or change from the common interpretation was deliberate and took place only after great thought and serious attempts at research into what is known about the surrounding culture at the probable time of these events. So if I have erred, it was in the attempt to approach the truth contained in the Bible, and never in disregard of it.

Here are some of the sources I used in preparing this book. They are all interesting and valuable books, even if I often drew conclusions that the authors might not have been pleased with, and even though some of the scholars, at least, were quite avidly of the rejectionist camp. I consulted many other books, but these were the ones I found most useful and trustworthy, and which I intend to use again as sources.

Donald B. Redford, *Egypt, Canaan, and Israel in Ancient Times* (Princeton University Press, 1992)

Gösta W. Ahlström, *The History of Ancient Palestine* (Sheffield Academic Press/Fortress Press, 1993, 1994)

Gay Robins, *Women in Ancient Egypt* (Harvard University Press, 1993)

Michael Rice, *Egypt's Making: The Origins of Ancient Egypt, 5000–2000 B.C.* (Routledge, 1990)

And for those who do not immediately recognize the source of some of the events early in the novel, those are based on the book of Abraham in The Pearl of Great Price, a book of scripture recognized only within the LDS Church.

Peter James and Nick Thorp, *Ancient Mysteries* (Ballantine, 1999). The great care these authors took in verifying speculation and drawing evidence from many disciplines made this a fascinating and useful tool—especially concerning the location of Sodom and the events surrounding its destruction.

If you have questions or comments about any aspect of this novel, you are invited to visit http://www.hatrack.com or http://www.nauvoo.com.